ReNEGADes

Also by David Liss

Randoms

Rebels

RANDOMS
3
RENEGADES

DAVID LISS

Simon & Schuster Books for Young Readers
NEW YORK • LONDON • TORONTO • SYDNEY • NEW DELHI

TWEEN

SIMON & SCHUSTER BOOKS FOR YOUNG READERS

An imprint of Simon & Schuster Children's Publishing Division

1230 Avenue of the Americas, New York, New York 10020

This book is a work of fiction. Any references to historical events, real people, or real places are used fictitiously. Other names, characters, places, and events are products of the author's imagination, and any resemblance to actual events or places or persons, living or dead, is entirely coincidental.

Text copyright © 2017 by David Liss

Cover illustration copyright © 2017 by Derek Stenning

All rights reserved, including the right of reproduction in whole or in part in any form.

SIMON & SCHUSTER BOOKS FOR YOUNG READERS

is a trademark of Simon & Schuster, Inc.

For information about special discounts for bulk purchases, please contact Simon & Schuster Special Sales at 1-866-506-1949 or business@simonandschuster.com.

The Simon & Schuster Speakers Bureau can bring authors to your live event.

For more information or to book an event, contact the Simon & Schuster Speakers Bureau at 1-866-248-3049 or visit our website at www.simonspeakers.com.

Also available in a Simon & Schuster Books for Young Readers hardcover edition

Book design by Lizzy Bromley

The text for this book was set in New Caledonia.

Manufactured in the United States of America 1018 OFF

First Simon & Schuster Books for Young Readers paperback edition November 2018

2 4 6 8 10 9 7 5 3 1

The Library of Congress has cataloged the hardcover edition as follows:

Names: Liss, David, 1966– author.

Title: Renegades / David Liss.

Description: First edition. | New York : Simon & Schuster Books for Young Readers, [2017] | Series: Randoms ; 3 | Summary: After many ups and downs, Zeke and his friends work together in a final effort to stop the evil Phands from taking over the galaxy.

Identifiers: LCCN 2016049271 | ISBN 9781481417853 (hardcover) | ISBN 9781481417860 (pbk) | ISBN 9781481417877 (eBook)

Subjects: | CYAC: Science fiction. | Conspiracies—Fiction. | BISAC: JUVENILE FICTION / Science Fiction. | JUVENILE FICTION / Social Issues / Friendship. | JUVENILE FICTION / Action & Adventure / General.

Classification: LCC PZ7.1.L57 Ren 2017 | DDC [Fic]—dc23

LC record available at https://lccn.loc.gov/2016049271

RENEGADES

CHAPTER ONE

I t's funny how you can change your life, mix things up, try new approaches to old problems, and still keep ending up in the same sorts of situations. It didn't seem that long ago that I was on a spaceship, surrounded by friends, cooking up a moderately insane plan to rescue some other friends. I have a tendency to overreach, so I was also working on a scheme to liberate my home planet, which had been conquered by the Phandic Empire. On top of that, I wanted to free the Confederation of United Planets from the clutches of an evil goat-turtle. Maybe a little ambitious, I know, but on the other hand, I had a spaceship, I had beings I trusted by my side, and we had all been upgraded with ancient alien technology that rendered each of us evil-crushing agents of mayhem. There were a lot of balls in the air, but I still figured we had a decent shot at fixing just about everything that was currently wrong in the galaxy.

So finding myself in a classroom with an oversized lummox hurling spitballs at me was not something I had planned for my immediate future.

I turned around and saw, about five rows back, a kid with a face like a potato. He had tiny eyes and stringy blond hair, and an evil gap-toothed grin. He had the same stupidly smug expression of every kid who had given me trouble all my life, but I couldn't figure out why this particular bully had it in for me at this particular moment. He didn't know me. I'd never spoken a word to him. I was a new kid, sure, but so was he—we all were. It was possible he didn't need much of a reason. Spitballs come from the heart, not the head. He seemed perfectly happy to sit with three or four other meatheads, moistening balls of paper in his mouth and then tossing them at me.

"Ignore him," Mi Sun said. She had that look on her face that meant she was sure I was about to do something stupid—which meant I must have had *that* look on *my* face. It was easy for her to tell me to ignore him. She wasn't the one getting pelted with saliva bombs. I doubted she'd be a model of restraint in my shoes. Mi Sun had never put up with anyone giving her a hard time, even without the ancient precursor-alien augmentations we had swimming through our blood. I also knew she wasn't the most patient person, but right now her impatience was zeroing in on me.

Maybe it was because I'd just been smacked in the forehead with a particularly moist wad, but I felt she was being a little unfair. I don't see myself as someone who goes around doing obviously stupid things. I may, on occasion, be a little reckless, but only when there is something important at stake. Yes, the thought of testing out my new nanotech upgrades on this kid— let's say, punching him so hard he flew into the air and through the ceiling—had a certain appeal. It might have fallen into the category of things that a reasonable person, such as Mi Sun, might call *stupid*, but I was only thinking about it. I had no real intention of unleashing the most humiliating beat-down in the history of nerd revenge. It was more like an emergency backup plan.

Besides, we had more important things to worry about and bigger bullies to take down.

Alice, who was on the other side of me, brushed some

strands of her unruly white-blond hair out her face, and peered at me over her glasses. "I can't believe you're going to sit there and let that guy lob spitballs at you."

Mi Sun glowered at her. "Don't give him any ideas. We're trying to blend in. Act normal."

Charles, who was on the other side of Mi Sun, now leaned over. "Would not a normal student resent this treatment?" he asked. "Is not confronting this ruffian a means of blending in?" There was real uncertainty in his voice. Charles was from Uganda, and he didn't know how things worked in American schools. Maybe spitball pelting was how kids said hello around here.

"Why are you encouraging him?" Mi Sun asked Charles.

A spitball came flying through the air and struck her in the face.

"I think that's why," I suggested. "He doesn't want to get hit."

Mi Sun was scowling as she used the nails of her thumb and index finger to remove the spitball that clung to her cheek. "You might have a point."

I was starting to get to my feet when Alice grabbed me by the hand and pulled me back down. "Hold on. Mi Sun was right. We're here for a reason. We need to lie low for a few more hours, even if it means putting up with a little humiliation."

I sighed, but I had no real argument. After escaping from Confederation Central, things had taken a bad turn: We'd arrived in my solar system only to find my home planet under Phandic control. Then they'd taken another bad turn, and here we were on Earth in this Phandic reeducation facility. Yes, the situation looked bad, but I was being an optimist. Imprisonment, brainwashing, and spitballs, I told myself, were speed bumps on our road to success.

I turned around to face my tormentor, who shrugged and grinned and gave me a *what are you going to do about it?* look. I glowered at him as best I could, because that was as far as I could go without giving us away. I remembered what it felt like to be powerless back when I was, literally, without powers. Now I was powerless even though I was incredibly powerful. If you ever have a choice, the second option is the better one, but honestly I don't recommend either.

Finally, the classroom door opened and the teacher entered, which I figured was good news only because the presence of an adult would end the rain of spitballs. The teacher was in his fifties, I'd guess, and his fringe of gray hair and gray mustache contrasted sharply with the deep brown of his skin. He wore khakis and a blue button-down shirt with a black tie. He also wore a grim expression that made it clear he would rather be anywhere else and do anything other than teaching this bunch of students. I'd seen teachers like this before, and they were best treated like wounded predators. Maybe a kind gesture would earn this man's friendship, or maybe he would bite my arm off.

"Good morning, students," he said in a tone designed to make sure we understood that nothing in our morning was going to turn out good. "I see we have some new faces today, so I'll introduce myself. I am Mr. Authoritarian-Hammer, and I have the honor/duty/compulsion to be your reeducation and obedience facilitator. You are here because your behavior has inclined toward nonconformity. In our new Phandic culture, individuality, experimentation, and exploration are all frowned upon, so I hope you will participate fully in this program designed to help you find your proper place in our benevolent society. Glory to the empress!"

We had been hearing this sort of insane talk since returning to Earth. The Phands had been capturing and subjugating worlds for centuries, so they had a reliable playbook for planetary domination. Though they'd been on Earth less than a week, things were already running like clockwork. They had procedures for every step of the conquest process, from establishing subspace energy relays to forcibly recruiting compliance instructors. Authority figures who resisted the Phands—from world leaders to policemen—were injected with behavior-modifying nanites, which compelled them to enforce the new order. Plenty of locals went along willingly, though. My guess was this man had not actually been born with the name Authoritarian-Hammer, but he had a hard look that told me that reeducation and obedience facilitator might just be the job he'd always dreamed of. Kids who lob spitballs need careers when they grow up.

"I have not been doing this very long," said Mr. Authoritarian-Hammer, "but I have high hopes for my students. Please be advised that those who fail to conform to Phandic ways will be shipped to Planet Pleasant, where their disobedience can be studied and understood so that future generations of youth may better serve the empress."

I'd been threatened with Planet Pleasant before. Junup, the previously mentioned evil goat-turtle who had somehow taken control of the Confederation, had brought it up the last time I'd been on Confederation Central. It was some kind of super-secret Phandic mad-science facility, and pretty much the last place anyone wanted to go.

"Before we begin today's lessons in subordination, service, and the proper disregard for our own feelings," said Mr.

Authoritarian-Hammer, "I'd like our new students to introduce themselves. When I read your name, please rise and tell the group about your crime against our benevolent and merciful empress, and how you most hope to change in order to earn the privilege of continued existence."

We'd known this was coming, and just as we'd already come up with fake names that would help us blend in, we'd also agreed to say what we had to say in order to get along. All we had to do was survive in this school, without making trouble, for one day. I figured that even I could manage something like that.

"Sally Applesauce," Mr. Authoritarian-Hammer said, narrowing his eyes suspiciously at the name on his printout.

Mi Sun rose to her feet. I gave her my best *that's your idea of an inconspicuous name?* glower, but she ignored me. Maybe she thought that *was* a normal American name. Having spent a fair amount of time on a space station full of countless alien species, you tend to forget how much the minor cultural differences of your own planet can trip you up.

"Yeah, hi," she said with her customary gruffness. "I am Sally Applesauce, and I am guilty of breaking curfew, refusing to report to my appropriate reeducation center, and showing disrespect to designated Phandic authorities. In the future, I promise to give all Phands and their representatives exactly what they deserve."

I hoped that those in the room who did not know her would not hear that the way I did.

Next came Alice, who had picked the name Betty Hill. She told the class she wanted to help the Phandic empire achieve greatness. She tried to sell it, but she sounded like she was choking on a chicken bone the entire time.

"Jean-Luc Picard," Mr. Authoritarian-Hammer called out, one eyebrow raised with suspicion.

I waved at the students who were now watching me with obvious curiosity. "Yeah, my parents—that is, Mr. and Mrs. Picard—were total nerds," I offered. Maybe the name was a little too nerdy, but I hoped we would be long gone before anyone had a chance to look into my background.

Finally it was Charles's turn. "Anthony Stark," said Mr. Authoritarian-Hammer.

Was the full name supposed to disguise the fact that he'd picked Iron Man's real name? It was too late to do anything about it now, and given that Mi Sun had taken a stab at a generic name by calling herself something that sounded like a My Little Pony, there was no point in complaining.

Mr. Authoritarian-Hammer proceeded with the rest of the roll call. After that, we stood, put our hands over our hearts and, along with the rest of the group, pledged allegiance to the war banner of the pacified planets of the Phandic Empire, and to the ever-expanding hegemony for which it stands, one culture, under the empress, with obedience and prescribed modes of conduct for all.

We resumed our seats and proceeded to learn how to be better imperial subjects and help our supreme viceroy, Nora Price, the most esteemed colonial administrator on our planet. These lessons kept us busy until lunchtime.

The Manhattan School and Reform Facility for Insufficiently Subservient Youth had obviously been put together in a hurry, but even so, it was already running smoothly. The Phands seemed to like working with existing social structures in the worlds they conquered, and since the family unit was a big part of human culture, the invaders cracked down heavily on people, especially children, who didn't seem to have a home. Alice, Charles, Mi Sun, and I had no families—according to our hastily-forged identities—so we had been sent to this facility, where we would live until we became adults and could serve the Phandic Empire by oppressing others, building things that aided in that oppression, or offering ourselves up as cannon fodder in one of the empire's many wars. I knew the Phands regarded children and adolescents as hardly better than animals—it was one of the reasons they were so irritated that a bunch of kids kept pwning them—so their main educational goal was to make sure we were fully indoctrinated before we grew out of our current larval form. Our goal was to be off the planet before the next sunrise.

But first: lunch period. After our morning lessons, trustees guided us through the bleak cinder-block halls to the cafeteria. All the students wore school uniforms—gray slacks and blue blazers for the boys, the same blazer plus a short plaid skirt and knee-high black socks for the girls. We were all required to wear ties, though the rules mandated that the girls had to wear theirs loose with the collar undone so that, in Mi Sun's words, they looked like they belonged in an anime.

The trustees, on the other hand, wore menacing black uniforms and moved through the halls with the confidence of storm troopers. Really they were just kids our own age who had demonstrated unusual loyalty or received high scores in domination aggression on their Battery of Universal Talents Test. Owing to their excellent BUTT scores (the Phands hadn't yet seemed to notice this acronym, and I wasn't going to be the one to point it out), these kids had been given the great honor of abandoning their own education to help keep possible trouble-makers in line. From what I'd seen, they performed these duties with what any Phand or Phand sympathizer would consider an entirely appropriate amount of shoving, name-calling, and jabs from lightly charged electrical prods. So far I'd avoided these punishment sticks, and my augmentations would keep them from doing any real harm as long as I saw the jolt coming. They looked like they were painful, though, if the wincing, teeth-grinding, and cursing of the kids on the business end of those things were any guide.

Once we reached the cafeteria, we lined up, collected our trays, and shuffled along until a machine squirted unidentified—and unidentifiable—nutritional goo into various tray compartments. We then found our way to a table.

"Jean-Luc Picard," Alice said to me, her voice low. Unlike most school cafeterias, in which shouting was pretty much required, here people spoke very quietly.

"I had to pick something, and I had to do it fast," I said, jabbing a thumb at Charles. "And why single me out? He picked Tony Stark."

"I picked *Anthony* Stark," he said. "I was subtle."

Mi Sun was about to say something, almost certainly in the *shut up* family, when a golf ball-size spitball arced through the air and landed in her tray of theoretically edible slop. Just to add an extra layer of grossness, it sprayed food all over her face and school uniform.

Mi Sun was the person in our group who generally advocated restraint, but now she was also the person with alien gruel dripping into her eyes, so there was a pretty good chance she might make a pitch for giving restraint a rest. Even without her upgrades, Mi Sun could have tae-kwon-doed her way through half the delinquents in the room, but doing something like that might cause our ordinary-kids cover story to come under a little scrutiny.

I checked to see where the spitball had come from. No guesswork required. I'd already figured out how to use my alien augments to track a missile trajectory to its source. I assumed the software had been designed to track actual weapons across large distances, but it worked perfectly well on a smaller scale. A red line appeared across my field of vision, tracing the saliva bomb back to its lunchroom table of origin.

"Take some calming breaths," I told Mi Sun. "Think of pretty flowers and sunsets while I deal with it."

"You?" she asked while wiping goo off her face with one of those school-cafeteria disposable napkins designed to resist ever absorbing anything. "You'll make it worse than me kicking him into tomorrow. Let Alice go. She's good at defusing things."

"I'm not sending Alice to deal with a bully," I said. "She's too nice. I can handle it myself."

"Then Charles. Or send a greeting card. A fruit basket. Anything but you."

I found this insulting. "You don't think I can handle it?"

She slumped her shoulders, defeated by life. "You'll go over there with the best of intentions. You'll even do and say all the right stuff, and then one of two things will happen."

"Someone will utter a straight line that you cannot resist, and you will say something insulting and mildly funny," Charles proposed, "thus snatching discord from the jaws of peace."

"Mildly?" I asked.

"Or," Alice continued, "in spite of being your own worst enemy, you'll somehow manage not to say or do anything wrong. You will play it by the book, and be on the verge of resolving all problems, when something unexpected will happen, something entirely out of your control, that will blow this whole operation."

"Wow," I said. "You guys don't trust me at all."

"Of course we trust you," Alice said.

"Let's not get ahead of ourselves," Mi Sun cautioned.

"Of course we trust you," Alice tried again, "but there's a pattern we can't ignore. When we're dealing with messy situations, you're totally dependable. You are the guy we want when things get crazy and dangerous. But delicate, diplomatic operations? Not your strength."

I gritted my teeth for a moment. "That's hurtful because it's true," I said, deciding to be completely honest. These guys were the best human friends I'd ever had, and there was no point in acting all defensive. "But I've learned a lot. I can defuse with the best of them."

"And we can always unleash our ancient-alien technological awesomeness and speed up the timetable if we have to," Charles suggested.

"That's a worst-case scenario," Alice said. "We don't know one tenth of what this tech can do. I don't think we're ready for a big fight."

"Besides, we want to be ghosts here," Mi Sun said. "Invisible."

"We can't be invisible with some jerk throwing spitballs into your lunchlike substance," I said. "We've got a long road ahead of us, and we have to trust each other, so you guys are going to sit there and watch me handle this like a pro."

I stood up, walked across the cafeteria, and sat down across from the hulking blond kid who, in my mind, I had already dubbed Mr. Potato Head.

"Hey," I said. "You're Gavin, right?"

"How'd you know my name?" He scowled at me.

I shrugged. "Roll call."

There are a couple of things I want on the record. At this point, though several seconds had passed, I had not addressed him as Mr. Potato Head, nor had I made a sarcastic comment about how those of us with working brains can listen to something like roll call and actually pick up information. I let these things go, because I was in diplomatic mode. I was Diplomacy Man. Conflict resolution was my superpower. I was going to show my friends, the world, the entire galaxy that I could be counted on to get things done without causing wars, explosions, or major political upheavals.

"Gavin, do you mind if I ask why you are throwing spitballs at my friends?"

"Didn't mean to hit your friend," he said. "Mostly I was just throwing at you."

"Okay, good. We're making progress. We are learning about each other. Why are you throwing spitballs at me?"

"Because I don't like your stupid face."

I smiled. I was an ambassador of peace, and ambassadorial people smile and do not take offense. I was playing a role. I was in character. I was like a S.H.I.E.L.D. agent infiltrating a secret organization.

"I get that a lot," I said. This part was easy, because it was true. "People see me, they want to smack me. They don't know why, but this kind of feeling can result in their saying things like what you just said. Of course, I don't have a stupid face, but you are looking for a way to express your feelings."

"No," Gavin said. "Your face is actually stupid."

This was coming from a guy who looked like a starchy tuber, though I did not make this point out loud. Diplomatic. "You know, we have an honest disagreement about my face, but we should set that aside. This isn't about you and me. It's about the greater glory of the Phandic Empire. The empress doesn't care about my face. She needs us both to be the best subjects we can be. Instead of being angry with me, be angry at those who oppose Phandic greatness."

"No one opposes the Phands," Mr. Potato Head reminded me—or at least he reminded me of the lies we were told. "No one is strong enough."

"Right you are," I said, snapping my fingers and pointing at him. "You are an excellent student of Phandic knowledge. No Planet Pleasant for you."

"The thing is," Mr. Potato Head said, lowering his voice, "I hate those alien creeps, and I hate the people who want to kiss their butts even more. So I'm going to keep throwing spitballs at you, because you are a lickspittle."

Number one, there is absolutely nothing I own that I would not have bet against this guy knowing the word "lickspittle." That was a plot twist for sure. Number two, he was on the right side of things. He hated the Phands, and I hated the Phands. We should be like brothers or something. In an alternate time-line, the team of Stupid Face and Potato Head could be a thing.

"Your best move is to play it safe," I said, keeping my voice quiet. "Follow the rules so you don't get in trouble."

"Phands captured my parents and put them in a reeducation labor camp," he said. "I'm not planning on getting along with anyone, especially not a collaborator like you."

So saying, he pushed me. If I'd had a second to brace myself, my nanotech augments would have easily guarded me against it, but it surprised me, so I went crashing into the next table. Trays and plastic went flying. Cups of water spilled. Lunch trays arced through the air. A few kids actually screamed. From somewhere behind me I could hear Mi Sun saying, "I told you!"

I was scrambling to my feet when someone reached out and grabbed my arm and hoisted me the rest of the way up. It was one of the trustees, the uniformed kids who helped to keep order. I was about to thank him, when his face went weird on me, shifting in an instant from curiosity to surprise to unmistakable happiness.

"Hey," he said, smiling like he'd just won the tormentor's lottery. "You're Zeke Reynolds, the most hated human in the Phandic Empire! I'm totally going to score some major points for bringing you in!"

It was then I decided, no matter how painful the advice, I was going to have to start listening to my friends.

CHAPTER TWO

How is it possible to go from having a spaceship that can, within all reasonable limits, take you to pretty much any inhabited spot in the galaxy to, less than twenty-four hours later, being trapped on Earth in a facility for insufficiently obedient children? A lot of things have to go wrong, and, though it was small consolation, none of these things had been my fault. There is actually a fair amount of evidence to support the theory that sometimes bad things happen without my direct involvement.

The day before the incident now known to history as the Lunchroom Catastrophe, we had tunneled into Earth's solar system in our stolen Former ship, emerging among the outer gas giants. That's where we learned that my home planet was now in the hands of the Phandic Empire. Rather than risk being seen by our enemies, Steve set a course for another quick jump to the nearest star on the ship's charts—less than half an hour away.

In the meantime, we'd cooked up a plan. We were going to figure out a way to rescue some prisoners from the Phands, a group that included our friends Nayana and Urch. More importantly, as far as the stability of galactic culture was concerned, it included Confederation Director Ghli Wixxix and Captain Hyi of the *Kind Disposition*. Both had information that could lead to the overthrow of Junup, who had seized power after

Ghli Wixxix's supposed death (at my supposed hands) and then secretly allied the Confederation, or at least his own power base, with the Phandic Empire. Given that the Phands had been at the Confederation's mercy—thanks to technology stolen by my gang of rebels, I might add—Junup's alliance was the only thing keeping the empress's oppressive lights on right now.

So it was actually pretty simple. Get a small band of kids who didn't know what they were doing, accompanied by an adult who kept telling them what they wanted to do was crazy, and infiltrate an evil empire, discover the location of a top-secret prison holding beings who were probably the most heavily guarded inmates in the galaxy, and break them out. Sure, there were some leaps of faith hardwired into this scheme, but we'd done crazier things. I know this is not the most convincing argument out there, but I thought it had more going for it than *Let's do nothing and hope everything works out swell*.

Besides, we had one serious advantage: We were now maxed-out superheroes. That definitely goes into the plus column. Our last fun-filled excursion through Confederation Central had taken us though the underground Hidden Fortress, an ancient facility established by the mysterious precursor aliens, the Formers. Before escaping, we'd managed to upload nanites that not only gave us the standard Confederation skill tree, but the newly rediscovered military tech tree. As soon as we'd gotten what we wanted, in what may be the worst act of vandalism in the history of the galaxy we destroyed all that Former technology in order to keep it from falling into the wrong hands, claws, or tentacles. If we hadn't done it, the bad guys might have gotten hold of some unstoppable weapons, so

I knew it was the right thing to do, but it still felt like destroying the library of Alexandria times a billion.

Once we had all these skill-creating and -enhancing nanites swimming through our bloodstreams, Tamret hacked in and maxed out both systems for everyone. None of us were entirely sure of all the crazy things we could now do. In fact, the system seemed designed to make it difficult for the user to learn about these skills except by experimenting. There was no clear tech progression, like there was with the standard Confederation upgrades. Instead, skills followed one another in what seemed to be random patterns, and I couldn't find a list or a map to let me know all the things I could now do. The best I could manage was to search for skills using my HUD and hope the skill I was looking for existed. It was a little frustrating, but I was looking forward to discovering new abilities while simultaneously making every Phand and Junup follower I ran into eat a little plastic cup of humiliation pudding.

Also on my mind was the question of whether or not Tamret, who had done said hacking, was my girlfriend. With all the escaping, destroying, and surviving-against-the-odds we'd been up to lately, we hadn't had the chance for an honest, heart-to-heart sit-down. The fact that it had been impossible for us to get more than three and a half feet away from her former fiancé had not helped.

Lots of things to juggle, yes, but I knew what we had to do. After what had felt like a long period of helplessness, a sense of purpose felt great. Defy a brutal military empire, redraw the lines of galactic power, rescue my planet, and sort things out with the alien cat-girl I liked. It was going to be a busy week. A good week, but busy.

At least I thought so until everything went wrong—which, honestly, I should have expected.

Steve piloted us out of Earth's system in a hurry. We hadn't had a chance to carefully review the galactic maps, but I figured there should be nothing much happening around Alpha Centauri. I was wrong. There were about a gazillion Phandic ships in the system. *Doing what?* you may ask. Good question, but no one on my ship was suggesting that we find out before we came up with a way to escape. And yes, a gazillion may be an exaggeration, but I wasn't counting. The actual tally was more than a few and fewer than infinity.

"There's like a gazillion Phands in this system, mate," Steve said in his inexplicable working-class London accent. He flicked his reptilian tongue like he was trying to taste the number of enemies in the air.

"Get us out of here!" Villainic screeched. He was staring at the viewscreen with his eyes wide and his catlike ears pressed back in alarm.

I would not have screeched, personally, and given that he'd been trying to marry Tamret, I wasn't so inclined to sympathize with Villainic, but I still understood his sentiment. The problem was that interstellar travel doesn't allow for quick and easy departures. You can't just zip merrily around from star to star on a whim. Punching a direct, navigable hole in reality and coming out on the other end is not, if I may make an analogy, like dusting crops. It's more like doing advanced math while playing Jenga on a pogo stick as you try to invent a new musical scale. It can't be done by normal beings. It can only be done, in fact, by beings who are both naturally gifted and have taken points in the appropriate skill trees while using computers designed by a long-vanished civilization of unfathomable intellect. It doesn't help when hysterical aliens, beings who are not really in your group of friends and who are trying to marry girls they should not have been trying to marry, are screeching.

Tamret and Charles were busy working the navigation and helm consoles, trying to figure a way out of the system, or at least a place to hide. The first priority had to be avoiding detection by the Phands. Meanwhile, I was warming up the weapons console. Rightly or wrongly, I was considered the go-to guy in our group for making things turn into fiery balls of destruction. Sometimes I only blew up what I was supposed to; sometimes things got a little more creative. All I knew was that the majority of beings I liked in the universe were on that ship with me, and I was not letting the Phands take us without a fight.

"Before we start giving our position away with weapons fire," Steve said to me, "I might have a bit of a plan."

"Let's hear it," I said. "Better yet, let's do it, and you can tell me about it after."

"It's these new skill implants, yeah?" he said, scratching his Komodo dragon head like he was trying to get a handle on this plan even as he explained it. "I think I may have figured out a way to get us out of here, but I don't really understand it."

Dr. Roop, the only adult on our ship, now peered over our shoulders, stretching his long, giraffelike neck between us. "The Formers had navigation skills we have only begun to guess at," he said in his curiously Dutch-sounding accent. "Your mind must have intuitively picked up on one of these possibilities and is urging you to take it. Perhaps you should listen."

"It shouldn't be possible based on what I know," Steve

explained, "but let's face it—I don't know all that much. I have this idea that I can reverse our tunnel, pretty much send us back to where we came from. Pretty close, anyhow."

"If you think you can do it," I said, "then it sounds like our best option."

"What good is that?" Villainic demanded. "We came here in order to escape from Zeke's conquered system. There were Phands there as well."

In spite of him having performed some inexplicable Rarel ritual that had made me his brother, I could always count on Villainic to complain about any plan I liked.

"The good thing," Steve said, "is that no one knew we were there. We tunneled out before they detected us. Here we're right on top of these blokes, so they're going to notice us in a matter of seconds. When that happens, they'll come looking to crack open our ship to get at the nutmeats inside. Do you fancy being the nutmeats, mate?"

Villainic did not answer, but I thought it was safe to take that question as rhetorical. No one in the history of creation has fancied being the nutmeats.

"So we go somewhere else after we get back to our system?" Mi Sun asked. "How do we know it won't be just as bad?"

"The galaxy is very large," Charles said, "and the odds of any particular place we choose having a gazillion Phands are relatively small. I say it is a risk worth taking."

It being a risk worth taking, we took the risk. Steve did a thing that he didn't understand very well and we understood even less, and with a half dozen Phandic flying saucers moving in with their metaphorical nutcrackers at the ready, we popped right back into tunnel.

Now we had to wait half an hour to get back to the place we didn't want to be. It made sense to have another destination in mind by the time we emerged so we could reroute in a hurry.

Dr. Roop suggested the nearby Wolf 359 system, but Charles and I vetoed it on the grounds that it was the site of a devastating Federation defeat by the Borg. "It's courting bad luck," Charles insisted. Instead we opted for the binary Luyten 726-8 system, which had no science-fiction connotations that I was aware of. It was uninhabited and uninhabitable, therefore with zero strategic value. It seemed as good a place as any for us to catch our breath.

We had to get there first. Once we reemerged from tunnel in my home system, Steve needed to plug in the new coordinates and tunnel out. With the engines hot, and the coordinates ready, we should have been able to evacuate in a matter of minutes.

And that is exactly what would have happened had not something much worse happened instead.

The trip back to my solar system was a little bit tense, sure. None of us knew exactly what to expect. I spent most of the time sitting at the weapons console, though there wasn't anything to target while in tunnel.

We were maybe halfway through the trip when Alice came over to me. "Can I talk to you for a minute?" She was busy taking her mass of nearly colorless hair out of a black elastic and then putting it back in.

Tamret looked up at us from her console but didn't say anything. Her lavender eyes seemed to glow against the background of her white fur.

I got up, and Alice and I walked to the back of the ship. "What's up?"

"I don't know if it's going to be possible now," she said, "but if there's any way you can do it safely, I want you to drop me off on Earth before you go on the rescue mission."

"What? Why?" This took me by surprise. Alice had been so desperate to get into space that she'd stowed away on a shuttle, risking her life just for the chance to see life in the wider galaxy. Since then, she'd been a valuable member of the team. I knew what we were going to attempt was risky, but no more so than things we'd already done. With our augmentations, maybe it was a whole lot less risky than the things we'd already done.

"Look," she said, "you guys have been great to me and everything, and I really want to be a part of what you've got planned, but there's an alien army on Earth. I have to believe they're not going to be too nice to people who used to be in the military. I'm worried about my dad and my Uncle Jacinto." She rubbed at her eyes, maybe to keep from crying. "Especially my dad."

Alice's father had been suffering from PTSD. He drank too much and generally seemed out of it. I knew she'd felt terrible about leaving him behind, but now that things had fallen apart on Earth, he might really need her help.

"The sooner we get the Phands off Earth, the safer he'll be. I understand if you want to go back, but you could be doing him more good by staying with us."

"Maybe," she said. "I don't know. But I think he might need me now. With my new abilities, there's probably a lot I can do to help Earth while you guys are taking care of the big picture. Besides, Tamret doesn't want me here." She glanced over at Tamret, who was pretending not to watch us.

"She'll be fine. She just needs to get used to having you around. If that's the real reason—"

"It's *a* real reason," she said, "but not the only one. I don't know if I can have my head in the game if I'm worried about my father the whole time. Getting everyone out of that prison isn't going to be easy, and you don't need a team member who's distracted."

I understood what it was like to worry about your parents. I'd gone to Confederation Central in the first place because I wanted to help my mom. "I get it. I hate to see you go, but if that's what you need to do, I won't try to talk you out of it. I mean, assuming we can even get you to Earth safely."

"Let's see how that goes," she said, "and then we can decide what to do."

A few minutes later, Tamret came over to speak to me. Like the rest of us, she was still wearing the clothes in which we'd been wandering around the Forbidden Zone. Most of the dust had worn off by now, though, and somehow she managed to look relatively neat.

"You're not going to give me a hard time about Alice, are you?" I asked her.

She smirked at me and her lavender eyes crinkled with amusement. "Seriously? Am I supposed to be jealous?"

Her response was not what I'd expected, and so I may have had a hard time making any sounds that didn't sound like sputtering.

Tamret's expression hardened slightly. "I don't need to be jealous, do I?"

"No, of course not," I said, maybe a little too quickly. She didn't, of course. Tamret was the most amazing girl I'd ever met. She was brazen and smart and maybe a little bit reckless, but the most important thing to me was that she made me feel like I was those things too. When Tamret was around, I could go places and do things I would never have had the guts to do before I met her, and she always made me feel like I could get the job done.

"Anyhow," I said, "Alice wants to see if she can leave when we get to Earth."

"Really?" Tamret's ears rotated slightly backward. "I thought she wanted to be in on the action."

"She does, but she's worried about her dad."

Tamret nodded. "I'd have given her a hard time if it were something stupid, but if my parents were still around, I'd want to make sure they were safe too."

Her parents had disappeared into the black hole of her country's prison system when she was a little girl. Tamret had no idea if they were alive, but I got the sense she assumed the worst. The way things were on her planet, she had no reason to be optimistic. I knew that was one of the reasons she had been fighting so hard for the Confederation. If she could get membership for her world, the oppressive rulers and tight caste systems of Rarel would come crashing down.

"She thinks you have a problem with her," I said, feeling like I was on thin ice.

"Maybe at first," Tamret admitted. "Things were weird with us when I got back to Confederation Central." "Weird" in this case meant she'd shown up with a total dork as her fiancé, but that was all in the past, so there was no point in dwelling on it. "But she's a good member of the team. I'd rather she stuck around, but I understand why she needs to go."

She looked relaxed, and I knew she was being completely honest. She usually was unless she thought she needed to protect someone from the truth. It was just one more thing I admired about her. I'd spent so much time on Confederation Central worrying about how intense she was, how she might hate Alice because she'd see her as a rival, and now, once again, I saw that I'd been an idiot to underestimate her.

I wanted to talk to her about whether or not we were a thing, and if she was still planning on coming back to Earth with me when this was all over, but it seemed like the wrong time. It always seemed like the wrong time, what with planetary invasions and upheavals in galactic civilizations and all that. Maybe, I thought, it didn't matter. She wanted to sit near me while we recovered from the last crisis and waited for the next one. For now that was enough.

We emerged back in Earth's system, just as Steve thought we would. That was good. We did not emerge at the exact same point from which we'd departed, in the void between Jupiter and Saturn. That was less good. Instead we emerged between the Earth and the Moon. Quick astronomy lesson: There is a lot less distance between the Earth and the Moon than there is between Jupiter and Saturn. That means the gravitational pull of the larger body, in this case my home planet, was going to become a factor, especially since the crew piloting our ship had anticipated popping into gravity-negligible emptiness and not next to something as big as a planet.

And, while we're at it, quick lesson in space-battle tactics: When you suddenly appear near a planet where there are dozens of enemy ships on the lookout for anything that doesn't belong, you don't have a whole lot of time to come up with a clever plan that doesn't end with capture or destruction.

Steve did not discuss options, because there were no options to discuss. We had nowhere to run, and there was no place to head but down. In order to avoid being spotted by the orbiting Phandic cruisers, he took us directly toward Earth.

The ship rumbled and lurched as we entered the atmosphere, but then quickly settled. The viewscreens revealed clouds and below us oceans. Inhabited planets tended to look similar from orbit, but there was still something unmistakable about my own world, even viewed from miles up. This was where I was from, the place I was fighting for—and it had been invaded by aliens who hated me.

"Head for someplace uninhabited," I told Steve. "We can't let the nonhumans be spotted."

"No!" Dr. Roop cried. He was rubbing his knobby horns, which he tended to do when nervous. "The Phands won't miss an unidentified spacecraft entering the atmosphere. You have to find someplace densely populated where the natives of this planet can blend in. Those of us from other worlds are going to be captured. There is no avoiding that."

I glanced at Tamret. "Forget that. We need another option."

"It's the only way," he said. He had opened up the holographic keyboard from his data bracelet and was typing rapidly while he talked to us. "I'm sending all of you my plan. The Phands always follow protocol, which is to wait two standard days before they begin interrogating prisoners. With your upgraded skill trees, that should give you ample time to find and liberate us. If we attempt anything else, we'll all be captured, and the situation will be much more difficult. We want to get off-world unhurt, but we also want to do it without revealing what we can now do, so I suggest you only use the Former military technology for concealment. Nothing ostentatious. The less they know about our new abilities, the better."

A message pinged in my HUD, and I opened it and glanced quickly at Dr. Roop's plan, which did seem to make sense. I looked at Steve and Tamret, who both nodded. If they were on board, then I had no choice but to go along with the scheme, however much I hated it.

"I can't agree to this," Villainic said. He was the only one among us who had not received the Former implants. He didn't even have a data bracelet, so Dr. Roop couldn't have shown him the plan. "On behalf of Tamret and myself, I insist that we find an alternative that does not involve capture."

As had become our custom, we ignored him.

"We are also going to have to destroy this ship," Charles said. "It is of Former origin, which means they'll be able to figure out exactly who we are."

"Yes," Dr. Roop agreed. He had already thought of it. He began programming a molecular decomposition program into the ship's computer. It was a lot less spectacular than an explosion, but a great deal more effective. The ship would dissolve into particles and drift away in the breeze. There would be no pieces left to examine or reconstruct. The Phands would know some aliens had landed on the planet, but it would take them time to identify their species and point of origin. If Dr. Roop's information was correct, Phandic protocol would require the prisoners to stew for two days before they began any questioning. With the aid of the stealth features of our upgrades, we'd use that time to find our friends, steal a ship, and be back to exactly where we were before we'd started spiraling out of control through Earth's atmosphere.

"Your world," Steve said to me. "You should take the helm."

I sat down and began to steady the ship as I figured out where we should go. If Alice, Charles, Mi Sun, and I were all going to blend in, we needed to be someplace that was ethnically diverse so none of us looked out of place. We were also wearing Confederation clothing, which wasn't that different from plenty of Earth clothing, but it would help to be in a place with lots of weirdly dressed teenagers. Maybe there were better spots on the planet than New York City for kids who'd gotten their outfits on a space station, but I couldn't think of any.

While I piloted the ship, Dr. Roop turned to address us humans. "We can't even guess at all the abilities we now possess, but finding us and rescuing us from the Phands is well within your power. I have no doubt you can do this. But you are going to need to protect yourselves from scrutiny. You have a camouflage ability, so use it to hide your data bracelet and any technology that could identify you as having spent time off-world."

I checked my HUD and saw this was pretty easy to do.

"Why do we need to wait to be rescued?" Villainic asked. "Why can't you use your new abilities to lead us to safety?"

"Because once the Phands understand what we can do, they are going to take us much more seriously," Tamret said. "If they realize we are basically walking weapons with the means and will to take down their empire, I think they'll find ways to make our lives more difficult."

"Exactly," Dr. Roop said. "However, those of you who are

from this world will have one disadvantage, and that is the people you know and care about. If the Phands identify you, they may try to use your families and friends against you. For that reason, I suggest you do all you can to conceal your identities and to avoid making contact with anyone."

This was a disappointment. Alice had wanted to check in on her dad, and I had been hoping to talk to my parents to make sure they were okay. We all wanted to know that our friends and families were safe, but we couldn't take the risk. The best way to protect them was to stick to the plan and get the Phands off Earth for good.

"Okay," I said. "I think we get it."

We were coming across the Atlantic and could see Manhattan now. My first impulse was to land in Central Park, and our course was projected on a holographic display above the helm station. When Tamret saw where I was heading, she shoved me away from the console. "An open field is going to make it impossible for you guys to escape. You need someplace crowded, where you can vanish quickly."

Tamret may not have known very much about New York, but by pure chance or clever instinct she picked a good spot, landing our ship at Astor Place, right by a big statue of a cube. I don't know what that cube is supposed to be, but I was pretty sure no one was looking at it too closely when our ship touched down. On our viewscreens we could see people staring at us but keeping their distance, not sure what fresh horrors were going to emerge. They probably thought we were more Phands, come to do something terrible.

"Everyone ready?" I asked.

"Not yet," Dr. Roop said. "We have a few minutes before the

Phands will likely be able to mobilize a response to an unknown spaceship landing here. Keep in mind that on occupied worlds the Phands use a system of passive security checks embedded into virtually all their technology. Inhabitants radiate an identification aura, which is constantly being verified. You will have to forge identifications in order to blend in, and this should be quite easy to do with our new upgrades, but you will first have to hack into the local security systems. That means you will not have the opportunity to generate proper identification until you are actually interacting with local authorities. Meanwhile, they will be attempting to read your aura before it exists."

Okay, so I'd be forging a new identity on the fly under impossible conditions. "Got it."

"Then I will open the hatch," said Dr. Roop. "Is everyone prepared to run?"

"Not yet," Tamret said. She threw her arms around me and hugged me. "Don't be long," she whispered in my ear.

"I won't," I told her. The last time we'd been separated, I'd promised to come get her, but I'd had no idea how I could make it happen. This time around, I was ready. The Phands were not going to get in my way.

Dr. Roop opened the hatch, and the gloomy light of an overcast day streamed in. We ran.

By unspoken agreement, the humans all stuck together, as did the aliens. It wasn't going to work in anyone's favor if we got separated.

I'd been to New York a few times with my mom, and I felt like I knew the city moderately well—I understood the difference between uptown and downtown and could read a subway map—but I'd never been to New York during an alien occupation. That changed things.

The streets were, as always, full of people, and I was pleased that none were Phands. I had no doubt there were plenty of them on the planet, but none were near me, and that was a good thing. Less good was the obvious influence they'd had on the place in the short time they had been on Earth. All the billboards and advertisements on buildings were now about the glories of the Phandic Empire. There were holographic projections in the skies promising peace, prosperity, and order. More than that, I saw human police officers in altered uniforms, changed so that they reflected the cut of Phandic military uniforms. On one of the police cars rushing toward where we'd landed I saw the motto TO PACIFY AND PRESERVE ORDER.

Worst of all were the billboards and posters showing the smug face of our supreme viceroy, Nora Price. I was annoyed, but not at all surprised, that she had risen to become top Phandic bootlicker on Earth. She had been the adult human representative during our first visit to Confederation Central, but it had turned out that she was a Phandic double agent. Now she'd received her reward for selling us out. Pictures of her were everywhere. We saw her glancing down at us wherever we went, smiling her humorless smile, as text accompanying the images urged us to ADMIRE AND OBEY or SUBMIT TO YOUR VICEROY—AND PROSPER!

Nora Price and I had a history, and it wasn't a pleasant one. I'd made her look bad in front of her Phandic masters, and I knew she would like nothing better than to see me face what she considered justice for my crime of not wanting to be murdered. I needed to rescue my friends and get busy putting an end to this invasion before she found out I was here.

I dared a quick glance behind me while police officers rushed out of their vehicles to inspect our ship. They seemed afraid to get too close, a decision they probably felt good about when the ship began to glow an eerie white color and then slowly dissolve into a wispy fog that blew away in the breeze.

I started to run again, but Alice grabbed hold of my arm. "Don't," she said. "No one else is running. Act normal."

"She means act like a normal person," Mi Sun elaborated. "Don't act normal for you."

Alice was right. A crowd had now formed at what had been mutually determined a safe perimeter around where our ship had landed. The police were cautiously walking around the now-empty spot, but there were no signs that anything had been there a second ago. Several of them were talking nervously into their phones, obviously unclear about how to proceed. My guess was that the Phands weren't particularly forgiving plane-tary masters, and none of these officers wanted to do the wrong thing in a completely unfamiliar situation. As far as any of them could know, they'd already made a thousand mistakes, and their new bosses were going to be very angry.

As for Tamret, Steve, Dr. Roop, and Villainic, I could see no sign of them. Maybe they hadn't been captured yet, but it was only a matter of time. Two cat aliens, a lizard man, and a guy with a giraffe neck were not going to blend in, not even in New York.

I glanced back over my shoulder and saw police officers moving crowds away from where the ship had been, and they weren't being too gentle about it. "I can't believe they're working with the Phands," I said. "New York cops should be leading the charge against the aliens."

"I did some research on the way over here," Alice said. "I figured it was a good idea to be prepared."

Especially, I thought, *since she plans to stay.*

"About ten percent of the population on Earth now has behavior-modification nanites," she explained. "Anyone in law enforcement or the military, or with any kind of leadership role, has them. It's not exactly mind control, but they make people want to help the Phands. It's not really their fault that they're cooperating."

"So we can't expect any local help," I said. "Good to know."

Alice looked around. "Yeah. So, now what?"

"Now we wait until they're captured," I said. "Then we find out where they're being held and go get them. Let's give things a few hours to settle down and then see if we can hack into the Phandic planetary computers."

"Okay," Alice said. "I'll help make sure everyone gets away, but then you guys are on your own."

"What?" Mi Sun crinkled her face in surprise. That was the first she'd heard of Alice's plan to leave.

"I'm just—" Alice said, cutting herself off. I guessed maybe she didn't want to talk about her dad's problems. "This is just more than I signed on for, you know. And I'm worried about my dad."

"Yeah," Mi Sun said. She seemed to be thinking about this. "I'm worried about my family too."

We began to turn away from the crowd when we noticed a police officer standing directly behind us. He was holding up his smartphone and moving it so it scanned each of us, like he was taking videos.

"Why don't you have loyal-citizen identification auras?" he demanded.

I haven't had a chance to forge mine yet was not an answer that was going to get me very far. "We forgot them at home?" I attempted.

I took some comfort in the knowledge that there was no response unstupid enough to get us out of that situation.

By now several other officers were coming toward us, getting out their handcuffs. We could either fight and run, which would only draw attention to us, or go along for now.

"It looks like we've got four more delinquents for reeducation school," one of the cops said as he cuffed my hands behind my back. "Don't worry. Pretty soon you'll learn all about the Phandic Empire. I know things must seem scary right now, but the behavioral-modification nanites they've given me have helped me to see that the Phands are really our friends."

And that's how we ended up going back to school.

CHAPTER THREE

In order to operate reeducation facilities for troublemaking kids, you need to have some kind of system of oversight. You need enforcers, sure, but a particular kind of enforcer—the kind who won't make friends because he's too busy punishing anyone who steps out of line. I have no doubt that there are adults out there who would love a job in which they got to punish a seventh-grader for failing to wear a HAVE YOU HUGGED A PHAND TODAY? button, but those adults were probably needed as soldiers or torturers or fry cooks. No, the well-oiled Phandic machine used other kids, and they were likely to be the worst bullies they could find.

The oversized lowbrow who stood in front of me, pointing gleefully, was named Tanner Hughes. He'd tormented me when I was in school back in Delaware, and now here he was, in a uniform, with license to torment weaker kids. Maybe the Phandic invasion wasn't good for everyone, but for the Tanner Hugheses of the world it was like winning the lottery.

"My name is Jean-Luc Picard," I assured him, trying not to make eye contact. "I have no idea who this Zeke Reynolds guy is."

"He sounds like a total troublemaker," Mi Sun said. She'd come over to stand near me, and had her arms folded, scowling at me like I'd done something wrong.

"Go back to your seat, Sally Applesauce!" Tanner Hughes commanded.

And here I laughed, because I thought that sounded kind of funny. Unfortunately, that pretty much killed any chance we had of keeping things from escalating. Tanner Hughes looked at me again, and I could see any doubt he had about my identity was gone.

"I know what your aura says, but you are definitely him," Tanner Hughes said as he took out his smartphone. "I recognize you. You were a dork back before the invasion, and you're a dork now. They say you're some sort of renegade and war criminal. Hard to believe a loser like you could make so many enemies."

"I've always had a problem getting along with dimwits," I said with a shrug.

"Yeah, well, I'm going to get a promotion when I bring you in. I hear they already have a medical-experiments lab with your name on it at Planet Pleasant."

He started to punch in a number on his phone, but only got about two digits in when the phone flew out of his hand and struck the wall with enough force to shatter into a cloud of plastic and metal.

I turned to see Alice pointing a finger like she'd just cast a magic missile. "Yeah, yeah, I know what Dr. Roop said, but I think we're done flying under the radar. Plus, did you guys see that? It was totally amazing!"

"Who are you?" demanded Mr. Potato Head, who was now looking at us with something like awe. Mostly he was looking at Alice, but that was because she'd just demonstrated some flashy telekinesis, which had the side effect of making her already-unruly hair frizz out.

"We are no one you need to worry about," Charles said.

Tanner Hughes's brow was wrinkled and his mouth reduced to a hard line. These were the classic signs of a bully about to charge. I quickly checked my HUD, and before Tanner had taken more than two steps, I went for a skill I'd previously discovered while trying to figure out my skill tree. I'd been worried I wouldn't have a chance to try it out, but every once in a while the universe tosses you a softball.

Not bothering to suppress a grin, I unleashed the molecular realigner, turning his sneakers back into their constituent parts, including petroleum. When you're moving forward and your footwear suddenly vanishes and is replaced with oil, there is only one possible result. Tanner slipped backward, his butt landing in the pool of what used to be his shoes. He continued to slide until he collided with a lunch table.

"That was amazing!" said Mr. Potato Head. "I want to join you guys."

"Very kind of you, Mr. Potato Head," I told him, "but you don't want to get into trouble. Keep your head down until we get things under control."

"No one needs to put themselves at risk," Alice told him. "But keeping this incident quiet for as long as possible will really help us."

"Forget that," Tanner Hughes said. He was on his feet and trying to look as intimidating as possible, which isn't easy when you're a shoeless kid with an oil slick on his butt. "If you think I'm going to be quiet when—"

That was as far as he got before Charles thrust out his palm, shouted "Repulsor blast!" and unleashed fifty thousand volts of Taser action into my old tormentor. Tanner convulsed for a few seconds and then collapsed into a silent, oily heap.

"Nice touch," I said.

"I found that very satisfying," he said.

And with our business in the lunchroom complete, we fled.

The original plan had been to wait until after lights-out and slip into the records office on the top floor of the building. Any Phandic computer system would be able to interface with its main communications network, which meant that we'd be able to locate Tamret and the rest of our alien friends. Then all we had to do was get to where they were being held and, using the stealth features from our military upgrades, break them out. We had hoped to be operating completely under the radar, but that part of the plan was out the window. Tanner Hughes was going to alert his superiors, and that meant they would know exactly who we were. The Phands were not going to miss the chance to capture me, not when I had become the public face of their galactic humiliation. Our maxed-out skill trees, which had made us seem invulnerable only a few minutes ago, were very likely going to be pushed to the limit before we got off Earth.

On the stairs we passed students, teachers, and trustees, none of whom eyed us with any suspicion. It was only a matter of time before someone in authority entered the cafeteria or a kid looking to earn brownie points blew the whistle, but every second we avoided notice was a gift.

We reached the top of the stairs and headed down the corridor toward the main records office. Standing in front of the door, holding a steaming cup of coffee in one hand and a book in the other, was Mr. Authoritarian-Hammer. He was engaged in a hushed conversation with another teacher, whose aura identified her as Ms. Institutional-Orderliness. I felt sure we could have walked past teachers we didn't know, coming up with some sort of convincing excuse for walking around, but our own teacher was going to want to know what we were up to.

Was it better to knock them out and try to raid the computer system as quickly as possible or invent a cover story that might buy us some time? I think we were all struggling with the same question.

"Will you excuse me?" Mr. Authoritarian-Hammer said to his colleague. "I need a moment with my students."

She nodded and headed down the stairs.

"What are you doing up here?" he asked us.

"We just wanted to check in the office to see if . . ." This was as far as I got before I realized coming up with a reasonable lie was harder than I thought.

"If our schedules have been finalized," Charles finished. "We were told that they were subject to change and our homeroom assignment might not be permanent."

"We've just really enjoyed your particular approach to reeducation," Alice offered, "and want to make sure we continue to learn from you about the superiority of the Phandic way."

He studied us for a long moment, blinking slowly. He took a slurping sip from his coffee. "For a bunch of delinquents," he said, "your lying game is weak."

Charles was about to repulsor blast him, but I shook my head. There was something about him that made me think we didn't need to electrocute him into unconsciousness. Maybe it was the fact that the book he was holding was the collected short fiction of Arthur C. Clarke. *How evil can you be if you're reading one of the greats?* I wondered if, as with Mr. Potato

Head, I might have misread Mr. Authoritarian-Hammer.

"What makes you think we're, you know, that?" Mi Sun asked.

"You guys are not really great at blending in." He gestured at me with his coffee. "Plus, you have this look on your faces like you're just putting up with this nonsense until you bust out of here. Also, *Jean-Luc Picard*? Come on."

"You have entirely mistaken us," Charles assured him. "We are most certainly enthusiastic about the Phandic Empire of prosperity."

He rolled his eyes. "I didn't see you up here, and I'm not going to notice you not returning from lunch. These behavior controllers they injected in me mean that that's the best I can do. If you step blatantly out of line, I'll be compelled to report you."

"Thanks, Mr. Authoritarian-Hammer," I said.

He forced a sad smile. "I would tell you my real name, but the mods make it impossible for me to say it out loud."

I remembered another neat ability I hadn't known if I'd be able to use. "Well, let's do something about that," I said. I put a hand on his arm and allowed a microneedle to emerge from my fingertip and pierce his skin. This device injected a few million nanokillers into his bloodstream on a mission to hunt down and dismantle all Phandic invaders. They needed about six seconds to complete their work, after which both invaders and defenders would break down into their atomic components and be harmlessly passed in the host's urine and feces. More information than maybe you wanted, but still—it's better to know than to wonder.

Mr. Authoritarian-Hammer was now looking at his arm,

where he'd felt the slight pinprick. "What did you just do to me?"

"You've been scrubbed clean," I said. "Act normal and they'll never know, but your behavior-modifying nanites are gone."

Mr. Authoritarian-Hammer looked into the distance, maybe thinking unkind thoughts about the Phands to see if he felt a jolt of nausea or discomfort. He then turned to me and grinned. "I'm Thomas Link," he whispered. "It worked. And you're not ordinary troublemakers. Who are you?"

"We're the invaders' worst nightmare," I said. "A bunch of middle-school kids with dangerous technology we don't really understand or know how to control."

Then we entered the office, where we had our first encounter with Phands since our return to Earth.

There were three of them in the office and as many humans as well. One of the Phands was typing furiously on a holographic keyboard that hovered in front of her. The other two were tossing a holographic football back and forth. Either the game of football was of evil Phandic origin or the invaders had taken a liking to it. I wasn't sure which was more likely.

"Human juveniles may only enter this restricted space with permission from a designated authority figure and in the presence of a designated order-enforcer of no less than level six," said the typing Phand, not looking up from her keyboard. Her squarish gray-skinned face was crinkled in concentration, and her tusks jutted out of her lower jaw as she scraped at her bottom lip with her teeth. "Your identification auras are not emitting any permissions, and I see no order-enforcer. Thus I am forced to conclude you have made an error and entered the wrong room."

"It's surprising these creatures ever enter a right room," said one of the ball tossers. His big, orc-like body seemed to have been made for football. "Their brains are less formed than even our adolescents'."

"They appear to be in a perpetual state of confusion," agreed the other as he caught the football. "But the adults are hardly better. Though she's all right." He gestured with his head toward a big picture of Nora Price scowling down at us.

"One of the few bearable ones," the other agreed. "Why did we invade this ridiculous world anyhow?"

"I just have a question," I said, trying to cut in.

"Your question can wait until your identification aura emits the correct permission," said the typing Phand. "Until that time, your questions will go unanswered."

"Sad, really," said the Phand tossing the football. "All those questions that will never be answered."

"Keeps me up at night," said the one catching the ball. "Where do the unanswered questions go?"

Then none of them were saying anything, because they were first twitching and then unconscious. The humans in the room had been silent the whole time, and now they were even more silent because, like the Phands, they were unconscious. I closed and locked the office door while Alice generated a holographic keyboard with which to interface with the main Phandic computer network. There were multiple layers of encryption, but having a maxed-out security-busting skill tree meant that she could eat through those firewalls in seconds and enter the most secure databases in the system without triggering any alarms. In about thirty seconds she shut down her keyboard.

"I know where they're being held. And while I was there, I

got the coordinates of the prison where they've got Nayana and the others. We're set."

We all exchanged looks. This was too easy. I knew that the Former enhancements we'd picked up at the Hidden Fortress were going to make our tasks possible, but I never thought it was going to be this uncomplicated. Getting Tamret and the others, stealing a ship, rescuing the political prisoners, and getting the galaxy back on track was going to be a piece of cake.

Then Tanner Hughes kicked open the door. Behind him stood about twenty other trustees, all of them armed with Phandic phased-particle-beam pistols. And they opened fire.

Big deal. There was some redundancy since we hadn't had a chance to work out a routine. Things could have gone badly, which I realized even as they were going well, and I vowed that we would have to assign tasks in the future. Fortunately, there *would* be a future, since in spite of the lack of planning, we had all the bases covered. Charles, Alice, and I all triggered plasma shields, establishing a blue barrier between us and the Phand wannabees firing their PPBs. The phased particles were handily absorbed, leaving them astonished, disappointed, and a little bit afraid.

They were right to be afraid. Mi Sun, the most intuitive fighter in our group, must have assumed one of us would handle defense—either that or she was just acting on instinct. A second or two behind us, she unleashed a barrage of voltage, stunning the entire group. Problem solved. One second you've got a bunch of thugs with energy weapons; the next you've got a big pile of nappers.

With our data in hand, escaping was no more difficult than

stepping over the sleeping adversaries. I grabbed some of the PPB pistols—you never know what might come in handy—and then paused briefly over the slumped form of Tanner Hughes. He was wearing new sneakers he'd picked up from somewhere, but he still had oil stains all over his rear. I crouched over him and quickly cooked up a set of nanites, which I injected into his neck.

Just like that, he would now be unable to control his bladder. Instant pants-wetter. You cross me, you pay. I'm not entirely cruel, so I programmed the nanites to self-destruct after two days, but by then he'd be the laughingstock of the Phandic Empire. Assuming there still was a Phandic empire, because Team Randoms was on fire.

I wasn't the only one feeling big on our new tech. There were smug nods and fist bumps all around as we casually walked down the stairs, passing students and teachers. Most of the trustees had been summoned to deal with us, and no one had noticed yet that they hadn't returned. The Phands, from my experience, favored overwhelming force as a military tactic, and they didn't tend to worry that their forces might fail.

Soon they would realize they were facing a genuine danger, and they would up their game in response, but they had no game that could beat ours, I told myself. We could block any assault they threw at us. We could stop any being who challenged us. We could become invisible or invulnerable or unstoppable, and all it took was the desire to make it happen.

"It is a good thing none of us are evil," Charles said evilly. He had evidently been thinking along the same lines as me. "We are almost too powerful."

"The Formers had all this and more," I said, "and they

didn't turn evil. They created worlds and life. They paved the way for galactic civilization."

"And where are they now?" Mi Sun asked.

It was a good question. The fact was that no one knew what had happened to the Formers. Some thought that they had left the galaxy entirely, finding new and, to our minds, inconceivable methods of travel that would allow them to cross incredible distances. Others claimed they had set aside the need for material bodies entirely and now existed as beings of pure energy or at a quantum level, experiencing life with an entirely new set of physical realities. Then there was the school of thought that said they had become so powerful, that they had experienced so much, that they'd grown tired of existence and allowed themselves to fade from reality.

Personally, I found this possibility depressing. I couldn't imagine ever growing tired of my new abilities, and these powers represented only the tiniest sliver of the things the Formers could do—that *we* could now do. How could they have grown bored with all of this? I could spend years doing nothing more than turning guys like Tanner Hughes into pants-wetters without getting tired of it.

We reached the school's main entrance, which was unlocked and unmonitored. The Phandic security auras regulated who could come in or go out, but our counterfeited auras told the door we were fully authorized to leave. Just like that, we were out of there.

Tamret and the others were being held at a police station in the East Village. Getting there was no problem. A quick peek into the new global data network told me that New York's cabs had been fitted with a Phandic computer designed to read the security auras of anyone who stepped inside, but we had all tweaked ours to show we were in good standing and had every right to be out and about. We hailed a cab, paid with an electronic transfer of fabricated money, and were on our way.

When we'd first landed in Astor Place, I'd been too busy trying to escape, and worrying about the well-being of our friends, to really take in the details of life on conquered Earth. Other than the billboards and signs, and the images of Nora Price's face everywhere, things weren't that overtly different. I knew that the Phands wanted kids going to school and adults going to work, so if you didn't look too closely, it could have seemed like an ordinary day in an ordinary city.

Now I saw the fear on almost every face we passed. While we sat at a stoplight, I watched as a woman holding a toddler's hand trembled when a policeman paused to look at her. We drove past another set of policemen who were rounding up homeless people and tossing them into the back of a truck.

The other major difference was the blue cylinder of light that rose up from the Empire State Building in midtown. Dr. Roop had explained that Phandic colonial efforts required massive infusions of power, and these came via some sort of subspace link with the home systems—a kind of tunnel for energy instead of for transportation. I figured that's what I had to be looking at.

Mi Sun broke my train of thought by sending a message via my HUD. *I'm worried about my family.* There was no way we were going to discuss anything important out loud in this cab. *Especially now that the Phands know we're on Earth. I get where Alice is coming from. I need to make sure everyone's okay.*

I'm worried about my parents too, I messaged her, *but*

you heard what Dr. Roop said. The Phands will have nothing to gain by messing with our families once we're off the planet. Besides, we can't take them with us. Our best bet is to get rid of the Phands as quickly as possible.

I'm just going to call them, she said.

She didn't need a phone to do it, and there was no way I could stop her if she really wanted to, but I felt sure it was a mistake.

No! I grabbed her wrist. *It's too big a risk. Stick with the plan.*

She yanked her arm away from me. *The plan to rescue your girlfriend? All your friends? You're the one who is tight with Steve and Dr. Roop, not the rest of us. Why is it that you get to call the shots?*

Maybe I am closer to Dr. Roop than you, I told her, *but he's still the only adult good guy we've got, and he knows what he's doing. He's the one who says not to contact anyone. Come on, Mi Sun. I get that you want to check on your family, but it's not the smart move.*

She snorted, but I could tell from her slackening expression that she was relenting.

I told the cabdriver to drop us off about a block away, since we needed some time to discuss our strategies. In part, I wanted to make sure that the next time we were attacked, we had a system for who blocked and who counterattacked. Also, we needed to figure out what we were going to do once we escaped with our friends. Earth might be part of the Phandic Empire now, but there were relatively few Phands on the planet, and so far I hadn't seen any other aliens. Our associates were going to draw a lot of attention.

"Now what?" Mi Sun asked, crossing her arms and staring at me.

"Did you two get into a silent quarrel in the cab?" Charles asked.

"I would never think to argue with our great leader," Mi Sun said. "He's always right, after all."

"Okay, then," Alice said in an effort to be diplomatic. "Moving on. While you guys took care of the important bickering, I was doing some wireless research on the way over. It looks like the Phands don't want to mess with local economies, so they haven't taken over the airport. Most of the space traffic is moving in and out of Central Park. It's destroying the actual park, but they don't care about that."

"Once we get everyone, we'll have to steal a van or something in order to get there," I said.

"And who is going to drive it?" Mi Sun demanded. "You?"

I grinned. "Steve."

CHAPTER FOUR

O ur plan was surgically precise. Mi Sun was still annoyed with me, but she got her head back in the game pretty quickly. We entered the precinct, and Alice went up to the policeman at the front desk to ask for help. She was probably best of all of us at appearing sympathetic, so while she told some story about a missing parent, the rest of us hung back like we were her friends there to support her. In fact we were all busy. Mi Sun hacked into the station's records to get the layout of the prison. Charles checked on the security-camera feeds, getting a sense of what sort of opposition we could anticipate. I, meanwhile, used the sabotage branch of my skill tree—yeah, I really had one of those—to create a communication-dampening field over the precinct building. No one could call for help or report our infiltration until we were long gone.

We all pinged Alice when we'd completed our tasks so she'd know when we were ready for the next stage. Then, in the middle of speaking to a bored and unsympathetic policeman, she stunned him. Charles, Mi Sun, and I took care of the rest of the room. We sealed the front door so no one could go in or out, and we moved on to where the prisoners were being held.

There were several layers of locked doors, which we blasted through until we reached the holding cells. Prisoners on either side shouted at us, and much of what they had to say wasn't very nice. Clearly these were garden-variety criminals—people hadn't stopped breaking the law just because there had been an alien invasion—so there was no way I was going to let them go free.

Beyond these cells we came to the maximum-security holding pen. I accessed the panel that controlled the electronic lock and broke through in a matter of seconds. The door swung open to reveal a room with no chairs or beds—no furnishings of any kind except a single metal toilet and sink. Sitting on the floor were Steve, Dr. Roop, and Villainic. They wore the same clothes as when we'd last seen them, and they didn't look like they'd been hurt.

"Where's Tamret?" I said.

"Finally, you are here," Villainic answered. "There is no private toilet, and I had to use the facilities in front of *them*. It was humiliating."

Steve was kind enough not to make me ask a second time. "They've kept her separate, mate—they said because she's female. She should be fine. They haven't bothered us since they threw us in here. Just a lot of sitting about. And watching him use the loo was no fun for the rest of us, let me tell you."

I heard something in his voice that I didn't like. "What happened before they threw you in here?"

"There were some unkind words," Dr. Roop said regretfully. "Some disparaging comments on our being nonhuman. The words were spoken with malicious intent, but I could not let them trouble me, and I hardly think Tamret would be vulnerable to that sort of thing."

"Let's find her," I said.

"One moment," Villainic said, his expression showing some obvious feline fear. "Most of us are now safe. Is it really advisable to go further into the enemy's compound to rescue just one more?"

"Are you serious?" I asked him. "I'd keep going even if *you* were the only one we hadn't rescued. You expect me to leave Tamret behind?"

"I merely point out that it may not be wise," he said. "We mustn't be reckless."

"Yeah, we must." Steve put a hand on Villainic's shoulder and pushed him forward.

We made our way farther into the facility, looking in cells and kicking down doors, but there was no sign of her. I couldn't shake the feeling of unease. It made sense that they might separate out the only female, but why keep her so far away? I tried to tell myself that I was anxious because I wanted to see her, because I wanted to know for a fact that she was safe, but something didn't seem right.

We came to another steel door protected by a keypad. I quickly hacked the encryption and the door swung open, revealing an antechamber—a dusty little room with a few filing cabinets, a table with a coffeemaker, and a metal desk at which sat a balding, middle-aged policeman.

"Where is she?" I demanded.

His eyes bulged as he looked at the aliens with us, so he had no doubt who I was talking about. "In there," he said. "But you can't get inside without the combination, and—"

That was as far as he got. I stepped over his unconscious body and quickly bypassed the security system—this was probably faster than entering the correct code. The metal door clicked open.

We were instantly met by PPB fire. Charles and Alice set

up the defensive shielding, as we'd planned. Mi Sun and I were to go on offense, and I had no doubt Steve would join us without a second thought.

There were two Phands in the room and one human. The Phands were the ones firing at us. The human was farther back. The room itself was large—a lab, not a cell—filled with computers, glass bottles and beakers, and shelves full of various equipment I couldn't identify. On a gurney toward the back of the room lay Tamret, eyes open but immobile. She was in the clothes she'd been wearing when she was captured, but her sleeves had been rolled up so IVs could be inserted. A tangle of plastic tubes pumped chemicals into her arms, and several thick straps held her bound tight to the gurney.

Standing behind her, a syringe in her hand, was Nora Price, the supreme viceroy herself.

This woman was now running a *world*, but here she was, taking the time out of her busy schedule to mess with Tamret. Could this be about our history? The fact that she'd been unable to deliver me to the Phands had made her look bad, but I doubted that whatever was going on here was about me or my friends and the things we'd done. Ms. Price was probably as evil as they come, but I didn't think she would be vindictive unless there was a payoff for her in the end.

These thoughts went through my mind as I saw two Phands, who had been raising their weapons, go down. Mi Sun and Alice had zapped them, maybe leaving Ms. Price for me. I aimed at her, but Dr. Roop put a hand on my forearm.

"We may need to know what she's done to Tamret," he said.

"I found something a bit more refined than just blasting her with electricity," Mi Sun said. She jerked out her hand, and a wave of blue energy hit the lower part of Ms. Price's body. She fell heavily to the floor but was still conscious, though now gasping for air like a freshly caught fish.

"She's temporarily immobilized from the waist down," Mi Sun explained.

I ran over to Tamret, who was lying completely still, but her eyes were darting back and forth. I could see the fury in them, but she seemed unable to speak, let alone struggle against her restraints.

"I'm going to get you out of here," I said. I looked down at Nora Price. "What did you do to Tamret?"

"Hello to you too, Zeke," she said through gritted teeth. I didn't know if the paralyzing effect somehow hurt or if she was just frustrated. I didn't much care.

"Answer the question," I demanded.

"Or what?" She laughed. "You're pretty tough when it comes to ship-to-ship combat, but I don't think you've got what it takes to actually kill another person face-to-face."

Dr. Roop stepped forward, maybe worried about what exactly I had planned next. Nora Price had betrayed humanity in general and me in particular. She had sided with the Phands out of a desire for power, and now she had hurt Tamret. I didn't know what I was prepared to do to help Tamret, but I wasn't going to rule anything out just yet.

"Whatever they're giving Tamret must be some sort of suppressant for her upgrades," he said quietly. "Otherwise I'm not sure they would be able to hold her against her will. She should be able to repair herself once the upgrades are allowed to do their work. I think if we disconnect her, she'll be fine."

"And what if you're wrong?"

"We have just overtaken a law-enforcement station in which the supreme viceroy was conducting experiments. It is only a matter of time before our enemies notice something is amiss and they come at us with overwhelming force. I believe it is time to take a chance."

I looked at Tamret, and there was something in her eyes that told me she agreed with Dr. Roop. It was like she was telling me that his plan was the way to go. I nodded and began to remove the IV needles from her arm.

The effect was almost instantaneous. Before I'd even finished unfastening her restraints, Tamret gasped for breath like she'd been held underwater. She raised her head to watch me, and as soon as the restraints were off, she sat up.

"Let's go," she said.

"Tamret, are you—"

"Forget it," she snapped. "I'll be fine, and I don't want to stand around and wait for whatever they're going to throw at us."

I glanced back at Nora Price, who flashed me a humorless smile. There was nothing I could do about her. We couldn't take her with us, and it wasn't as though I was prepared to execute her. Besides, she was only a lickspittle, if I may use that word, working for more powerful, if not more evil, beings. If she weren't around, the Phands wouldn't have any problem finding someone else to stand in as their head human. I told myself she was unimportant.

"You can't keep doing this forever, Zeke," she called out to me. "You're going to make a mistake."

I wanted to make some kind of snappy comeback, to tell her that she would be the one running from us, but I didn't want to say anything that even hinted at our plans, so I walked away, saying nothing.

I put a hand on Tamret's shoulder, but she shrugged me off. "I'm fine," she said. "You don't have to keep checking on me."

She wasn't fine—I could see that—but I couldn't make her talk to me.

We hurried past the prisoners and then through the precinct full of unconscious policemen. Other than the two who had been in the lab with Nora Price, we hadn't seen a single Phand, but I told myself that didn't mean anything. I was sure they didn't hang out, drinking coffee and playing darts, with the local humans. When they finally decided to show up in force, we'd be facing some real opposition.

We found the stairs leading to the parking garage and selected a van. No keys required when you are fully loaded, as we were. Steve uploaded some basic instructions on how to operate the vehicle, and he played tentatively with the gas and brake pedals while we all nervously buckled up.

"Seems pretty basic," he said thoughtfully, while he examined the gearshift and tried to get comfortable with a standard driver's seat. He couldn't sit all the way down, and his tail was pressed against the back of the seat and dangling over his own shoulder. "Using my feet will take some getting used to, but I'll learn as we go." So saying, we lurched out of the parking spot and onto the main street.

"Turn on the flashing lights and siren," Charles suggested. "It will be very exciting."

"No, don't," Alice corrected him. "We don't want to draw any attention. We keep a low profile."

"Focus on caution," said Villainic, "not excitement."

I sat between him and Tamret. She wouldn't meet my eye, and though I wanted to take her hand, I got the feeling she wanted to be left alone. Being drugged and nearly experimented on seemed pretty traumatic, and I wanted to help her, not be locked out.

To take my mind off all of that, I turned to my Former upgrades and began searching for new skills we might use, things that could help us right now. After looking through a bunch of things I didn't understand or couldn't use, I stumbled on something possibly very useful.

"You know, I'm pretty sure I can get this van to fly," I said. "Using, you know, my brain."

"Oi!" Steve shouted. "I'm driving here."

"I'm just saying. I think I can create a localized gravity-dampening field, which I should be able to keep stabilized while someone else generates propulsion. Obviously, we don't want to go zooming around the city in a flying police van, but if things get hairy, it's good to have choices."

"I cannot help but think it is a mistake to run too freely with these newly obtained powers," Dr. Roop warned.

"If the Phands try to recapture us," Tamret said, her voice dark, "then the mistake would be not to use everything at our disposal."

"That is certainly true," Dr. Roop said. "However, unless there is real need, I do not think we should meddle with abilities we do not yet understand. Unless . . ." He looked at Tamret. "Did they discover anything about your capabilities? Is that what they were doing to you?"

She shook her head. "It's what they were *trying* to do. They were definitely probing and experimenting, trying to learn what

I could do and how they could stop me if they had to. But they didn't get anywhere. I figured out there was a way to use my nanites to shut them out. They didn't learn anything from me."

That was pure Tamret, I thought. She might have saved us all—maybe the entire galaxy—by making sure Nora Price didn't learn what we now had within us and what we could do.

"How can we hope to understand our abilities if we don't use them?" Charles asked.

Dr. Roop nodded. "It is a good question, but I think study and experiment, under safe and controlled conditions, is the best approach. As I told you back at the Hidden Fortress, there is something about the code in your upgrades that does not seem right to me. I would hate for anything to go wrong unexpectedly in a life-or-death situation."

"I don't think we need to worry about that anymore," I told him, "We've already used the new abilities under fire. We show up, and we pretty much eliminate any threats we come across."

"That's the sort of thinking that will lead to sloppiness and disaster," Dr. Roop warned.

"Normally, I'd agree with you," Mi Sun said, "but Zeke may be right this time. I'm not saying we should let our guard down, but so far we haven't faced anything we couldn't handle, including Phands. We've got overwhelming force to use against them."

From the seat in front of me, Alice turned around. "So we get the ship and that's it, right?"

I nodded. I knew Alice wanted to stay and look after her father, but I was still hoping that when the time came, she might change her mind.

As we approached Central Park, I told Steve to pull over. I

accessed my high-range scanning ability to take stock of what lay ahead, and I saw that the fields the Phands were using as a temporary spaceport were well defended and heavily patrolled. There was no way we were going to be able to drive up to a spaceship and take it.

I explained all of this and told the others we were going to have to go the rest of the way on foot.

"I hate to point this out," Steve said, "but we're not exactly going to blend in."

"We don't have to," I said. "Look, some humans are going to see you, but they already know the planet has been invaded, so they'll figure you're just some other kind of invader. They're not going to look at you and think, 'I bet that's some outlaw kid who's been working against the Phands! I'd better go report this!'"

"He's right," Tamret said gruffly. She didn't sound like herself, but at least she was weighing in. "If this isn't a stealth operation, then we need to go in and get it done as quickly as possible."

"Why isn't this a stealth operation?" Villainic asked, clearly irritated that we weren't doing things his way. "Is there some reason you could not have rescued us under cover of night? Does this planet even have a night?"

"Yes, Villainic." I sighed. "Earth has a night. It gets dark and everything. Unfortunately, our timetable got pushed ahead."

"Zeke started a fight with a bully," Mi Sun said.

"You really must learn to control your temper," Dr. Roop told me.

I was not going to get into this. "Look, stuff happens. You can't always control every little detail. What I can control is how awesome we all are. So let's go steal a ship and get away from this planet, since that's the only way we're going to be able to liberate it."

"So we simply rush ahead, guns blazing?" Villainic demanded. "That sounds like madness!"

"In the absence of Nayana," Charles observed, "the role of C-3PO will be played by Villainic."

"Totally," I agreed. I then sent everyone the data I'd been collecting this whole time. I had tactical layouts of every Phandic position in the park, including military personnel, weapons, and vehicles. "Upload the file into your HUD. All the hostiles we'll encounter are tagged as glowing red, like in a video game. Our sensors are monitoring their movements, which means we'll know where they are at all times. We can keep track of every unmanned weapon, barrier, and obstacle, so this should be simple. We raise our personal shields, we go in blasting nonlethal power, and we get out of here. It's kind of brash, sure, but if anyone has a better idea, then I'm open to suggestions."

Charles was busy examining the data on his HUD. "This is amazing, Zeke. How did you figure out how to do this? I haven't had nearly so much success in discovering the specifics of our new abilities."

I shrugged. "You learn by trying. I hoped there would be stuff like this, so I searched until I found what I thought would work."

Mi Sun nodded. "Okay, I'm impressed. I hate to say anything nice about you, given how bossy you're being, but you nailed this."

I felt myself relax a little. It was good to have everyone on the same side. "We are so used to being outnumbered and outgunned, to always being behind the curve, that we keep thinking like we're the underdogs. But we're not underdogs anymore. We're the overdogs, so let's go mess with an empire."

I thought it was a pretty good speech, so I yanked open the side panel of the van and stepped onto the street.

We made pretty much exactly the sort of splash you would expect. People stared and pointed. There was some screaming. A child pulled on his father's hand and said he wanted to hug Dr. Roop. We ignored it all and entered the park feeling good about our chances.

That said, I knew things were about to get complicated. The area was too large to dampen all communications without creating some kind of major alert, so there was nothing to do about people snapping photos of us. I figured it would be maybe thirty seconds before our images started showing up on Twitter and Instagram, which meant that any Phands monitoring human communication networks would know we were on the planet. At the very least, they would know unauthorized aliens were on the loose and moving toward their spaceships. The danger dial had just been cranked all the way up.

We entered the park and my HUD showed three Phands patrolling about a hundred feet ahead of us. Steve, Tamret, and I snuck quietly ahead, and we each zapped one of them. Easy enough, but I'd done my homework and knew that Phand soldiers' status aura would report if they lost consciousness. Their movements were also probably being monitored by some sort of security system, so if three guys suddenly fell asleep, someone was going to notice. Alice and Mi Sun were in charge of tweaking the nanites in their auras to give false readings. Once we knocked them out, the soldiers would continue to register as conscious and mobile indefinitely. At some point, a clever monitoring program would notice that they seemed to be walking in the exact same pattern at the exact same pace over and over again, but I hoped to be very far away before any red flags went up.

We steadily worked our way into the interior of the park. We would advance about a hundred feet, take down Phandic patrols, and alter their status so that no one would know we were there. Then we would do it again. It was slow and methodical work, but it felt familiar, like clearing a level in a video game, and it meant that we were, piece by piece, eliminating all resistance. I wanted to have a little breathing room when we picked the ship we were going to steal. Ideally, we'd want something with long-range capability and strong offensive and solid defensive structures, but also a ship that could be operated with the smallest possible number of beings. There weren't enough of us to handle one of the larger ships.

After exactly fourteen minutes and thirty-four seconds, according to my HUD, we'd cleared the outer perimeter, and we were ready to move into the main landing area. Seven ships sat on the field, and now there were only four guards remaining. From what I'd been able to binge-learn about Phandic operating procedures, several of the patrols would already be a few minutes overdue, and the remaining guards would soon start getting worried. We needed to move.

The whole time, Steve had been accessing a Phandic database for information on all the ships, and now he gestured toward a saucer-shaped long-range shuttle. "That one's probably our best bet."

I nodded and messaged the others that it was time to move in. The four of us—me, Steve, Tamret, and Mi Sun—took down the guards almost simultaneously. While Dr. Roop and Villainic held back, Charles and Alice were working to tweak their auras and keep what we'd done from showing up on anyone's monitor. Phandic occupation forces had way more security checks and protocols than anything we'd seen back on the prison world where we'd rescued my dad, and it would be better not to face them. I wanted to be on that ship and heading away from the planet in five minutes or less.

It had been a long day, and we'd accomplished some incredible things, but it had all been so easy. I can't even say I walked toward our ship. I strutted. I felt equal to anything, and not only was I not afraid of what the Phands might throw at us, but I was looking forward to it.

And then, as we approached our ship, they threw some stuff at us, and I actually didn't like it all that much.

CHAPTER FIVE

Fire, explosions, sulfuric-acid mists, the ground crackling with electricity: These are sure signs that someone does not want you around.

A lot can go through your mind in a fraction of a second, and a lot went through mine. The Phands had figured out we were trying to steal one of their ships, and they'd worked out we were not your typical troublemakers. You don't lead with acid mist for a few teens with cans of spray paint.

I couldn't be too surprised. It seemed likely that Nora Price had informed her security forces about our rescue, and they had figured out—not too hard, when you think about it—that we would be interested in stealing a ship. Now they were taking no chances on letting us get away. They might not have known exactly what we had and what we were capable of, but they knew we were skilled and dangerous. That would explain why they decided to front-load the lethal attacks. I guess they figured we could handle it, but the assaults would knock us back long enough for us to be captured. Either that or they didn't want us captured and were perfectly content to kill us.

Here's another thing that went through my head: *Protect my friends*. With the exception of Villainic, everyone there had the same abilities I did, and I knew they could take care of themselves, but we'd each explored our new upgrades in our own way, and I couldn't be sure what the others did or didn't know. I couldn't depend on their being able to defend themselves against everything the Phands were throwing at us. The instant my security systems warned me about the first micro change in temperature, the first molecules of toxin in the air, I went on high alert, and time slowed down.

I'm not saying that time *seemed* to slow down. It wasn't like how you have a whole bunch of thoughts that run through your head in a split second of crisis. I'm not talking about my reflexes growing sharp while adrenaline kicked in—though there was plenty of that as well. No, this was some kind of defensive protocol I didn't know existed, which caused my senses and reflexes to speed up while creating the illusion that the world around me was moving at about one-eighth normal speed. My best guess was that sometimes the upgrades suggested solutions to problems even when I wasn't looking for them. Maybe it was like how Steve had known how to reverse a tunnel back when we'd stumbled on all those Phand ships. I hadn't been searching for a skill to use, but one had popped up on my HUD, and I ran with it.

It was like being in *The Matrix*. I looked up and saw that two small Phandic assault saucers had spun in from out of nowhere, but I took in every detail from the pitting on their hulls to their wobbly movements as they flew. Paratroopers were leaping out. Light flashed from weapons fire. I instantly activated a defensive bubble around all of us. My HUD was advising I go with a sphere, not a dome, and I wasn't about to argue. I wanted to kiss my HUD, because I watched as the ground around us sizzled with electricity even as fire and acid rained down and small, intense explosions pocked the ground around us.

Alice and Charles had also set up defensive spheres, but

better too much protection from acid than too little. I immediately sent out a message. I wanted the two of them to continue to shield us, and I'd put everyone else on offense. I directed Steve and Tamret to focus on the attacking saucers. Dr. Roop and Mi Sun began to pick off individual fighters.

They came looking to squash us like bugs, but they weren't prepared for the bugs being unsquashable. Obviously they knew we had upgrades, but they had no idea of the extent of our abilities. They probably thought they were coming in with overkill, but other than almost catching us by surprise, they had nothing we couldn't handle. They'd had one chance—to hit us before we detected them—but our tech made even that impossible.

The sense of slow motion made everything easy. While I sent individual paratroopers reeling into unconsciousness I was aware of Steve and Tamret, summoning spheres of plasma energy out of the ether and lobbing them at the incoming attack saucers. They seemed to be using a targeting feature, because I saw one of Tamret's energy spheres hit an engine exhaust directly. Hot metallic chunks of the saucer were ripped away, and the vessel began to spin wildly toward the ground. Another saucer looked like it had been struck by an enormous baseball bat, and it went twirling toward the cosmic fences. My enhanced perception picked up the splash of it landing in the Hudson River.

All the paratroopers were unconscious before they hit the ground. They lay motionless in their protective suits while the fire, acid, and electricity dissipated. We stood silently in our bubble as the flow of time returned to normal, but I felt anything but ordinary. Excitement seemed to tingle across my skin.

They'd found us and they'd hit us hard, and we hadn't taken a scratch.

We remained motionless and silent for more than a minute, until our environmental sensors told us it was safe to shut down the protective bubble. Then, with nothing else to slow us down, we began to hurry toward the ship we'd selected. I'd not gone ten feet before I saw something streaking across the sky toward us. At first I thought it was a missile, that they were looking to take us out with a massive explosion, and I directed my sensor tech to lock onto it.

It wasn't a missile, though. It was a single-person vehicle—a sort of militaristic hoverboard like the Green Goblin used in the old Spider-Man comics. The being who rode it, however, wasn't cackling or tossing novelty bombs. I didn't know what it was doing, and I didn't care. There was no way to knock the hoverboard out of the sky without killing the rider, and I didn't want to do that. I also didn't want to wait around for whoever it was to get closer and do what it intended to do.

"Let's run," I shouted, and we all took off toward the ship. We could have gone at superspeed and shaved thirty seconds off our time, but that would have meant leaving Villainic behind, and while I might have said I would be okay with that, actually doing it was another thing.

I held back, making sure the others got on board. Everyone but Villainic had reached the safety of the ship when my HUD warned me of a building energy wave from the hoverboard—it was heating up a weapon that required at least a few seconds before it was ready to fire. I raised a protective plasma shield behind us and grabbed Villainic, but my HUD flashed another warning. The countermeasures I had deployed were not going to be effective. The attacker was using a new kind of weapon, one designed to cut through plasma shields. We'd faced the prototype of this back on the *Dependable*, and the Phands had nearly destroyed us. This enemy was apparently using a portable model of the same weapon.

There were two things that concerned me. One was that the ship we'd chosen, or maybe even all the ships docked on the field, were going to be damaged to the point of being useless to us. The other was that we would get killed.

It was time to prioritize. I could slow things down to look for a solution, and if there was a countermeasure, I'd be able to find it in time. If a solution didn't exist, we were cooked. I also knew that I could not send the entire group my message. If Tamret knew what I had in mind, she'd never go for it. She might even interfere with the others, wasting precious seconds. If there was one person I trusted to act in the best interests of all of us, without sentimentality, it was Mi Sun. I told her to get the ship out of the blast radius. I'd slow this attacker, but sticking together wasn't going to do any of us any good if we didn't have a way of getting off the planet. Our little infiltration trick had worked because no one had been expecting us. If we didn't get away right now, the Phands were going to come at us again, and the next attack might destroy any chance we had of getting away with a ship.

Mi Sun acknowledged my transmission, and my temperature sensors registered our ship's engines warming up. It took long minutes to set an interstellar tunnel course, but only a few seconds to get the conventional engines operational. I had to use that time to distract the Phand on the hoverboard.

The first thing I needed to do was find a way to interfere

with the plasma-piercing energy blast that was soon going to be coming my way. With time slowed, I toggled through the simplified data my HUD provided. Back on the *Dependable*, Captain Qwlessl had had neither the time nor the resources to do what I could now do in a fraction of a second. She'd been too busy keeping her crew alive to try to develop countermeasures. Besides, it would have taken hours, maybe days, to figure out a work-around even if she'd had the analytical capabilities of the Former tech tree, and the Confederation didn't have anything like it. I could figure out how their shield-piercing tech worked and select from a series of possible counters all in the blink of an eye.

The problem was that they were all *possible* counters. They all involved tinkering with various subatomic fields in the plasma, and they would all likely be effective to various degrees, but some would be more effective than others, and some would provide more protection to either organic or inorganic matter.

I had an instant to decide. Every part of me wanted to put up the strongest barrier to protect myself, but my friends were on that ship behind me, and that ship was the only way any of us were going to get off the planet. The window of opportunity for escape was closing fast.

I altered my shields to provide some protection for living beings, but more for the ship itself. I raised a wall between me and the upcoming blast, and I turned to shield Villainic. I saw the ship just beginning to move out of the way as I turned.

That's when I saw Alice was no longer on the ship. She'd come to face the attacker. It seemed that since she had no intention of leaving the planet, she'd decided to back me up.

Her faraway expression told me that she was desperately

scrolling through options on her own HUD. Maybe she was looking for a shielding solution that I'd overlooked. Whatever she was up to, she didn't have the time. The blast wave hit us.

I felt myself turned around, my head slamming into Villainic's stomach. This was pleasant for neither of us. Alice was knocked back onto the ground, driving a divot into the grass before I lost sight of her in my own wild, painful tumble with Villainic.

And then, almost without my even trying, my tech helped me right myself. I was on my feet and turning to face the being on the hoverboard. In that instant, I realized I knew him.

It was Ardov, and now—like the Green Goblin—he was laughing.

All around me was smoke and heat and scorched grass. Hovering twenty feet above it was Ardov, looking triumphant.

How many times was this guy going to show up at an inconvenient moment? A Rarel, from the same planet as Tamret and Villainic, he had the good looks of a guy from a cat-alien boy band and the smug attitude of a thug who believed he was untouchable. He'd tormented us during our first visit to Confederation Central, but back then he'd been little more than a particularly tough and nasty bully. When we returned to the station, he'd become Junup's henchman, ready to follow any orders, including killing us. Fortunately, we'd been able to prevent that, but I still felt like we owed him some payback.

"You've learned a few new tricks," Ardov said. "Something you picked up at the Hidden Fortress?"

Those concerns I'd had about not wanting to kill my attacker were swirling down the drain. I raised my hand and projected a stream of metal-eating nanites at his hoverboard.

He saw the blast coming and leaped off, somersaulting in the air and landing safely on the ground. Junup had illegally maxed out Ardov's Confederation skill tree, and that made him like Captain America. I, on the other hand, had the Former skills, and that made me like Superman. I didn't even care if I was mixing Marvel and DC—I was going to kick his butt from one continuity to the next, and there was nothing he could do about it. His hoverboard was gone, and it was now a fight, plain and simple. He was sure he had the advantage in a straight-up brawl, but he was in for a nasty surprise.

Alice was on her feet, looking battered but not seriously hurt. Her hair was a wild mess of tangles and twigs. Her glasses were crooked on her face but still intact. Did she even need them with her upgrades? I'd have to ask her that later.

"Zeke, forget him!" she called to me. "He can't hurt us. You need to grab Villainic and get out of here."

"You're still pathetically trying to make everything in the universe work out just right," Ardov said to me, planting his feet like he was ready for me to charge him. "Don't you get it? Even if you were to get everything you want, then what? You bring Tamret back here, where she'd be a bigger freak than she is on Rarel. How do you think your fellow humans will take to having an alien criminal living among them? No matter what you do, you'll still end up miserable. I get a certain satisfaction out of that."

I was about to launch myself at him, but Alice blasted me with another communication, this time through my HUD. The words *Go! I'll cover you!* appeared before me in gigantic glowing letters.

She was right. It would have been nice to deliver a superpowered punch to Ardov, sending him flying over the tops of trees. I knew he could survive it, and I had no doubt the memory would keep me happy for years to come. Even so, I turned away. I'd just risked my own skin, and Villainic's, too, I suppose, because I'd let Ardov get to me. Escaping from Earth was our priority. Maybe I'd get a chance to humiliate Ardov in the future. Hopefully I'd never have to face him again, though. Making sure he was on the losing side would be revenge enough, I decided. The most important thing was getting everyone out of here.

I turned to help Villainic up, but my HUD detected another incoming weapon. I raised my new shields, but this wasn't an energy attack. It was a physical weapon. A projectile, like a bullet, though the readings I was getting made it clear it was something much more advanced.

I realized, too late, that the defenses we had might not be good enough. The projectile was partially phased, cycling rapidly from energy to matter and back again, and it pierced through the shields as though they weren't even there.

It hit Alice in the shoulder.

She spun around and hit the ground, rolling as the momentum of the blow knocked her across the blackened grass.

I'm okay, she messaged me almost instantly. *It's not serious. You need to move.*

Even with just the Confederation skill tree, a bullet wound to the shoulder would mean nothing. The nanites would already be working to expel the bullet and repair any damage. Nothing short of a direct hit to the brain or heart would be deadly. I tried to suppress the rage coursing through me. He'd shot my friend, someone I cared about. Maybe he was trying to goad me into a fight. I had to find the will to resist taking the bait.

I would have, too, if it weren't for the readings I was getting from Alice. My scan showed me that her wound wasn't healing. The damage to her cells was spreading, defying the ability of the nanites to repair the damage. That was bad enough, but there was more. Whatever Ardov had shot her with, it was transmitting data somewhere, cutting through our communications blackout.

When they'd had Tamret in the lab, she had been able to conceal her nanites to keep the Phands from figuring out how they worked. Now they'd devised another way to try to get that information. They'd had to hurt Alice to do it, but I had a feeling both Ardov and Nora Price were perfectly fine with that.

While I'd been showing off, reveling in what I could do, the Phands had been using the time to figure out how to study our abilities. If I was right, they were getting detailed information on how we had hacked the Former tech tree. Alice was hurt, maybe dying, and the Phands were learning everything they needed to know in order to eliminate our advantage.

There was one person who could tell me what I needed to know to stop all of this, and he just happened to be the being I hated most in the galaxy. Or maybe second most. Definitely top three. It was between Ardov, Junup, and Nora Price for sure. I stopped worrying about the rank, and I charged him.

There was nothing Ardov could do about it. He grinned when he first saw me coming, but then he noticed my speed. He might have observed that I was glowing and that fire was shooting down my legs and away from me like rocket exhaust. I was creating these effects intentionally—while they didn't actually make me any more dangerous, they looked menacing, and I figured they had to intimidate him. If he wanted to mess with me, he was going to see what he was up against.

He not only held his ground, but he charged me. He was slow by my standards, but he shifted from a tackling stance to something more aggressive, and he took me by surprise. He swung at me, and while I managed to avoid the full impact of the punch, his fist clipped my nose, which sprayed an alarming amount of blood. I expected Ardov to press the attack, but instead he rushed past me. He had my blood on his hands, and he was wiping it on a piece of cloth, which he quickly deposited in a plastic bag that he placed in his pocket. Having then finished this bizarre process, he turned to face me again.

My nanites were already healing my nose. There was nothing left of the damage now but some drying blood. It wasn't what he had done to me, but to Alice, that fueled my rage.

I charged him again, more quickly this time, and grabbed him before he could evade me. I was done messing around, and, operating purely on instinct, I created a localized gravity-dampening field, the sort of technology I'd been examining when I'd proposed making the van fly. I pressed my feet against the earth and shot up into the air.

I really was a superhero now. It would have been so amazingly cool if my friend weren't lying on the ground below me, possibly dying, while nanites in her body recorded and transmitted data that would doom the Earth and the galaxy to tyranny.

"What did you do to her, and how do I stop it?" I asked Ardov when we hit about three thousand feet.

"Maybe I misjudged you," he said. "Have you lost interest in Tamret already? The novelty of another species has worn off?"

"Tell me what you did to Alice!" I demanded.

If he was afraid, he hid it well. "I'll never tell you anything," he said with a sneer.

"Then you're no good to me," I told him. And so saying, I let him drop.

Watching a guy you really hate—who has bullied you, hurt your friends, and become a foot soldier in an evil empire's war—fall a thousand feet, screaming and limbs flailing, is very satisfying. It's an experience every decent person should have. I was in no mood to enjoy it, though. The clock was ticking.

I cut off the antigravity effects and dove down and plucked Ardov out of the air, directing my energy field to stabilize his skeletal structure from the sudden halt in velocity. I needed him alive, and I couldn't afford for him to go the way of Gwen Stacy.

"Let's try this again," I said. "How do I stop what you did to her?"

He laughed at me. I was flying him hundreds of feet above the ground. I'd just let him fall almost to his death, and he thought it was funny. This guy didn't easily lose his cool. "You showed me that you care about the human girl more than Tamret. Better yet, you showed me you won't kill me. I know all your weaknesses. Why should I tell you anything?"

It was a good question. I had to think about it for a second. "Because I can pull your arm right off your body. You will heal in seconds. You won't die, but that arm won't be coming back. And keep in mind, you've got four limbs. Maybe you won't tell me what I want to know after the first arm, but you will when I go for the second one. You've got three seconds to decide."

Then I saw what I was looking for. Fear. He needed to be important, vital, active. I'd come up with a way to get what I wanted without risking his death. I could keep him alive, but hurt him enough that he would be useless to Junup—and he seemed to fear that more than death.

Was I actually going to tear off his arm? I have no idea, but Alice did not look good, and the data was flowing fast. Hesitating was not an option.

I was distracted by a ping from Tamret. *Forget him. We need to get out of here. Once we hit tunnel, the data stream will cut off.*

That was a good point. There was no way to transmit data across the vast distances of space, only physical objects. Smacking Ardov around had been satisfying, but maybe a waste of time. There was still the matter of Alice's health, but he could tell us about that on the way. As much as I hated the idea, Ardov was coming with us.

Get Alice in the ship, I sent back. *I'm coming in, and I'm bringing a prisoner.*

I touched Ardov's neck and injected him with a sleeping agent. I then turned toward the ship and began zooming toward it.

I hadn't been thinking clearly. I had allowed my hatred for Ardov to cloud my judgment, and I'd been lured into making what was pretty clearly a tactical error. We'd lost time, maybe for Alice and maybe for all of us, and I hoped that I hadn't just handed Ardov his biggest victory over me yet.

I flew toward the ship, the air stinging my eyes. Maybe there were some tears of rage and frustration there too. I'd been an idiot. I'd put it all on the line so I could show off, so I could make Ardov see that I wasn't a victim.

Then, suddenly, I was no longer thinking about my mistakes,

because I wasn't flying. I was falling. I'd lost all ability to control my flight. My HUD was offline and I was looking through normal, human eyes. With no warning I'd gone from being a superhero to a guy who just happened to be a thousand feet in the air, gripping a cat alien he hated. And we were both tumbling toward the ground.

CHAPTER SIX

amret saved me. She leaped up and plucked me out of the sky. She probably could have saved Ardov too, but she didn't bother. Maybe she knew that Steve was going to grab him. Maybe not.

"I've got you," she said, but her voice lacked the glee I'd come to expect when she saved me from one of my stupid mistakes. Maybe she was angry with me for getting drawn into Ardov's trap. Maybe she was worried about how much danger we were in. I was worried about all those things too, but I was relieved she'd been there for me.

"Thank you," I said.

"Thank me later."

She landed hard on the ground and unceremoniously rolled me out of her arms. I found my footing, just barely. I felt wobbly, like after a carnival ride that spins you around.

Charles was at the entrance to the ship, waving us in. "Alice is on board. We must go."

I felt like vomiting and passing out, and I was more than a little freaked out about not being able to activate my HUD, but I managed to propel myself forward.

Steve was at the controls, and he didn't wait for me to stop staggering, or even for the doors to close, before he began to lift off the ground. "Everyone not strapped in might want to grab something," he said.

I managed to take hold of a metal ring, possibly designed for that exact purpose, just as I was thrown to near horizontal, like a flag in the wind. Steve simultaneously turned hard and accelerated. The dampening fields had not yet kicked in, and without them travel at these speeds was going to feel like being flung through space inside a hollow cannonball. The effect didn't last long, though. We began to level out around the time we exited the atmosphere. I looked over and was relieved to note that the door was now closed.

"We've got Phands on our tail, and it'll be a minute before we can tunnel," Steve shouted. "I need to keep them distracted. Zeke, you want to take the weapons console?"

I wanted to be able to step up, but I felt like I'd just been rattled around inside a jar for five minutes. Besides which, my upgrades were still not functioning. Anyone with the Former skills, even someone who had never seen a weapons console before, would be faster and more accurate than I could be right now.

"Can't do it," I said, shaking my head as I slid down to the deck. I was still nauseated and dizzy, and I put my head between my knees in order to keep from puking. Before I did that, though, I managed to catch a look cross Steve's reptilian face. Concern? Disappointment?

Without a word, Charles sat down at the weapons station and began to lay down a barrage of suppressive fire at lightning speed. I glanced up at the monitor showing the aft view and saw Phandic cruisers spiraling wildly as they tried to avoid our PPB blasts. I wasn't getting the job done, and that felt terrible, but the job *was* getting done, and maybe that was all that mattered.

In another few seconds Steve was able to open the tunnel

aperture. The disorientation that accompanies dropping out of relativistic space was more than I could handle, and at the very moment our ship violated the laws of ordinary physics and we punched a hole into the fabric of reality itself, I barfed on my shoes.

One thing I will say for the Phands: As a species of recreational pukers, they know how to clean up their messes. Little robots appeared out of nowhere and scrubbed the floor while nanites broke my upchuck down into a molecular mist. A brief spray of something citrus-smelling misted from the floor. No harm, no foul.

By the time these machines had finished their work, my nausea had started to ease up, so it was time to take stock of the situation. I could now deal with exciting developments like Ardov being along for the ride. Hooray. He was currently unconscious, and his wrists and ankles were bound with blue plasma cuffs that someone had generated. I knew that even with his enhanced strength he couldn't break out of them, but somehow that didn't make me feel any better about having him around. I wouldn't breathe easily until he was off the ship, preferably locked in the Phantom Zone, though I'd settle for a concrete bunker at the bottom of an ocean on a distant planet somewhere.

As bad as that was, there were even more serious issues to contend with. Alice was unconscious, lying on the deck of the ship, with Dr. Roop and Charles hovering over her, looking disturbingly doubtful. There was also the matter of my upgrades being offline, but I would deal with that later.

I went over to where they'd set Alice, some blankets under

her head. Her eyes were closed, and her skin had become pale and slightly waxy-looking. "What's wrong with her?" I asked. Besides all the other terrible things I was feeling, I could now add guilt. Alice had wanted out. She had been willing to see us to the ship, but then she'd planned to go find her dad. Now we were taking her away from Earth, against her will. We didn't have much of a choice, but I still felt terrible about it.

Dr. Roop shook his head. "I'm not entirely sure. When Ardov awakens, he may be able to provide us with more information, though I doubt he will choose to be cooperative. As near as I can tell, the weapon disoriented the operations of Alice's nanites while simultaneously transmitting data about their function back to the Phands. I do not know if the weapon was meant to harm her or if that was an unintended side effect. However, the projectile that struck her did considerable damage, and now her metabolism appears to be slowing at an alarming rate."

"Is she going to die?" I asked.

"If the process does not stop, or if we do not find a way to stop it, then yes."

"How long does she have?"

"A week, perhaps," he said, shaking his head. "Maybe less."

That was not good. I told myself there was good reason to hope we could restore order to the cosmos within a week. We could get Alice to a friendly Confederation hospital and have the best medical minds in the galaxy working to help her. I hated the idea of putting her health on hold, but I wasn't sure what else we could do. Until we solved some bigger problems, there was no safe harbor we could take her to—at least not that I knew about.

"How could they know how to do this?" Charles asked. "We haven't even begun to understand our abilities."

"It seems that they *have* begun to understand them," Dr. Roop said. "Remember, Zeke's father stole the code for the military tech tree after the Phands uncovered it. They have already had a chance to study it at length."

"Then why did they need to get data from us?" I asked.

"Because we hacked the system and learned how to maximize the available abilities," Dr. Roop explained.

Tamret, who had been working the navigation panel, turned around and held up her furry hands in protest. "Look, I know I'm good, but I'm just one girl. I can't believe that in all of the Phandic Empire they can't find someone who could pull off what I was able to do pretty quickly—and while under a lot of pressure."

"I have no doubt that they tried," Dr. Roop said, "but remember, Tamret, you hacked a particular version of the code, and you did it from a Former computer. There were almost certainly avenues and back doors available from that console that would not be found elsewhere. It is also true that, as adolescents, your brains are more pliable than those of adults. You see things differently, and that may have helped you to exploit elements in the Former code."

"Then why do the Phands not use their own young hackers to crack the code?" Charles asked.

"They may not have any," Dr. Roop said. "Theirs is not a society that tolerates beings such as Tamret, who do not flinch at breaking the rules in order to do what is right. And even if they did have hackers, using adolescents for such a purpose would not have occurred to the Phands. You will recall they regard young beings as barely even sentient."

"So before all this," Mi Sun said, "we had an advantage that we've now lost?"

"Yes. They must have had their suspicions, which is why they tried to isolate Tamret's nanites." He glanced at her.

She shrugged. "They put something in my food to make me fall asleep, and when I woke up, I was in that lab, unable to move. I guessed what they were after, and I just sort of figured out a way to keep them from being able to get hold of any working nanites."

Dr. Roop nodded. "On Confederation Central, you experimented with hacking your own skill tree long before altering anyone else's. They must have assumed that you, of all their prisoners, would most likely have a hacked version of the Former tech tree. Maybe they knew your blood yielded nothing, maybe not. But then Zeke and the others demonstrated their abilities at their school, and they decided to try to get information from the other humans."

"So I handed them exactly what they needed?" I asked.

"You could not have known," Dr. Roop said, his voice kind.

"I *should* have known," I said. "Ardov lured me into a fight, and I walked right into his trap. I should have gotten Alice back to the ship right away. Now we've given an advantage to the enemy, Alice might die, and I'm—I'm broken. My upgrades don't work. I can't even access my HUD."

Dr. Roop looked at me and blinked sympathetically, which did not make me feel good about my prospects. "We have already realized that this is the case. Your falling from the sky alerted us to the error, and we ran some medical scans on you immediately."

"Then you've been looking into it?" I asked.

Tamret nodded.

I looked at her. "Can you fix this?"

She let out a breath, and her ears flattened. "I don't know. Right now we have no idea what went wrong with you. We don't understand why your abilities have gone dark or if it can happen to the rest of us. I've downloaded all your data, and I'm comparing it to the rest of us, but it may be a while before I learn anything. You can still understand our languages, which means your nanites are still there and partially working, but beyond that, you don't seem to be gaining any benefits from either the original or the Former upgrades."

"I would not read anything into the translation abilities continuing to function," Dr. Roop said. "They have always been separate systems. That was why, when you were first exiled from Confederation Central, it was easy for me to keep your translation nanites working while temporarily neutralizing everything else."

It was bad news, but it could have been worse—not being able to understand any of the aliens on this ship would have been a disaster. The fact that I'd been in a similar situation before, and clawed my way back, gave me some hope. I made a decision not to get upset. We were going to fix this, not accept it. "Okay. So what's the plan?"

"The plan remains unchanged," Dr. Roop said. "The original approach is still the only option we have, both for removing Junup from power and for saving Alice's life. We are on our way to rendezvous with Captain Qwlessl. She has been using her time to search for Former artifacts. Perhaps her efforts have revealed new technology that will help defeat the Phands. Regardless, we need her ship and her expertise. Once we are on board, we will go to the planet where they are holding Director Ghli Wixxix and the others."

I nodded. "Do we have a plan for what we do once we get to the prison?"

"I'm afraid there is no 'we,'" said Dr. Roop. "Not for you. You cannot participate in any operations. You and Villainic, with no Former abilities, are too vulnerable."

I stood there, unable to speak. After everything we'd been through together, it had never occurred to me that I might be sidelined for the most important operation my friends had ever attempted. I understood their reasoning, of course. I would be virtually helpless, a liability to the rest of the supergroup. I knew I had nothing to offer, but even so, it stung.

"Isn't that just perfect," said Ardov, who was now awake. He leaned against a bulkhead, his arms bound behind him, his legs spread out with his feet manacled. "Poor little Zeke getting kicked out of the club. But now, at least, we know what you're up to. Director Junup asked me to find out, and now I have."

"Is he transmitting?" I asked the group. I felt so powerless. I hadn't been using those Former skills very long, but they'd become almost second nature in a short amount of time. Now I felt like I was missing a sense—maybe all my senses.

"Not a chance," Steve said. "There is no data coming in or out of the ship. We're in tunnel, which means communications are a no-go, but even if we were in normal space, it wouldn't matter. We're on full communications blackout."

"We'll have to keep it that way," Mi Sun said. "We need about five layers of redundancy on his restraints if we want to keep him from breaking free, and this means we can't maroon him anywhere until we've completed the operation."

Dr. Roop walked over to him. "Perhaps you can tell us how your weapon is harming our companion?"

He managed to shrug. "They gave it to me and told me to shoot her. That's what I did. Other than that, I have no idea. But I'm glad it's messing her up."

"If he cannot help us," Charles said, "then I think he should be rendered unconscious for the remainder of the voyage."

"I agree," Dr. Roop said. "Are you willing to cooperate? All we want is to help our friend."

"One more of you running around wouldn't make a difference to me," he said. "I'd tell you how to help her if I could. Let's find some other reason to keep me awake. Ask me something else."

"Not interested," Tamret said, getting up and walking over to him.

"Now hold on, Snowflake," Ardov said. He looked at her and she stared right back, almost as though she'd been slapped. There were a lot of things about Rarel culture I did not understand, but I had seen Tamret, usually fearless and defiant, bend and almost break under the weight of her society's codes and traditions. I started to walk over to get between them, when Tamret touched Ardov's arm, injecting him with something to render him unconscious. Almost immediately, his head slumped forward.

"That may have been premature," Dr. Roop said. "There's a chance he could have helped us."

"He made it pretty clear he wanted to be conscious," Tamret said, "and he still said he couldn't help Alice, so I think he was telling the truth. And while he's awake, he's dangerous."

Dr. Roop nodded thoughtfully. He probably agreed with her, but I guessed he didn't like her acting so impulsively.

I watched as Tamret walked back to where she had been

sitting, but her expression was darker now, distracted, and she wouldn't meet my eye.

No one would, and I knew they were thinking that I could have avoided this whole mess. Alice would still be hurt, maybe, but if I'd played things differently, Ardov would be back on Earth, he wouldn't know our plans, and the group would have one more superhero with which to carry out the operation. The only good news to come out of all of this was that the Phands hadn't guessed what we were up to yet, and that meant they wouldn't be waiting for us at the prison. It might well be that security would be tight everywhere, but we knew we wouldn't be walking into a trap—or at least *they* knew *they* wouldn't be walking into a trap. I'd be sitting on a ship, watching Ardov for signs of wakefulness and listening to Villainic complain.

"Oh, no."

It was Mi Sun's voice, hardly more than a whisper, but it cut through my thoughts. She was sitting by a console, scrolling through some images, and I could tell from how she sounded that she'd found something very bad.

I started to walk over to her. "What is it?"

She almost leaped from her chair and turned to me. "What is it? It's *you*, Zeke. This is your doing." She was pointing to an image on the screen. It showed a man and a woman, along with two teenagers, being led into a police van by uniformed officers. Watching over them were two Phands.

"That's my family," she said. "I captured a bunch of news feeds before we went into tunnel, just to see if the Phands were going to lash out at our families for what we did." She switched to another image. A haggard-looking man I recognized as Alice's father was also being arrested. There were pictures from India—Nayana's family being taken away. From Uganda, where the head of the boarding school Charles had attended was being led away in handcuffs by grim-faced men in uniforms. And then my own mother and father, being put in the back of a police car. Off to the side, two Phands looked on, and standing with them was Nora Price herself. She was looking at the camera, smirking, like she knew we were going to see this.

"This is your fault," Mi Sun said. "You said they would be okay. You said that we didn't have to worry about them, but your stunts back there forced their hand."

I opened my mouth to speak, but nothing came out. I felt like my throat was closing up. After all my parents had been through, they were finally safe and together. Now they were in the hands of beings who would hurt them just for the pleasure of causing me misery. And the rest of them. I never wanted anyone's family to get hurt, but I didn't know how to say any of it.

Tamret watched this exchange. I expected her to snap at Mi Sun, to tell her to be quiet, but she said nothing.

It was Charles who came to my defense. "You cannot say this is Zeke's doing."

"Then whose is it?" Mi Sun demanded.

"*I* asked that you not contact your families," Dr. Roop said.

Mi Sun turned to face him, hands on her hips. "And like a good little boy, Zeke did what you said. And he bullied me into doing it. I knew it was wrong. I knew I should have told them to hide, but I listened, and look what's happened."

"Mi Sun," I began.

"Save it," she said, waving a hand dismissively. "What do you have to tell me that will make a difference? That we'll save the galaxy? That we'll go on some stupid rescue mission and that will help our families hundreds of light years away? Let's just hope they're still alive by the time you get what you want."

She turned away from me, and I knew there was no point in trying to talk to her. Not now.

"Phands are far more likely to hold prisoners until they are useful than to execute them needlessly," Dr. Roop said, his voice soft.

"And what is Nora Price likely to do?" Mi Sun demanded.

Dr. Roop had no answer to that, and we found ourselves in an uncomfortable silence.

I coughed awkwardly. The Phandic ship was small, and there weren't private rooms or even bunks—apparently Phands considered sleeping an inexcusable weakness—but the aft section included an escape pod that could provide a little privacy, and I told the others that I needed a little time alone.

I went into the escape pod and shut the door. It was small, with just enough room for five or six Phands to sit with a tight squeeze. There were two emergency medical bays along the walls as well, but they were closed, I guessed to prevent the spread of possible contagions. There weren't even viewing windows, but it had probably never occurred to the designers that sick people might want to look out or their friends might want to look in. The pod gave every appearance of being minimally comfortable. On the other hand, it did seem to be maximally functional, and I noticed several boxes along the walls, including a portable medical kit, food rations, and a weapons locker.

These supplies, designed to aid survival under desperate conditions, only made me feel more isolated. They were like a sign that I was on my own. Maybe most of the others weren't angry with me, but they felt sorry for me, and that was almost as bad. No one had blamed me for Alice getting hurt, but as I recalled what had happened during the attack, I felt sure that I ought to have done something to keep her safe. Now it was too late, and I had no way of making things right.

Mi Sun had accused me of being a bully, of having a hero complex. Could she be right? I made a case when I believed I knew what we had to do, but so did everyone else. No one called Steve a bully when he insisted on steering the ship through some insane escape route. No one accused Alice of having a hero complex when she wanted to take a crazy risk to keep the rest of us safe.

I felt sure I had a lot to contribute to the cause, that the team was better with me than without me. Now I was going to be sitting out the most important operation we'd ever attempted. Maybe it was selfish, thinking of things this way. What did it matter who saved the galaxy as long as the galaxy got saved? I believed that, but I also felt that I could make a difference, and somehow, without meaning to, I had ruined my chance to help my friends. If one of them were to be hurt or killed, if the operation were to fail, then I would spend the rest of my life blaming myself.

The door to the escape pod hissed open and Tamret stepped in. She looked uncomfortable, like she wasn't sure she should be talking to me or if I would want to be talking to her. She brushed her hair out of her face, and I was struck once again by how pretty she was. She still frightened the poo out of me, and she probably always would, but I wasn't sure I would have it any other way. No matter what kinds of powers and ancient alien knowledge we brought to the table, I was still sure she was the most dangerous weapon we possessed. I thought back to all the times our enemies had underestimated her and paid the price.

She was going to go into battle one last time—I hoped— and more than anything I wanted to be by her side. Instead I'd be hanging back where it was safe, and that made me worry that maybe she would be disappointed in me. In the past I'd earned Tamret's respect by facing problems, not hiding from them. I'd stood up to enemies stronger and more dangerous than I was. How would she feel about me now that my job was to stay out of everyone's way?

Tamret came and sat down across from me. "Are you okay?" Her voice was strangely neutral, like an overworked nurse checking on a patient.

I shook my head. "I'm worried about my parents—about everyone's families."

"I know," she said. "But Mi Sun is wrong. It's not your fault. We're doing what we can to help them."

"But I feel like I messed up," I said. "You guys are about to attempt the most insane thing ever, and I can't be there."

"We'll somehow manage without you," she said, and there was no mistaking the hard edge in her voice.

"Are you angry with me?"

She looked away. "I just wish you hadn't messed around with Ardov. You had to go play hero, so now we've got a weaker team when we go into that prison."

Nothing could have stung me more. I hated that Mi Sun was angry with me, but hearing this, from Tamret, was almost more than I could take. "I thought you, of all people—"

"I'm not a *person*," she said. "You use that word when

you're talking about your own species. I'm a *being*. A Rarel. I'm not like you."

Where was this coming from? When had Tamret ever cared that we were from different worlds? There was a lot we didn't understand about each other's cultures, but that had never mattered before. Her coldness now, the obvious accusation in her voice, shocked me.

"So what?" I demanded. "Why should that suddenly make a difference?"

"It made a difference on Earth," she said, "when we were locked up for being aliens. It mattered when that woman was pumping me full of chemicals so she could try to unlock my secrets. And that was just the beginning, Zeke. She had plans for me. She was going to *dissect* me. She told me that with a smile on her face, and I was powerless to stop her."

Nora Price could be cruel—I knew that—but had she really planned to dissect Tamret? I didn't even want to think about it. The important thing was that we'd gotten Tamret out of there before she had the chance. "I'm sorry you had to go through that," I told her, trying to keep my voice calm. I didn't want to sound defensive. "You knew we would come for you."

She shook her head. "I didn't know you would come in time. I had no idea your species was so nasty to other species. It wasn't just Nora Price, you know. All the humans seemed to find being cruel to aliens pretty hilarious."

"There's good and bad everywhere," I told her. "I've seen some members of your species who aren't so nice."

"And some who are," she said, "even though you treat them like dirt."

"Wait a minute," I said, feeling like I'd just been transported into an entirely different argument. "Are we talking about Villainic now?"

She nodded. "I've decided that when this is all over, I'm going back with him. After all we've been through, there are ways that I can get caste protection from his family without being engaged to him. If there's one thing I've learned, it's that I belong with my own kind."

Her own kind had tried to talk me into leaving her behind when she hadn't been housed with the others in the police station. It felt like cheating to bring that up, but Tamret had to know she was safer with me than she would be with him, no matter how powerful his family.

She must have seen the disbelief on my face, because she crossed her arms and planted her feet as though I might try to shove her off her opinion. "I'm better off going home."

I couldn't believe what I was hearing. I thought we had worked all of this out back on Confederation Central, and now she was telling me she was going to return to Rarel, not because she was obligated to—which had been the situation before— but because she wanted to. It made no sense. "Tamret, have you forgotten how they treated you on Rarel? You're not safe there."

"After we save the Confederation, I'm sure they'll give Rarel another chance to join, and then things will be different. They'll have to be. All I know is I can't live somewhere I don't belong."

In the last hour I'd lost my powers, learned my family had been arrested, and been tossed aside by Tamret. When my powers cut out and I'd been plummeting toward the ground, I hadn't felt half this scared or helpless.

"I need to get back to working on the code," she said. "I haven't given up on getting you up and running. I know you want to be part of the team."

There was nothing I could say. I mean, there were a million things I felt, but I couldn't figure out how to say any of them. They all stuck in my throat. I sat there silently, looking down while Tamret stood up and left the pod.

CHAPTER SEVEN

About an hour after Tamret left, Steve came into the escape pod. The seats weren't built with Ish-hi in mind, and he shifted uncomfortably and moved his tail around so that he wasn't putting too much pressure on it.

"You look like rubbish," he said.

"I'm having a bad day," I told him.

He patted me on the shoulder. "Yeah, I kind of figured. The enhancements, your families, and Tamret giving you the old heave-ho."

I looked up. "She told you."

"Didn't have to," he said, his tongue tasting the air. "All those emotions hovering about. I smelled the whole thing."

"She wants to go back to Rarel with Villainic," I said.

"That's daft," he said, sounding genuinely surprised. "There's something else going on. You can count on it. That girl is emotional, even for a mammal, but she's not barking mad, and there's no way she'd throw over a relatively choice bloke such as yourself for a git like Villainic."

"Thank you for saying so."

"The thing is, upgrades or not, you're part of the team, yeah? You can't sit in here and mope all day. Also, if I know anything about girls, you don't want to let her see she's got to you. Act like it's no big deal. Maybe get a little chummy with Mi Sun. Make her jealous. That'll bring her around."

"All it will do is get me kicked in the face."

"Probably true, but the point is to act like you don't give a toss. That's what works for me."

"You're cooler than I am," I said.

"I'm a reptile, mate. Do we need to review the whole warm- and cold-blooded thing?"

I sighed. "I just don't see why I should even be out there. I have nothing to contribute at this point."

"Nothing if you're feeling sorry for yourself. Look, there's not a stupid, reckless, and irresponsible thing this lot has done that you weren't at the center of. You think we've gotten this far because of the technology? It helped, but in the end we did all that because you're always there saying we need to go off on one mad romp or another. Even if you can't be on the ground, we need you with us to figure out what completely daft approach is going to get the job done."

"Thanks for saying so, but—"

"There's a strategy meeting in ten minutes. And you'd bet- ter be there or I will mock you."

No mockery was required. I was there when the meeting began. Neither Tamret nor Mi Sun would look at me, but Villainic was friendly—so, bonus there. We were still about two hours out from the planet where we were to meet Captain Qwlessl. Meanwhile, the agreeably comatose Ardov was put in the escape pod. Dr. Roop didn't want to take any chances with him, so at the first sign we couldn't control him, we could simply jettison him into the void.

"We have all been very concerned about what happened to Zeke during his battle with Ardov," Dr. Roop said. "Why did his Former enhancements shut down, and why can they not be reactivated? Might the same thing happen to the rest of us? We have some answers, and I'm afraid the news is not good."

"Did Zeke somehow damage our systems?" Mi Sun asked.

"Don't be stupid," Tamret snapped. "How could he have done that?"

She shrugged. "I wouldn't put anything past him."

Tamret rolled her eyes. "As near as I can tell, he burned out his upgrades. He used too many abilities in too short a time, and the nanites that control the Former upgrades stopped working. They took out the standard Confederation skill tree as well. The only thing that didn't shut down was the translation technology. I think it's because, as Dr. Roop said, it's an entirely separate system."

"It appears," Dr. Roop said, "our ability to integrate this technology is limited. I told you back at the Hidden Fortress that there was something I did not like about the code. It appears to be unstable."

"Will these nanites harm us?" asked Charles.

"Only if you are in a dangerous situation when you experience a malfunction," Dr. Roop said.

"You mean like pretending you're Superman?" Mi Sun asked.

"Just back off," Tamret said. "This is my fault. I should be able to fix it, but I can't figure out how to repair the code."

I was grateful to Tamret for defending me, but she still wouldn't meet my eye when I looked at her.

"No one is to blame," Dr. Roop said, his voice very kind. "The Formers were perhaps the most advanced beings ever to exist in our galaxy. They built a sophisticated civilization that regarded millennia the way we regard months. Tamret, that you cannot solve a problem with technology they engineered is hardly to your discredit. In any event, given what we know about the Formers, it is possible that the code may not be flawed at all. It may have been designed this way."

"It may have been designed to malfunction?" Charles asked. "That makes no sense."

"To beings like you and me, perhaps," Dr. Roop agreed. "Our knowledge of the Formers is very limited, but we do believe they were experimenters, compulsive tinkerers on a cosmic scale. They were possibly even capricious by our standards. Some legends portray them as cosmic tricksters who loved nothing more than to put beings, worlds, even entire civilizations in difficult positions to watch what happened next. Planting technology that gives beings astonishing powers—and then taking those powers away—is entirely consistent with what we know of the Formers."

That made sense to me. Smelly—full name Smellimportunifeel Ixmon Pooclump Iteration Nine—an artificial consciousness who had spent months living inside my head, hadn't been a Former, but it had come out of Former society, and it had loved putting me in difficult situations just to see how I'd deal with them. I didn't think it would have ever allowed me to come to real harm, but it hadn't minded testing my limits.

"But what about the rest of you?" I asked. "Are you going to just shut down at some point?"

Tamret sighed. "The short answer is yes, and there are two ways it can go. The first is that these nanites will fail under heavy use. That's what happened with you, Zeke. You overtaxed them, and the code went into some kind of self-destruct loop.

It seems to be a mechanism that, as Dr. Roop says, is worked directly into the source code. From what I can tell, it may be too deeply embedded in the tech tree's operating system to remove or modify or work around. And like with Zeke, it will take out Confederation skill tree abilities too. Everything but translation will be wiped out."

"I understand," Charles said. "This limits our options, but it does not change the overall plan. We must simply avoid conflict, use less-taxing, stealth-based skills rather than combat skills, which tend to require multiple uses simultaneously—weapons, shields, speed, and so forth. Might that not solve the problem?"

"Unfortunately not," Dr. Roop said, "for there is an additional flaw. I fear that time is also a factor. The code is in a constant state of decay, and any of us could find our skills nonfunctional at any time."

"So," Mi Sun summarized, "using these abilities too much could shut down the system, but saving them might not do any good because the system could shut down on its own anyhow."

"Yes," Dr. Roop agreed.

"Then either approach to managing upgrades—aggressive or cautious—could be equally flawed?" Charles asked.

"That pretty much sums it up," Tamret said.

"So, how do we get everyone out of prison without risking our lives?" Mi Sun asked.

"I'm afraid we don't have an answer to that yet," Dr. Roop said.

Something then occurred to me. "Wait a minute. If everyone is vulnerable, then there's no reason why I can't go along with you."

"I do not think so," Charles said. "Every one of us *might*

be vulnerable, but if I understand all of this, we might also get through an operation without any of us experiencing problems. We certainly had no difficulties at the police station."

"We might experience difficulties, but we might not," Dr. Roop said. "It is not the same as bringing along someone who we know is entirely vulnerable. I'm not sure I can agree to anyone taking that sort of risk."

"And who put you in charge?" Mi Sun asked. "Zeke thinks he can tell us what to do, and so do you, but I don't remember agreeing to that."

"Let's hold on—" I began.

"No," Dr. Roop conceded. "It's a fair point. I have been presuming that I should be in charge, at least until Captain Qwlessl is among us, because I am eldest. It seemed the most natural arrangement, but I do not wish to force this hierarchy on you."

"Of course Captain Qwlessl should call the shots," I said. "She has the most experience. Nothing else makes sense."

"Easy for you to say," Mi Sun said. "You guys are always the ones making the decisions. I don't see that it is getting us very far."

"Back off," Tamret told her.

"She may have a point," Villainic offered. "Perhaps it is time for some new voices to be heard."

No one responded to this.

It wasn't that I didn't get where Mi Sun was coming from. She'd never asked for any of this. She'd agreed to go to an alien space station as a kind of cultural ambassador, and now she found herself in constant danger—space battles and prison breakouts were not for everyone. She was tough, but even she could only take so much. Now that her family was in danger, maybe she'd reached her breaking point. I knew that thinking about my family being held by Nora Price made me sick.

"Look, Mi Sun," I said, "I understand what you're saying. None of us knew what we would face when we left Confederation Central, and maybe things are worse than we expected. It's hard, but we're in a situation where we can make a real difference, and I think we have to try. Letting the beings with the most knowledge and the most experience make the calls is the smart move."

"I agree with Zeke," Charles said. "Doing nothing and waiting is not a choice we have. The headmaster of my school, who has been like a father to me, has been arrested, and I want to help him, but we are doomed to fail if we do not get the Phands off Earth. Alice is growing weaker, and our own prospects of helping anyone diminish, rather than grow, with time."

"Doesn't it bother you that Zeke and his alien friends are always the ones deciding where we go and what we do?" said Mi Sun.

"I have no need to be the one to make the decisions if the decisions are sound," Charles said. "And I think that Zeke's record, when you factor in the difficulty of our situations, is quite impressive. I am certainly content to have Captain Qwlessl take charge once we reach her. Swift action, under her leadership, is surely still our best option."

"Unless Captain Qwlessl has an idea of how we might fix the Former skills," Dr. Roop said. "What if she has a way for us to be back to full and dependable strength, but doing so will take weeks or months?"

"And what about Alice?" I asked.

Dr. Roop looked away. "We may have to make some difficult decisions."

"I'm not signing on to any decisions that involve letting one of us die," I told him.

"Of course not. There are always options, but every option may involve additional risks." He sighed. "That is all we know for now. When we transfer to Captain Qwlessl's ship, the medical staff may be able to help Alice. At the very least, we should be able to place her in medical stasis. We will see what our choices look like at that time."

"Maybe we should put this to a vote," Mi Sun said.

"All those in favor of handing the operation over to Captain Qwlessl," I said, and raised my hand. So did everyone else, including Mi Sun. I knew she was frustrated, and I figured her pushing back against our decision-making was just her way of expressing it, but she still wasn't going to argue against reason.

"I'm going to go over the code one more time," Tamret said.

"Perhaps you should sleep," Dr. Roop said.

She snorted. "Like that is going to happen."

Tamret went over to work the console, and I followed her. The things she'd said before had hurt me, and I felt uncomfortable trying to have a normal conversation with her, but I could see she was being hard on herself.

By the time I reached her, she was already at a workstation, streaming through lines of code. I put a hand on the back of her chair.

"Not now," she said to me.

"Look, give yourself a break," I told her. "Dr. Roop is right. You can't be expected to be able to figure out something like this. You are putting yourself up against the Formers."

She shook her head. "You don't understand. This is the

moment when everyone is counting on me, and I'm letting them down."

"What do you mean *the* moment? What about all the other moments? What about all the times we needed stuff done and you just did it and made it seem like no big deal? It's not like this is your one turn at the plate."

"I have no idea what that last part meant," she said. "I'm getting something about team-based recreational .activities, which sounds pretty stupid. I don't have time for that sort of thing."

"Why don't you take a break—at least until we get to the new ship?"

"No," she said with a sigh. She brushed hair out of her eyes. "I'll be miserable if I stop working. I appreciate your trying to make me feel less bad about myself, but it's really not your concern."

Not so long ago, I'd believed we were going to burst into whatever prison held our friends and shut down any resistance. I'd known what it felt like to be almost unimaginably powerful, and now we were all powerless—or close to it.

I sat by myself, trying not to think about how miserable I was, watching Tamret work. I was also trying not to think about how miserable she obviously was. She was always so hard on the beings she didn't like, but I realized now that she was a thousand times harder on herself. I also had to admire how she would not quit. Maybe her tenacity, her single-mindedness, could get her into trouble, but it had also saved her life, and our lives, plenty of times. If anyone could fix this problem with sheer intellect and force of will, it would be her, but I worried that it would be out of her reach.

I lost track of time, but then Steve snapped me out of my thoughts by telling us that we were coming out of tunnel. I braced myself for the weird, disorienting feeling as the ship shifted from who knows what or where and back into the universe as we understand it.

We emerged in the outer fringes of a solar system typical of those the Formers had touched. There was a single yellow dwarf star at the center and several large gas giants pulling dangerous space debris into their gravity wells. We zoomed passed these until we saw an Earthlike planet ahead. At first glance it seemed almost identical to Earth, but there were more, smaller continents, and while there was plenty of blue water, there were few patches of green to be seen through the cloud cover. Most of the land looked brown or dull yellow.

Tamret looked out and sighed. "You know, I feel like [*marine predator*] poop, but seeing that actually kind of puts things in perspective."

"What?" Steve asked. "Some fringe planet no one has ever heard of?"

She shook her head. "We're so wrapped up in our own problems—which are pretty big, I admit—that it's kind of easy to forget the bigger picture. We're traveling on a spaceship in a galaxy full of amazing life. We're playing with the technology of beings who were so smart we can only gape at them like morons."

"I never gape like a moron," Steve said. "My gaping is always dignified."

I smiled to myself. Tamret could come across as the most negative being, but then she would say something like that. Maybe she was really an optimist. I needed to be an optimist too, I decided. I didn't really understand her reasons for wanting to go back to Rarel, but I had to respect them. At the same time, I hoped I could change her mind.

She turned and saw me smiling at her.

"What?"

"I just like how you think about things."

For an instant she smiled, and then, as though she was remembering something, her expression turned cold and she looked away.

She was hiding something from me, I was sure of it now, and if her decision to go back to Rarel was a problem, then it could have a solution. I was going to find it, and I was going to fix everything. Maybe that was a little ambitious, since I had no idea how I was going to fix myself, but I felt sure I could come up with something.

Things were going to work out, I told myself. They always had, and they would again. Maybe Tamret would crack this problem, or maybe Captain Qwlessl would know what to do. If it came right down to it, I still had the Smelly option. Before leaving, it—Smelly had no gender—had given me a small metallic disc, an entangled quantum signaling device, which I still had in my pocket. Smelly had promised it would come help me one time if I needed it. Given my history of getting into horrible life-or-death situations, I hated to call in that favor until I was really desperate, but if it was the only option left on the table for resolving the current crisis, I wouldn't hesitate.

I actually felt a little less terrible. We were going to make it through this, I decided. We'd won before and we would win again.

"This is a bit odd," Steve said. "Captain Qwlessl was supposed to meet us, but I don't see any ships, Confederation or otherwise, in this system."

Dr. Roop looked up, alarmed. "Let me take a look." He began to walk over to the console.

That was when everything went black.

Often when people say everything went black, they are using the term metaphorically. Not this time. I wasn't hit on the head or given a knockout injection. No, everything went black because there were no lights. Not only had all shipboard illumination shut down, but all equipment as well. Our viewscreens were not real windows, but image projections, so there was no ambient light from outside. We were in total and complete darkness. There was also no gravity, I was both blind and weightless.

There are places you don't want to be when you experience complete and utter system failures, and among these is a spaceship. This was a relatively small one, and there were nine beings on board. I had no idea how long the air would last without life-support systems, but I knew the answer wasn't *a really long time*. Maybe hours, maybe minutes.

I reached out to grab on to something. Anything. I took hold of the back of a chair so I wouldn't float around like space junk. Everyone else would be able to use night vision, and they would need to get around to try to figure out what had gone wrong. If I started flailing about in the dark, I'd just get in someone's way.

I heard Tamret say something in her own language—it sounded strangely guttural and sharp.

"My HUD is down," Mi Sun said in English. "And it sounds like even the translator nanites are offline."

I didn't answer, but I felt a tightening in my chest. If the ship and the tech trees were down, and even basic functions like translation weren't working, it could only mean one thing.

"We may have been hit with an electromagnetic pulse," Charles said, echoing my thoughts.

I knew a little bit about EMPs. The good news was that as soon as the attack was over, the ship, and presumably the people in it, would reboot and the systems would come online again. That meant I could expect my translation abilities to return eventually. The bad news was that someone was deliberately attacking us.

Ardov! I thought. He had been restrained only by plasma bonds created by the Former tech. They would now be offline. So in addition to our other considerable problems, we had a dangerous enemy running loose—or at least floating loose—on the ship.

Someone said something in a series of hisses and clicks. I presumed it was Steve.

"We need operational silence," Mi Sun said.

She was right. If Ardov was loose on the ship, in the dark, the last thing we wanted to do was to give ourselves away by talking.

Knowing that it was probably true was one thing, but it didn't give me any idea of what to do about it. I still couldn't see, and even if I could, what good would it do me? Ardov's tech would be offline too, but he was still a lot stronger than I was.

There was also the possibility that his tech would not be down. Maybe he had some kind of EMP-proof implant that would protect him from the effects of the attack. That seemed like the sort of things the Phands might develop, though I was just guessing. If he had something like that, we were in huge trouble.

I had to stop and think—though I didn't have much of a choice. There wasn't much else I could do.

Maybe Ardov is up and functioning, I reasoned, *but what good does it do him? He can't operate a nonfunctioning ship. That means he needs to incapacitate us before shutting down the pulse and reactivating the systems.*

Would he kill us? Had he started killing already? If his original skill tree was maxed out, he would have lots of nonlethal combat options at his disposal, but that didn't mean he would use them. Being pummeled unconscious was better than being killed, but it was still something I wanted to avoid.

I closed my eyes—not that it made a difference—and listened. I heard a faint click somewhere and the sound of a body bouncing against the wall. I knew the sound. It was a medical dispenser. He was administering some kind of injection, presumably to make people sleep. I had to hope it was not something deadly.

How would the dispenser work? Was it purely mechanical, designed to function during an EMP attack, or did Ardov have some sort of override?

Assuming he had a way of insulating himself from the effects of the EMP, he would have all the abilities that came with a maxed-out standard Confederation skill tree. That was the bad news. The good news was that I had a pretty good idea of those skills and their limitations. I knew, for example, that he would have excellent, but not perfect, night vision. If I moved slowly enough, and was lucky, maybe I wouldn't draw his attention. Once he believed we were all unconscious, he might reactivate the system. When the lights came back on, I would have a chance—one chance. I would have a moment of surprise when I could hit him with something. There were PPB pistols on board, and while one shot would not take Ardov out, it would slow him down long enough for me to shoot him as many times as it took. I had to find a weapon.

The one place I was sure I could get one was in the emergency weapons locker on the escape pod. It was also the best place to hide so Ardov wouldn't find me. I knew where the pod was relative to my current position, but once I started moving, I would lose all sense of direction. On the other hand, I could push myself off and float. I would look no different from an unconscious person. The only way he would be able to tell if someone was conscious would be by watching their movements or listening to their breathing.

Hoping I was not giving my location away, I pushed off against the wall and, keeping my breaths slow and shallow, gently directed myself across the ship toward the open hatch of the escape pod.

My hands found nothing but wall, and I was sure I'd miscalculated, but as my fingers probed, I felt the slightest of indentations. Then, moving farther in that direction, I hit empty space. This was it. It had to be. I grabbed what I believed had to be the doorjamb of the escape-pod area and twisted my body so I would swing back in the other direction. Once I'd completed the arc, I let go and drifted back, until a few seconds later I bounced gently off the bulkhead.

I now knew I was in the right place. There was nothing to do but probe along the walls until I found the emergency weapons locker. I began doing this, working my way slowly from one end of the spherical space to the other. It was tedious work, but there was nothing to be gained by rushing.

At last I found the box, which was held against the wall with a material that seemed a whole lot like Velcro—I assumed to keep it in place during weightless incidents. Fortunately, it had no electronic components. I slid the the unlocking mechanism and, gently opening the box, maneuvered my hand into the narrow crack to feel around for the pistol. I had to hope I didn't get the business end of something sharp by mistake. At last my fingers moved along the familiar pistol shape. I grabbed the weapon and closed the box.

Now I had a gun that did not work to use on a target I couldn't see. I probably had a fifty-fifty chance of escaping Ardov's notice. My best bet, I realized, was to stay where I was. When the lights came on and the gravity kicked back in, anyone still conscious, including Ardov, would have a moment of disorientation as they tried to figure out where they were and what was going on. I would know exactly where I was. Up and down were tricky things without gravity, but I used the doorjamb to maneuver myself to a position where I could put my feet on the floor quickly. While Ardov flailed and fell, and while he looked desperately around and tried to figure out who was where and what they were doing, I would be able to spot him and start firing.

I didn't know if his skill tree would be up and running as quickly as the rest of the ship systems, but I had to assume the revival would be instantaneous. I would need, therefore, a fraction of a second to adjust the weapon's settings so I did not accidentally kill him. What I wanted was the highest stun setting, and I wanted to hit him at least a half dozen times.

So, as prepared as I could be under the circumstances, I waited motionless and in silence. In absolutely darkness, it's hard to tell ten minutes from two hours, especially when you are holding on to a doorjamb with one hand and a pistol with the other, waiting for a target to appear. My hands began to ache. I felt the air growing heavy and stuffy, warm from so many bodies in close proximity, but I still gripped the wall. I didn't see that there was any other choice.

Then, in an instant, there were lights and gravity and sounds of machinery kicking back to life, of grunts and groans of the semiconscious who had been too high up crashing down. The cool breeze of circulating air swept across my face. I'd been ready for this, poised and waiting, but the light still shocked my eyes, and the sudden existence of gravity hit me like I'd been tackled.

I stumbled as my feet made awkward contact with the floor, but I then planted myself and glanced around the ship. I saw Tamret, Steve, Dr. Roop, Charles, and Mi Sun, all unconscious—though, I hoped, unharmed—as they fell to the deck. Some distant part of my brain registered that I did not see Villainic, but I assumed he had found a tight spot in which to hide. I'd figure out what happened to him later.

I did see Ardov, though, at the navigation console. He had positioned himself so he would land in the seat when the gravity came on, and he was now plugging in what looked like tunneling coordinates. His plan had clearly been to incapacitate our crew and redirect the ship.

That was not about to happen. I couldn't tell how far along he was, but he would not be able to finish once I'd blasted him into unconsciousness. I raised my pistol, confirmed the setting, and took an instant to double-check my aim. His reflexes were a million times better than mine, so if I missed with the first shot, I might not get another chance.

I had him. I squeezed off the shot that I was certain would stop him in his tracks.

Except it hit the interior of the escape pod.

It did that because the door to the escape pod had hissed closed a fraction of a second before I pulled the trigger.

There was no porthole—I've seen such things in movies and comics and games, but you really don't want a glass window in a small craft that is going to be ejected from a ship under dangerous conditions—and I had no idea what was happening on the other side of the door.

I glanced around, looking for the control panel that would let me open the door, but it was a Phandic ship, and my understanding of their technology was patchy at best. I saw what I hoped was the main control board, and a switch that seemed likely to operate the main door. I moved toward it when I felt a deep rumble. The pod lurched hard to my left, and I had to grab on to the wall to keep from falling over.

My first thought was that the ship had been hit by enemy fire, but then I realized that that couldn't be right. The impact had been too soft, but also too immediate. It came from right under my feet, vibrating through me.

Then I understood what I'd felt. The escape pod had been disconnected from the ship.

I grunted in frustration and dashed for the control panel, scrambling to find a way to somehow reestablish the link. The pod was no longer coupled to the ship, but the ship had been holding a stationary orbit, so that meant inertia would keep us near each other, at least for a little while. All I had to do was find a way to dock. I saw nothing that looked like basic controls, so I would need to access the main computer. I worked out how to get to the top of the operations menu, and I was looking for some kind of docking command when I felt a sudden lurch and the momentary sensation of weightlessness before the pod's own gravity and inertial compensators kicked in.

The escape pod was moving away from the ship. I was being separated from everyone I knew.

Do not panic, I told myself. *There is no reason to panic, and therefore I won't.* This was what I chanted to myself even while I completely panicked.

All I had to do was turn this thing around. Maybe it was just a standard protocol to move a safe distance from the ship. I had to hope so. If the pod had any kind of default programming, such as to find the nearest planetary body, things could get trickier, so I needed to act fast and make sure I didn't drift too far away.

I found the navigational-control access and shifted it to my workstation. That also activated the main viewscreens, so I could see the ship on one screen, growing increasingly distant. From another I watched the long-uninhabited planet, growing ever closer.

I worked my way through the confusing Phandic commands and ordered the pod to come to a full stop. That would give me a moment to breathe while I figured out how to return it to dock.

A message popped up on the screen. PROTOCOL VIOLATION. PLEASE ENTER OVERRIDE CLEARANCE.

Only the Phands would require an override clearance in an

escape pod, a vehicle you use if things are in utter chaos. Were they looking for a password of some kind? I had no idea. Tamret would be able to figure it out in seconds, but I didn't have her skills or her confidence.

Tamret. She was trapped on that ship with Ardov. She was unconscious and helpless, and he was in control and clearly meant to take my friends somewhere they wouldn't want to go.

I thought about my data bracelet. I could try contacting her, but taking the time to do so would mean less time to crack my own control problems. If Tamret was conscious, I might distract her from any life-or-death struggle in which she was involved. If not, I'd be wasting my time.

I had to take the chance. Tamret could probably remotely patch into the pod's security system and override the programming. If I didn't act soon, I would enter the atmosphere and be trapped on an abandoned planet. I knew there was no intelligent life down there, but I had no way of knowing what kind of dangerous creatures might prowl the surface. I didn't know what my food or water options would be there. The time for delay was over.

I keyed my bracelet to contact Tamret, and waited the second I would have expected her to respond if she could. Nothing.

Then I heard her voice, her tone breathless and urgent, like she was mid-struggle. "Zeke, where are you? I need help—"

Then her transmission cut off. There was a flash of light, and the ship vanished into a momentary rip in space. They had tunneled out of the system. Tamret needed me, but now she was gone, and I was spiraling toward an uninhabited planet, utterly alone.

CHAPTER EIGHT

I t was time for some inventory taking. With the fate of the galaxy on the line, and with Alice seriously injured, maybe dying, on board our ship, I was now separated from my friends, who were dealing with my greatest enemy's most loyal and vengeful servant. Back on Earth, my parents were in the hands of the invaders who hated me, led by a woman who would not hesitate to hurt them if she thought it would bring her some advantage. Meanwhile, I was plunging toward a planet so worthless that even the Phands hadn't bothered to conquer it. I was alone, with limited supplies, food and drink designed for aliens whose nutritional needs might not be compatible with mine, and heading into dangers for which I was totally unprepared.

These were all bad, but they were not the worst thing. Tamret had said she needed help, and I couldn't do anything for her. I'd promised I would always be there, and now, because I was the genius who'd thought it was a great idea to hide in an escape pod, I could not help her.

This was one of those disasters that everyone always felt sure was my fault. In the past, those had always been decisions I'd made. In tight spots I'd chosen to act, and I felt like almost every time those actions had been right, but they'd also had unintended consequences that had made beings across vast expanses of space hate my guts.

This time it was much worse. Those other mistakes I could

look back on and tell myself that I'd done the right thing. This time I had somehow accidentally launched an escape pod, separating myself from the others. I didn't know where they were heading, and it was entirely possible they hadn't yet figured out I was on the escape pod.

In the meantime, they were heading off to some unknown location, but I had to think Ardov was sending them back to Junup or even directly into Phandic hands. Although I knew virtually nothing about it, I thought of Planet Pleasant and shuddered.

What could they do to protect themselves? There was no way they could change their destination once in tunnel. The most they could do would be to gain control of the ship and drop out of tunnel entirely. Assuming they were awake and could overpower Ardov, that is. Otherwise, they would be facing a whole lot of Phandic forces when they got to where they were going.

What if they did get away? With time running short, they were hardly going to take a detour to rescue me. They were going to have to figure out what had happened to Captain Qwlessl or go after Ghli Wixxix and the others directly. Those were the only logical choices, and that meant that the best-case scenario was that I would be completely sidelined until Junup was either out of power or my friends failed.

Now, I realized gloomily, it was time to think about the worst-case scenario. I was heading toward an uninhabited planet full of unknown dangers and limited, possibly inadequate, resources. While my Former upgrades had been working, I'd been playing in creative mode, but now the settings had been switched to survival. I had to shut down the part of my brain that was worrying about my friends. I needed to figure out what sorts of supplies I had, what sorts of dangers I might face, and how I could stay alive.

Maybe no one lived down there anymore, but it was the site of a secret dig for Former artifacts, which meant there might be stuff on the planet for me to use. That sounded promising until I remembered I was talking about finding things on a *planet*. It wasn't that long ago that I'd had a hard time finding overdue library books in my own bedroom. I wasn't Luke Skywalker, and I couldn't count on crashing my ship within strolling distance of Yoda's hut.

It was time to try to figure out the Phandic computers. The only other times I'd tried to make sense of their systems, I'd been desperately searching for just the right thing with no time to spare. Now, at least, I was under a little less pressure. I checked the pod's inventory of supplies, and found there were enough food and moisture packs to last eight beings eight days. I did a quick analysis on the contents of the packs and found they were biologically compatible with my physiology. I had hoped to go my whole life without having to taste Phandic food, and I didn't think it would be good, but at least it would be edible, which was definitely a plus. I couldn't remember the last time I'd eaten, and only adrenaline and terror were keeping my hunger from distracting me.

I grabbed one of the food packs, but I couldn't bring myself to eat yet. I needed to get a better sense of what I was dealing with. I had a weapon, and I wasn't going to die of hunger or thirst in the next few days, so that sort of counted as good news. The next issue was figuring out what I'd be dealing with on the planet itself, and things there were less cheery. The pod's database had no detailed information about the world I was about to call home for an indefinite amount of time. It only listed it as "uninhabited and undesirable." I was going to a place Phands found undesirable, and that did not fill me with hope. On the other hand, I was sure they would find a candy store undesirable, so maybe the planet would be a wonderland of chocolate.

The pod rumbled as it entered atmosphere, and then I felt the automatic attitude controls kick in. I was then able to activate both a topographical map, which would be useful for helping me to find the most ideal landing sites, and a viewscreen that provided images of the surface.

The chocolate-wonderland theory was not holding up. I saw mostly desert and vast oceans whose water, the computer told me, was undrinkable. I surveyed the planet for possible landing sites, but I lacked a clear sense of what I was looking for. There wasn't a whole lot of variety in the terrain—sun-blasted valleys, rocky outcroppings, waterless mountains. I then scanned for Confederation technology. Whatever Captain Qwlessl and her team had been doing here, they must have left some of their equipment behind. Their camp might contain useful supplies. There might even be some Confederation comm beacons I could use to let them know what had happened to me. I doubted if those things could get me off-world in time to help the others, but at least they would know they needed to save me after they were done saving civilization.

I picked up what might have been residual signs of Confederation technology. They were faint and indistinct—certainly not something that would scream out to a passing Phand vessel, but I was running a thorough search for something I thought might be hidden away. I scanned the surrounding areas, and the ship's database told me that there was a suspected Former historical site nearby. There were no guarantees, but I figured I had a pretty good idea of where the dig might have been. I next selected a reasonable place to land within hiking distance. I found a place with a high density of vegetation, which was of the tough, desert variety, but this was better than nothing. Also, this area seemed especially light on the carnivorous plants that appeared to be the planet's dominant life form.

There was no avoiding the fact that I was heading into the desert—not like Sahara sand dunes, but more like the expansive scrubland that I'd passed through when traveling across New Mexico: rolling hills of dirt and sand, hardy (and likely inedible) plants, little water, and few animals. However, my scans detected the presence of underground springs, and I downloaded the information to my bracelet. There were a few places where a strategic blast or two with my PPB pistol would get me plenty to drink.

I was feeling marginally less miserable, but the move from total to mild desperation didn't bring me a ton of comfort. I was still alone, isolated, worried about the others, and hoping against hope I would find . . . what? Another fully operational spaceport like the one at the Hidden Fortress? There had been one, I supposed, so there was no reason to believe there could not be another. On the other hand, if there had been that much technology lying around, the Phands would not have ignored this planet, which was on the border of their territory. I had no idea what Captain Qwlessl had been doing here, but it must have been important for her to let it occupy her time in this period of crisis. It seemed like a safe bet that she hadn't been looking for emergency transport.

Maybe she'd found something. Maybe what she'd learned would lead her to a place where she and her crew would discover technology that would utterly crush the Phands or Junup—technology like we had discovered, and destroyed, at the Hidden Fortress. It would be nice, but none of that felt exciting to me. I wanted to bring Junup down. Now. I didn't want to spend my time digging through the dust of a forgotten planet while the real battle was being waged elsewhere, while my friends were in danger. Frustration seethed inside me, ready to explode, but I had to keep calm. I couldn't let my feelings take control. If I let the cork out of that bottle, I'd never be able to survive.

I tried to clear my mind, to calm my breathing, while the autopilot worked its way through the planet's atmosphere. I opened the cap of the food packet, which was a long tube made of some synthetic material similar to plastic. I braced myself for the worst—the package boasted that it was made with 100 percent genuine carapace!—and squeezed the contents into my mouth.

It was not terrible. It tasted like a blander version of peanut butter, though I was getting slight notes of beetle. There were only a few spoonfuls in the pack, but I guessed it was nutrient dense, since my hunger more or less vanished after the first taste, leaving me free to concentrate on all the ways my life was now a complete disaster.

Finally I thudded to a soft landing in the planet's soil. I sat very still for a moment, looking at the flashing lights of the readout, trying to clear my mind. I didn't want to think about how this was the worst situation I'd ever been in. I had never been so helpless and so alone. I didn't want to listen to the voice inside my head telling me I was going to be lost forever. I didn't want to give in to the fear and the anger and the misery. I silently chanted that I was going to get through this.

I clenched my teeth and took a deep breath, and then I got to work.

First I performed a series of environmental scans to make sure the air was safe, there was no dangerous radiation, and no Zeke-devouring predators. As near as I could tell, I wouldn't run into anything but small creatures once I stepped outside—nothing larger than a rabbit. Many of these animals were poisonous, but if I didn't step on, kick, or otherwise antagonize them, the data suggested they were likely to leave me alone.

The hopelessness of my situation washed over me again, but I pushed it back. Feeling sorry for myself, or worrying about Tamret and the others, was not going to help me survive, and it was not going to help me find a way to get back in the game. If there was a way to do that, it was outside this pod, and so saying, I opened the doors and prepared to go out and find it.

I felt the rush of warm, fresh air, the sharp scent of herbs, utterly unfamiliar but somehow not unlike things I had smelled before. Light, impossibly bright, streamed into the pod, and I had to squint and turn away. I already felt thirsty, so I grabbed a couple of moisture packs and stepped out the door.

Sand, rocks, weeds. Repeat in one direction toward rocky hill, and in the other toward rocky valley. The heat felt like it was weighing down on me, like it was penetrating all the way to my bones. The sun itself, looming bright and orange and unrelenting in the sky, somehow gave the impression of being twice the size of Earth's. Gravity was about normal, typical for a Former world, but otherwise everything about this place was miserable. It felt used and dried up, like I was visiting it a few billion years after its prime.

I was about to begin a preliminary exploration of my landing site when I heard it. The slight mechanical whir and click of a compartment opening. It was coming from inside the pod itself.

I spun, hardly knowing what to expect, but ready for anything. I raised my pistol as my heart pounded in my chest. Without my upgrades, combat was completely terrifying.

One of the emergency medical bays was sliding open with excruciating slowness. Someone or something had been in the pod with me. Had there been Phands on board the ship the whole time? Had whoever was in that medical compartment helped Ardov get free? I backed up, ready to make my escape if I needed to. I tried to steady my arm, and make myself ready to fire. The door continued to creak open, lifting inch by painful inch.

Then I saw his familiar tall form, his goofy face grinning with bewildered good cheer. Villainic poked his head out. "Is it safe for me to emerge?"

I'd thought there was nothing worse than being utterly alone on a dead world, but now, it seemed, I had discovered that I was wrong.

CHAPTER NINE

I tried to compose myself. I could not, after all, be angry with Villainic for having found a place to hide during Ardov's attack. I would have preferred for him to have found another place, *any* place other than where I was, but it wasn't as though this situation was his fault. I was now saddled with him, which meant someone completely useless would be using up my limited supplies, but there was no helping that.

"How did you even get in there?" I demanded, trying to make sense of this impossible situation.

"As soon as the difficulties began, I realized the escape pod was where I wished to be. This containment unit must have opened automatically as the power switched off, and I wedged myself within so that I would not float away while the gravity was not working."

Given that he had no abilities he could have used to help us, and that he might have otherwise just been in the way, I had to admit that it had been a reasonable thing to do.

"When the power returned," he continued, "the door to the unit closed. I called out to you, but by then you could not hear me. I saw through the video feed that your pistol was out, however, so I knew there was danger. That was why I decided to activate the emergency jettison option."

A ball of rage, ice cold, began to build inside my gut. The sound of my breathing made me think of a rhino about to charge. I slowly turned to Villainic, unable to believe what I was hearing. "*You* jettisoned the escape pod?" I asked through gritted teeth.

"Oh, yes!" He looked incredibly pleased with himself. "I knew we would want to get away from the danger as quickly as possible, and I thought it best to get far from the ship. Are you not so very pleased with me?"

And that, your honor, was when I shot him.

Okay, I didn't shoot him, but given that I was holding a pistol, not shooting Villainic at that moment was among the most incredible acts of restraint ever shown in the history of galactic life. If Villainic had not launched the escape pod, I would still be on board that ship, still with my friends, still able to stop Ardov and join the fight against Junup. Instead we were now alone, in a brutal desert. We were on the outer fringes of nowhere while the beings I cared about were at Ardov's mercy.

I put my pistol down so I would not be tempted to do something I might later not regret. "You are a complete idiot!" I may have shouted this part. "We're stuck here because of you."

"I think you have not considered the matter very carefully," he said, sounding sad about my inability to keep up with his reasoning. "Ardov would not have attempted to take control of the ship unless he had a reasonable chance of success. Everyone else up there is in possession of many wonderful skills, but you and I are ordinary people. We are more brothers than ever, united in our uselessness. Had we remained, we would only have been in the way."

We were in no way equally helpless. At least, that's what I wanted to believe. "We might have helped them," I snapped.

"You can't convince me that abandoning our friends and running away is the right thing to do."

"Of course it is," he assured me. "You clearly haven't thought this through. As soon as they are done dealing with Ardov, they will come rescue us, and we will be on our way. It is really quite simple."

"It's *not* simple," I told him through clenched teeth, "because they tunneled out of this system. Ardov was able to send them somewhere, and assuming they can get control of the ship and then escape from whoever is waiting for them at the other end of that tunnel, then they are going to have more important things to worry about than rescuing us."

He looked momentarily concerned, but then rediscovered his trademark chipper attitude. "Surely the pod is equipped with a distress beacon. We must launch it so someone else can rescue us."

"We're on the border of Phandic space," I snapped. "Who do you think is going to respond to a beacon?"

"Oh," he said, for a moment unable to come up with anything to say. He stepped out of the portal and cast a look at the desert scrub surrounding us, blinking at the brutal brightness. "You certainly picked a desolate place for us to land."

"This is the garden spot of this stupid planet!" I shouted at him.

"Then how are we supposed to survive here, Zeke?" he demanded, hands on hips, as though he had not been paying attention to the rest of our conversation and somehow missed that it was his fault we were here. "What shall we do for food and water?"

"Maybe you should have thought of that before you launched the pod!"

"There is no need to raise your voice at me," he said, sounding infuriatingly calm. "I am just trying to explain to you the difficulties we face."

"I'm aware of the difficulties we face," I grunted. I wanted to say more, but there was no point. I'd already learned that there were diminishing returns in talking to Villainic, especially about his own behavior. I had braced myself for being a story of survival, like *The Martian*, but now, suddenly, it was an unlikely-buddy story. It was *District 9*, only I was the cool shrimp alien and Villainic was the clueless corporate stooge.

There was nothing to do about it, though. The mission remained the same. I had to find out everything I could about this place, especially the Former dig, and figure out a way to get off-world. It was just that I now had the additional challenge of not killing Villainic, which so far I'd been remarkably good at. I would have to find a way to keep that up.

I stepped back inside the pod and Villainic followed me, like a puppy eager to see what game we would play next. When he saw me stuffing supplies into a backpack, he came over and peered at me. "What are you doing?"

"I'm getting ready to go exploring," I said in a tone that could best be described as "civil under the circumstances."

"Oh, that's an excellent idea," he agreed. "Well done, Zeke. Pack me a bag as well and I shall help you explore."

I made the strategic decision of not looking at him. "Do I look like your servant?"

"Deities, no!" he said with an easy laugh. "My servants are Rarels—and they have much better manners. Still, there is no one else to do it."

"There's you," I pointed out.

"I am unused to packing my own things," he said mournfully.

I stood up and glowered at him. "You'd better get used to it. It's just the two of us on this planet, for I don't know how long. Whether we live or die, stay here or escape, depends on us being smart and resourceful. You are going to have to step up and figure out how to contribute or you are going to become a liability to me, and that's not going to be pretty. Do you hear me?"

"Of course I hear you," he said with a sad shake of the head. "How could I not with your voice so loud? You certainly like making speeches. Perhaps that energy could be put into packing my supplies."

"I'm going to wait outside," I told him, "where the chances of strangling you are lower. If you're not out and ready to go in five minutes, I'm leaving without you, and I'll see you when I get back. Assuming I decide to return."

Villainic stared at me as if daring me to actually make him pack his own supplies, and when I turned away from him, he actually gasped.

Outside the pod, the air was hot and dry. I took off the reeducation-school blazer and tossed it back inside the pod. The sun was above us, so at least this heat—bad but not unendurable—was likely the worst we'd have to face. Still, there might be other problems down the road. On Earth, deserts get cold at night, and I had no way of knowing how low the temperature was going to drop. I also didn't know where we were in this part of the planet's seasonal cycle. If this was the middle of winter, it meant that the summers we would later face could be brutal. I hated the idea that I would still be on this world months from now, but I knew it was a genuine possibility, and the sooner I resigned myself to it, the better.

Maybe my friends would be back to pick us up soon. Maybe they never would. I could shut out the implications of what complete abandonment would mean, but not the burdens that would fall on me. I had to stay alive and I had to get away, and now, as much as I hated it, I was responsible for keeping Villainic alive. A better version of the story might be keeping him alive until I needed to kill him for food, but somehow I didn't think I could bring myself to do that. Roast Villainic sounded even less appealing than 100 percent carapace. At least it did at the moment. A few months down the line could be a different story.

While waiting for Villainic, I spent a few minutes exploring the area surrounding the pod, moving in widening circles. I had synched my data bracelet to the database on the escape pod's limited computer, and I'd adjusted for my own physiology as best I could—a sloppy, trial-and-error method of listing foods I could and could not eat—so I was able to scan plants for food and medicinal value. So far my bracelet was telling me that everything that grew here would either, in a best-case scenario, cause me to vomit painfully, or, less good, produce painful vomiting followed by death. One plant would cause death followed by corpse reanimation. Great. I'd found a zombie plant. I made a mental note to make sure Villainic didn't eat it. It would be just my luck to have him follow me around after he was already dead.

He took an inexplicably long time to pack his bag. A blind goldfish could have completed the task more quickly. He finally emerged fifteen minutes later, his pack slung jauntily over his shoulder, beaming with satisfaction. "My bag," he announced with a great deal of pride, "is packed!"

Knowing I could be trapped with him for an unspecified amount of time, I decided to hold back any commentary about how long the packing had taken Villainic. We were going to have to get along, and, unlikely as it might sound, my life might at some point depend on his help. I didn't need him nursing any grudges.

"Where shall we begin our explorations?" he inquired with great cheer. "Is there a temperate place with more vegetation we might visit?"

"Didn't you hear what I said about this being the nice part of the planet?" I asked him.

"Still, perhaps someplace indoors, with an eatery . . . ," he mused.

"It's an abandoned planet."

"I have been to abandoned places where there were once eateries."

I steadied myself and gestured toward an area below, through a maze of jagged rocks. "Somewhere around here is where Captain Qwlessl was digging for Former artifacts. We're going to try and find the site."

"Why did you not land the pod precisely where you wished to go?"

"Because the rocks give us cover. If there's anyone already at the dig site, we can sneak up without their seeing us." I gestured with a nod of my head. "This way."

He considered the landscape ahead of us. "It's much too rocky." He pointed off in another direction. "We should go that way."

"Is this a joke?" I demanded. "Are you trying to be funny? I'm not walking off into the middle of the desert because the ground is level. We're actually going to look for things we can use, not to stretch our legs."

"You have a habit of explaining your ideas at great length," Villainic noted. "On my world that's often a sign of insecurity."

"On mine," I said, speaking slowly to control my frustration, "it's a sign of being trapped in a discussion with someone who needs basic concepts explained to them. I'm heading that way. You can go wander off into the desert for no good reason and get captured by Jawas if that's what you want to do, but otherwise, come with me and keep quiet."

He looked like he was about to say something, but thought better of it, and he followed along as I moved toward the outcropping.

It was, admittedly, a difficult path to follow. The jagged rocks along the ground made each step uncomfortable, and there were many points at which I had to stop and use my hands to help me climb down steep drops. The sun, which seemed to grow more intense by the minute, glowed a fiery orange like a massive Eye of Sauron. Heat blasted me from above and radiated from the ground below us. As a Rarel, Villainic was a much better athlete than I was, and apparently he was more resistant to heat. He handled these challenges with an ease I could only admire and envy.

After about an hour, having made relatively little progress, I proposed we take a rest beneath a shady overhang. I pressed my back against the cool stone and slid down to a rock that served as a reasonable bench. After taking a few minutes to wipe the sweat off my face with my sleeve, I fished in my bag for a moisture pack and drank down the concentrated hydration.

"An excellent idea," Villainic said. "May I have one of those?"

I stared at him, unable to believe what I was hearing. "You didn't bring any moisture packs?"

"You did not say I should expect to get thirsty."

"It's a *desert*."

"I have very little experience with such places," he told me. "My father says desert inhabitants are uncouth."

"You were with us in the Forbidden Zone," I reminded him. "That was a desert."

"And you provided the moisture packs."

I'd brought more than I would need, and there were plenty of packs left on the pod, but I still resented his failure to bring his own. Still, as much as I enjoyed the idea of his passing out from dehydration, the next image that popped into my head was me having to drag him to the pod and then nurse him back to health. Giving him a pack was the better option.

I handed it to him, and he placed it in his bag. "I shall save this for later," he announced cheerfully. "Should I grow thirsty, I now have recourse. You see, Zeke, I am every bit as capable of planning ahead as you are."

Soon we were under way again, and after another two hours we reached the bottom of the slope, which was protected by a series of natural pillars that jutted out from the ground like the jagged claws of a monster. By this point I was exhausted. Only the dry air kept my clothes from being soaked through with sweat. I felt myself dragging, but Villainic, infuriatingly, seemed no worse off than when we'd left the pod.

Further downhill from where we stood lay a roped-off area,

marking the entrance to the dig. A hole in the cliff face wound underground, much like the cave entrance we'd found in the Forbidden Zone on Confederation Central. This was clearly where we needed to go.

I was no longer the sort of person willing to enter an enclosed dark space without a ray gun at the ready, so I pulled my PPB pistol out of my back. "Better grab yours," I told Villainic.

"Was I supposed to bring one?"

I turned to him. "We're talking about basic supplies for an expedition. Did you bring food?"

"No, I was not hungry when we left, though all this exercise has worked up an appetite. Do you have any?"

"No food, no drink, no guns. What exactly did you put in that bag?"

"A change of clothes," he said, "in case these get soiled, which they have. Also, my stomach has been bothering me a bit, so I threw in some toilet paper as well as—"

I held up my hand in a stop gesture. "I really don't want to hear any more. You can go first. Use your bracelet for illumination."

"What if something jumps out at me?" he asked.

"Duck, and I'll shoot it."

He studied my face for signs that I was joking. Finding none, he resigned himself to my strategy and we entered the cavern.

As with the entrance to the Hidden Fortress, this cavern had a set of stairs, which were dangerously small and descending sharply. The ceiling was high enough that I didn't have to worry about hitting my head, and somewhere in the distance I could hear the drip of water. That was good to keep in mind for the future. Also, the cave was about thirty degrees cooler than the outside air. When I stepped into the shade and breathed in the scent of earth and damp rock, I felt reenergized.

Villainic, though larger than I was, had less difficulty moving down the stairs, probably because Rarels can see better in the dark than humans. He also seemed not terribly concerned about what we might find in an ancient cave on an alien planet. Other than a comment about how pleasant the temperature was within, he had little to say.

It had taken us a long time to descend to the bottom of the Hidden Fortress, but this location was clearly not so far from the surface. We reached the bottom of the stairs within half an hour, and the cavern we found was small by comparison. Perhaps thirty feet high and a quarter mile across, it was still very spacious, but it was also mostly empty. I found no signs that Captain Qwlessl's team had been here, but that did not surprise me. I'd hoped they might have left equipment and provisions behind, but I also knew it was likely they would have been careful to clean up after themselves.

We began to search the area—or, at least, I did while Villainic trailed after me. There were the crumbling remains of what appeared to be very ancient stone structures—really just remnants of walls, sometimes close enough together to give the impression that they'd once been a room of some kind. These ruins were entirely empty. We found no robots, computers, communication devices, or anything else that could be of use. Whatever had been here, either from the Formers or those who had come looking for them, had been cleared out.

I bit the inside of my cheek, trying to keep my disappointment and sadness under control. I knew that finding an operational spaceport was too much to ask, but I'd been hoping for *something*, some hope for getting off this planet or making contact with my friends. The only thing we'd discovered was shelter from the heat.

There was nothing to do but head back up with Villainic. The two of us could look forward to sitting in the pod together, eating our rations, until there was nothing left but to scrounge for vaguely edible plants. After all I had been through, all I had endured, I was now completely and utterly out of options for either saving my friends or being saved by them. It was now time to face the very real possibility that everyone I cared about was in enemy hands and that I would spend the rest of my life on this planet.

CHAPTER TEN

D id you find what you were looking for?" Villainic asked as we climbed back up the stairs.

"Yes, Villainic," I said with a sigh. "I was looking for absolutely nothing, and that's what we found, so I'm super pleased."

"Ah, I see. So you were hoping something you did not wish to see would not be there, and now your wishes have been answered. That is excellent."

"No, it's not excellent," I growled. "There was nothing there. And nothing's exactly what we have now. Whatever we have on that escape pod is all we have to live on until it runs out, and then we die."

Villainic was quiet for a moment. "I have been thinking, Zeke. As I was the one who thought to launch the escape pod, does it not seem more logical that I should have more of the supplies? After all, your being here is a mere accident. It seems unfair that my chances of survival should be endangered when you have no wish to be here in the first place."

Keep in mind that I was standing behind him, and holding a pistol while he said this. I suppose I might have been angrier, but I'd grown used to Villainic being clueless, and his idiocy was really the least of my problems.

I would need to go back through the supplies on the pod as well as do a more thorough scan of local plant and animal life.

I now believed that finding a source of water would not be too difficult, and there was a purification unit on the escape pod, but food would be an issue, and I didn't want to wait until we were starving to find a new source of things to eat.

What would I be surviving for, though? I supposed it would be the eventual hope of rescue, but if my friends weren't able to come back here for us before the supplies ran out, I wasn't sure they would ever be coming. The best I might hope for would be to live out my days with Villainic as my only companion.

The more I thought about it, the more miserable I became. Still, I couldn't give up. I would not let myself. There had to be a way. I was on a planet, an entire planet, and if Captain Qwlessl was right, and the Formers had lived here, that meant there had to be more archeological sites somewhere. And I knew that the Formers always kept hidden ships on their planets. That was what Smelly had told me.

That's when it hit me. Smelly! I still had the little metal disc that would let me signal my completely unreliable AI buddy. I could call Smelly, and it would be here in an instant through some kind of ancient technological wizardry. The way I understood it, when I activated the device, the quantum entanglement with its counterpart would not only relay the signal, but do so in what, to me, would seem to be the past, so that Smelly would receive my request in time to show up pretty much the moment I pressed the button.

There were a couple of reasons to hold off on using the signal, though. First of all, Smelly could be kind of a jerk, and while it owed me a favor, it had warned me not to use the device unless my life was in genuine danger. If I called it asking for rescue, it might say I'd bothered it needlessly and leave me here—or leave me here until I was in real danger of starving. If I waited until the food ran out, it might show up with supplies but refuse to transport me. Smelly wasn't evil, but it enjoyed messing with people, and the idea of trapping me forever with Villainic might prove too funny for Smelly to resist.

Finally, I didn't want to call it unless I had no other choice, because an ancient Former AI is a powerful ally, and, until recently, I'd actually been at the center of a major galactic conflict. If something went wrong and I needed a get-out-of-jail-free card to help bring down Junup or save my friends' lives, I wanted to have Smelly in my back pocket—so to speak. I needed to take some time to think about this, and time was one of the few things I had.

We came up the stairs with Villainic lurking just behind me. The desert heat began to warm the chamber, and the bright light streamed through the cavern's entrance. Villainic suddenly put a hand on my shoulder. In general, I didn't like him to touch me—or speak or look in my direction—but the expression on his face was fairly serious. His ears kept pivoting toward the entrance. "There are voices ahead."

Rarels have superior hearing, so the fact that I didn't hear anything meant nothing. I held up a hand, indicating that Villainic should stay put, with the implied additional meaning that he should not do anything stupid. I crept forward, keeping my back to the wall and deep in shadow. Anyone peering into the cavern would see nothing but darkness, but I could see out.

Approaching the entrance to the cavern, still about a hundred feet away, were three Phands.

They appeared a little odd to me, and it took a moment for me to figure out what it was. They were the only Phands I'd ever seen in anything other than military uniforms. All three wore what I could only imagine to be Phandic casual wear— button-down long-sleeved shirts tucked into loose pants held up by suspenders, and over that, ankle-length coats with high collars. Their clothes were all muted colors—what people back on my home planet called "earth tones"—as if they wanted to blend in with the desert. Most surprisingly, they wore gigantic, wide-brimmed hats that were almost like cowboy hats.

These looked ridiculous perched on top of their big, rectangular heads, but I'd never seen a Phand who hadn't filled me with horror. Their corpse-gray skin and jutting tusks made them look fierce, but it was their cruelty, their drive to conquer and dominate, that made them terrifying. I also disliked the fact that every single member of their species seemed dedicated to dumping as much misery on me as possible.

I stayed in the shadows watching them, making sure it was only those three, and waiting until they were turned away so that I had the best chance of retreating without anything catching their eye. I knew I would not have been able to see anything in the cavern's mouth, but I had no idea what Phandic vision was like or how these particular Phands might have been augmented.

Having three Phands coming toward you is almost always a bad thing. *Almost*, but not in this case. Well, the fact that they would probably want to kill or capture me on sight was bad, but less bad was that they were here on this planet. That meant supplies, shelter, and at least one ship. In other words, I now had at least a hope of getting off this world and finding my friends.

I crept back toward Villainic, who was leaning against the wall, looking less concerned than bored, like I was keeping him from something he'd much rather be doing.

"There are Phands out there," I said in a hushed voice. "Three of them. We need to wait until they go away, but if it looks like they might be entering the cavern, we'll head deeper inside." I was going to have to figure out where they were camped, but I would do that later, and preferably without Villainic leaning over my shoulder. Right now I had to make sure we weren't captured or killed.

Villainic put down his pack and began to rummage through it. "I may have brought something that can help us should they decide to come in here," he whispered.

"Like what?" I demanded, unable to hide my frustration. He hadn't brought food or water. I seriously doubted he had brought anything of use. "You didn't happen to bring a stun grenade, did you?"

He pulled his furry hand out of his bag and held up a metallic sphere about the size of a baseball. It was a Phandic stun grenade.

Had he activated the grenade and, you know, actually *stunned* me, I could not have been more stunned. That is admittedly an exaggeration, since if he'd done that I would have been unconscious, but the metaphor was sound. Villainic had brought something useful, and my brain was having trouble dealing with this turn of events.

"I thought you said you didn't bring any weapons," I hissed.

"No, *you* said that," he answered. "I said I didn't bring a pistol. I didn't bother to correct you because you get very irritable when someone says you are wrong."

I grabbed the grenade out of his hand before he could do something more Villainic-like and activate it or toss it into the dark for no reason or retract his jaw and swallow it whole. I put nothing past him, and I knew this moment of competence would be brief and unstable. "Why did you bring a stun grenade?" I demanded. "We're on a deserted planet. What possible use could a stun grenade be?"

"Obviously the planet is not deserted," Villainic said. "And the use would be to incapacitate those Phands. Clearly this is another example of how you must always be right about everything."

I swallowed a couple of dozen responses. Villainic had brought something that should have been entirely useless, but it turned out to be something that could save our lives. My mother has a saying: *Even a stopped clock is right twice a day*. I decided that was as good an explanation as I was going to get.

I crept back along the wall, keeping in shadow, and watched the Phands. They had completed some kind of survey of the dig area and were now in the process of pointing at our footprints and discussing them. They were too far away, and the wind was blowing into the cave, creating a whistling sound, so I couldn't make out any of their words. Pointing toward the cavern was explanation enough, though. They were coming inside.

Ideally I would not have to use the grenade—I'd rather retreat back to the escape pod without their knowing we were here—but if they were going to enter the cavern, I didn't see that we had much of a choice. I'd rather they knew *someone* was here than for them to know our species and our number. Most of all, I could not let them know who I was. There was no way I was going to let myself be captured. I'd rather die of hunger and thirst in the desert than let them parade me all over their news outputs.

The three Phands were about twenty feet from the entrance when I armed and tossed the grenade. They stared at it as it landed by their feet, kicking up a little cloud of dust. Then it detonated, with a flash and a rumbling blast that rattled my bones even though I was outside the area of effect. The Phands fell over, unconscious, like someone had hit their off switch, and that was good enough for me.

"Assume there are more out there," I said to Villainic, "so keep low and keep quiet. We need to get back to the pod, but we have to scout it before approaching in case they've discovered it already. You have to follow my lead and do everything I tell you."

"Of course," Villainic said. "Don't I always?"

I moved over to the Phands and searched them quickly for weapons. Surprisingly, they had none. No food, either, just some old-fashioned canteens with water in them. I hated Phands, but I wasn't going to abandon them in the desert with nothing to drink, so I left the canteens and hoped I didn't later regret the decision. When I'd given up on finding anything useful, we headed toward the uphill slope we would need to climb in order to get back to the pod. To anyone watching from a distance, we would be visible and slow, but there was only one way back, and we had to take it. At least it was starting to get dark, so it was cooler. It would probably be cold soon, and that would be its own challenge, but I had enough problems to face now without worrying about the problems that were going to crop up.

The climbing was difficult, and though Villainic kept quiet, I could hear the complaints vibrating off him even though his species was more athletic than mine. Still, he didn't give them voice, and that showed some improvement on his part. We reached the top of the climb and kept our backs to the outcroppings as we risked scans of the expanse ahead, but there was no sign of any Phands or their vehicles.

It took twice as long to get back as it had to get to the dig in the first place. Night had almost completely fallen by the time we were in visual range of the pod. In spite of Villainic's implicit protests, we crouched low and watched the pod for another hour, until the desert had descended into full darkness. The temperature moved from refreshingly cool to uncomfortably cold, and I regretted having left my blazer behind.

I heard the sounds of nocturnal creatures beginning to crawl and skitter and belch bullfroglike cries. These last, I think, came from carnivorous plants. I realized that there might well be things far more dangerous than the Phands out there, and that it would be a terrible irony if I were to be taken down by an alien vine bite, but I couldn't protect myself against every unknown.

Finally I decided it was as safe as it would ever be, and we made it back to the pod. I closed the door, put on my blazer, ate a food packet, and turned to the main control panel. It had to be possible to look for the heat signature of something like another ship. An escape pod would be designed to seek out friends and avoid foes.

I wrestled with the main computer for a few minutes until I found exactly what I was looking for, but in order to run the kind of search I had in mind, the pod had to be in the air. I was tired, maybe too tired for safe flying, but I didn't think it was safe to wait.

Unfortunately, it looked like I was going to have to. Power reserves, the computer told me, were too low for flight. That was the bad news. The mostly good news was that the pod would recharge using solar energy. I hadn't realized this, and so I hadn't set the pod to charge. I could do that in the morning, and, if I was reading the data correctly, we'd have enough power to be airborne by noon. I hoped it would be enough time to avoid detection.

I would sleep for a few hours, I decided, get up early and start the charging process, and lift off as soon as we possibly could. There was a plan now. It was a vague plan at best that involved stealing a ship of unknown size from a Phandic force of unknown number, so it was hard to say just how hopeless this plan might be. I didn't care. I'd thought I'd run out of options before, but it had turned out I wasn't done yet. I had a chance, and that was more than I'd had when we searched the Former cave.

I opened one of the emergency medical bays to use as a bed, and slipped inside. I closed my eyes and began running through the morning's tasks, but I couldn't concentrate. My brain was fried. Things began to run together. Somewhere in the distance Villainic was talking, but his words were too distant to hear. I could, I thought dreamily, escape him in sleep.

I awoke with a start but somehow managed not to sit up fast and hit my head. I checked my bracelet. It was now well past dawn. I'd overslept. I was annoyed with myself for having missed at least an hour of solar recharge.

I also had to pee, and while there was a sort of emergency

onboard toilet, I was not about to go in front of Villainic. I pressed the button to open the door, and morning sunlight streamed into the pod.

Standing outside the pod, as though they were about to knock, were the three Phands we'd stunned the day before.

CHAPTER ELEVEN

I knew I should have brought my pistol with me. I'd never needed to bring weapons to the toilet before, but times had changed, and I marked this down as a lesson learned. Besides, there was probably not a whole lot I could have done even if I'd had my pistol. There were three of them and one of me.

Instead of shooting them with a pistol I didn't have, I stared at them, which was not terribly intimidating.

One of the Phands stepped forward and did something with its mouth that, were it to come from any other species, I might have thought was a smile. He took his hat off his head and pressed the brim to his chest.

"Good morning," the Phand said. "I hope we're not intruding."

This is not the sort of greeting one typically expects from a Phand. I wasn't quite sure how to respond.

"Ah, yes," the Phand said uneasily, as if he realized he *was* intruding and felt terrible about it. "I am being rude, aren't I? You don't know our names. I'm Nimod Plood Adiul-ip. This is Usmoor Jope Thindly-bak, and the pretty lady is Plovim Roove Hopir-ka. We noticed that this is a Phandic escape pod, but you are clearly not Phands. I recognize your species—at least I think I do—and I'm not entirely certain what you are doing here. We're also pretty sure you tossed a stun grenade at us yesterday. They're reusable, you know."

He held out the stun grenade as if he was offering it to me. Unsure how to respond, I reached out and took it. I was now holding a weapon, so that seemed like a step forward. I still had no idea what was going on, though.

"Would you mind answering a few questions?" Adiul-ip asked. "We are very curious about who you are and how you came to be here."

I was still trying to process all this information when Villainic appeared behind me. Then he shoved me out of the way and bowed in almost a single movement. He proceeded with his weird Rarel introductory gesticulations—hand and head movements, plus lots of footwork. "I am Villainic, Fifth Scion of House Astioj, Third Rung of the Caste of the Elevated."

"Terrific!" the Phand called Thindly-bak said cheerily. "I love his little ritual."

"It's charming," Hopir-ka agreed.

"And this," Villainic continued, "is my ritual brother, Zeke Reynolds."

So, here's something to keep in mind. The Phands hated me. They hated everything about me. You know the expression to hate someone's guts? They hated my guts. My other organs too. They hated my *lungs*. That's how much they hated me. Maybe this sounds a little self-absorbed, but it seemed like their entire imperial policy was built around the question *What would make Zeke most miserable?* With that in mind, I felt like it would be a good idea not to tell the first Phands you saw that the guy standing in front of them—with no gun and in desperate need of a urinal—was the being their species most wanted to execute. That was how I saw it.

"Seriously?" Adiul-ip asked, his orcish face brightening like he'd just heard a new torture chamber had opened on his block. "You're Zeke Reynolds? For real?"

"Of course," said Villainic before I could devise a convincing lie that would somehow make them forget what they'd already been told. "Why would anyone pretend to be Zeke Reynolds?"

"For the attention?" Thindly-bak proposed.

"I bet everyone wants to be his friend!" Hopir-ka said. These two seemed just as excited as the first Phand.

"You must get free things in the mail all the time," Adiul-ip suggested. "Invited to parties. Stuff like that."

I was starting to feel like I was in one of those nonsensical dreams where your telephone turns into a pineapple. These Phands were not trying to capture or kill me. This was just the sort of thing that should not be happening.

"He looks like he is confused," observed Hopir-ka.

"He is also tapping his foot in the manner of someone who needs to urinate," said Thindly-bak.

"That bush over there provides excellent cover," said Adiul-ip.

It seemed likely that they were not going to shoot me, and as I needed my head clear, I did not wait for the suggestion to be repeated. By the time I returned, Villainic had invited the Phands inside and was offering them food packets. I'm all for hospitality, but giving away our limited supply of food to our sworn enemies seemed to be a pretty poor policy.

"Oh, no, thank you," Adiul-ip was saying. "You are very kind, but we have already had breakfast. Still, if you don't mind, we would like to take your supplies and put them in our stores. It is good to have emergency rations set aside. You never know what the future will bring."

"You expect us to give you our food?" I asked, beginning with outrage. I've found it to be a winning strategy in most social circumstances.

"Only if you don't mind giving it to us," Adiul-ip said.

"What, exactly, do you expect us to eat after we give you everything we have?"

"You won't want to eat these emergency rations," said Thindly-bak. "We can offer you something much better in the settlement."

"Settlement," I repeated. "There is no settlement. I scanned the planet before landing."

"Oh, we have it cloaked," Thindly-bak said. "This close to the Phandic Empire, on a planet with Former artifacts, we have to conceal ourselves or we would be caught."

"Of course," Adiul-ip added, "we would be found very quickly if anyone ever searched specifically for a cloaked outpost, but no one has bothered. Why would they? So, yes, there's a settlement, and a rather nice one."

"And you expect me to simply surrender to you?" I asked, though I didn't really see that I had much of a choice besides doing exactly that.

"No one said anything about surrender," Adiul-ip said. "You will be our guests."

"Our honored guests," Thindly-bak corrected.

"I don't understand," I finally admitted, finding no choice but to lay things out on the table. "You guys are Phands, aren't you?"

"According to my primary health-care provider," Adiul-ip said with a guffaw.

"Then why aren't you being, you know, meaner to me?"

"I don't think you understand," Thindly-bak said. "Yes, we are Phands, but we don't serve the Phandic Empire."

"Surely you don't think all Phands share the exact same political beliefs," Adiul-ip said good-naturedly. His tone suggested that of course I couldn't have thought something so absurd. I didn't tell him that it was exactly what I'd thought. The idea that there might be non-evil Phands had somehow never crossed my mind.

"Like you," Hopir-ka said, sounding pleased with herself, "we are renegades. Outlaws. Part of the resistance." She made a couple of finger guns with her hands and fired them off in rapid succession at imaginary enemies. I was grateful that she did not make zapping noises.

The news that there was a Phandic resistance took me by complete surprise. I'd never even suspected something like that, but if it was true, and Phandic renegades were on this planet, then this was better news than I could have hoped for. I tried to control my excitement. Depending on the kindness of Phands seemed to me a bad idea, but these particular Phands were clearly unlike any I'd met before.

"Well, let's not make ourselves out to be more than we are," Adiul-ip said. "We're not heroes like you, of course, but we aspire to be. Zeke Reynolds, you are our role model, and you have inspired our resistance, breathing new life into a movement that has been doing little or nothing for decades. We are seeking to topple the corrupt and cruel government that rules our world and dominates so many others. We wish to live in a society in which we are free to think and express ourselves as we choose."

"For a long time," said Hopir-Ka, "the movement had given

up hope. We'd become little more than a social club for misfits, but since you began your adventures, we have recruited new members and new leadership, and we believe we are on the cusp of striking a devastating blow, one that will change our lives forever."

"When we have deposed the empress," Thindly-bak said, "I will pursue my creative side, though I am now forbidden to do so."

"He makes giant sculptures of fruit out of the desiccated corpses of insects," Hopir-ka explained. "They're charming."

"But forbidden," Thindly-bak said sadly. "Art that does not glorify the empire is always forbidden. I am creatively stifled, and so instead of being an artist, I am a rebel. For art."

"Now that you are here on this world," Adiul-ip continued, "we would be honored if you would share with us some of your ideas. Perhaps you could review our operations and offer some advice. After we serve you breakfast, of course."

Almost from the first moment I went into space, I dealt with people who didn't want me around, who thought I was in the way or dragging them down. Then things got worse, and I had to grapple with powers that saw everything I did as disastrous and destructive. No matter how much my friends and I accomplished, we were called troublemakers and criminals. Now there were beings—Phands!—who not only understood the truth, but wanted to exaggerate it and be inspired by those exaggerations. The fact that they were kind of dressed like cowboys in no way diminished the importance of the moment for me.

This one time I was glad that Villainic was there to step forward and speak for me.

"We would love some breakfast," he said.

• • •

They did not use vehicles, since too many emissions might be spotted from space and give away their location, so it would be about a three-mile walk to the nearest micro-tunnel transport hub they'd established.

One of their scientists had invented this technology, according to Adiul-ip. Unlike the transporters from *Star Trek*, these mico-tunnels could only take a being from one prearranged position to another, and instead of dematerializing and rematerializing a body, it simply moved a being or objects from one location to another, much like ships tunneling through space. When a ship tunneled, it created a temporary wormhole that closed as soon as the ship emerged into normal space. These were tiny, stable wormholes.

"Why not use these to get from planet to planet?" I asked, marveling at the idea of being able to travel across the stars without even having to use a ship.

"It can be done," Adiul-ip explained as we walked, "but this method of transport, while necessary for us, is not without risk. Unlike a temporary tunnel that a spaceship creates, these fixed tunnels can occasionally become unstable. If that happens, the tunnel collapses uncontrollably, forming a singularity."

I might not know all that much about science, but I know a lot about science fiction, so I understood what he was saying. "You mean a black hole?"

"Yes."

"One that would consume the entire planet?"

"That would be the most likely outcome."

"And this doesn't worry you?"

"Oh, the inventor—you'll meet him back in town—thinks

the odds are very likely that such a thing will never happen. You can choke to death on your own spit, you know."

"Nice transition," I told him.

"Maybe he can't," Thindly-bak proposed.

"Of course he can," Adiul-ip said. "All species with spit can. You do have spit, don't you?"

"I do have spit," I told him. "Thank you for asking."

"Get him excited about something, and it's likely to fly in your face while he talks!" Villainic announced, clearly pleased with his wit.

"If you have spit, you could choke to death on it," Adiul-ip repeated. "It's in your mouth, and things can go wrong. Still, you don't spend your days worrying about choking to death on your spit, do you? Of course not," he answered, not giving me a chance to disagree, though I would not have. "Similarly, we don't worry about our entire planet vanishing within a matter of hours into a microsingularity."

These struck me as very different kinds of concerns, but I couldn't really do much about whatever experimental technology they were using to get around the desert planet. Were these Phands totally nuts, which was starting to look like a real possibility, or just your regular old Phands up to no good? They could be trying to lure me into a false sense of security. I couldn't guess why they would do that, but I'd faced too many disasters to let my guard down, no matter how sincere this bunch of space orcs might seem.

"There's an escape hatch," Adiul-ip said. "To a planet, I mean. We do not like to use this system for interstellar travel, since we wish to keep it a secret, but we have an emergency anchor portal to a distant location. We have chosen a planet where we might further our rebellion so we could still be useful should this world be, you know, on the cusp of vanishing into a vortex of nothingness."

To be clear, there was not one second of conversation I'd had with these Phands that I had not been thinking about whether or not they could provide me with a way off this planet. I was using the word "provide" in the loosest sense. Maybe I'd been spending too much time with Steve, and maybe I didn't want to live the rest of my life, or even pass the rest of the conflict, on this desert planet, but I'd be perfectly willing to steal a ship if that was what it took. Tamret was out there somewhere, and if she was not coming to help me, there was a pretty good chance that she needed help herself. My parents needed help. Alice needed help. I was not going to sit around while a bunch of weirdos talked about black holes and spittle when I was needed elsewhere.

Now, of course, I was thinking that maybe no spaceship theft was required—at least not immediately. If there was some kind of portal to another planet, perhaps that would be enough.

"Where does it lead?" I asked in my most casual voice. "This escape hatch?"

"No doubt Zeke is thinking he could use it to escape from this planet," Villainic explained helpfully. "He wishes to be back in the conflict, you know, though I'm quite pleased to be away from it."

It seemed to me that bashing Villainic's head with a rock might create the wrong impression with our new hosts, so I smiled like an idiot and hoped the moment would pass without them thinking too much about how I'd do just about anything to get away from them.

"You don't need to run away from us," Hopir-ka said. "We're on the same side. Besides, if aliens start popping up unexpectedly in strange places, it might draw attention, and then the escape hatch would no longer serve its purpose. We don't have the resources the empress has, so we need to keep our secrets until we absolutely need to use them."

I decided that maybe subtlety was not my strong suit, and even if these Phands seemed to think I'd rolled a natural eighteen in charisma, I was still going to have to deal with Villainic lobbing truth bombs at my best efforts at subtlety. These renegades claimed they admired me, so maybe I should be straight—or at least straightish—with them.

"Look, I know you don't want to give away your secrets, but I can't stay here."

"What are you even doing on this planet?" Thindly-bak asked.

I told them briefly about Ardov taking over our ship, through what I suspected was an EMP attack.

"Yes, we have those devices ourselves," Adiul-ip said. "Some large enough to take out an entire planet. This Ardov you speak of must have had an insulating device on him. He could neutralize your ship while his data bracelet and various nanite upgrades remained functional."

"Yeah," I said. "I kind of guessed as much. But that's why I need to get out of here. My friends are in trouble, and we were on our way to do important things."

"We know all about doing important things," Adiul-ip said with a laugh that I could only describe as being full of bravado. "We mean to strike a killing blow against the empress, and we would be mad—"

"Mad!" Thindly-bak echoed.

"We would be mad," Adiul-ip continued, "if we did not take full advantage of the presence of Zeke Reynolds, the Hero of Ganar, Rescuer of Prisoners, Bane of the Empress. If you would be willing to aid us, Mr. Reynolds, we know precisely where you can do some good."

It was a weird thing. In the Confederation, a civilization I loved and believed in, they'd called me the *Butcher* of Ganar because I'd destroyed a Phandic cruiser that was trying to destroy us. Now there were beings who saw everything my friends and I had done as glorious and heroic. Not only were they willing to let me back into the fight; they *wanted* me there. This should have been a happy moment. It would have been if I had not been so worried about the beings I cared about most. Also, I couldn't help but be troubled by the possibility that my new allies were a bunch of crackpots.

We reached a completely ordinary-looking crevice in a rocky outcropping, and the Phands gestured for us to stop. The heat of the day was starting to bear down on me, and my eyes hurt from the glaring sun, so I was hoping this would be the entrance to the tunnel. Adiul-ip gestured toward it with one of his meaty hands, and when I hesitated and Villainic drew back, Thindly-bak stepped forward, not a care in the world, and literally vanished into the dark.

"We know the other side of the portal is completely safe," Adiul-ip said, "so we prefer to go last, so our most precious guests are protected."

I was going to face much greater dangers than a stable wormhole if I had my way, so I supposed there was no reason to hesitate. Still, no one likes stepping into an abyss. I sucked in a deep breath and walked into the crevice, hoping I'd come out on the other side.

I did come out on the other side. The trip was, or at least seemed, near instantaneous, and when I came out, I felt only a little off-kilter, like my guts had been forcefully rearranged, but the sensation was pretty similar to what I felt when a ship went into or out of a tunnel. I struggled for a second to find my balance, but then I felt perfectly normal, and the sense of being out of synch with reality was less vivid than a memory—more like a memory of a memory.

Once it was gone, the disorientation I experienced was from what I saw around me. I was in some sort of town square. Dusty streets shot out from the square in four directions, and on either side were haphazard wooden buildings that looked like they'd been thrown together hurriedly. There were more Phands walking the streets, and other aliens too, beings I had never seen before, but they all had the same rough homespun-looking clothes that Adiul-ip, Thindly-bak, and Hopir-Ka wore. They had boots on their feet—at least those who had feet—and cowboy hats on their heads . . . at least the ones who had heads.

I felt a sudden shove from behind as Villainic came through the portal and bumped into me.

"Zeke, it is very discourteous of you not to step out of the way," he said, sounding deeply disappointed.

I was too distracted to be annoyed. This, I realized, was an Old West town. My world had gone full *Firefly*.

The sky was clear and deeply blue, streaked by only a few wisps of cloud, but the air also sparkled with occasional flashes of energy that manifested as patches of blurriness. This, I had to believe, was the settlement's cloak, which kept it from being discovered by the imperial Phandic forces. As a pleasant side effect, the air must have been thirty degrees cooler.

The town wasn't large by any means, really little more than a permanent camp with a couple dozen wood and stone buildings for, I guessed, maybe a couple hundred beings. The buildings themselves seemed to be thrown together from local supplies—mostly stone and plant fiber. The streets—which was a generous term—were just obvious straight lines in the dust between buildings. Even so, given what they had to work with, it was an impressive achievement.

What struck me the most, though, was that these rough buildings, combined with the dirt roads, the desert environment, and the wide-brimmed hats that just about everyone wore, made this seem like a frontier theme park. It was like one of those *Star Trek* episodes where they beam down to discover a world that is exactly like some period out of Earth's history, one generally familiar and American—only the aliens in those episodes didn't have tusks.

I wanted to be gone, and I wanted to be gone hours ago, chasing after Tamret and the others, but the truth was I had no idea where they were and what I could possibly do once I found them. If these guys had information, resources, weapons, and muscle, it was very possible they could be my new best friends. I took a deep breath, told myself to be patient, and turned to Adiul-ip.

"You said you have some kind of plan to end the empire's rule," I said. "Can you tell me about it?"

"Of course," Adiul-ip said. "We would be honored if you

and your trusted companion would hear our top-secret plan for breaking the empress's grip on this region of the galaxy."

"About that," I said, drawing Adiul-ip away from Villainic. "The thing is, he's not really my companion. Or trusted."

"But your friends are legendary," Adiul-ip said, sounding very disappointed. "The clever and resourceful children of your home world, and the heroic randoms of Ish-hi and Rarel. Surely he is one of these."

"No," I said, speaking as quietly as I could so that Villainic's excellent hearing would not pick up what I was saying. It wasn't that I was afraid of him hearing so much as, for reasons I could not have explained, I preferred to avoid hurting his feelings. "Look, my friends are amazing. You're right about them. Destroying the cruiser at Ganar, for good or bad, that was me acting alone, but everything else you may have heard about me was a team effort. You should admire those guys, but he isn't one of them."

"Then who is he?"

"He's an idiot," I said. "Really, I don't know how else to put it. He's a mostly well-meaning guy who comes from an important family and who until recently has never had to confront the fact that he isn't terribly bright. He's not bad, just kind of dim. He's also a blabbermouth. I've never known anyone to blurt out more secrets than this guy, and I don't even think he's aware that he's doing it. You don't want him in on your briefings."

Adiul-ip looked over at Villainic, who was in the process of doing his little introduction dance to a guy who looked like a humanoid with an octopus head. "He seems harmless enough to me."

"Believe me," I told Adiul-ip, "in the two seconds they've been talking, I bet he's told Cthulhu over there every secret thing he's been exposed to since he arrived on Confederation Central."

"That is unfortunate, Mr. Reynolds," Adiul-ip said sadly. "Our organization is built on trust."

"Then you see why you have to keep him out of any briefings."

"If we do that, then our organization is no longer built on trust."

I was starting to think I liked the narrow-minded, blood-thirsty Phands better than the kind and trusting ones. I was also starting to detect some disappointment in Adiul-ip's expression, as though he might be wondering if Zeke Reynolds might not be the hero he'd previously believed. I had to put the brakes on that, and do it quickly. I didn't need to be admired by the greater galaxy, but I wanted to be trusted by the beings who could help me get to my friends.

"You guys have built all this," I said, "so I have to think you know what you're doing. We'll do things your way."

Adiul-ip bowed at me. "I am so glad to hear it. Now come with me. There are some beings you must meet."

The building we entered could only have seemed more like an Old West saloon if the word "saloon" had been painted above the door. Inside was an assortment of aliens to rival Maz Kanata's castle. They sat at tables talking, laughing, eating, drinking, and, in one instance, pouring some sort of sludge into what looked like a blowhole. A machine that vaguely resembled a tractor played music on an instrument that looked a little like a bathtub filled with rubber balls. The sound was nothing like a player piano. Frankly, it was less like music and more like someone pouring buckets of nails on a marble floor, but the beings inside seemed to enjoy it. Behind the bar, a gigantic sympathetic-looking bumblebee wearing a leather vest and a bandolier was pouring a drink for a depressed-looking alien of the same species. Its antennae were drooping.

As soon as we entered the saloon, the music and conversation stopped. It was *that* moment, like in a movie, where the guy who obviously doesn't belong steps into the place where he absolutely should not be. For a brief instant I got to feel like the good-guy sheriff making his first appearance in a crooked town, but then everyone went back to their food and drink and conversation, which was fine by me. I didn't want to have to get into any shoot-outs.

Adiul-ip led us to a table and brought us "biologically appropriate" food and drink, which was welcome. The two other Phands who had escorted us had drifted off somewhere, and the conversation went into suspension mode while I ate and drank. The food and moisture packets had kept me alive and given me energy, but they hadn't really satisfied me the way an actual meal and an actual drink would have. This food was some sort of bread with some sort of cheese. A little dry, but not bad. The drink tasted like a combination of sweet tea and pineapple juice, and hit the spot like maybe nothing else I'd ever had.

When I was done, I wiped my mouth and turned to Adiul-ip. "I really appreciate the hospitality, but my friends are in trouble, so if you have a plan to help them, I'd like to hear about it, and sooner is better than later."

"I am not the one to brief you," he said. "But here is the being you want to speak with."

I had not seen anyone walk in—maybe I'd been too focused on eating and drinking—but now a being stood by our table, silent and motionless in a way that it had to know was intimidating.

From the neck down, it sort of looked like a classic *Star Trek* alien—it had a vaguely humanoid body, with clothes of an inexplicably retro design but made from a shimmering "space age" fabric. These included a form-fitting silvery tunic that went all the way to the floor so I could not see its feet. Over that was a robe that went all the way to the wrists and had a high, pointed collar that overlapped the back of its head. Its hands were covered with silver gloves, so no part of its body below the gown's high collar was visible.

I thought of the alien as an "it" because there was nothing about this being to indicate maleness or femaleness. Absolutely nothing in its face, because it didn't have a face—no eyes, mouth, nose, or ears that I could see. It did, however, have a head, which sat resting on top of the collar, probably connected by a neck, though I could not see it. The head was covered with material that looked neither natural nor artificial—smooth and skinlike and vaguely synthetic all at once. Its color changed constantly, not in flashes, but more like a gentle shift from one point on the spectrum to another. Red easing into yellow into green into blue.

Also, it is worth pointing out that its head was shaped exactly like a twenty-sided die.

"This," Adiul-ip announced, "is Convex Icosahedron. Convex Icosahedron, may I present Zeke Reynolds."

"The Hero of Ganar!" cried Convex Icosahedron in a voice so deep it almost made my teeth rattle. It definitely sounded masculine, so I'd assume he was male unless someone told me otherwise. The being's voice seemed to somehow emanate from the being's entire head, as though the words were formed through vibrations. "It is good to meet you, for my analysis of the data suggests our efforts will be thirty percent more effective simply because you are part of our organization, Zeke Reynolds."

Anyone who has ever traveled in deep space knows the awkwardness of that moment when you meet a stranger and want to ask it what exactly it is. This was that moment. I had no idea what kind of biology, if any, was going on with this being.

After my encounters with Smelly, a construct from the age of the Formers, whose nature had remained an almost complete mystery while it was living in my head, I had realized that the universe was a stranger place than I had even begun to suspect. Now, with this faceless being in front of me, I realized I had to up the strangeness quotient another notch.

"Hey there," I said with a halfhearted wave, hoping someone would explain something to me.

"In my culture, Zeke Reynolds," said Convex Icosahedron, "there are conditions when it is customary to speak a being's name when addressing him, her, it, thrum, flikim, or ixmo."

There are things I want to learn about, but at that moment, the nature of an ixmo was not one of them. "Hey there, Convex Icosahedron?" I tried.

"Hey there unto you, Zeke Reynolds." he replied, bowing deeply. "Great tales have been told of you, Zeke Reynolds. Songs have been sung, Zeke Reynolds. Puppet shows have been performed, Zeke Reynolds."

"That is super excellent, Convex Icosahedron," I said, wondering how quickly and politely I could get out of this conversation. "I'm really honored to hear that."

Everyone stared at me like I'd just belched at the cotillion.

"I'm really honored to hear that, Convex Icosahedron."

The sighs of relief were audible.

I now officially hated this guy. There was nothing appealing about having to say his stupid name every time I spoke to him, but everyone seemed to think it was utterly vital, so the only solution I could think of was to avoid speaking to him entirely. I hoped I didn't have to do the name thing when talking to everyone. Honestly, I wasn't sure I could remember all three Phands' full names.

"While you're with us," Adiul-ip said, "Convex Icosahedron will be your main liaison with our operations. He will be the being you speak with most frequently. Isn't that wonderful, Convex Icosahedron?"

"I'm so pleased to be able to assist you, Zeke Reynolds. I hope you are also pleased, Zeke Reynolds."

"You bet I am, Convex Icosahedron," I said, and tried with all my strength not to groan.

Convex Icosahedron suggested that I might want to sit in on a strategy meeting with some of the other high-ranking renegades.

"I'd like to see my room first," Villainic announced. "I want to be sure I'll have a nice place to sleep, given how uncomfortable I was last night. That escape pod of Zeke's is very inhospitable."

Adiul-ip led Villainic off to Old West Motel or whatever while Convex Icosahedron took me out of the saloon and down the street toward some other building. We walked in the heat, and I looked around at the variety of aliens who were going about their business. Toward the far end of the road, a tall, broad-shouldered being with a head like a weasel used a stick to guide a couple of dozen cow-size creatures into a pen. They were four-footed and seemed docile enough, but instead of hair they grew what looked like thin planks of wood on their sides.

"What are those animals, Convex Icosahedron?"

"Those are nerfs, Zeke Reynolds. We harvest their spiny growths to construct our buildings, Zeke Reynolds."

"Nerfs," I repeated. "So, that guy is a nerf herder, Convex Icosahedron?"

"Precisely, Zeke Reynolds."

The wonders of the universe truly never cease.

"Do you mind if I ask you a question, Convex Icosahedron?"

"I cannot know the answer to that until I hear the question, Zeke Reynolds."

That was fair enough, though at the same time completely annoying. "I am sorry if this is insensitive, but are you alive or an artificial entity of some sort, Convex Icosahedron?"

"I don't see why that would be offensive, Zeke Reynolds."

Because you have a game piece for a head might not have been the most polite answer, so I just shrugged, which got me out of having to say his name.

"We are the Geometric Upstarts, Zeke Reynolds."

"That's the name of your species, Convex Icosahedron?" I asked. It sounded more like a mathematically inclined street gang.

Convex Icosahedron assured me that it was, in fact, the name of his species.

"And are you guys, uh, biological or artificial, Convex Icosahedron?"

"We are both and neither, Zeke Reynolds. But really, are any of us truly biological, Zeke Reynolds?"

I kind of felt that I, for one, was truly biological, but instead of making this point, I decided to smile like this was an insightful philosophical point and all my questions had been answered to my complete satisfaction.

I really hoped that this Geometric Upstart was better at providing an operational briefing than he was at making chitchat. Otherwise we were in serious trouble.

We entered an unmarked building that might have been someone's home, but unlike the saloon, on the inside it appeared modern—or futuristic, I guess. Whatever it was that you expected from space-traveling aliens, this was it. The floors were made of a smooth white material, like tile but not quite so slippery. There were computers everywhere, screens displaying data and readouts, and stations were being worked by both Phands and other aliens. I did not see anyone else who might have been a Geometric Upstart, though. We moved through the room, and all the aliens turned to offer polite and respectful greetings to Convex Icosahedron. He might have been difficult to talk to, but he seemed to get a lot of genuine respect from the other renegades.

We entered what looked like a meeting room, and Convex Icosahedron told me to have a seat. "I will summon the others, and then we will begin the meeting, Zeke Reynolds."

"I feel like we're just wasting time," I blurted out. "I don't need all this formal stuff. I want to know what's going on. I want to do something to find my friends and to help them." Then, under pressure, I added, "Convex Icosahedron," as though I merely hadn't gotten to that part yet.

"I understand, Zeke Reynolds. This meeting should answer your questions and give you a clear sense of our intended direction, Zeke Reynolds."

After an endless delay of about twenty minutes, the other participants began to file in, including Hopir-ka and Thindly-bak. Adiul-ip soon followed with Villainic.

"I hope all is to your satisfaction, Villainic," Convex Icosahedron said.

"Of course," he answered. "But I'm not fussy."

I waited for Adiul-ip to press him to say Convex Icosahedron's name, but the Phand didn't seem to notice the lapse. Neither did the Geometric Upstart. Why was I not surprised that Villainic could somehow get away with violating that annoying rule?

A few more beings entered the room, mostly Phands, but a few other alien species I didn't know. Then another human walked through the door. Under normal circumstances, this would have been a reason to cheer, but not this time. This was an older man, wearing an Earth military uniform. He had a head full of silver hair buzzed into a crewcut, and a patch over his right eye.

It was Colonel Richard Rage, the man who had betrayed me and my friends to Junup.

CHAPTER TWELVE

launched to my feet, pointing like a pod person. "What is he doing here?" I demanded.

Colonel Rage made a patting gesture with his hand. "Calm yourself, Zeke. I know what you must be thinking, so let me just put all my cards on the table. You were right and I was wrong. I made a bad deal with Junup, and I came to regret it."

That was, in my view, putting it mildly. While the rest of us had been trying to find the Hidden Fortress and uncover the code for the Former military tech tree, Colonel Rage had made a secret bargain to turn us and the code over to Junup. I knew why he had done it. He wasn't like Nora Price, evil and power-hungry. Colonel Rage was so focused on his duty to protect Earth that he would side with anyone, no matter how evil, if he thought things would turn out better for his home world. I partly understood this, but I also understood that when you cut deals with cruel and ambitious bad guys, you never get what you bargain for.

So while I didn't hate Colonel Rage in the way I hated Nora Price, I didn't want him around, either. He could be useful and smart and resourceful, but as soon as he had to choose between the right thing and what he believed to be his mission, he could be counted on to toss the right thing under the bus.

Besides, when a guy you don't trust shows up at a top-secret facility, it's time to get suspicious.

"How exactly did you just happen to end up here?" I demanded. "Am I supposed to believe this is coincidence? Because you being a spy for the other team seems a lot more likely to me. Maybe another deal with Junup? Or the Phands this time?"

"I didn't happen to end up here," Colonel Rage explained, still using his reasonable voice. "I was recruited."

"I identified this alien as an insider who would be willing to work for our cause," Convex Icosahedron said. "Given his military background and his motivation to weaken the Phandic Empire, bringing Colonel Rage into our group seemed a wise choice."

I looked at him, waiting for him to say my name. He didn't. Had I offended him somehow?

"The name-at-the-end-of-the-sentence thing isn't proper etiquette when discussing military or tactical matters," Adiul-ip whispered in my ear. "The protocol dropped as soon as Colonel Rage entered the room."

I silently thanked the universe for this small mercy. "So Convex Icosahedron sends you a message saying to come to some desolate planet on the border of Phandic space, and you grab a space Uber?"

"He didn't send me a message, son," Colonel Rage said, making no effort to hide his impatience. "He came and got me. He was waiting for me when I got out of the john one morning and said I could come with him and fight our mutual enemies or stay and be Junup's stooge. After what happened at the Hidden Fortress, I didn't have to think about that one for long."

If Convex Icosahedron could identify Colonel Rage as someone who would be willing to help his cause, I figured he must have a pretty good intelligence network. Even better, if he could position himself so he was ready to pounce the moment they got done washing their hands, he had to have the technology to infiltrate enemy facilities.

I looked around the room and saw a bunch of Phands, a few aliens I didn't know, Colonel Rage, Convex Icosahedron, and Villainic. Of all of them, Villainic was the guy I trusted most, which said something about my situation.

Obviously, I didn't get a vote about Colonel Rage, or anyone else, being involved in whatever they were cooking up. It was better to go along for now.

"Okay, so let's hear what you have to say," I told them.

In the center of the room, a holographic projection of Confederation Central appeared above the table. "As you all know," Convex Icosahedron began, "the ability of the Phandic Empire to expand and conquer was halted after Zeke Reynolds and his allies provided the Confederation with technology that brought the era of Phandic military superiority to an end. That act also revitalized this resistance movement. The period of imperial containment did not last long, however. Following the murder of Director Ghli Wixxix, the being known as Junup rose to power. He made a secret alliance with the empress, allowing her once more to pursue the expansion of her borders in exchange for her covert support of Junup's position. We know he encouraged the empress to conquer the planet Earth, Zeke Reynolds's home world. It is my assessment that the best way to restore the more favorable balance of power is to remove Junup from his office and return Confederation leadership to a traditional pacifist who will, once more, limit the empress's ambitions."

Everyone nodded sagely, including Villainic, like this analysis so far measured up to his exacting standards. I ground my teeth.

Responding to some unseen cue, the image of Confederation Central began to rotate, so we could see the underside. "I have been able to infiltrate secret Confederation databases to acquire this detailed schematic of Confederation Central. My analysis has revealed a cluster of power nodules that make the entire structure vulnerable. A single small ship, if armed with a dark-matter torpedo, could enter an access port here." He gestured with a gloved hand, and a square tunnel on the underside was now glowing red. "The torpedo, if fired at precisely the right point, will cause a chain reaction, destroying Confederation Central, thus removing Junup from the equation." The graphic now depicted a missile moving forward through the shaft and stroking the power nodules. Animated waves of energy radiated outward, and the animated Confederation Central began to break apart before being consumed by flames.

The various aliens in the room murmured with approval.

"The destruction of this city will produce numerous beneficial results," Convex Icosahedron continued. "Power will shift elsewhere, and based on my analysis of the surviving politicians, the Confederation will fall into more traditional, peaceful hands. The Phandic Empire will once more be contained. This is, without doubt, the most certain method of restoring order to the Confederation, the consequence of which will be greater galactic stability. Any questions?"

No one had any. They all nodded like this plan made complete sense. I, however, had many questions, but none more pressing than whether or not they were completely insane.

"Are you telling me that you want to Death Star the capital of the Confederation?" I asked, somehow keeping my horror out of my voice.

"Your fantasy stories aren't really relevant to our cause, Zeke," said Colonel Rage gently. "Do you have a point to make?"

"The point," I said, "is not that this plan comes right out of *Star Wars Episode Four: A New Hope*. The point is that it's bonkers. You want to destroy the capital of the Confederation, a city with millions of beings, just to get rid of Junup? Doesn't that seem a little excessive?"

"I have run the numbers," Convex Icosahedron said, "and this plan provides a near one hundred percent chance of success. Nothing else even comes close to that level of certainty."

"If you're so bent on killing beings, why not send someone to Confederation Central to take out Junup?"

"We're not assassins," Convex Icosahedron explained with an unmistakably insulted tone.

I took a deep breath and tried not to sound hysterical. "Then send someone to kidnap him! Put him in jail! There are better options here than destroying an entire city!"

"I'm afraid there are not," said Convex Icosahedron. "I appreciate your earnest desire to preserve life, but you cannot suppose we have not considered what you propose. I reviewed all possible projections, and the numbers don't support those approaches. The assassination scenario has a 47.0978 percent chance of either failing outright or resulting in a similarly inclined politician rising to power. The numbers on the kidnapping scenario are even worse. In both cases, the likelihood of the Phandic Empire discovering our operation is unacceptably high. When you project these numbers out over just the next century, the loss of innocent life is nearly triple that involved in the destruction of Confederation Central. The plan I have proposed is by far the least costly in terms of bloodshed, and that is only over a hundred years. Over two hundred or five hundred the number of lives saved becomes astounding. There really is no other option. I hope you will see that, because your skill with dark-matter missiles is legendary, and we wish for you to pilot the ship that will destroy Junup's power base."

Calling it Junup's power base did not change the fact that it was a city full of millions of beings going about their business. I was not about to play any part in their ridiculous plan. I'd sabotage it if I had to, though I hardly knew how I could do that. "Don't you see that if you try to carry this out, you become evil? Colonel Rage, haven't you learned that lesson yet? If you want to be one of the good guys, you have to act like one of the good guys. You don't kill innocent beings because some computer program tells you the numbers say it's the best way to go."

"You've got a good heart, son, and I appreciate that," Colonel Rage said, "but these folks are the resistance. It's their show. If they think this is how we get the aliens off Earth, then I'm in favor of it."

Once again, Colonel Rage was only worrying about Earth. It was natural, maybe even smart, to put his own planet first, but he kept thinking of our home world as an isolated speck in the galaxy. It wasn't anymore. We were part of this community now, and what happened in the Confederation mattered to us. I wanted to try to explain this, but I knew he wouldn't listen. They had all decided that I was some idealistic kid who was too starry-eyed to see the hard truths.

"You want everything to be black and white," Colonel Rage continued, "but you don't know how politics and politicians works. Once Ghli Wixxix died, there was a powerful shift in how the Confederation saw Earth and its place in the galaxy. I understand these things in a way you simply can't. I even tried to talk them into helping Earth."

"It's true," Adiul-ip said. "He did."

"They had a plan," the colonel told me. "The planet's conquest was a high-profile deal in the Phandic media, so they thought that if they could liberate Earth, it would set off a chain reaction that would destabilize the empire and bring down Junup. I even talked them into opening one of their transporter tunnels to Earth."

"That's your obscure escape planet?" I asked Adiul-ip.

"It served our purposes," he said, "and if we had to get away in an emergency, it made sense to go someplace we could help to create an uprising against the empress."

"So let's do that!" I said. "I like that plan!"

"Sadly, the projections do not look promising," Convex Icosahedron said. "You will see that there are too many ways for things to go wrong. Too many risks. The elimination of Confederation Central is much cleaner and more precise. More predictable. The numbers are always truthful."

I stood up, because I realized I had them. I knew something they didn't know, and that meant that all their predictions were out of whack. "Yeah, well, your numbers are wrong, because your information is wrong. Director Ghli Wixxix is still alive."

This had their attention. Everyone turned to look at me with utter fascination. Everyone but Villainic, who was cleaning his fingernails and humming softly.

"How can you know this?" Adiul-ip demanded. "What is your source?"

"Dr. Roop," I said. "He dug into the files when he was holed up in the Hidden Fortress. Our plan was to rescue Ghli Wixxix. Once she was restored to office, Junup would be exposed, and then things would go back to the way they were. We still have the problem of the Former military tech tree, but that's a long-term one. In the short term, the Phands are back to being contained. And it's done with maybe no violence at all."

Convex Icosahedron cocked his twenty-sided head as if giving the matter some thought. Maybe it was my imagination, but the colors seemed to be cycling more rapidly. "If this is true, and if the rescue mission were to proceed successfully, then the operation would have nearly as high a chance of success as the one already proposed. Unfortunately, even a preliminary review of the numbers indicates that there are too many things that could go wrong during a rescue attempt. There is even a roughly thirty-two percent chance of Ghli Wixxix being killed while escaping, our operatives being captured, and this base being discovered before we can return to the original plan. No, destroying Confederation Central remains the best option."

"Hold on," Colonel Rage said. "You made it clear that even without Junup the political situation was too unstable to play out dependably. But if the old director is alive, then it changes everything. It *guarantees* a return to the way things were before."

"Yes, the numbers trend toward stability," Convex Icosahedron agreed, "but that does not alter the fact that the odds of getting to that point of stability are unfavorable."

"It sounds to me like it's a chance worth taking," the colonel continued. "I wasn't going to oppose this operation if we were going to trade Junup for another alien just like him, but if Zeke is right, and we have a shot to return things to the status quo prior to Junup's rise to power, we should take it."

"It is a risk," said Thindly-bak. "If Zeke's plan were to fail, then we would have lost everything and exposed our movement."

"I'm inclined to agree," Adiul-ip said. "We have an opportunity before us, a genuine opportunity to reshape galactic politics for centuries to come. Think of it—an end to conquest and war. I will remind everyone that Convex Icosahedron has projected that if Confederation Central is destroyed, there is an eighty-seven percent chance that within twenty years the Phandic Empire will transition to a peaceful, representative government on the Confederation model. No one wants to destroy a city, but think what we gain. Future generations will thank us."

There was a murmur of assent all around the room. They actually meant to blow up Confederation Central rather than rescue Ghli Wixxix. No, it was more terrifying than that. This wasn't some thought experiment. I was sitting in on a meeting with a bunch of lunatics who loved the idea of destroying the greatest place that ever existed because a wacko without a face thought that the numbers looked pretty good.

I slowly sat back down because I was afraid I was going to barf. There was no way I would fly the mission, but my sitting it out would not stop this terrible thing from happening. The renegades would just find another pilot. Maybe I could sabotage a ship, or even a base, but this thing was bigger than I was. I'd made my best arguments, and they had ignored them. I had been outvoted, and I did not see any way their minds were going to change.

Convex Icosahedron was now inclining his gigantic head toward Villainic. "What do you think?"

Villainic looked up from his very interesting fingernails. "I beg your pardon. What was the question?"

"Do you agree with Zeke or the rest of us?"

Villainic smiled. "Oh, my opinion? Of course. Well, I know Zeke's interpersonal skills are quite poor, but in the past his schemes have proved remarkably successful. I think we should do things his way."

Convex Icosahedron appeared to consider this. You can't really tell with a guy who has a geometric shape for a head, but he put one hand on his hip and put another on a spot that might have been his chin. It looked sort of thoughtful.

"That being the case," Convex Icosahedron said, "we should look into Zeke's plan more carefully."

I was about to object on the grounds that there was no rational reason to pursue a plan just because Villainic liked it, but then I realized I would be arguing against my own position. The only thing crazier than wanting to destroy Confederation Central was Convex Icosahedron changing his mind because Villainic had chimed in. Something about this did not sit right with me. I was going to have to keep an eye on things.

"I will need to meet with Zeke privately so I can learn more about where Ghli Wixxix is being held," Convex Icosahedron said. "Once we formulate a plan, we will discuss putting together a team."

"I already have a team," I said quickly. This could be my chance to help rescue my friends. "Or at least I did. The first step is finding out where they are and getting them back."

"I'm sure you have faith in your friends," said Colonel

Rage, "and you've all done some impressive things, but they're just kids. I don't think you can make the case that they're vital to any operation."

"I can make that case," I said. "My friends have maxed-out skill trees, both original and Former." I neglected to mention that the augments were unreliable because, well, that was private, wasn't it? And my pronouncement got everyone's attention, so there was no point in undermining it.

"These are going to prove to be very interesting numbers indeed," said Convex Icosahedron.

"So, will you help me look for my friends? There was this guy, Ardov, and he managed to gain control of our ship. I don't know where it went."

"Yes," said Convex Icosahedron. "We know about Ardov and we know where he took your friends. Unfortunately, I don't think you are going to like it."

CHAPTER THIRTEEN

Planet Pleasant. I'd been hearing about this secret and horrific Phandic research facility for a while now. It was where they sent beings who wouldn't get with the program so they could be galactic guinea pigs in scientific experiments. It was where beings were tortured and sacrificed to the Phandic war machine.

I felt myself gripping the side of the table. I needed to be out of that room and on a ship headed for Planet Pleasant now. An hour ago. I couldn't stand the thought of my friends being there—of Tamret being subject to their experiments. Again.

"Why are they there?" I asked. My voice sounded raspy, almost broken. "What's going to happen to them?"

"I suspect the Phands wished to understand how you could have maximized the Former tech tree," Convex Icosahedron said. "It only makes sense that they would bring your friends to their premier research facility to understand how this goal was achieved."

"I've got to get them out of there," I said.

"Hold on, son," Colonel Rage said. "It's commendable that you want to help them, but I don't see how a suicide mission gets the job done. We're talking about a top-secret military research facility. What makes you think you would be able to successfully exfiltrate them?"

"I don't know, but I have to try."

"You are on the cusp of becoming a victim of your own success," the colonel said. "Just because you've made it this far doesn't mean that you can succeed at whatever you want."

"Then let's figure out a way," I said, "because I'm not leaving my friends there to be experimented on. I am going to get them out and then we are going to get Ghli Wixxix. We are going to defeat the Phands without blowing up Confederation Central. That's the deal."

They all stared at me, no doubt wondering who this kid was who was giving them orders. I wondered the same thing. I also wondered what I could possibly be thinking. Getting everyone out of the Phandic research facility was even crazier than breaking into a Phandic prison. I had no special skills, no amazing team to back me up. I had, in short, no reason to think I wouldn't be killed or captured within seconds of arriving at this high-security research facility, assuming whatever ship I arrived on wasn't destroyed before I got close.

I realized that Colonel Rage was right. I was so used to succeeding with my wild stunts that I had lost all perspective. I couldn't do whatever I wanted just because I wanted it. With my previous successes, I'd had a ton of help—Tamret, Smelly, and, most recently, the military tech tree. The feeling of being invulnerable wouldn't fade away, but the actual invulnerability was long gone.

It was time to stop telling these beings what to do. They were actual freedom fighters who had put together a base and a plan, and who had real knowledge of the enemy they faced. I would do what they wanted and follow their lead—unless that lead involved leaving everyone on Planet Pleasant and destroying Confederation Central. In that case, I'd do whatever I could to sabotage them.

Realizing I was, once again, making big plans I could not follow through on, I sat still, uncomfortable and miserable. I used to try to be a well-behaved kid. I liked following the rules and flying under the radar. I always wondered at kids who seemed to want to get into trouble. Now I'd become just like them.

I would have been perfectly content to sit back and let these beings make their decisions, to listen to those with more knowledge and experience, but every time I told myself to quit making trouble, I thought of my friends in that Phandic facility. I thought of Tamret.

"Look," I said. "I'm sorry I keep making demands. You obviously know your stuff, though destroying Confederation Central makes no sense. Otherwise, though, I'm sure you're on top of things. I just want to help my friends. I want to get them away from Planet Pleasant, but I have no idea how to do that."

"This is war, son," Colonel Rage said gently. "I understand that you want to save the people that matter to you, but what counts is the mission, not the people who carry it out. In this case, any attempt to rescue your friends would end in disaster."

"Actually," said Convex Icosahedron, "I'm not quite sure that's true." I couldn't say for sure, because his booming voice didn't come with a whole lot of inflection, but he seemed to find this exchange amusing. Maybe it was how he held his big game-piece head slightly to one side, the colors shifting across its surfaces in undulating waves that somehow reminded me of laughter. He bounced on his heels and wiggled his gloved fingers. "There are certain design exploits in the facilities at

Planet Pleasant that we have known about for some time, but we lacked operatives who were able and willing to make use of them or targets of sufficiently high value to make it worth our while to try."

"Of course!" said Adiul-ip, suddenly quite animated. "His youth will confuse their sensors."

"What does that mean?" Colonel Rage demanded.

"In Phandic culture a being is not considered to be, well, an actual being until it becomes an adult," Adiul-ip explained. "Their sensors are calibrated with this bias in mind. It makes it much easier for adolescents to infiltrate even a high-security facility like Planet Pleasant."

I knew about the Phands' disregard for young people, but I'd had no idea that this bias could become a strategic advantage.

"Wait a minute," I said, suddenly realizing something. "Does that mean the only reason we got away with rescuing my father and stealing those ships was because we're kids?"

"As I understand it," said Adiul-ip, "you performed intelligently and with great courage during that mission. You managed to avoid detection entirely. Had you made some strategic errors, however, it is likely they would have been less costly for you than they would have been for adults."

"I believe we can take advantage of this weakness and get you to the planet surface undetected," Convex Icosahedron said, "but from that point, it will be up to you. You must find your friends, rescue them, and make your way to the prison to free Ghli Wixxix. Because of the nature of this operation, we will have to maintain radio silence, which means we will not be able to coordinate with you. You will be entirely on your own."

"Let's slow down," I said, even though I didn't want him to slow down at all. I wanted him to speed up. I wanted to know everything, and I wanted to know it at once. Unfortunately, it didn't work that way, and I knew I had to hear more about this plan because these guys could very easily have something entirely impractical in mind. "What do I do once I'm there? How do I get them out?"

"We will review with you the intelligence we have on Planet Pleasant, though it is limited," Convex Icosahedron said. "Once you are on location, you will have to improvise, and you will have to find your own transport. Unfortunately, with our tight timeline, we can't help you any further than that."

"What timeline do you mean?"

"If you cannot succeed within ten standard days, we will have to proceed with the original plan," he said.

The original plan was to destroy Confederation Central.

They were asking me to do the impossible—to save my friends and then rescue the prisoners. If I couldn't do this undoable thing, millions of beings were going to die. I was about to tell them that they needed to come up with another plan, but I realized what it was that I would be walking away from. Alice could still be unconscious, for all I knew, slowly dying from whatever Ardov had done to her. I needed to show Mi Sun that she could count on me, that I would get her back to her family. I couldn't leave Steve and Charles and Dr. Roop to whatever cruel experiments and tortures the Phands devised for them.

Most of all, I thought about Tamret, and how she planned to go back to Rarel with Villainic. If I could rescue her, if I could show her that even without upgrades and Former powers

I could still look after her, maybe she would change her mind. That was selfish, and I knew it, so in my own defense I'll say I was also thinking about how much I couldn't stand for her to be subjected to the Phands and their experiments. Even if I knew I had no chance of impressing her or changing her mind, I would still risk anything to save her.

That was the reality, though. I had no reason to think I could succeed where someone else, anyone else, might fail. I wasn't Zeke the hero anymore. I was just an ordinary kid who was neck-deep in trouble.

I was about to speak—to say something just to buy myself more time—when something flashed before my eyes. It was just an instant, a bit of static, and then it was gone, but I knew what it was. My HUD. It had, for the merest instant, flickered into existence with a bit of static, a few readouts scrolling data. It was there and then it was gone, but maybe it was coming back. Maybe it would return with all those upgraded abilities, and if it did, nothing at Planet Pleasant would slow me down.

"I'm in," I said, forcing out the words before I could change my mind. "If there's a chance, I'll take it."

"Good," said Convex Icosahedron as he rose from his chair. His silvery tunic shimmered excitedly in the room's light. "I will let Adiul-ip brief you on what we know about Planet Pleasant. The two of you need to be prepared to leave in six hours. Every moment counts."

I looked at Adiul-ip. All this time I'd presumed he was an adult. Had I gotten that wrong? "I thought only children could go on this mission."

"Not Adiul-ip," said Convex Icosahedron. "Villainic. He goes with you."

"I think it would be better—" I began, but Convex Icosahedron shook his massive, inexplicable head.

"That is how it must be, Zeke Reynolds. Villainic goes with you or I must cancel the mission."

"Once more," said Villainic quite happily, "we shall be buddies."

CHAPTER FOURTEEN

Seven hours later, Villainic and I were sitting in a ship even smaller than the escape pod. I was practically in Villainic's lap, something I didn't particularly enjoy. Villainic smelled a little bit like orange soda. I'd never noticed that before. I really could have gone my whole life without knowing anything about Villainic's odor.

Convex Icosahedron's plan was actually a pretty good one. It had an *Empire Strikes Back* feel to it. The service ships in and out of Planet Pleasant followed the sort of orderly, predetermined route favored by evil space empires, both real and fictional. The pod we sat in had been dropped near that route and given an inertial push. Moving, as we were, without any sort of engine power, we'd look like nothing more than space junk. If all went well, a supply ship would pass by us, and we would magnetically attach to its hull, after which we could then get into the facility without anyone noticing us. The downside was that we had no chance of rescue, so if things went badly, I would be stuck drifting with Villainic forever.

I still had no idea why he was coming with me. I understood that he was the only other being in the renegade camp who was young enough to avoid whatever sort of sophisticated grown-up detector the Phands used, but that didn't make him an asset. I had tried to explain that. I'd made it clear that Villainic was not part of my team, just some cat guy I was stuck with, but Convex Icosahedron said that the numbers showed Villainic needed to go with me, and—evidently—there was no arguing with that particular Geometric Upstart once he started talking about the numbers.

The renegades certainly prepped me for the trip. They gave us both fresh clothes—dull brown jumpsuits that made us look like prisoners, but that had been treated with PPB-resistant armor. I liked that. They provided backpacks with food and moisture packets and weapons—including injectors tailored to Phandic physiology that would produce almost instantaneous unconsciousness. It would be far better to proceed stealthily than to go in with weapons blazing, so I knew these would come in handy. Finally, toward the end of Adiul-ip's briefing, Convex Icosahedron reentered the room. With great ceremony, he held out a gloved hand to show me what looked like a little noose. It was a circle of silver rope, knotted at one end, with a long string dangling from where the rope closed. The whole thing was about as wide as a coffee cup in circumference.

"What is that?" I asked.

"It is very old," Convex Icosahedron said. "Technology belonging to those you call the Formers. You may need to interrogate beings on your journey, and it will help you to know if they speak the truth. This item is a piece of code given physical form, but it can incorporate into your data bracelet. The Lariat of Veracity, as it is called, will alert you with a mild buzz whenever a being lies to you."

"The Lariat of Veracity," I repeated. "You mean a Lasso of Truth? Like Wonder Woman's?"

"I could not say," Convex Icosahedron responded thoughtfully.

The colors began to shift more rapidly along his many-sided head. "Perhaps."

"Why would the Formers make a lie detector in the shape of a lasso?" I demanded.

"Why would they make cockroaches?" he countered. "Why would they make kiwi fruit, which are delicious but difficult to peel? Do you want something that will help you, or do you want to ponder the mysteries of the cosmos?"

I held out my arm. Convex Icosahedron placed the Lariat of Veracity around my data bracelet, and I watched as it seemed to meld into the device. In a matter of seconds it was gone, leaving no sign that it had ever been there.

"I am a very pretty flower," announced Convex Icosahedron.

I felt a mild buzz, slighter even than a cell phone on vibrate, but still noticeable. "This could come in handy," I said.

"I have no doubt you will use it wisely," said Convex Icosahedron.

I waited for the buzz, but surprisingly, he seemed to really believe what he'd said.

After Adiul-ip's briefing and Convex Icosahedron's presentation of the cool gadget, I'd had a moment alone with Colonel Rage. I still hadn't forgiven him for betraying us back at the Hidden Fortress. I never would.

I therefore put my most burning question to him. "What is the deal with Convex Icosahedron?"

"Son, I wish I knew. I can't even figure out if he's a living thing or some kind of talking toaster. All I know is that these aliens seem to trust him, and they appear to be on the up-and-up, so I am going along with them for now. I don't have any better options if I want to get those invaders off our planet."

"But why does he want me to take Villainic along?"

"No clue about that one either. As near as I can tell, that alien is nothing but a liability. Either he's got a skill set none of us have seen yet, or Convex Icosahedron is keeping something from us. Based on what I've seen, I'm more inclined to think it's the second one. He's definitely playing his own game."

"You think he's a bad guy?"

The colonel shook his head. "No, if I had to guess, I'd say he's not working with the Phands, but I do think he may have his own agenda, something other than which of these two civilizations comes out ahead. After all, we don't know who his people are or what they want. No one will tell me much about him, or how he got to be their leader."

All of which meant I was heading into a very dangerous situation with a guy I couldn't count on because another guy I didn't much trust insisted on it. The only thing that gave me any comfort was the fact that there was no way Villainic and Convex Icosahedron could possibly be working together.

"I still don't know why you gave up on the plan to liberate Earth," I told him.

He cocked his head, and his good eye narrowed with suspicion, like I was fishing for information. As it happens, I was. I hadn't forgotten that the Phandic renegades had a portal that opened to my planet as well as a fully formed plan for freeing it. I wanted to know what they'd worked up in case I needed more options.

"I didn't abandon it," the colonel said. "Convex Icosahedron did. As far as liberating Earth went, the plan was solid, but in terms of destabilizing the Phandic Empire, it was less of a sure thing. Apparently, the Phands use a kind of faster-than-light technology to provide energy to their conquered worlds."

I nodded. "The subspace energy relay. I saw it in Manhattan."

He looked at me, maybe remembering that I wasn't just some dumb kid. "The plan was to shut it down. Deprive the Phands of their power source, cut them off from the empire. They only have a few thousand soldiers on Earth, so without the technological advantage, human numbers take care of the rest."

"What's to keep them from just sending more ships?" I asked.

"The hope was that enough other planets would follow Earth's lead, and there would be too many uprisings to put down. A domino effect. The numerical projections looked pretty good, but then they came up with the idea for destroying that space station, and those looked even better."

"Once we get Ghli Wixxix back to Confederation Central, you won't need either of those plans," I told him, though I wished I were as confident as I sounded.

We drifted for hours. Villainic spent the beginning part of the trip chatting endlessly, until I finally pretended to fall asleep. He gave up talking after a while. Finally we received a notice on my data bracelet that our ship was closing in. There was always the chance that it would see us for what we were, and if that happened, the odds were pretty good it would decide to fire weapons at us. Alternatively, we could be captured.

Neither one of these possibilities appealed to me, and I was starting to think this mission had been a huge mistake. Since that moment in the meeting, I hadn't had another flicker from my HUD. I'd spent most of my pretending-to-sleep time trying to coax my skill system back to life, like John Carter wishing himself to Barsoom, but it clearly wasn't a matter of will. I began to worry that the flicker I'd seen had been nothing more than my imagination or, less humiliating but not less dispiriting, a momentary glitch in a system that had shut down entirely. If my HUD did not come back to life, I had no idea what I was going to do when we got to Planet Pleasant.

The good news was that the transport ship didn't seem to take notice of us. The pod behaved just as it was programmed to do. It moved in behind the ship and attached itself near the engine exhausts, where the plasma wake would make us invisible to any scans. Now it was time to get to work.

Using the equipment Adiul-ip had given me, I set up an automated drill that began to cut a hole about four feet wide in our hull and then the supply ship's. Our pod created an airtight seal between the two vessels, so that when we breached their hull, the Phands would not receive a structural-integrity warning on their bridge, since there would have been no loss of atmosphere. Adiul-ip had explained that any readings produced by our actions would look like normal hull stress to be noted in their maintenance logs.

We would be emerging in one of the cargo bays, where no crew were generally assigned. That meant we should be able to enter unseen, but I had my PPB pistol ready for an emergency.

This operation took perhaps fifteen minutes. Once we were through, I crawled into the cargo bay, saw that it was empty, and signaled Villainic to come through. I then activated the nanotech hull sealant we'd been given. It took about thirty seconds to create a new, equally strong hull plating over the hole.

With that complete, I keyed my bracelet to disengage the pod. It fell away, leaving nothing behind except a few near-microscopic cameras. Once the pod detached, it would begin to disintegrate, leaving no sign of our entry. Unless someone walked in and saw us, we would remain completely undetected.

We now had a whole other series of problems, such as not knowing where in the compound our friends were being held—and how we would get from this ship to that unknown location. I had a schematic of both the transport ship and the research facility uploaded to my bracelet, but unless I could crack into the computer system or interrogate a prisoner, I would be operating blind. Adiul-ip had provided me with some hacking tools, but there was still a strong chance any attempt to breach the computers would send off alarm bells.

I used my bracelet to call up the cargo manifest that Adiul-ip had provided, and scrolled through the cargo. Villainic hovered over my shoulder, peering at the information.

"Much of this is fairly ordinary," he noted. "Food, bedding, toilet tissue. Things of that nature. However, if there were equipment related to the research on Tamret and the others, then we might be able to follow those shipments."

I stared at him. "Villainic, that's actually a great idea."

"You know I want only to help."

"But this time you're actually helping. This is a huge step forward for you."

I reviewed the manifest, and it seemed like there were a few boxes that contained equipment related to reverse engineering nanites. These crates were, I discovered, quite large. It turned out to be fairly easy to open them, crawl inside, and close them up again. Now we had to hope they wouldn't be opened immediately, since if some eager scientist wanted to peer inside at his new goodies, we'd be in major trouble.

Once again I was stuck in a cramped space with Villainic. We waited for what must have been at least three hours until I felt a rumble I recognized as a ship entering a planet's atmosphere. Using my bracelet, I projected a visual so I would have some idea what we were getting into. We came through the upper atmosphere and flew over a vast ocean, low enough that I could make out gigantic creatures—they looked like monstrous emerald-green eels, twice as big as any whale—leaping out of the water, snapping their jaws at us, though we were thousands of feet above them.

We then flew over a vast and uninhabited forest region. Finally we approached what looked like a small city, almost totally uninhabited, made up of mostly squat rectangular buildings. It looked more like an industrial park on Earth than anything fantastically science-fictional. The structures were windowless, covered in a reflective coppery substance. Around the perimeter were dozens of towers—for defensive purposes, I assumed. There also seemed to be a rail system connecting different parts of the compound. The Planet Pleasant facility was depressingly huge. I had to hope we were right about our crate and we ended up somewhere near where we needed to be. Otherwise we were in big trouble.

Once the ship came to a halt, we had to wait another two hours for anything to happen. We heard movement and dull voices outside, but our crate remained motionless. Finally, some sort of antigravity device lifted our container and began to move it. We were taken off the ship and set in a waiting area, from which we were eventually placed on a flat car of the train.

From there, the transport itself took maybe fifteen minutes. We were then set down in what—through the slats—appeared to be a lighted space. Most likely the storage room off a lab.

No one appeared to be around. I waited another half an hour to be safe, and then signaled Villainic that it was time to move.

We exited the crate, and while I expected sensors and proximity alarms to start screaming, we managed to avoid attracting any attention. Of course, the Phands could have had silent alarms and might have been closing on our position at that exact second, but I decided to remain optimistic.

I scanned the room looking for cameras or other security measures that would trip us up, but I didn't find anything. I knew that the Phands had a strict culture, one in which creative thinking and indulging in wild speculation were frowned upon. During the pre-mission briefing, Adiul-ip had explained that that was one of the reasons their highest-level scientific research was conducted at a remote facility. They wanted their scientists to feel free to experiment without facing the sort of scorn and condemnation such freethinkers were generally subject to in Phandic society. The security to get in—and especially out—of the facility was very tight, but once inside, I could rely on my own senses to make certain I was unobserved.

All around me were workstations, mainly pale green countertops. Many of them had clear plastic boxes, subdivided into drawers, for storing materials of various sorts, but these stations were otherwise empty. I guess they didn't need computers since, like in the Confederation, the Phands had personal data devices that could produce a screen and keyboard at will.

All of that meant that there would be nothing here to give me a clue about finding the others.

I turned to Villainic. "Don't you have like an amazing sense of smell or something?"

"I have never won any sniffing competitions, if that's what you're asking."

"Okay, on my planet we don't have sniffing competitions, because sniffing is something no one is good at. I have to think even an embarrassingly mediocre sniffer like you could give us an edge. Can you smell any of them?"

He pointed his face upward and sniffed the air. "No," he said.

"Well, then. Let's just give up and go home."

"Aren't we here to find them?"

"Yes, Villainic. That's why we're here. Maybe we should go sniff in some other places."

"I see," he said, grinning. "You are being funny. We're joking, as buddies are inclined to do!"

We approached the door, which hissed open to reveal a deserted hallway. It was another instance of the Phand scientists needing to feel free of scrutiny in order to indulge in scientific creativity. I felt sure that if we were seen, plenty of guards would come pouring out of nowhere, but for now we were safe.

Villainic sniffed the air like a werewolf ready to maul a minor character, and then walked quickly away from me. I followed along, forcing myself not to ask questions. I didn't want to mess with his sniffing mojo.

Villainic passed about five doors and then stopped in front of one. "There's something in here," he said.

"What sort of something?"

"I'm not certain. It smells sort of like you."

"Like me? One of the other humans?"

Villainic didn't answer. He just kept sniffing.

I raised my wrist to the door scanner, and the security override that Adiul-ip had given me did its work. The door hissed open. The room inside, like the one we'd come out of, was deserted. It was a similar space of workstations, but this one looked less neat. There were materials spread out all over the various surfaces, like someone wanted to continue with what they were doing when they started their next shift. There were no prisoners. That did not stop Villainic, though. He kept walking around the room, sniffing.

I was about to tell him to knock it off, since none of our friends were here, but he seemed to be seriously engaged, and I was curious. What, exactly had he been smelling?

He went over to a workstation and picked up a glass container, bulbous on the bottom but narrow at the top—basically an alien test tube. It contained what appeared to be blood. "This is it," he said. "I believe it's yours."

I walked over and picked up the container. It certainly seemed to be blood, but I had no way of knowing whose. "Are you sure?"

"It smells exactly like you."

How had Phandic scientists gotten hold of my blood, and what did they plan to do with it? The second part was easy. After I'd shown them how much butt I could kick back on Earth, they wanted to figure out what my nanites were up to so they could reverse engineer Tamret's work. Maybe they hadn't even realized our skill trees were hacked. Maybe they approached augmentation from a purely mechanical perspective rather than focusing on hardware.

That left the question of where this blood sample had come from. I remembered back to the fight with Ardov in Central Park. I'd seen him put a cloth with my blood on it in a little plastic container. I had not been bleeding nearly this much, but it was possible they'd been able to replicate more blood from the few drops Ardov had taken. The only reason they would want to do that would be to study the nanites I'd received at the Hidden Fortress. I seriously doubted they were looking to make an army of Zeke clones.

I was about to put down the test tube when I noticed that the blood was moving. I almost dropped it, because moving blood is, pretty much by definition, gross. Little tendrils of the stuff were pushing up along the sides of the glass, like they wanted to return to the business of circulating. There was no way I was going to let that stuff back inside.

Then I realized it wasn't trying to return to me. It was trying to get away from something. I had been holding it close to another container, one filled with a yellowish powder, and the blood seemed not to like it. Experimentally, I moved the blood a little closer, and it pushed away from that side of the glass.

"I wonder if it's magnetic," I said.

"I don't think so," said Villainic. His voice had an unusual tone, like he was actually thinking about stuff. He took the vial from my hand and moved it back and forth, closer to the powder and then away, several times. "It's not a consistent movement like you would see with a natural force such as magnetism. It's more like a fear response."

I took the vial away from him again and tried the experiment. "I think you're right." I stared at him. Every once in a while, I thought Villainic might not be as much of an idiot as he seemed to be. Either that or he'd simply noticed something completely obvious that I'd missed, which by no means made him a genius.

I moved the vial around experimentally a few more times, not quite sure what I was looking for. This seemed to be important, though. During one pass, I moved it a little too close to another powder—this one pale blue in color—and the blood reacted entirely differently. It seemed to want to get closer to the blue powder.

I found a pair of metal tweezers and grabbed a few grains of the blue powder. I dropped it into the blood. There was a little bit of swirling, but otherwise nothing happened. I then moved it closer to the container of blue powder and the blood moved toward it, only this time more forcefully. I moved it closer to the yellow powder, and it pushed away.

"You know what I think?" I said. "They are experimenting on ways to strengthen and weaken nanites."

"Perhaps that is how they shut down your system," Villainic suggested.

I turned to him, again thinking I might have underestimated his intelligence. "What makes you think they shut me down? Tamret decided that the tech was in a natural state of decay."

"That's true," he said, "but it seems a bit strange that you suffered such a complete and embarrassing failure while fighting with Ardov—the very same fellow who took our friends and brought them here. And here is where you find this material. It seems more likely that you were exposed to something that harmed you during that fight."

I grabbed the container of blue powder. "Maybe if I eat some of this, I'll go back to full strength."

"I can think of nothing wiser than consuming an unknown chemical found in an evil alien lab," Villainic said.

Now he was calling me out for being stupid. This was a new low. At least he was developing a sense of humor. "Do you have a better idea?"

"No," he admitted, "but you don't know what that is. Too much, or even too little, might kill you. Maybe it is meant to be injected or turned into a cream that's rubbed on your skin. You can't simply eat mysterious experimental chemicals and hope for the best."

"On the one hand, you are making a lot of sense, but on the other, I don't care." I found a small vial and scooped a bunch of the powder inside. The vials had screw-on lids, so I sealed it and put it in my pocket.

The moment the vial made contact with my skin, I saw it again—the flicker from my HUD. It was just for a second, but it was there—the flash of static and the scroll of text. It was real. There had been none of this powder back at the renegade base, but I had no doubt that this time the powder had caused that moment of life. It was like my augments were trying to reboot.

As much as it pained me to admit it, Villainic was right. This stuff could kill me or turn me into a raving lunatic. Or, in the tradition of the most classic origin stories, it could turn me into a superhero.

For now I would simply keep some with me. Maybe we would be able to gain access to the files. If I could see the research notes, it was possible I could figure out a way of restoring my abilities. In the meantime, I was wandering around a Phandic research facility with no one to depend on but Villainic. Admittedly, he'd done pretty well so far, but I wasn't anxious to give him enough time to do something dim-witted.

"This is all interesting," I admitted, "but we still need to find the others."

Villainic nodded. He went back into the hallway and took some deep sniffs, but he shook his head. He wasn't getting anything, so we walked a little longer.

I checked my data bracelet, which was automatically set to adjust to local time. It was still deep in the middle of the night, which was good, but we couldn't keep wandering forever. Pretty soon we were going to have to deal with early risers, and that meant conflict.

After about half an hour of hapless exploration, Villainic picked up on a scent. We went through a few hallways until I heard what sounded like movement. I gestured for him to stop and be quiet, and miraculously, he understood. Pressing my back to the wall, I peered around the corner and saw two guards standing in front of a heavy door. It had to be the entrance to where the prisoners were kept.

The two Phands were wearing some kind of body armor— quite possibly something that would resist PPB fire. On the other hand, maybe it wouldn't. Two quick shots, and we could be past them. There was also the chance that weapons fire would trigger an alarm. Adiul-ip didn't have any details about the specifics of their security setup, and he'd warned us not to use energy weapons except in an emergency.

What were my other options, then? We had the injectors Convex Icosahedron had given us, but there was no way to get close enough to these guys without them seeing us. What we needed was some sort of distraction. If this were a video game, I could toss some rocks or something and the guards would blunder out to investigate, but I had a feeling that this technique didn't work so well in real life. Besides, there were no rocks to throw, and no way to toss them except by revealing myself to these guys.

I hated to risk a frontal assault, but with every minute that passed, we had less of a chance of succeeding with this rescue. I was about to turn to Villainic to begin explaining this to him, but I realized he was already moving past me, PPB pistol out. He squeezed off two shots, both of them quite good. He hit the guards in their heads, and they went down.

I turned to him. "Why did you do that?" I demanded.

"I didn't see that there was any other option," he said, "and I thought you might be having difficulty making up your mind to proceed. I decided to take the burden on myself."

"And if it set off an alarm?"

"Then it would be my fault," he said, "and you wouldn't have to feel bad about making the mistake."

I took a deep breath. "That is very nice of you. I guess. But maybe we should discuss decisions of this magnitude."

"I am trying to be more like Tamret," he said. "She does not overthink things. She acts."

"She thinks plenty," I said. "That's why the things she does tend to work out."

He gestured toward the guards. "This worked out."

I did not have the energy to argue with his success. "From now on, we discuss. But thanks."

We went over to the door and used our bracelets to trigger the lock. It clicked open, and there were no guards waiting for us on the other side, so that was good. I crouched down to pull one of the sleeping guards into the other room when I saw that his eyes were open. I almost jumped back, thinking he was about to get up and go Phandic crazy on me. Then I saw that his eyes weren't moving. They were still and blank, like dull marbles.

I turned to Villainic, and I had to force myself to choke out the words. "Did you kill these guys?"

"Of course. You can see they're dead."

I felt revulsion crawl through me, but at the dead body or what Villainic had done—or both—I couldn't say. "But why?"

"They're Phands," he said simply.

"So is Adiul-ip."

"These are *enemy* Phands. If we give them a chance, they will kill us."

"That's not the point," I said, my voice hard. I couldn't believe he had killed them. That wasn't how I did things, how the beings with me did things. "They're grunts," I told him, trying to keep from sounding hysterical. "It's not their fault they were born into this culture. They think they're doing the right thing. You can't just kill anyone who gets in your way. Not if you have another choice. Don't you feel bad about doing this?"

"Of course not," he said. "They're aliens."

"I'm an alien from your perspective."

"This is a silly conversation, Zeke. I understand your objections, but we no longer need to worry about these two waking up. They are dealt with. Forever. Now, can we please move on?"

"No more killing," I said to him. "You have to give me your weird Rarel deity word."

"Very well," he sighed. "If it will make you happy, I promise not to kill anyone unless I see no alternative."

We dragged the dead Phands inside and closed the door again. Out of the corner of my eye I watched Villainic, realizing how little I knew and understood him. I'd thought he was just an idiotic bumbler, a guy fate had stuck me with because fate thought it was hilarious. It turned out he had a dark streak, or possibly an amoral one. Maybe it was Rarel culture, but I had never seen Tamret show this kind of disregard for life, and she was the least rule-bound person I'd ever met.

It was true enough that I'd played a part in events in which beings had died, but those had been space battles, when I'd been fighting to keep myself and my friends alive. You don't really have the option of knocking an enemy ship on the head. There are huge weapons involved, and ships can explode or leak oxygen or do all sorts of things that you can't control. The first time I'd used weapons on another ship, I'd gone after the enemy with everything I had, but I'd learned my lesson. In my second battle with the Phands, when I'd understood more about how the weapons worked, I'd done my best to keep the damage to a minimum.

More importantly, while I knew I'd acted justifiably, that I'd done the best I could each time to save my own ship, I still felt bad about the beings who died. They had been my ene-mies, and they had been doing their best to kill me and beings I cared about, but most of them had still just been doing their job. Maybe they knew the Phandic Empire was a bad place, but it was their culture. They had friends and relationships and children to go back to. They weren't evil, cackling villains. That made a difference to me.

It didn't seem to make a difference to Villainic.

There was a security station a little farther down, and given that we'd already started killing beings who worked in this compound, it seemed a bit late to go with the subtle approach. After I made sure that Villainic had put his PPB pistol on stun, we shot the two guards and dragged them away from their post, sticking them in an empty room. This station had an actual computer console, and using a hacking tool that Adiul-ip had provided for my data bracelet, I bypassed the password prompt and was able to pull up data on the prisoners. There were hundreds of prisoners being held in various parts of the facility, but only six in the building with the nanotech labs. Hopefully that meant everyone I was looking for was nearby and in one place. Unfortunately, the prisoners weren't labeled, and if there were cameras monitoring them, I couldn't figure how to access them. I was going to have to open each cell and look inside.

I'd been so intent on getting to this point that I hadn't allowed myself to worry about what everyone might have been through. Had they been tortured, experimented on? Planet Pleasant was notorious for that sort of thing. I had known from the beginning that I might manage to make my way inside and not like what I found. If my friends had been truly hurt—if the Phands had done something to Tamret—I wasn't sure I would be able to deal with it.

I told Villainic to keep watch. We needed to know if someone was coming, but I also didn't want him around. I needed to do this on my own. I reached the first cell and keyed it open, my PPB pistol at the ready. Maybe it would be one of my friends. Maybe it would be a deranged lunatic, frothing at the mouth. I would face the worst if I had to, but I wouldn't think about it until then.

The door clicked open and swung inward, revealing a small chamber with bare walls. There was a bathroom area in one corner and a cot against the wall, and little else. In the gloom of the unlit chamber I saw a figure lying still on the cot. I crept forward, using the light on my bracelet to illuminate the form.

It was Steve. He was on his side, wearing the tunic I'd last seen him in. There was a gentle rise and fall of his chest, indicating he was alive, but he did not stir.

I grabbed his shoulder and shook him gently.

Nothing.

Maybe they had sedated him. That was a possibility I hadn't considered. I gave him another shove, this one much rougher.

Steve darted up, grabbing me under my armpits and lifting me into the air. Still seeming to be asleep, he slammed my back against the wall. Then he paused to blink at me through reptilian eyes. "Oi. It's you. Took you bloody long enough."

"Can you put me down?" I gasped. "You're kind of crushing my rib cage."

"Sorry, mate," he said as he set me down. "You startled me."

"Clearly, they didn't hurt you," I said breathlessly. "What about the others?"

"They did something to us so our tech trees are shut down, but we're fine otherwise." He thought about it for a second. "Tamret's pretty ticked off."

"Yeah, I'll bet. But I'm glad she's okay. She is okay, isn't she?"

"Yeah, we're all fine. They haven't let us sit about and chat, but we've seen each other passing in the hall, and I would have been able to smell if there was anything seriously wrong. They left us alone—I mean, other than turning us into regular beings."

I thought of the lab and what I'd found there. "The powder?"

Steve nodded. "Yeah, they just blew some of that yellow

nonsense in my face. I inhaled it without meaning to and I was just switched off, yeah?"

So Villainic had been right. Ardov must have somehow exposed me to the powder when we were fighting, and that's why my system shut down. The real question was if we could do anything to switch ourselves back on. I still had the blue powder on me, but I couldn't believe that the answer would be as simple as that. Still, in an emergency, if all else was lost, it was good to have a crazy, last-ditch effort to give me hope.

"What about the others?" I asked.

He nodded. "Same with them. They're all back to being ordinary."

I nodded. This was bad news, but if everyone was healthy, then things weren't as bad as I feared.

"So, what's the plan, then?" Steve asked. "How do we get out of here?"

"One step at a time. Villainic and I snuck in, and we're making the rest up as we go along."

"I'm surprised you haven't killed him."

I looked at Steve. "He's the one doing the killing. Two guards we could have just as easily stunned."

Steve cocked his head. "That's surprising."

"No kidding. He's darker than I thought."

Steve let his tongue taste the air "Speaking of dark mammals, Ardov is still around here somewhere, and if he catches wind of you, he's not going to play nice."

"Yeah, good point. Let's get the others and then improvise a way off this planet."

This was easier said than done, and I knew it. The security apparatus on Planet Pleasant didn't seem all that interested in keeping out intruders, since the reputation of this place meant no one ever wanted to come here in the first place. The security setup was designed to make sure none of the staff—a bunch of Phandic misfits and freethinkers—didn't escape with their technology or research. That meant that even though we'd made it this far, there was still a pretty good chance it was going to be a one-way trip, and all I'd done was hand myself over to my enemies.

Steve had no idea who was in which cell, so I opened them in the order I came to them. In the first one I found Alice, who was in the process of sitting up as she heard her door open. She was still in her school uniform, which was now wrinkled, and she'd lost her tie. On the other hand, she was no longer in a coma.

"You're okay!" I said, rushing into the room. I kept my voice quiet, but I don't think she had any trouble mistaking my enthusiasm.

She nodded. "Yeah, they fixed me up when I got here. I guess they were able to undo whatever they'd done to me in the first place." She rubbed at her eyes sleepily. "Zeke, what happened to you? Why did you leave the ship? Where did you go?"

"It's a long story," I said. "I never meant to ditch you guys, but I'll tell you the rest later."

She nodded, pushing herself off her cot.

"Alice," I said. "I'm sorry this happened to you. I didn't forget that you wanted to stay on Earth, but we couldn't leave you. You were hurt, and you would have been captured."

"I know," she said. "No one thinks you're running around just doing what you feel like."

"That seems to be what everyone thinks," I told her.

"That's what they *say*," she told me. "Not what they think. Look, we're all frustrated and scared and angry. Everything we do puts us one step back. If Mi Sun or, I guess, someone else vents a little, you need to toughen up. They unload on you because you're the leader."

"I thought I was the leader," Steve said.

"Of course you are." She patted his arm and turned back to me. "If we were at home and things were normal, we'd be annoyed because our parents were telling us what to do, but we expect our parents to do exactly that, and if they stopped, we'd be terrified."

"But we're supposed to all be equal," I said.

"And we are," she said, "but when we get into a jam, you usually tell us what to do."

"I make a suggestion," I said. "I don't want to be the leader. I just want to do what we need to do to make sure everyone is safe."

"Then maybe we should do that instead of standing around and talking about it," she said.

"Thinking too much just gets you into trouble," Steve said. "I like to act first and think about it later."

The next cell we came to contained Dr. Roop, who appeared mildly alarmed that I had broken into the Planet Pleasant facility, but somehow managed to keep himself from lecturing me on being foolish. After that we got Charles, who was just happy that there was a rescue underway.

I opened the next cell, and there was Tamret, sitting on her bunk, like she'd been awake and waiting for something like this to happen. She looked at me and her eyes went wide. I saw her twitch, like she was about to leap up, but then she held still. Her expression became dark. "What happened to you?" she demanded. "How did you get off the ship?"

"I slipped into the escape pod to avoid Ardov and to get a pistol," I explained. "Once the power came back on, Villainic jettisoned the pod before I could get a clear shot. After that, things got weird. I'll explain it later."

"That was good thinking on his part," Tamret said.

"No, it wasn't. He panicked. That's all."

"Maybe so," she said. "But if he hadn't, we'd all be locked up, and none of us would ever be getting out of here."

That was probably true. Come to think of it, Villainic had stumbled into a number of fortunate blunders.

I shoved the notion to the back of my mind as we moved to the last cell, which I assumed held Mi Sun. Tamret, it seemed, was still angry with me. I thought about what Alice had said, but I wasn't sure it made sense. Tamret was putting up walls, and I had no idea why. I also had no idea how I was going to find out if she would talk to me.

We opened Mi Sun's cell, and she greeted me more warmly than Tamret had, which was maybe a new low for me. "I hate this place," she said as she got off her cot and put on her school blazer. "Let's get out of here."

It seemed like a good idea to me. The major problem was that I had no idea how we could do that. I decided not to tell her that, because Alice's words were weighing on me, and I didn't want to disappoint everyone. On the other hand, I was suddenly struck by the stupidity of this plan. Convex Icosahedron had somehow encouraged me to try to break my way out of a facility specifically designed to prevent anyone from escaping, and I was now starting to feel like maybe I had walked into some kind of a trap.

I couldn't begin to guess what the purpose of the trap might be. Had Convex Icosahedron been trying to get rid of me? I couldn't see why. He could just as easily have ignored me. Could he have been working all along to deliver me into the hands of the Phandic Empire? If that were true, though, the Phands would know I was here and I would already be in custody.

I had to conclude that he believed I could get off this planet. That meant there had to be a way to do it. Now it was just a matter of figuring it out.

CHAPTER FIFTEEN

W e only had two PPB pistols. I pointed mine toward one end of the corridor. Tamret grabbed the gun out of Villainic's hand and covered the other end. She looked determined and ready for anything, but with limited weapons and no upgrades, we were firmly on last-stand territory here. They'd found us and they were coming for us, and there was no way the top research facility in the Phandic Empire wasn't going to be able to handle a few lightly armed runaways.

I tried firing my pistol at the wall. *Who knows?* I thought. Maybe it would open into a convenient garbage chute. No luck. The wall absorbed the blast harmlessly. I returned to standing ready. Maybe they were going to get us, but I vowed to make it as difficult for them as I could.

Then an orange gas began to waft up from the floor. It smelled like burned plastic and rotten meat. I turned to look at Tamret, but her eyes were already growing heavy. In an instant she slumped to the floor, along with everyone else except Villainic and me.

I didn't feel anything at all from the gas. I had to assume that they'd treated the prisoners with something to make them react to it so they could deploy the gas without affecting their own people.

For a second I considered pretending to be affected, but I

wasn't sure what that would get me. Mostly it would be a form of passive surrender, and I wasn't ready to go down that path yet. The guards began pouring in from both sides now, heavily armed, with big PPB weapons, like futuristic shotguns, aimed at us. Villainic's hands shot up in surrender, but I wasn't about to give up. I took aim at the first guard.

It turned out, a trained Phandic soldier is a quicker draw than I am.

Though it may be hard to believe, after all my adventures in space, this was my first experience with being stunned. I didn't enjoy it. When I came to, I had no recollection of being hit by the blast that took me down, but now I felt stiff and nauseated. My head pounded and my fingers and toes tingled.

I found myself not in a cell, but in a lab. My wrists and ankles were bound with plasma restraints to the oversized chair, no doubt designed with Phands in mind. I could hear someone moving equipment around, rearranging things made out of metal or glass. The footsteps sounded light and graceful. I kept straining my neck to try to see behind me, but I couldn't get a good look.

Finally I heard a voice, and I wished again for silence. It was Ardov.

"I don't think I've ever seen you go this long without speaking," he said. "Does it hurt you not to talk nonsense?"

This was not a situation I wanted to be in. Ardov had total power over me. We were on his turf, and he had every advantage. Somehow I didn't think cracking wise was going to get me very far. "Hey, Ardov. You sure get around, don't you?"

He smirked his evil-cat smirk. "I figured it was only a matter of time until you showed up here, looking for your friends. And now we're all reunited. Kind of nice, actually."

"So, it's one thing to be working for Junup, who's taken you under his wing and all, but now you can't even pretend you're not one of the bad guys. Doesn't that bother you?"

"There are no good and bad sides, Zeke. There are just the powerful and the powerless, and I'm siding with the powerful. That's what I've always done."

"And you've always lost," I said, "which maybe kind of tells you something."

"There is an old saying from my city-state," Ardov said. "'Declare no battle won until the war is over.'"

"So all those times I handed your butt to you were just strategic withdrawals?"

"Temporary setbacks. Necessary steps to get us to where we are today. I have the upper hand, and you are utterly defeated, like the powerless weakling you are."

"I'm still not clear on why it's taken so many strategic withdrawals and setbacks to get the upper hand on a powerless weakling," I said. "Can you walk me through that part?"

"You are not going to be laughing soon."

"I'm not actually laughing now. Mostly I'm really nervous. I don't have any problem admitting that. It's the way I tend to feel when I'm tied to a chair in an experimental lab with a wacko speechifying in my general direction. But here's the thing, Ardov. You don't have to be that wacko. You don't have to be the bad guy. All the things you've done, the beings you've hurt, you can put that behind you. Untie me. Help me get the others out of here, and it can be a whole new life for you. Doesn't that seem more satisfying—helping beings instead of hurting them? Wouldn't you rather work for the good of the many instead of the power of the few?"

He smiled at me, a pitying sort of smile, and I knew that there really was nothing there to save. Maybe he had a sad story—a childhood trauma or a cruel parent. Maybe Ardov had endured terrible things and was now broken. Maybe he'd been seduced to the dark side by Darth Junup and had been brainwashed beyond redemption. It didn't matter. I knew I could never reach him.

Unfortunately, this realization did not get me anything, because I was still tied to a chair in an experimental lab. I guessed that when Ardov started to torture me, I could take comfort in the knowledge that there hadn't been much I could have done to prevent it, but there's not really all that much comfort to be had from that.

Then from behind me I heard a door hiss open. "You're not supposed to be in here," a female voice said.

"I didn't know that," Ardov said.

"I find that unlikely," the voice answered. "You are dissembling. If you wish to serve the Phandic Empire, you must never dissemble."

"Yes, of course you are right."

"Your rivalry with this being does not further the empress's cause. Go purge yourself of these feelings."

"Yes," Ardov said. "Right away."

I heard him step toward the door and exit the lab.

So now I was alone with a being who frightened Ardov. Things just kept getting better and better.

I heard her approach from behind and then come around the front of my chair. It was a female Phand wearing a turquoise lab coat. She had thick hair pulled back into a long braid, and she wore big silver rings on almost all her fingers. I'd never seen a Phand with jewelry before.

She placed her hands on her hips and jutted out her lower jaw slightly "You're awake at last," she said with an unexpected amount of cheer. "I'm so excited!"

I tried not think too much about what she might be excited about. Any being who worked here was probably a big fan of torture. I was part of a group that had killed two of their guards. There was no way they were going to go easy on me.

"If I take off your restraints," she said, "do you promise not to try to run away?"

"I pinkie swear," I assured her. If I had the chance to get away, I'd take it. She could drag me to pinkie court later.

"You've been treated with nanites to make you susceptible to the control gas," she said, "so if you do run, you'll be quite easy to stop this time. But you won't want to run, because I'm your friend. You know I'm your friend, don't you?"

"It sure is looking that way," I agreed. "Can I ask who you are?"

The Phand smiled. "I am Investigator Kossnarian-iz, and I am so excited to finally meet you."

"This is a big day for me too."

Investigator Kossnarian-iz pressed a button and the restraints vanished. I began to rub one wrist with the opposite hand while my captor watched me with the delight people on Earth reserve for Internet cat videos.

"My superiors haven't figured out yet who you are," she said. "If they had, they wouldn't have let me have you. I suspect your friend Ardov might inform them if he decides it will be to his advantage, so I'll have to be quick."

"Okay," I said cautiously. "What is it we need to do?"

Investigator Kossnarian-iz came over and crouched by me, putting her tusked face uncomfortably close to mine. "I'm a great admirer of yours," she said, sounding giddy. "Zeke." She said my name quietly, like it was a secret. Then she giggled.

A giggling Phand fan is not something you see every day. Still, I'd been meeting lots of different kinds of Phands lately. "Are you with the renegades?" I asked.

"Oh, no," Investigator Kossnarian-iz said, keeping her face uncomfortably close. I guessed this sort of proximity had some meaning in her culture. All I knew for sure was that it made me squirm. "I've heard of them. Traitors to the empress. I don't have the time for such silly things. I'm not political. I'm in it for the science. I love science. Don't you?"

"Science," I assured her, "is super great."

"It is," she assured me, with a creepy look in her eye. "Super and great."

Okay, so this Phand was not looking to destroy the renegades with a sweep of her mighty arm. That was good. She was, however, extra weird.

"Hey," I attempted, "you seem like a really nice being. I'd love to introduce you to my friends. Do you think you could get them out of their cells?"

She brightened at this. "Your friends! Including the Rarel girl, yes? The whole galaxy knows about you two. It is the great romance of our age."

"We've held hands a few times," I said. "Anyhow, I think she's done with me."

"No!" gasped Investigator Kossnarian-iz, putting a hand to her tusked mouth. "What did you do to her?"

"Why, exactly, is it my fault?" I demanded. "She just suddenly started giving me the cold shoulder, so how am I to blame?"

"You must be, because she is so devoted to you," Investigator Kossnarian-iz said, scrunching up her face judgmentally. "Anyone can see that."

"Yeah, well, things have changed. Now she's into getting as far away from me as possible."

"You know, young ladies are complicated beings," Investigator Kossnarian-iz began.

"Look, I appreciate the advice and all, but do you have any thoughts on how I could get out of here and maybe bring Tamret and the rest of my friends with me?"

"I do," she said. "That's what we're here to discuss."

That was easier than I thought. "Just so I understand, if you think the beings who are working against the empress are silly, then why would you want to help me?"

"I've followed your exploits," she said, "and I want to see what you can do. You are my special experiment, Zeke. And the universe itself is my lab. How do you like that?"

"I love it," I said, because *I think you're out of your mind, and you are totally freaking me out*, while honest, might not have gotten me the results I wanted.

Investigator Kossnarian-iz clapped her hands together several times rapidly. "I'm so glad. Now, I've made great progress with this ancient technology. I have a prototype, you know. Prototypes are so much fun to play with. They are full of promise. If things go well, I should be able to deploy in a matter of a few months. We would never have gotten so far if not for you. Your blood sample made it all possible, Zeke. Won't that make you happy, being responsible for such big changes across the galaxy?"

"I'm already a pretty happy person," I said, having no idea what she was talking about. I suspected she wasn't really listening to me anyhow.

"I searched you, you know," she told me, her expression sly. "While you were unconscious, I looked through your things. I checked your pockets. What kind of person walks around with a stun grenade?"

Just when you think the creepy factor can't go any higher, life defies your expectations. "That was a very reasonable thing to do," I assured her.

"I see you found the powder."

Was I in trouble? If I tried to act innocent and asked *What powder?* she might get angry or be disappointed. For whatever reason, this freaky Phand scientist had decided she liked me for being me, so I decided to take a gamble on being honest.

"I thought it might help me get my abilities back," I said, "but I wasn't sure what to do with it. I was afraid if I used it wrong, it might kill me."

"As it turns out, if you use it right, it might kill you. Oh, yes. It might indeed." She nodded rapidly. "Do you know what the chances of it killing you are?"

I shook my head.

"It is very simple to take the powder. Just put a few grains on your tongue. The dose is actually not terribly important. It is almost impossible to take too little, and you can't take too much. Once you ingest the powder, it will work instantly. You will then have a fifteen percent chance of dying. Do you know another way of expressing the number fifteen, Zeke? Three out of twenty. You have seventeen chances out of twenty of surviving, but this is Former technology, so it's not that simple. You'll still have access to the abilities, but the powder will kill you in a few hours if you don't immediately check to see if you will survive."

"What do you mean, 'check to see'?"

"The powder, the nanites—they are both designed with quantum entanglements. And this is the object with which they are entangled."

She opened her grayish hand and showed me a black twenty-sided die, which she dropped into my hand. Anyone who has ever played a tabletop role-playing game would recognize the object. This one was heavy, made out of stone or possibly even an alien metal.

"You put a few grains of powder on your tongue," she said, "and then you roll the die. If you get a four or higher, you will live. If you get a three or lower, your body will shut down when the benefits of the powder have worn off."

"There's a *saving throw*?" I asked. "That's what you're telling me?"

This was a classic tabletop RPG move. Let's say your character has been zapped with a sleep spell that has a 30 percent chance of working. You roll a six-sided die, and if you get a three or higher, she's safe. Different percentages require different dice, which is why there are also dice with four, eight, twelve, and twenty sides.

"Why would this stuff be designed this way?" I asked.

"Who knows?" she answered. "The Formers are mysterious. Perhaps this was just second nature to them, pure logic to their minds. Some think they took pleasure from creating tricky rules and forcing lesser beings like ourselves to follow them. I don't know why, but that's how the system works. So keep the die and the powder. You will want both."

"Couldn't I manipulate the throw?" I asked. "Like maybe load the die?"

"The die will automatically calculate what the correct outcome would have been had you not interfered, and that number will be the one that drives the outcome, even if you don't know it. Believe me. We experimented on many subjects. I know this to be true."

"And how long will the effects last?"

"Approximately one eighth of a day—Confederation standard, that is. I have used a frame of reference for your convenience because I am a kind being."

That was a little over three hours. Plenty of time to get us out of here. "Okay. Fine. Then what happens now? Are you really going to let me power up and save my friends?"

"If you have the courage to risk death and use the powder, then yes. I will observe and take notes. I will then post about it on my [blog]! Anonymously, of course. Otherwise I would be arrested for treason, but that's silly, as my first loyalty has always been to knowledge!"

"Isn't there some way to turn the nanites back on without risking death?"

"A method like that wouldn't much interest me," she said. "I did my graduate-school work in quantum entanglements, so you can see why I'm so excited."

"Sure," I said, "but is it possible?"

"I don't think so," she said.

This wasn't true. The lie-detecting software that Convex Icosahedron had given me buzzed softly against my wrist.

"Come on," I said gently. "You can tell me the truth."

"Fine," she said. "I probably could work something up if I wanted to, but it would take weeks, maybe even months. If you want to get out now, this is your only choice."

No buzz from my wrist, so Investigator Kossnarian-iz was telling the truth.

"Let's deal with reality as we find it, shall we?" she proposed, placing a finger on her chin as though posing for a photograph entitled *Thoughtful Phand*. "In just a few seconds, I'm going to alert the guards to who you are and let them know you've escaped. If they recapture you, you will be treated much more harshly than you were the first time, and I will not be able to meet with you again. I'm afraid that if you hope to remain free and liberate your friends, you have but one chance to succeed."

I was going to have to roll the die. Literally. I tentatively unscrewed the vial and put a few grains on my tongue. It tasted like nothing, but I knew now the clock was ticking. I was, as of this second, doomed to death unless I pulled off a saving throw.

I could not remember how many times I'd done this with friends, goofing around as I cast game dice. I wasn't goofing around now. I took the die in my hand and let it drop onto the table. As I did so, something snapped into my head, and I suddenly recalled that in math class I'd once learned the geometric name of a twenty-sided die. It was a convex icosahedron.

I kept my head turned away. I couldn't bring myself to look.

"Seventeen!" I heard Investigator Kossnarian-iz shout gleefully. "Safe with room to spare!"

I snatched up the die and put it in my pocket next to the vial of powder. I also saw Villainic's stun grenade on the table, which I grabbed. You never knew when that would come in handy. Just then the door opened, and five guards charged in. The scientist screamed and backed up.

"He broke free!" Investigator Kossnarian-iz shouted. "He's a monster! A glorious alien monster! Destroy him." And then, with a twinkle in her eyes, she added, "If you can."

They raised their weapons, and I looked at them, realizing almost instantly that my HUD had reactivated. I was back. I was not going to die, and I had several hours of superheroic ability with which to get my friends out of here. Things were looking up.

I slowed time but sped myself up. I must have looked like a blur to the guards as I approached, grabbing the gun out of the hands of the closest one. I checked to make sure it was set to stun, and then opened fire on the remaining four. Maybe two seconds had passed since the door had opened, and the guards were down.

I turned back to Investigator Kossnarian-iz, who was giving me a big, tusky grin. "That was what I was hoping for."

"I'm glad you enjoyed the show," I told her.

"I look forward to following your exploits, Zeke. Up until a roll of the die kills you."

"What makes you think I'll ever use the powder again?"

She smirked. "You won't be able to resist."

She was wrong, I told myself. I'd be able to resist plenty once the Confederation was safe and Earth was free. I wasn't a thrill-seeker by nature. I kept finding myself in these situations through no fault of my own, but once things calmed down, I would be ready to go back to being a normal kid. I told myself that this was completely true, and maybe part of me believed it, but I also knew that the scientist was right about one thing. Going back to being a normal kid was not going to be easy.

Getting my friends off Planet Pleasant, I hoped, would be.

I made my way back to the prisoner wing, encountering a beefed-up security presence, but that was no obstacle for me. I won't belabor the details. Guards with guns: disarmed. Locked doors: smashed. Electronic security measures: neutralized. In very little time I had the cells open, and I was reunited with my friends.

It took a few nanoseconds to interface with a computer terminal to find the nearest usable ship, which was on the other side of this complex. It would only take us a few minutes to get there. I would go a little slower than my best speed to make sure everyone else stayed safe.

"How are you up and running again?" Charles demanded.

"I don't know," I lied. "It just happened, so I'm not going to stop to wonder why." The last thing I wanted was for everyone else to start gambling with their lives. If I could take the burden on myself, I would do it.

"One of the scientists was tinkering around with my nanites," I said. "She must have accidentally triggered something. Let's worry about how later, because I don't think it's going to last. The question for now is how quickly we can get out of here."

"Zeke is right," Dr. Roop said, though his expression made me think he hadn't bought my explanation. "Our first order of business is to get away from this place."

The computer I'd tapped into had identified a docking bay across the compound, and I began to lead the others in that direction. There were a few more obstacles I had to get rid of, such as a small platoon of guards, some mechanized death turrets, and a few robotic sentries armed with dark-matter blasters. I had the gang hold back while I handled these minor issues.

Outside the docking bay, there were no guards. Either every guard in the facility was now unconscious or recovering from broken bones, or there was a last stand waiting for us inside. I couldn't even bring myself to hope it was the first option. I told everyone to hold back. Tamret was reluctant, but she'd seen what I could do and was willing to try things my way while she and Steve peered around the corner, holding PPB pistols just in case.

Bracing myself, I hacked the electronic lock and opened the double doors that led to the hangar. It was massive—large enough to hold a few long-range ships as well as a number of smaller, shorter-range shuttles. The huge ceiling made it feel like a cathedral. I did a scan for life signs, but determined it had been completely abandoned, so I waved everyone forward.

We made it halfway to the nearest ship before we saw Ardov.

He stood fifty feet in front of us. I had no idea why I hadn't been able to see him when I scanned the room. Maybe he had some sort of cloaking device, like the one the Phandic renegades used. Maybe he hadn't been inside yet and had just entered from a door I couldn't see. It hardly mattered. He was here, and I was going to keep him from hurting anyone.

Ardov stepped forward, wearing dark pants and a dark shirt, and a long coat that flared villainously. He grinned at me as he placed the tip of his finger on his tongue. Then he opened his hand and tossed something high into the air.

It was a twenty-sided die.

In the blink of an eye, I went through all the ways that this was completely terrible news. If Ardov was taking the time to roll a die, it wasn't because he was trying to get in a quick game of Pathfinder. He had the Former military tech upgrades. I was about to fight a guy who could do everything I could do—except he was a lot meaner than I was.

That was the immediate problem. In terms of the big picture, it meant that this technology wasn't just for those of us who had unlocked it in the Hidden Fortress. The Phands had figured out a way to reverse engineer Tamret's hack of the tech tree. When I'd fought Ardov back on Earth, I'd more or less handed our greatest enemies the tools they needed to conquer the galaxy. Now I understood what Investigator Kossnarian-iz had been saying about the tests she was conducting. Months, she'd said. The Phands would have complete control of the Former tech tree, be able to distribute it to all their soldiers, in months. If we didn't get the Confederation out of Junup's hands soon, there would be nothing to stop the Phands from expanding as quickly and as mercilessly as they wanted. It would be the end of the Confederation forever. I wasn't even sure that the renegades' plan of destroying Confederation Central would be enough to stop the Phands from getting these abilities.

That was the situation I was facing: beat a guy who had every advantage over me—who had those advantages *because* of me—or allow the galaxy to enter a potentially endless era of bleak oppression. Not too much pressure.

I slowed time so I could think. How could I defeat Ardov?

I couldn't simply slug it out and hope for the best. I had to figure out some angle, or everything I cared about would be lost. Tamret and Steve and the others could die, right here, if I didn't come up with a plan.

One option would be to share my abilities with some of my friends. Ardov might be tough and evil, but he would be no match for an augmented team including Steve and Mi Sun. It was a nice thought, but I didn't have the time to explain to the others about eating powder and rolling a die. Even if I weren't so rushed, I wasn't about to ask one of them to risk death. If the throw didn't come up high enough, I would be responsible for one of my friends dying, and I couldn't handle that.

The only other thing I could think of was to manipulate Ardov's throw. The wacko Phand scientist had told me that nothing I did to the die would change the outcome—the actual number was determined the moment the die left the thrower's hand—but maybe Ardov didn't know that. If I messed with this throw and he thought I'd doomed him, it might distract him enough to make him vulnerable.

I looked at the die, now spinning in midair. I calculated its trajectory and determined that it was going to land on the number twenty. Wow. Good for him. If he were on offense, he'd get a critical hit.

I then tracked its arc, calculated the exact angle and pressure required to produce the result I wanted, and executed. I darted forward, and before Ardov had time to realize what I was up to, I had gently tapped the die, altering its spin. It landed on the floor, bounced twice, and came to a stop—on the number one.

He paused, looked at the die, and looked at me. He blinked in disbelief. There was a moment of utter silence. We all stood, staring at the die. No one besides me and Ardov understood what it meant, but they still somehow recognized that something important had just happened.

"You just killed me," Ardov said, his voice hushed.

"Sorry, Ardov." I shrugged, going for the stone-cold-killer effect. I wasn't sure I could pull it off in general, but it helped that Ardov thought we were discussing something I'd already done. "You keep messing with our plans. Things will be a lot easier when you're out of the picture. No hard feelings, right?"

Maybe this was cruel, making light of his doom, but I figured he had it coming. He'd tried to kill, capture, or humiliate me enough times. A few hours would go by, and he'd realize he wasn't dead. Besides, the only chance I had of beating him was to be smarter than he was.

"One of your stupid tricks," he said, "and it's killed me."

"It's actually a clever trick," I said, "the sort that gets you every time. You never learn. And now you never will. Because you'll be dead and all."

His eyes turned dark and terrifying, and I began to wonder if, instead of evening the odds, I'd given him an edge. I'd just given this dangerous bully nothing to lose and every reason to want to hurt me and everyone I cared about.

The instant that thought crossed my mind, Ardov charged.

Tamret and Steve were firing their weapons on him, but he ignored the impacts like they were raindrops. I looked around, trying to find an angle, some way to survive the onslaught of an enraged Ardov who now appeared to want nothing so much as to avenge himself.

Maybe the trick with the die hadn't been as smart as I'd

thought it was, but Ardov had reminded me of something fairly important. Up until I'd faced him on Earth, he had always been bigger and stronger and more dangerous than I was, and I'd always found a way to get the upper hand. The only reason he'd gotten the better of me in our last two encounters was because he'd had the advantage of cleverness—even if it was cleverness supplied by Phandic scientists. On Earth he'd had the antinanite powder that had shut down my upgrades. On the ship he'd had the EMP device. Now he had nothing but pure power and rage, and that meant, historically speaking, that the odds favored me.

Even so, with him running toward me at almost a hundred miles an hour, I didn't feel like the stats told the whole story.

"Scatter!" I shouted to the others. "Take cover!" He might try to hurt them in order to throw me off, so if they were in different locations, it would make things harder for him.

I leaped forward, planning to take him out at the knees. I could hit him with the force of a freight train, and it probably wouldn't break anything. If it did, the injuries would heal almost instantly, but physics still affected us, and he would be knocked over, buying me a few seconds to work out a broader strategy. In our heightened states, seconds could seem like hours.

The problem was that Ardov, while no genius, wasn't actually stupid. He could project my movements as well as I could project his. More significantly, it had looked like he was coming to tear off my head, but I realized, an instant too late, that he wanted, instead, to tear out my heart. He was going after Tamret.

There was no point in her running. She knew that she couldn't outpace him, so she turned and fired her gun into his face. The blast did nothing, but the light distracted him, just for an instant. It was the only advantage I would get, so I took it.

I grabbed him and leaped up into the air, moving like a rocket. I smashed his head into the ceiling, which erupted in a burst of dust and wood and metal.

He was, I realized, stuck. While he tried to pull himself out without separating his own head from his body, I hovered in the air, slamming his torso with punches that I delivered with lightning speed. This might seem like poor sportsmanship, but the guy had just tried to kill my maybe ex-girlfriend, and I was in no mood to play nice.

Ardov managed to wiggle free, and he tumbled to the ground with chunks of ceiling falling after him. Dust clung to the fur on his face.

Maybe he had not figured out how to fly yet. He had the same abilities I did, but he still had to explore them and discover what they were. I'd had more time to tinker. This was not an advantage I was going to squander. I turned around and, with one fist extended in the classic Superman pose, I sped toward him like a rocket. He leaped out of the way in time to avoid the impact, but I was still able to grab him by his shirt. I spun rapidly, twirling like a discus thrower, and tossed him across the hangar so he landed hard against the wall. The wall dented but did not break.

I used the momentary lull to look around. I didn't see any of the others. That was good. If I didn't see them, then Ardov didn't. I was going to scan for life signs, but I held off. Maybe he didn't know how to do that yet either, but he might be able to detect what I was doing. I didn't want to teach him any new tricks—especially now that he seemed to have picked up on flying. I realized this because he was zipping through the air, coming directly toward me.

"I'm going to make you watch me kill them!" he screamed, his face twisted with rage.

I waited until the last second and super-sped out of the way. Ardov tried to stop, but he ended up colliding with the hull of a shuttle. I knew from my own experiences that the Former tech didn't dull the pain of a blow like that, but it made it easier to deal with, like you could put it in a box and forget about it until later. Pain aside, a blunder like that was humiliating, and I could see that Ardov was taking it kind of hard.

"That was fun," I said. "Let's do that a couple more times before your bad die roll kills you."

He howled and came at me again. This time I went low, under his reach, and rolled like a ball into his legs. He toppled like a bowling pin. I grabbed his ankle, leaped into the air, and spun until we must have looked like a whirling propeller. I let him go, and he crashed into the wall again. This time he did go through it.

"I could do this all day!" I shouted. "Up until you're dead, I mean. Tossing your corpse around won't be as much fun."

By the time I finished speaking, he was back and almost upon me, moving through the air like a missile. I tried dodging left, but he anticipated me this time, and he pulled me up by the arm.

Even with the tech repairing damage almost the instant it was inflicted, the pain was incredible. It shot up my arm and through my whole body. I hardly had time to call out, because he was tossing me against the wall. I hit with a solid impact, and everything went white and hot for an instant before the nanites dulled the pain and restored the damaged tissue.

No serious harm done, but it was a lot more fun being on the other side of the toss.

Ardov was on me again, lifting me up and hurling me back into the center of the hangar. I landed with a heavy thud, and I had hardly lifted my head off the floor when he came at me and punched me in the face. My head knocked against the hard floor and bounced up back into his fist. He hit me again.

This was bad. The punches were coming fast—too fast for the fraction of a second my nanites needed to compensate for injury and pain. It was like in a video game where you corner an enemy into a wedge in the landscape and you keep hitting or shooting him each time he tries to make a move. I was in a feedback loop, and I could not get out.

"If I'm going to die, you're going to die first!" he shouted as he punched me. My head kept hitting the floor. It felt like my face was turning into a hot mash. My arms and legs twitched, and I couldn't control them.

Everything started to recede. Maybe I was losing consciousness. Maybe the nanites were tinkering with my brain so the pain wouldn't make me black out, but the world felt like it was floating away. It was almost like falling asleep, but with a lot more face-pummeling.

This was really it. Ardov was going to kill me, and even if one of the others had been willing to use the powder to save the Confederation from the Phands, they would never be able to because I hadn't told them about it. In losing to Ardov, I had just lost the war.

I needed to find a way to turn this around, but I couldn't. It was like my body didn't belong to me anymore. I was this passive thing that watched through a red haze as Ardov's furry fist cocked back and then came at me again and again. It was an endless repetitive motion, like a mechanical piston, firing away, destroying me. And it continued until something big and metal hit Ardov in the side and he went flying off of me.

I looked up to see a shuttle now parked inches from where I lay. Steve had to be piloting it. He'd hit Ardov with a shuttle.

Arms were grabbing me. I couldn't see who it was—my vision was too foggy—but the arms weren't hitting me, so I was going to assume they were friendly. I was set down somewhere, and there was a vague sensation of movement. I heard gasping. It was Alice, maybe, and from somewhere far away I heard Tamret telling someone to shut up. And then I passed out.

When I came to, my HUD's chronometer informed me that I had been unconscious for eighty-seven seconds so that my body could perform some necessary maintenance. That felt like an understatement. The nanites had put those eighty-seven seconds to good use though, because I could see now, and it seemed like we were on a small Phandic ship—probably another long-range shuttle. I did not feel great by any reasonable standard, but I was feeling a lot better than I had been when Ardov was beating me into oblivion.

"Hey," I heard Mi Sun say, "his face grew back."

"It is an improvement over the pulp," said Charles, turning around from his position at the navigation console, "if not a major one."

Tamret was hugging me. "You looked awful. You looked like you shouldn't even be alive."

"I felt like that," I said, trying not to think about the fact that Tamret seemed no longer to be angry with me. "But I'm okay now. Where are we?"

"There are orbital patrols," Steve said from the helm station, "so I'm flying in atmosphere until Charles can calculate a safe path. Once he figures out a blind spot, we're going to make a run for it."

Tamret was still hugging me, and I wasn't complaining. I had almost died out there. I had almost lost everything, and I would have if these guys hadn't saved me. Steve had hit a bad guy with a space bus. That seemed like the height of friendship.

Then an alarm went off.

"We are experiencing hull degradation," Charles said.

"What could cause that?" Alice asked.

"I have no idea," Charles said. "I am putting it on the monitor."

I'm not really all that good with the technical stuff, but I could see at once what the problem was. Ardov was on the top of the shuttle, holding a drill of some kind, trying to burn his way through the hull.

"We have perhaps seven minutes until he breaches," Charles explained, "but only ninety seconds until he does enough damage to make the ship unsafe for space travel."

I pushed myself to my feet. I felt a little light-headed, but almost as soon as I put a hand to the bulkhead to steady myself, I started feeling better. Now that I was no longer being beaten mercilessly, I was getting stronger by the second. "I'm going out there. I'll get rid of him." I might not have been at maximum capacity yet, but I was close, and someone had to stop Ardov.

"Relax, mate," Steve said casually, as though having a guy on your hull with a drill was no big deal. "You don't have to do everything. Just sit down, and everyone buckle up."

We did as he said, and then as soon as we were ready, Steve simply rotated the shuttle. Ardov looked up, startled. He made a sudden effort to hold on, but he didn't react quickly enough and simply fell off like a bean tipped out of a can. He fell toward the sea, still holding his drill. We watched in fascination and horror as he plummeted, limbs flailing.

Why wasn't he flying? Had I hurt him too much in our fight? Was he too disoriented? Too distracted by his belief that I had doomed him with a bad saving throw? I kept expecting him to halt himself in the air and zip back toward us, but he didn't. He fell.

I wanted to turn away—I didn't want to see the impact— and yet I could not stop watching. I saw that, in the last instant, he seemed to stop struggling and relaxed, as though accepting his fate. Then there was a sudden gust of sea spray as a giant eel exploded out from the surface, its great jaws open. It let Ardov land softly against its massive yellow tongue, with barely a bounce, like he'd landed on a pillow. The eel then snapped its mouth shut and disappeared beneath the waves.

We all remained silent for a moment.

"I am attempting to think how this might qualify as poetic justice," Charles said quietly, "but I can come up with nothing."

"No poetry required," Steve said. "He was a bad bloke, and now he's eel food. Sometimes literal is best."

No one else said anything. There was nothing left to say. I'd wanted Ardov out of my way, but not dead. Not that I questioned what Steve had done. He'd saved the ship, which meant he saved us. Maybe, in doing so, he'd saved the Confederation. I supposed Colonel Rage would say that this was war, and in war you have to do terrible things in order to stop worse things. Ardov had put us in the position of having to drop him into the ocean, but I knew this would haunt me later. I just hoped there would be a later in which to be haunted.

A moment later Charles quietly told us that he had calculated our escape vector. We departed Planet Pleasant and tunneled toward the prison facility where we would, finally, rescue Ghli Wixxix and, I hoped, put everything right.

CHAPTER SIXTEEN

t would take a little more than a standard day to reach the prison facility. When we got there, I was going to have to take another dose of the powder, and I wasn't looking forward to rolling the die again. I also wasn't looking forward to powering up again. The beating I'd taken from Ardov may have done no permanent damage, but it left me feeling a whole lot less invulnerable than I'd thought I was. Maybe that was a good thing. I would be more cautious, less likely to make a careless mistake. Still, I couldn't get the sensation out of my head—powerless, unable to move in spite of all those augments, while Ardov pounded on me.

Everyone wanted to know how Villainic and I had avoided getting captured. They also wanted to know how I had managed to revive my power. I assured them I had no idea why my HUD had turned back on and why it had, since we left Planet Pleasant, turned off again. As for why we weren't on the ship when it was taken, I left it to Villainic to tell the story. I was genuinely exhausted after my ordeal, and I needed to sleep so I could recharge. I also had a lot to think about.

There was a small room with a bunk in the back of the shuttle. I closed the door behind me and lay down. I felt sure I would be lying there for hours, my worries competing with one another for my attention, but the moment I closed my eyes, I was out. My body must have needed sleep more than I needed to dwell on every single thing that worried me.

I awoke because someone was hitting my arm. "Wake up. You're a liar."

It was Tamret, She was sitting on the side of my bed, looking angry. She was wearing the same practical clothes she'd had on since our expedition to the Hidden Fortress, and they weren't holding up so well. Her pants were tattered at the cuffs; her shirt was wrinkled and stained and stretched at the collar. Her hair was unkempt and in need of a washing, and even her short fur was ruffled in places. Heavy bags hung under her bloodshot eyes. She looked like she hadn't slept in days, and she probably hadn't, but she was still the prettiest girl I'd ever seen.

"Let me sleep," I said. "I think my body is about to shut down."

"You can shut down when I'm done talking to you. I know when you're not telling the truth, and I know you were lying about not knowing how you got your powers back. Maybe you don't want the others to know, but you can tell me."

She was wrong about that. Of all the people on the ship I didn't want to tell, she was number one on the list. Tamret was the most likely to use the powder and not care about the consequences. She was the most likely to think she could outsmart or outmaneuver quantum entanglement, but even she couldn't rewrite the laws of reality.

Of course I didn't want to tell her what was going on, but it's also very tricky to lie to someone when they've just told you they know when you're lying. My limited ability to keep my face neutral was now completely compromised.

I must have gone too long without saying anything, because her eyes narrowed and her ears rotated back, a sure sign she was thinking through something. "Everyone sort of forgot about it because of how intense stuff got afterward, but what was the deal with Ardov and that thing he tossed in the air?"

Leave it to Tamret to get to the heart of the matter. I couldn't tell her what I knew about the twenty-sided die without explaining how I knew it, so I just shook my head. "I need to get some sleep. We can talk about it later." Delay seemed to me my best bet. If I could keep her from finding out until after the danger was over, there was a decent chance she would never use the powder.

I started to lie down again, but she grabbed my arm and pulled me back up. "No way. You're in some kind of trouble."

I turned away from her. "What do you care?" I asked. "You're going back to Rarel with Villainic."

"I'm not going to Ish-hi with Steve, and he isn't mad at me."

"That's different," I said. "*We're* different. I thought we were, anyhow."

She raised a hand to touch my shoulder, but then pulled it back. "You need to grow up, Zeke. We're supposed to be part of a team. We're supposed to be friends. It's . . . it's sweet, I guess, that you wanted me to come to Earth with you, but that isn't going to happen, so we need to move on."

I hated how I was acting, and I knew I needed to snap myself out of it. I thought Tamret was insane for wanting to go back to Rarel, and I hated that she didn't want to stay with me. I understood that if Rarel joined the Confederation, things would change there. She would want to help guide her world's process. It was admirable, but it still hurt. I couldn't let her see it, though. More importantly, I couldn't let her know the truth about how I'd gotten my Former upgrades to work again.

"You're right," I told her. "I'm sorry if I'm being difficult. I need more time to heal. We'll talk later."

"That's fine. I'll leave you alone. As soon as you tell me what you did to Ardov. I know you, so don't think I haven't figured out you're keeping secrets to protect me."

"Tamret," I began, but I had no idea where to go.

"I can't believe you would treat me that way. I'm not some fragile thing you need to hide away. I'm not going to shatter if I hear something I don't like."

"Tamret, believe me. I know you're not fragile."

"I can handle whatever you have to tell me."

"I know you can," I said. And then for good measure I added, "I don't have anything to tell you, though."

I was getting backed into a corner now, and with her sitting next to me, staring at me, it was becoming increasingly hard not to tell her what was going on.

"Look at me," she said, "and tell me if you know how to activate the Former tech."

This was now impossible. I wasn't going to be able to convince her if I lied to her face, and saying nothing wasn't going to get me anywhere. Telling everyone I didn't know why I had been reactivated had been a mistake. I should have told a better lie—maybe that there had been something back at the facility that had switched things on, something we no longer had. Now it was too late.

"If there is something you don't want me to know," she said in a quiet voice, "you can just tell me that. I trust you, Zeke, but you have to trust me too."

"There's something I don't want you to know," I told her. "And it's not about trusting you. I know you think you can handle anything, and maybe you can, but I just need to know you're safe so I can do the things I have to do."

"Are you in danger?" she asked me.

"What kind of question is that? We're in the middle of a fight between an evil empire and a really, really small rebellion. I'd say that counts as dangerous."

She nodded. "Does keeping your secret make you safer?"

"Yeah," I said. "I think it does." Maybe having more people by my side with abilities would be an advantage, but worrying about Tamret would distract me. I felt pretty sure that I was not actually lying to her.

She took a moment to consider this, and then her face set, like she'd made a decision. "Then I'll trust you."

"If everything goes well, this will all be over soon, and in a good way."

She stood up and opened the door. "Yeah," she said. "But when has everything ever gone well?"

The nanites working inside me must have given me a sedative, because I fell asleep almost as soon as she left. I woke up a few hours later, feeling a little bruised and still tired, but it was nothing I couldn't handle. I went out to join the others, who were also in various stages of sleepiness.

Dr. Roop immediately grabbed me and took me aside. I thought he was also going to interrogate me about my abilities, but he had something else on his mind. "Villainic told me about your time with the renegades."

"Yeah," I said, looking up at his face. I still felt tired from all the repair work my body had been undergoing, and straining my head to get past his long neck was giving me a cramp.

"I never knew there was a Phandic resistance."

"There has been for a long time," he said, "but our best information suggested that they were largely ineffectual. Phandic culture promotes strict conformity, so the resistance has tended to attract dreamers and misfits. They have always been most earnest, but they rarely accomplished very much. From what Villainic tells me, they have not much changed, but in sending you to Planet Pleasant, they may have saved all of us."

"I was just desperate for them to abandon their plan A."

"Which was what?" he asked.

"Villainic didn't mention that part?"

"No."

I shook my head. That was just like him. Maybe he'd been daydreaming when the renegades were discussing destroying one of the greatest cities in the history of everything. "They were going to destroy Confederation Central," I explained. "They still are if we can't get Ghli Wixxix out and back in charge within the next ten days. Maybe nine now. They have this idea that Junup's corruption runs so deep that there's no other way to get rid of his influence."

Dr. Roop took a moment to think about this news. "Can they do it?"

"They have the station schematics," I said. "They definitely believe they can."

He shook his head. "They understand little about Confederation politics," Dr. Roop said. "Junup has been very successful at deceiving a large number of beings, but he has few genuine allies—those who know his true goals. Destroying Confederation Central may ultimately produce the results they desire, but it is rather like destroying an insect with a dark-matter bomb."

"They seemed to feel that in a thousand years, it would all even out."

"I prefer to work with a shorter timetable. We will have to make sure we can rescue Ghli Wixxix; then we will have done all we wished to do, and with a minimal loss of life. Otherwise . . ."

"Otherwise what?" I asked.

"We will have to warn Junup of the attack, and you'll have to send a complete briefing of all you know about it."

I felt a sharp pain, which I realized was me biting my lower lip. Betray the renegades to Junup? It was crazy, but then so was letting the renegades destroy Confederation Central. I decided it wasn't worth thinking about. We were going to make our plan work so I wouldn't have to make a choice between two horrible things.

"There's something else," I said quietly. Maybe I just wanted to change the subject. "I understand why Steve shook Ardov off the shuttle: We didn't have a lot of time or a lot of options, and it was us or him. I know sometimes we have to do things we don't want to, but Villainic killed a couple of guards at Planet Pleasant when it was totally unnecessary. He could have stunned them, but he seemed to think killing them was a better idea."

Dr. Roop rubbed at his horns. He looked genuinely worried. He also looked tired. None of us were at our best. "Soon enough Villainic will not be our problem, and with any luck, he won't be in such a situation again anytime soon."

"I'm just saying that he has a dark streak that took me by surprise. I think he's got more going on in his head than he lets on."

"I hope never to find out," Dr. Roop said. "But as your experiences with the Phand renegades have shown you, not all cultures share our values. One of the goals of the Confederation is to spread our philosophy of tolerance and the preservation of life. Those Phands you met, and Villainic, prefer to find the most expedient way to achieve their goal. I think that the means must count as much as the end."

I agreed with him, which is why I said nothing about the powder and the die in my pocket.

"Tamret is planning on going back to Rarel," I said. "With Villainic."

"I know," Dr. Roop said quietly. "Her time on Earth did not present the most welcoming impression of your people."

"Do you think that's why? Is this about what Nora Price did to her?"

"Tamret has also experienced the worst of her own culture, but there are many wonderful things about Rarel and its inhabitants," Dr. Roop said. "She knows that too. I believe Rarel will be given another opportunity to join the Confederation, but joining is only the first step in the process, and there is no one better than Tamret to help her world succeed as it tries to move toward full membership. A being who has lived as she has, suffered as she has, will want to make sure that it is the good that triumphs over the bad."

"That's why you think she's going back?"

Dr. Roop stood up. "It may be that she has chosen her world over her attachment to you. If so, it must have been a difficult decision. Friendship is important, of course—look what you and your friends have accomplished together—but loyalty to one's world is also a virtue. Her choice may be painful for you, but I suspect it must be equally painful to her, and very likely, she would benefit from your support."

"Maybe I have been selfish," I agreed. "You're right that I should encourage her if she's trying to do the right thing for her world, but what if that's not the real reason?"

"I think Tamret is the most loyal being I've ever met, and if you want to understand anything she does, you have to figure out who she is trying to help."

Three hours later, Steve announced that we were ready to come out of our tunnel. We had no idea what to expect, but we were far enough from the planet that housed the prison to believe that we would be able to make our initial approach unnoticed. From there, I had no idea what the others had in mind. We were only ordinary people now. I was planning on taking the powder once we learned as much as we could about the prison below, but I had no idea how I was going to do that without revealing everything.

I might have to confess the truth if we were going to get Ghli Wixxix, Captain Hyi, Urch, and Nayana out of that prison. The only way I could think of telling the truth, while keeping my friends from risking death, would be to flush the powder out an airlock after taking it and before telling them. That meant that whatever we did would have to work, because it would be my last chance to use my Former skills. If I rolled a three or lower, it would be my last chance anyhow.

I hoped I might have a decent amount of time before having to do all of this, though. The clock was ticking with the Phandic renegades and their ridiculous plan to destroy Confederation Central, but I hoped we could take the better part of a day, at least, to learn more about the prison. That seemed like a safe bet.

It was a losing bet, though. The moment we emerged from tunnel, ships were firing on us.

Steve punched in some immediate evasive maneuvers, and we were thrown hard against the side of the ship.

I felt my shoulder slam against the bulkhead, but I ignored the pain, which was very real. Any injuries I sustained I'd have to heal the old-fashioned way, given that my upgrades were now a memory.

Steve banked hard again, too fast for the artificial gravity to compensate, and I was thrown in the other direction. A deep rumble told me we'd just been hit by something—more likely grazed, since we weren't spiraling chaotically or exploding. Still, our ship was little, and any damage was likely to be bad news.

There was another quick turn, and I threw up my hands in time to prevent myself from slamming headfirst into the bulkhead. Then, in a moment of relative stability, I scrambled up and pushed myself over to the weapons controls. No one had to suggest it. We'd been through this enough times that I knew how it went.

I checked my readout to see how bad things were. Things, as it turned out, were bad. There were four Phandic cruisers in our vicinity, all of them firing weapons. They were making no effort to communicate. These ships wanted to destroy us—not stop or capture or interrogate. They wanted us dead.

I thought about the powder and the die in my pocket. I could try to augment my abilities, but I wasn't sure it would do me much good. I was limited by the speed and power of the shuttle itself. Any advantage I might gain in increased reflexes would be lost by the time I took to ingest the powder and roll the die.

I fired a few PPB bursts at a passing saucer. They were direct hits, but we were no match for their defensive capabilities. We were a simple long-range shuttle up against four death machines. We were not going to win this battle. We were not even going to survive it. Our only chance was to get out of here, and I had no doubt that Steve and Tamret were working on that.

"Can you do that quick-reverse thing again?" I asked Steve.

"We've taken some engine damage," he grumbled. "I can't get the readings I need to execute."

So a quick and easy escape was not in the cards. We were going to have to get through this the old-fashioned way—with space weapons. I checked our armaments, hoping we had something more powerful than PPB cannons. There were no dark-matter missiles, but there was something simply marked CLASSIFIED. Planet Pleasant was, after all, an experimental research facility. It was entirely possible that this shuttle was fitted with a cruiser-busting prototype. On the other hand, it could be the latest and most advanced model of self-destruct features. There was no way of knowing.

Steve took us into a steep dive, and I felt like my stomach was squeezing itself out of my nose as his evasive maneuvers pushed the artificial gravity to its limits. He'd managed to dodge a killing blow, but the PPB grazed one of our engines, and I felt the ship lurch out of control.

"I'm losing navigation," Tamret said, punching furiously at the console. "I can't even begin plotting a tunnel until the nav system reboots. Six minutes." Her voice was hollow. We all knew that Steve was good, but even he couldn't dodge weapons from four different saucers for six minutes.

"There's a hidden weapon on board," I told Tamret. "If you can unlock it, maybe it will save us."

"Or maybe it will kill us," Mi Sun said.

"That is a real possibility," I agreed. "But those four ships out there will kill us for sure if we don't pull a rabbit out of our hat."

Tamret nodded and began working to decrypt the secret weapon. Meanwhile Steve did his best to avoid more blows, but we still took a few hits. I fired off our weapons as best I could, but we were barely even scratching them. As near as I could tell, they weren't even trying to avoid our fire. We were a mosquito fighting a bear. We might get a few stings in, but sooner or later we were going to get squashed.

I kept looking over at Mi Sun, who was working the communications station. Surely they were going to call on us to surrender. I didn't much like the sound of that, but we had escaped from enough tight spots to think of it as a reasonable option. If they would stop shooting at us, I could take the powder and hope for the best. That was a situation I could deal with. But Mi Sun sat staring at nothing. No one seemed interested in asking for our surrender.

Then two things happened simultaneously. "I've got it!" Tamret shouted. "It's some kind of shield-buster. This looks like just what we need."

The other thing was that we took a direct hit that knocked out all remaining propulsion systems.

Losing the navigation had been bad. Losing altitude control was catastrophic. The ship careened through space, knocking us around the insides like popcorn inside a popper. I was strapped to my chair, as were Steve, Tamret, and Mi Sun, but the others were getting hit hard. I lost all ability to lock on with my weapons. If I had taken the powder when it had first occurred to me, I might have been able to fire the superweapon even under those circumstances. Now I couldn't even get my fingers to hit the right buttons. I'd made the wrong call, and now we were all going to die.

Somehow, miraculously, Steve righted the ship. "I'm holding everything together with temporary plasma clamps," he told me, "but they're not going to last long. Power is low. If you've got something to fight back with, do it now."

I wasted no time. I accessed the secret weapon, hoping that it would somehow be enough to slow them down, and I tried to establish a hold on the nearest cruiser. I got a perfect lock and fired.

Nothing happened.

A weapons-malfunction message was flashing across my console. The text was advising me to check the operations manual, but we weren't going to live long enough to even find an operations manual. With nothing else to do, I fired a volley of PPB bursts, hoping to slow the attacking ship down. I watched, expecting the five shots to bounce off like they were completely harmless. One. Two. Three. Four.

The fifth one caused a massive explosion along the side of the saucer. Flames spewed out of a gash in its side as oxygen gushed into space. An instant later the flames were gone as emergency plasma shields sealed the leak, but the saucer was wobbling through the void. It was out of commission.

I checked my readings. I had no idea how I'd done that. A more powerful PPB against a weaker ship, hit in just the right circumstances, might cause a noticeable amount of damage, but a crippling blow like that? Impossible.

I looked over my screen, trying to figure out why those blasts had been so effective. The shield busting tech hadn't deployed, so why had we been able to damage that ship? Was it some sort of experimental PPB? Had I somehow hit a dark-matter missile just as it was launching? It would have been like hitting a bullet with another bullet—it could theoretically happen but I doubted we would be that lucky. It had to be something else.

While I frantically reviewed the data, another of the Phandic cruisers took a hit. A blast of energy hit it from below and burst through topside, spewing flame and debris. The ship, a second before illuminated with thousands of lights, went dark. It had suffered a complete power loss, and I hadn't even fired at it.

Slow though I was, I now understood at least the basics of what had to be going on. There was another player involved, and if it wasn't working with us, it was at least working against our enemies.

While I stumbled to my feet, Mi Sun pulled up an image for our viewscreen. A rectangular Confederation ship was now rearing up behind us, firing at the two remaining cruisers, both of which were withdrawing rapidly.

A second later Mi Sun announced that we had an incoming transmission. An image came up on the screen from the inside of the Confederation ship's bridge.

"You look like you could use some assistance," Captain Qwlessl said, her massive, protruding eyes sparkling with delight. She raised her trunk and pointed toward us. She was one of the first aliens I'd ever met, and she was still one of the strangest-looking beings by Earth standards, but I didn't know that I'd ever been happier to see anyone's face. Captain Qwlessl showing up under any circumstances was good news—in an emergency it was great news.

"Your timing could have been better," Dr. Roop said, looking very pleased. "But it could hardly have been more dramatic."

"We've had some delays," Captain Qwlessl said, "and things have been quite dangerous, but everything is now under control. In fact, we were escaping the system when we picked up your fight and had to backtrack to get you. You tunneled in directly in front of our pursuers."

"What are you even doing here?" I asked.

"I guess you didn't get our comm beacon," she said, "so you don't know that this part of the plan is no longer necessary. We received some intelligence that prompted us to act immediately, so we were not able to meet you at the agreed rendezvous."

"I don't understand," Dr. Roop said.

"One moment," said the captain. "Some friends want to say hello."

Nayana and Urch stepped into the image.

It's hard to describe what it was like to see them, safe on the bridge of Captain Qwlessl's ship. They looked unharmed and happy—at least Nayana looked happy. It was hard to tell with Urch's warthog alien face, though his mouth was open in a way I thought might be a smile.

They had been with me on the *Kind Disposition*, and when it was destroyed, I was sure they were dead. Then I'd learned they were actually being held prisoner, and while that's certainly an improvement over *dead*, it was no reason to celebrate. Since then, all my energy had been directed toward breaking them and the other prisoners free. Now there they were. The enormity of what it meant washed over me, and I had to grab on to the back of a chair to keep my still-wobbly legs from buckling.

"Zeke, I'm very cross with you," Nayana announced. "I told you this trip was not going to be safe." She looked a little thin, and like everyone else around me she probably hadn't been getting much sleep, but otherwise she looked fine.

"You were right," I told her, feeling myself choke up a little.

"I always am."

"It's good to see you, Nayana," I managed.

"I imagine it is."

"Captain Qwlessl," I managed, "if you have them, does that mean you have the others?"

The captain nodded at someone and the image broadened. Also on the bridge were Captain Hyi and Ghli Wixxix. The rescue had been successful. Captain Qwlessl had gone in with a Phand-crushing battleship and yanked out the director by force. We now had exactly what we wanted. We were going to topple Junup, save the Confederation, and liberate Earth. It really was all over. I would not have to take the powder and roll the die again. I could stop feeling like the lives of millions rested on my actions.

The good guys had won.

"We're going to lance you in, and then we shall return to Confederation Central," Captain Qwlessl said. She must have understood the look on my face because she added, "I believe about ten minutes after we arrive, this conflict will be resolved."

CHAPTER SEVENTEEN

Y ou're disappointed that you don't have to do anything, aren't you?"

We were sitting in one of the crew recreational lounges, finally wearing clean clothes—Confederation styles, but the almost chino pants and long-sleeved almost T-shirts might not have looked too out of place in a big Earth city. I'd transferred my die and powder to my new pockets. I was also still holding on to Villainic's stun grenade, which I now thought of as good luck, though it might just as easily have been bad luck. I decided to go for the optimistic interpretation. After all, we were enjoying an extended period of time with no one trying to experiment on us, lock us up, or generally make us dead.

That was just the beginning of the good news, though. We were all together and we were all safe. Sure, a bunch of Phands could try to attack us, but from what I'd seen of this ship, we didn't have much to worry about. Captain Qwlessl had stopped four Phandic cruisers in their tracks. Nothing short of an armada could take us on.

Our enemies could, I supposed, be putting together an armada at this very moment, but right now there were no signs of that. It would have taken an effort to remember the last time my life had been this stress-free. I sat with a glass of alien soda in my hand, talking with my friends. I was even happy to be talking to Nayana—maybe especially happy. I didn't care if she was criticizing me. What was a little teasing when compared to safety, cleanliness, and alien soda?

"Admit it, Zeke," she said. "You've reached the point where you cannot imagine a major event unfolding on the galactic stage unless you have a hand in it." Nayana still looked a little frail to me, but already less drawn than when I'd seen her over the viewscreen. Back when we'd first met, she'd had the radiant self-assurance of a Bollywood star, and while her appearance hadn't changed much, she seemed somehow less confident, less certain the world would automatically bend to her whims.

That didn't stop her from giving me a hard time.

"He *did* have a hand in just about everything," Tamret said. "You missed a lot after you let yourself get captured."

"Yes, I heard about all that silliness," she said, dismissing our last stay on Confederation Central, and the hunt for the Hidden Fortress, with a wave of her hand. "And that is part of what I mean. I am not being critical, you understand. I don't deny that you've participated in certain aspects of recent galactic events. That is why I think being put on the sidelines must be challenging for you."

If I had to be completely honest, I'd admit she wasn't entirely wrong. After everything we'd been through, having a bunch of adults show up and simply announce that things were now under control was a little disappointing—like someone had gone back on a promise. I didn't feel left out so much as I felt like the rules had suddenly changed without warning. I had thought there would be no choice but to risk death, yet again, by rolling the twenty-sided die and then going down to some supermax Phandic prison to rescue, among other people, the one being who could bring the Phandic empress to her knees.

I wasn't disappointed that I'd been spared having to go on that mission; I was relieved, and that relief made me feel guilty, like I was trying to get out of something that was my responsibility.

Fortunately, no one said I had to be completely honest, so I felt free to admit nothing. Besides, I knew the situation was in good hands. These weren't just any adults who were now in charge. It was Dr. Roop and Captain Qwlessl—with Urch backing them up. Plus there was Director Ghli Wixxix, who had once crossed the galaxy to ask for my help, and whom I had crossed the galaxy to rescue. The fact that I hadn't needed to rescue her, or do anything else, was okay by me. Kids doing nothing while adults took care of a crisis—that was the way it was *supposed* to be.

I couldn't shake that feeling of waiting for the other shoe to drop, though. I told myself there would be no other shoe. There were no more shoes left. The shoe supply was depleted, and the galaxy was unshod. I just wished I could really believe it.

There was also the fact that I wanted one more chance to show Tamret what I could do. If I were busy Hulking my way through an enemy prison, rescuing our friends and prisoners of cosmic significance, I wouldn't have to think about how she'd chosen her world over staying with me.

"I'm with Zeke on this one," Steve said. He was drinking a glass of water in which dozens of little fish were swimming. He took a sip, chewed for a bit, and set the glass down. "I want to be doing something. This sitting about on our bottoms is for tossers."

"I never said that," I told him.

"You didn't have to, mate. I understand."

"Count me in," Tamret said.

Alice, who had been sitting with her legs folded under her, now stretched out and looked excited. "Awesome. The sooner we get everything on track, the sooner we can all go home. What's the plan?"

"There is no plan," I told them. "We're with the good guys, and they're doing good-guy things. All they have to do is get to Confederation Central and tell everyone Ghli Wixxix is alive and Junup destroyed the *Kind Disposition* while trying to kill her. No fighting or breaking in or out of places. We can trust them to handle this."

"You sure about that, mate?" Steve asked. "They haven't been so keen on talking to us since we came on board, have they?"

"There's plenty we don't know," Tamret agreed. "Why didn't Captain Qwlessl meet us when she was supposed to? Why did she decide to rescue the prisoners herself?"

These were good questions, but so far there had been no answers. We had been welcomed aboard and given the run of the ship, but when I'd told Captain Qwlessl and Director Ghli Wixxix I wanted to let them know everything we had experienced, they had dismissed me. They hadn't been unkind, but they had seemed busy and distracted, and after all I'd done, I didn't like being treated as though I were an annoying kid trying to pretend he belonged with the grown-ups.

Still, I knew they had things to do, and while the information I had was useful, it wasn't vital to the next phase of the mission. The fact that a bunch of rebel Phands wanted to destroy Confederation Central in order to get rid of Junup wouldn't matter if we got rid of Junup first. It was only going to become important if we couldn't expose Junup, and if that happened, there would be a lot of other bad things going on.

"I am rather surprised they do not wish to hear our after-action report," Charles said.

"And so, to show our displeasure, you think we should mutiny against Captain Qwlessl?" Nayana asked. "Do I understand you correctly?"

"If necessary." Steve nodded thoughtfully. "I'd love to see how something this big handles. And Zeke here wants a go at those weapons."

I sighed. I knew they were kidding, mostly. "We're just going to have to live with being civilians. At least for a little while."

They all knew what I meant. When this was over, and we returned to our homes, nothing would be the same. Everyone would now know about alien life, but almost everyone on Earth who had real experience with galactic culture was sitting in the lounge on board this ship. The chances were good that we were all going to be asked to play our part as our worlds adjusted to being part of a wider galactic culture.

Just then our data bracelets pinged us. Captain Qwlessl and Director Ghli Wixxix wanted us in a briefing in half an hour. "Looks like we're back in the inner circle," I said.

"I'll table the plan for taking over the ship," Steve said. "For now."

Before I could respond, a second message came through on my bracelet. Dr. Roop wanted to talk to me privately before that meeting. He asked me to meet him immediately in the conference room.

He didn't say to keep it a secret, so I told the others where I was going.

"I'll go with you," Tamret said.

"We'll all go," Steve said.

"Then it isn't really a private meeting," I told them, trying to avoid looking guilty. I knew what Dr. Roop wanted. He wanted to know about my Former abilities and the die. He was too smart not to have figured out that something was up, and I was surprised he hadn't asked me before. Maybe he'd been getting questions from Captain Qwlessl and the others, and now he wanted to know if he needed to cover for me. "I'll let you guys know if he has anything interesting to say."

"You sure?" Steve asked guardedly.

"We're talking about Dr. Roop," I said.

Steve didn't respond. Did being benched make him suspect even Dr. Roop of being up to no good? He was the one adult I was always going to trust, and the truth was, I was happy to be able to tell him about the powder and the die. Maybe he could use the information as a starting point to figure out how to get our abilities back.

"He'll be fine," Tamret said. "I'll be there to protect him."

"What about it being a private meeting?" Alice asked.

"I'm sure he didn't mean to exclude me," she said.

Nayana rolled her eyes. "Dr. Roop is just being practical. He knows he can convince us to see reason, but Tamret is going to do what she wants no matter what anyone says."

"And don't forget it," she said with a smile.

"I don't have any secrets," I lied, "but I think it's probably better to do what Dr. Roop says. If there's anything important, I'll let you guys know."

Without waiting for a response, I left the room. I didn't dare turn back to see Tamret's expression.

I used my bracelet to guide me through the ship, which

was enough like other Confederation ships I'd been on to seem familiar, but different enough that I would get lost if I weren't paying close attention. When I reached the conference room, Dr. Roop was already seated, but he rose to greet me. He then closed the door, locked it, and activated a keyboard from his data bracelet. After about thirty seconds of typing, an electrical blue charge seemed to coat the walls. The effect lasted less than a second and then was gone. I didn't know for sure, but my guess was that Dr. Roop had just deployed some sort of antisurveillance technology.

"Who is it you don't trust?" I asked.

"Everyone," he said, his giraffelike face looking very serious. "I know I can count on you children, and Captain Qwlessl's loyalty is beyond question, but otherwise, I am not inclined to be trusting. We are discussing the most dangerous and volatile technology in the known galaxy."

"And why do you want to discuss that with me?" I asked, trying to sound like I had no idea, probably coming across as guilty.

"Zeke, only you were able to reactivate your Former abilities," he said. "I'd like you to brief me on what I don't know so I can decide how best to protect you and, possibly, all life within the galaxy."

"Why do you need to know suddenly?"

"If we had been poised to try to rescue the prisoners ourselves, you may feel quite confident that I would have asked you during a pre-mission briefing. Now there are larger, more political issues that I must contend with. I need to know precisely what happened."

His point was, beyond doubt, valid. Getting rid of Junup and shutting down the empress's ability to expand were great things, but if they only meant a brief delay while the Phands perfected the Former military technology, we'd have gained nothing.

I walked Dr. Roop through the major events following Villainic's jettison of the escape pod. I had already told him about the renegade Phands and their plan to destroy Confederation Central, but now I told them how they planned to do it. I was in the middle of describing one of the briefings when he stopped me.

"This Convex Icosahedron, who is he?"

"He seems to be their leader, but I don't know anything about his species. He was weird, though. I don't mean in personality, though that is definitely true. I mean I couldn't tell if he was alive or artificial. His head was a big geometric shape—with no face." I avoided likening him to a twenty-sided die because I was hoping to avoid that subject for as long as possible.

"He was one of the Geometric Upstarts," Dr. Roop said as if talking to himself.

This surprised me. "You've heard of them? What can you tell me about them?"

"They're not something you need to be concerned with," he assured me. "Please continue."

And I might have done so without giving the matter another thought if I hadn't felt that gentle buzz. Convex Icosahedron's lie detector had kicked in. Besides my parents, Dr. Roop was the adult I trusted most in the galaxy, and he had just lied to me.

I was grown up enough to know that this didn't need to be a big deal. After all, I'd just withheld information from Dr. Roop about the twenty-sided die, and that didn't make me evil—I hoped. Still, I was supposed to be able to trust him. I understood that maybe there were things he thought I shouldn't know about, but I wasn't some innocent bystander. I was pretty deeply involved in everything, I didn't like being boxed out.

"I kind of feel like you're holding something back," I said.

Dr. Roop rubbed his horns, as he did when he was anxious. "I don't know that we need to get into this now, Zeke. It's not pressing, and honestly, it's not my story to tell. Ask your father when this is all over."

No buzz from the Lasso of Truth, but that now seemed beside the point. "My father? What does this have to do with him?"

"I'll give you the short version," he said, "but that's it, because he needs to decide how much of this story to share. But in return, you tell me everything you are holding back."

I nodded. "Deal."

"You know that you were led to believe your father died in a vehicle accident, but of course you later learned that, in reality, he left Earth. Have you never wondered how he came to be on Confederation Central, and how, once there, he managed to rise to a position of such prominence?"

My father had promised to tell me all about it at some point, but since we'd been reunited, our conversations had tended to be brief and of the *I'm glad you're out of prison* and *Don't get killed doing what you're about to do* variety. The heart-to-heart had not yet happened.

"What do you know about it?" I asked.

"The car accident was real," said Dr. Roop. "Your father was critically injured, and for reasons we don't understand, he was rescued by one of the Geometric Upstarts, who happened to be on Earth at that time. I do not know why, but he was there, and he took an interest in your father. The Geometric Upstart duplicated your father's genetic material so that it would appear he died in the accident. He then took your father to Confederation Central. There the Geometric Upstart provided him with a new appearance and identity and put him on a course to advance in the world of politics."

"But why? Who was he, and why would he pick my father, of all the people on Earth, to take to the Confederation?"

"I don't know," Dr. Roop said. "I never got the full story. I'm not sure your father knows either, but I always believed he knew more than he told me."

"But you have a guess about what it all means."

"I have some unproved theories," Dr. Roop said. "Nothing more. Now, tell me about the Former tech."

I sighed. It was less information than I wanted, but Dr. Roop was right that it wasn't vital to the current crisis. Besides, my lie detector hadn't piped up, so I figured whatever else he knew, he would tell me when things settled down.

I went back to my story, and I told him about the scientist on Planet Pleasant, the powder, and the die.

"So you risked your life to fight Ardov."

"It was either risk my life or be certain of getting killed," I said. "It seemed like a reasonable decision at the time."

"I understand," Dr. Roop said. "Do you still have this die?"

I reached into my pocket and handed it to him.

He turned it over and looked at it from different angles. "Do you know what this shape is called?"

I nodded. "It's a convex icosahedron."

"Interesting, isn't it?"

"What are you saying?" I asked. "That this Geometric Upstart sent me to Planet Pleasant just so I would find an object that had his name? That makes no sense."

"There is a lot here that makes no sense," Dr. Roop said. He handed the die back to me. "When Junup is out of power and the Phands are once more contained, I hope you will let me run some tests on the die and the powder."

"Sure," I said. "Maybe you could figure out how to reactivate the Former tech."

"Possibly," he said, "but right now I don't think that's a good idea. There is a reason, I suspect, that the tech tree was lost for so many millennia. It is too dangerous, and hacking it creates beings of almost unimaginable power. I'm glad the technology is unstable, and I hope no one figures out how to repair it. In the meantime, the information about the powder and the die must be kept secret."

"Are you worried about something?"

"I am worried about almost everything," he said, "and I worry all the time. However, I don't see any reason that we need to worry about any of this until after we return Ghli Wixxix to her rightful place. Once we have restored the government of the Confederation, we can depend upon our best minds finding answers to all these questions."

We finished talking in time for Dr. Roop to turn off the antisurveillance tech and unlock the door, so we just looked like early arrivals when the others showed up. Even Villainic, who was rubbing his eyes like he'd just woken up from a nap, showed up for the meeting. Captain Qwlessl and Urch looked a little harried, but were very friendly when they came in. Urch slapped my shoulder and the captain gave me a hug even though she'd just seen me the day before.

"I've been very busy getting this ship in order," she told me, "so I'm sorry if you feel neglected, but it is wonderful to have you on board. All of you."

"I know what you planned to do for me," said Ghli Wixxix, "and for the Confederation, and I am very grateful." I hadn't seen her since her rescue, and I was glad that she was looking healthy. At least she was as far as I could tell. I'd never seen any other beings of her species. The Confederation director was small and blue and eyeless, though that didn't stop her from getting around. I presumed she navigated by way of sound, through her big batlike ears. Or possibly through scent, or some other sense, picked up by her nasal slits or the many small waving tendrils just below her forehead.

I felt an almost uncontrollable gratitude toward her. Yes, I would not have experienced all the danger of the past week if Ghli Wixxix hadn't come to Earth, looking to recruit me for her mission to the Hidden Fortress. On the other hand, she'd risked a lot to trust me, and she'd paid for that risk with the loss of her ship and the time she'd spent in a Phandic prison. If she hadn't trusted me and wanted my help, Tamret would still be stuck on Rarel, engaged to Villainic. I would have been stuck on Earth. None of us would have had another chance at joining the Confederation.

She stuck out one of her small blue hands for me to shake, Earth-style. "The Confederation owes you a debt, once again."

"Well, we didn't actually do anything," I said. "I mean, I would have done my best to rescue you, but we never had the chance. My mom would say we were a day late and a dollar short."

Steve cast me a knowing look. "Mainly because we were stood up on our way to the party, yeah?"

"I apologize for that," Captain Qwlessl said. "You have to understand that while we were willing to accept your help if we had no choice, we were uncomfortable asking a group of children—no matter how powerful—to attempt a prison break such as you had planned. We have been building our own contacts and insiders for years. While we were waiting for you, an opportunity to effect the rescue presented itself, and we took it. We left a coded communications beacon for you, but apparently you had your own troubles when you entered the system, and you never found it."

"Captain Qwlessl struck first," Urch said, "but I understand it was your plan, which Dr. Roop relayed to her. I consider us to be in your debt. I was going crazy in there. They kept the director separate from the rest of us, so I had no idea what was going on with her, and I feared the worst."

"It is true," Nayana said. "He kept breaking things out of frustration."

I knew Urch to be extremely loyal and equally determined. If he had been worried about the highest official in his civilization, he must have been difficult to be around.

"I was separated from the others, but not poorly treated," Ghli Wixxix said. "Though I appreciate the concern and all that you have done."

"So, what's the plan now?" I asked as we all took our seats. Tamret was next to me, but she didn't look over at me.

"The plan is your plan, Zeke," Captain Qwlessl said. "We arrive on Confederation Central unannounced, and we broadcast a message from Director Ghli Wixxix. Junup will be disgraced, and either he will be arrested, or he will flee. In either case, he and his followers will be out of power, since the actual elected director will now be back in Confederation territory."

"At that point," Dr. Roop said, "the director will exercise her authority to mobilize the Confederation military. Our forces will drive the Phands from Earth and any other territories they may have taken since my capture. Your world should be free within three or four standard days."

I nodded in thanks. Once Junup was out of power, the Phands would have more important things to care about than our families, whom they were holding prisoner, but the sooner Earth was liberated, the happier I'd be.

"We wanted to brief you because there are inevitably going to be hearings," Captain Qwlessl said. "The charges against Junup are serious, and in order for the Confederation to move forward, there will have to be hearings that expose precisely what happened and how. It is our intention that we learn from our mistakes so we do not repeat them. Your voices, your experiences, are important to that process. That means it may be some days, possibly even weeks, until you can return to your home planets."

"What!" Alice half rose out of her chair before controlling herself and sitting back down.

"No way," Mi Sun said. "I've been away long enough, and I'm worried about my mom and dad." She glowered at me.

"We would like to cooperate," Charles said, more diplomatically, "but you must recall that our planet is in a terrible state. Mi Sun and Alice are not alone in their concerns for those back home."

"That is, in large part, what I wanted to discuss with you.

We understand you are worried, and we want to do everything we can to help." The captain gestured at Ghli Wixxix.

"Once we have overseen a safe and peaceful removal of Phandic forces from your world," she said, "we will help in detaining their collaborators, who will be handed over to your own judicial bodies. We would like to invite your families to send communication beacons back to the capital. You will have to provide us with contact information, of course, but it should be relatively easy to track down any names you give us. It may be longer than you would like before you can see them again, but we will enable the sending and receiving of messages from them. Finally, in appreciation for all you have done for the Confederation, I will recommend that all your planets be allowed to bypass the initial step of providing candidates for the application process. I intend to argue that Earth, Rarel, and Ish-hi be granted preliminary Confederation membership."

Mi Sun looked skeptical at best. I knew she wanted to see her family, but maybe knowing they were okay would be enough. The rest of the humans looked considerably happier. We had been promised another chance to apply for Confederation membership, and while I believed Earth would have every chance of succeeding, this was even better. Skipping the year of evaluation meant a fast track to advanced technology and medicine, things that would make a huge difference, especially in the aftermath of the invasion.

Even so, there were things here I did not like at all.

"That sounds great," I said, "it really does, but I guess I worry it won't be so easy. I mean, Junup is just one guy, but there are a lot of members of his Movement for Peace, and he has followers throughout the government."

"I know you haven't always had reason to be impressed with Confederation justice," said Captain Qwlessl. "Neither have I, but you've seen only our worst side. I think now you will see us at our best."

"I'm glad you are optimistic about this," I told her, my voice icier than I intended, "but I'd like to hear Director Ghli Wixxix's assurances."

"Here we go," said Mi Sun, and she smacked her palm against her forehead. It sounded like a whip crack. "There's no need to turn everyone against you. Just take the win and move on."

The other humans were staring at me, looking anxious or embarrassed or angry. Even Steve was gazing at me with curiosity, his tongue flicking into the air as he tried to figure out what I was up to. Tamret turned to look at me, her ears back and her eyes slits of suspicion.

"Zeke," Dr. Roop said quietly, "your tone is a little forceful when speaking with the director."

"It is fine," said Ghli Wixxix, her tendrils waving vigorously at me. "As Captain Qwlessl observed, we have perhaps not earned Zeke's trust as well as we might have, but we certainly owe him, and his associates, our gratitude. I don't mind explaining. Yes, Junup has managed to build up a large faction, and they have been loyal, but popular opinion will turn against them when they are exposed. I have been through enough political cycles to know that those who were loyal out of expedience will change allegiances. Those who are true believers will flee. None who supported him will retain their positions following the next election. There will be no bloody revolution, but there will be a sweeping away of Junup's supporters."

"And what about Junup himself?" I asked.

"He has done more than support a political position," she assured me. "He has engaged in criminal activities, including murder, attempted murder, and sabotage of a Confederation vessel. He will face criminal charges. That is one of the reasons you must remain with us for a little while—so we can take your statements for his trial."

"And you're okay with this," I pressed. "I remember you telling me that the two of you were friends once."

I have learned, sometimes the hard way, that you can't read too much into alien body language, but her ears shot up and became broad, and her nasal slits were flaring. She didn't like these questions.

"That was a long time ago," Ghli Wixxix assured me. "He has changed. I feel nothing but disdain and pity for both him and his foolish ambitions."

"And you won't make any kind of alliance with the Phands?"

"Zeke," Dr. Roop snapped. "That is quite enough."

I understood why he reacted that way. It seemed like I was being rude. Maybe I was being rude, but I had to ask.

"I would like to hear the answer," Villainic said sleepily. He then covered his mouth so he could yawn. "We have a right to know."

I could do with less help from that quarter, but I supposed I should be glad someone was backing me up.

"Perhaps you could tell us why you are asking all this?" Captain Qwlessl said gently. "Is there some specific reason you want to press these points?"

"I just want to make sure things are going to be different this time."

"Very well," said Ghli Wixxix. "If it makes you feel better

to hear it, I promise you I have no intention of making any sort of alliance with the Phands. My goal has always been to stop their expansion and, ultimately, liberate the worlds they hold. This latter part will be a slower process than I would like, but I intend to dedicate the remainder of my time in office overseeing what I hope will be the beginning of the end of the Phandic Empire. As for Junup, I feel no loyalty to him whatsoever, and I intend to work to make certain he is captured and punished."

"Does that satisfy you?" Dr. Roop asked. I could hear the impatience in his voice. I understood that we were all seen as his responsibility, even Alice and Villainic, whom he had not brought into the Confederation, and my pushing the director had seemed disrespectful.

"I think I heard what I needed to," I said.

My interrogation of the most important elected official in the known galaxy had clearly soured the mood of the meeting, which broke up not long after. Dr. Roop looked at me sadly, and I wondered what he was thinking—that I had become too full of myself, or that I'd lost perspective. I would have to do damage control with him later. For now I was too worried about what I had learned.

As soon as we were away from the adults, Mi Sun rounded on me. "What were you doing in there? Why do you always have to make trouble?"

"We've got to get off this ship," I told her. "We need to steal a shuttle. If we don't, Confederation Central will be destroyed and Earth will remain part of the Phandic Empire."

"What are you talking about?" Alice asked. "Why would you say that?"

"Because I had a lie detector implanted in me by a guy with

a twenty-sided die for a head," I told them, "and nothing Ghli Wixxix told us is true. I don't know about you, but I can only think of one reason she would lie about that stuff. She's working with Junup and the Phands, and she's been on their side from the beginning. We've all been played."

CHAPTER EIGHTEEN

I was still putting the pieces together, but I thought I had a pretty good idea of how things had happened. As near as I could figure out, Junup's takeover had not been planned, but when the *Kind Disposition* was destroyed, and Ghli Wixxix presumably along with it, Junup had seen it as an opportunity to bolster support for his Movement for Peace. That I, an unruly primitive, could be blamed for the destruction and the death of the Confederation's leader only added to his cause. Ghli Wixxix had gone off with the other prisoners, ready to be returned if necessary. She had been held apart from the others not so she could be interrogated or given more intense security, but so she didn't have to live in the same conditions as the rest of them. In the meantime, the Phands had what they wanted—one of their own in power. It didn't matter to them if it was Junup or Ghli Wixxix.

I had no idea what Ghli Wixxix really intended to do when she returned to Confederation Central. Obviously, Junup was not going to prison. It seemed more likely that the rest of us would be locked away while Junup and Ghli Wixxix cooked up another story to feed to the public. I had no doubt that Dr. Roop, Captain Qwlessl, Urch, and Nayana would all disappear.

The bad guys getting their way was bad enough, but if we didn't do something, the Phands would stay on Earth. Meanwhile, the lunatic Phandic renegades would go back to their original plan of destroying Confederation Central.

I explained all of this as quickly and clearly as I could. The others all stared at me, maybe shocked by what they were learning, maybe upset to know that I was a walking polygraph machine.

"So what do we do, mate?" Steve said. "Let's say we do steal a ship and get out of here. I admit not being on Confederation Central when it blows up is probably a good idea, but it doesn't exactly feel like victory."

"Plan A for the Phandic renegades was destroying Confederation Central," I said. "Rescuing Ghli Wixxix was plan B, but there was, at one point, a plan C. The renegades wanted to liberate a world held by the Phands. The idea was that once the Phands lost their grip on one planet, beings all around the empire would notice and rise up at the same time. A well-publicized revolution will set off a domino effect. They even had a plan for pulling it off—on Earth. They have a stable wormhole leading directly there from their settlement."

"Hold on," Mi Sun said. "You're telling me that this group of renegades just happens to have a magic teleporter from their obscure, forgotten desert planet to Earth? Either you're lying or you've been lied to, and you were gullible enough to believe it."

"Because you know everything?" Tamret snapped. "The galaxy isn't big and varied enough for you that everything still needs to fit into your idea of what is and isn't likely?"

Tamret would still not meet my eye unless we were discussing strategy. She didn't want to talk to me about anything that wasn't super important, but she still wanted to defend me. I really needed to know what was going on with her, but maybe this wasn't the best time to dwell on it.

"There's a lot going on here that feels a little coincidental," I told Mi Sun, "and I'm not going to pretend to understand it all, but I'm telling you these Phandic renegades have a direct portal to Earth. We *can* use it, and we need to."

Mi Sun was worked up now. She was stomping toward me like she meant to give me a spinning kick to my face. "Why, Zeke? Why does it have to be us? Why are we the ones who have to do this crazy, dangerous thing? Isn't there someone else, in this entire galaxy, who is willing, just once, to step up so we don't have to?"

Her face was inches from mine by the time she stopped, her eyes wide and glistening. I didn't know if the tears she was fighting back were of rage or frustration or fear.

I shook my head. "No, Mi Sun. There isn't." I was speaking quietly now, trying to sound reasonable. "Do you think I want to do this?"

"Yeah," she snapped. "I do."

She didn't know about the powder and the saving throw. She didn't know that if we did this, I was going to have to take a leap of faith, to face a 15-percent chance of not living to see if our efforts saved the galaxy or not. Worst of all, I couldn't tell her, because if I did, she would probably take that risk on herself. Mi Sun wasn't a coward. I knew that she would do what needed doing, but I also knew she was tired of running and scheming and worrying about her family.

"I don't want to have to," I said. "I know you all gave me a hard time when I thought our part in all of this was over, but you have no idea how relieved I was. I don't want to head back into the thick of it and take on another crazy mission, to take chances with my friends' lives. I wish there were another way, but if we don't do this, if we don't find some way to shake things up, then Confederation Central is going to be destroyed. Millions of innocent beings will be going about their business one second and just be gone the next. Maybe the renegades are right and that will lead to galactic peace, but that price is too high. I will always know that maybe it didn't have to be that way. Do any of you want to spend the rest of your lives wondering what we could have done?"

Mi Sun blinked at me a couple of times. She stepped back a little. "If I understand what you're saying, and the Phandic renegades blow up the station, we'll probably be on it when it's destroyed."

"There's that. If you want to take a selfish approach."

"I do," Steve said. "It's not the only approach I want to take, but it's one of them. Also, for the record, I'm keen on the idea of a crazy, stupid adventure."

"Not helping," I said to him.

Mi Sun shook her head. "It doesn't matter. You already made your point. I guess we really do have to do this."

"I hadn't thought about the part where we would be killed along with the millions of beings on the station," Nayana said. "That changes my outlook considerably."

"You should have led with that," Alice said.

Mi Sun and I sat back down. We were all quiet now, like something that had been hovering over all of us had been blown away.

She let out a long sigh. "Zeke, I'm sorry I've been blaming you for what's happened to our families. I know you were only doing what you thought had to be done, and the truth is, I didn't have to listen to you. I could have contacted them without your okay, but I didn't because I knew you were right. I just wanted to blame someone."

"This is a mistake," Nayana whispered loudly for all of us to hear. "Never acknowledge fault. It puts you at a tactical disadvantage."

I nodded to Mi Sun. "I know that—"

Mi Sun shook her head. "It's probably best not to say anything. I'm sure whatever it is will just make me angry. Accept the apology and move on."

"I accept your apology, Mi Sun," I said.

"How very big of you," she grumbled, rolling her eyes.

"So," Alice said brightly, "I wonder if there's anyone else mad at Zeke for no apparent reason who wants to clear the air."

Tamret glowered at Alice, who tried to vanish into her chair.

"Right," Steve said, clearly out to break the tension. "So, the plan to liberate your planet—let's get back to that bit."

Nayana folded her arms. "We should think this through. I'm sure the basics of Zeke's plan are more or less coherent, but the devil is always in the details. I understand that liberating Earth will make the Phands look bad, and perhaps reflect poorly on Junup, but that hardly ends their collaboration. Any kind of rebellion we initiate will take months, maybe years, to run its course. In the meantime, there is nothing to stop the Phands from reoccupying Earth, no doubt more harshly."

"As someone who also comes from a country that was once held as a colony," Charles said, "I share Nayana's concerns. Rebellions are often dealt with brutally, and they can take generations to succeed."

"We need to get Captain Qwlessl and Dr. Roop on board," I said. "I have to convince them I'm right and then get them to expose Junup and Ghli Wixxix. If we can take control of Earth, we will be able to gain access to Phandic computers and records. That should provide all the evidence we need to link Junup to the Phands."

"Your plans keep getting stupider," Mi Sun said. "Last time you wanted to go to an empire and free maximum-security prisoners."

"And that plan worked!" I said, trying to muster more enthusiasm than I felt. "I mean, it would have if Ghli Wixxix had been what we all thought she was. It's not my fault she's a traitor."

"I agree with that," Alice said. "But just because your last crazy plan made sense, that doesn't mean all your crazy plans will."

"I'm as keen on a crazy plan as the next bloke," Steve said, "but everything we've done before hinged on small, stealthy operations. You're talking about war here, Zeke. A long, bloody conflict without a clear path to victory. A lot of beings on your planet will get killed. Is that really what you want?"

I slumped down in my chair and put my head in my hands. Of course I didn't want that, and I had to concede that when Steve thought a plan was too insane, it was time to take stock. The real question was if there was some way I could, with my augmented powers, single-handedly make a difference. I did not want an actual war. On the other hand, if I did nothing, then Confederation Central was going to be destroyed. Maybe Earth would be freed of the Phands and the empire would lose its grip on the galaxy, but that was too high a price to pay.

I thought about what I knew about the Phandic operation, and I began to see that there might be a way to pull this off without an actual bloody war.

"Look, I know that a guerilla action against an occupying army sounds like a lot to take on, but the Phands are using this high-end technology that requires a quantum-level energy link to their empire. If we cut it off, they run out of power to fuel their ships. They'll have to retreat or risk getting stuck on Earth forever."

"Their weapons will still work," Charles said. "What is to stop them from hurting a lot of people and doing a lot of damage before they go?"

"They have our families, in case you've forgotten," Mi Sun said. "I know I haven't."

"I haven't forgotten," I said. "Not for a second."

"If we launch some sort of attack, don't you think they'll take it out on the people we care about? That's the whole point of having hostages. How do you plan to protect them?"

"I have no idea," I said mournfully. I was hoping that the renegades would have a suggestion, but I knew this was a long shot. Sparing innocent lives didn't seem to be their particular strength.

"I do," Tamret said. "I know exactly how you do this. How many Phands do you think are on Earth?"

"I don't have an exact number," I said. "The Phandic rebels told me no more than a few thousand."

"So there are at least a million humans for each invader," she said, grinning. "The Phands dominate because they have the technology. The trick is to take away the technology. You make the numbers matter."

"Clearly you were not listening," Nayana said. "They will still have their weapons."

Alice looked up, getting it. "Not if they don't."

Tamret nodded. "Exactly. If these renegades are as handy as you say they are, then they can help us out with a planetary EMP. We'll do to the Phands what Ardov did to us, only on a bigger scale. We will shut them down, and we will keep them shut down until they agree to leave peacefully. Without their guns, they're no match for a few billion humans with big sticks."

Nayana nodded, stroking her chin to show she was giving this a lot of thought. "That is very clever," she said dubiously. "I have no doubt I would have thought of it myself had I been there for Ardov's attack."

"High praise," Tamret said.

"You are very welcome."

"Perhaps," Villainic suggested, "I should stay behind. If you'd like, I could serve as a special ambassador to Director Ghli Wixxix."

And tell her exactly what we don't want her to know, I thought. There was no way we could risk leaving Villainic behind. Besides, as strange as it was, the Phandic renegades seemed to like him. Having him along might actually help.

"No way, Villainic," I said. "We're adventure buddies. You are coming with me."

"This could actually work," Steve said. "Except what's to keep the Phands from coming back as soon as things settle down?"

"The idea is that there will be similar uprisings all over their empire," Charles said. "But we can't guarantee that. Things could go perfectly, but then we'll only be back where we started in a matter of days or weeks."

"We'll need to get the word out, then," Alice said. "In the Confederation. Dr. Roop and Captain Qwlessl will have to let everyone know that Junup and Ghli Wixxix are allies, and that they're both working with the Phands."

"How does that work?" Alice asked. "They are not exactly going to let the good guys hold a press conference. Ghli Wixxix will act like everything is normal until they approach the Confederation, and then they'll strike before any word can get out."

"But we know that," Nayana said. "We know their next move, and they don't know that we know it. That gives us the advantage, not them. If we are going to escape from this ship, we will first have to drop out of tunnel, yes?"

I nodded.

"Then Dr. Roop and Captain Qwlessl can secretly launch comm beacons to various news outputs on Confederation Central. They can make sure the truth gets to the station before they do. Perhaps not everyone will believe what they have to say, but they are respected, and their charges will have to be investigated. That gives us time to get the proof we need from the Phandic computers we capture."

"All right," I said. "So, here's the rundown on the operation. Escape from this ship with a stolen long-range shuttle, convince the Phandic renegades to help us out by giving us all their intelligence plus lots of dangerous technology, then have them open a wormhole to get us to Earth, where we'll drive off the most ruthless conquering force in the galaxy. At that point, we have to hope for more revolutions to spring up elsewhere, which will slow any Phandic response to our uprising. Meanwhile, we raid the Phandic computers for proof that Junup and Ghli Wixxix are working with the bad guys. Any questions?"

"Just one," said Charles. "How do we drop out of tunnel long enough to launch these beacons and steal a shuttle?"

Steve flashed one of his openmouthed, spiky-toothed grins. "I'm thinking sabotage."

The plan was for me to go talk to the adults I trusted while Steve tried to figure out how to get the ship to drop out of tunnel. That was something he couldn't do alone, and somehow we were divided into two teams, with everyone but me and Tamret working with Steve.

That meant Tamret and I were alone.

"You know, you can talk to me about what's going on," I told her, trying to keep my voice neutral.

"So could you," she snapped back.

"I told you why I can't. I'm trying to protect you."

"Maybe that's what I'm doing," she said.

"And maybe it isn't," I countered. "I don't know if you don't talk to me."

"Yeah, well, maybe you ought to know without being told."

"That's stupid," I said.

"I know," she agreed.

We were passing by an empty conference room, so I pushed her inside and closed the door behind us.

"Do we really have time for this?" she asked, hands on her hips. Her whiskers shot back in a way I knew meant she was irritated.

"I don't know," I said, "but I really don't want to go into a dangerous mission distracted by the fact that you're shutting me out. I know you have things on your mind, responsibilities, but I don't get why you're angry with me."

"I'm not angry with you," she snapped.

"That would be more convincing if you didn't sound angry," I told her.

"Well, I'm getting angry now because you won't stop insisting that I'm angry."

I sighed. "Come on, Tamret."

"Fine," she said. "You tell me how you reactivated your abilities, and I'll tell you why I'm not angry."

I turned away.

"That's what I thought," she said.

"Look, it's not safe, okay?" I blurted out without meaning to. "I have to eat this stupid powder and then I roll a die, and if I don't get a four or better, something bad happens."

"What kind of something bad?"

"The death kind," I admitted. Before she could say anything else, I cut her off. "It's only a fifteen percent chance, and I haven't used it except when there was no other way. I'm not being reckless or anything."

"Why didn't you tell me?" she demanded.

"Because I didn't want you to worry," I said, "and because I was afraid you would do it yourself."

"Oh, Zeke," she said, throwing her arms around me. "Every time I think I know how stupid you are, you find a way to surprise me."

There were some things in our future—some terrible, dangerous things—that I did not want to think about, but knowing Tamret was on my side somehow made it all easier. No matter what was going on with her, she cared about me.

I broke away from her hug. I didn't know how much time I had to spare, but this was important. "What is going on with you, Tamret?"

She shook her head. "I can't stay on Earth, and I just didn't want to, I don't know, get too comfortable."

I couldn't help but laugh. "I'm the one who's stupid? That's the dumbest thing I've ever heard. We don't know what's going to happen. Why plan for something you can't control? When all of this is over, maybe you'll want to stay on Earth."

"But Ardov said—"

"You're getting life coaching from Ardov?"

"Not anymore, since he was eaten by a sea monster, but he said that he'd spent time with the beings on Earth, and they would always hate me for being different. And they would hate you for being my friend. The humans are going to be suspicious of aliens after the invasion, and it's one thing for me to be treated badly, but you're going to have responsibilities once Earth joins the Confederation. You won't be able to do that if everyone on your planet hates you. If I stayed, you'd have to choose between me and your own world."

"And this is what Ardov said?"

"He said it, but I already suspected it."

"Why not ask me what I think? I maybe know more about Earth than either of you."

"Because you always want to see the best in beings, and Ardov might have been unpleasant, but he wasn't easily fooled."

I took her hand. The whole reason she didn't want to come to Earth was because she thought it would make my life difficult. "Let's not make any decisions, okay? Let's just see what happens, and we'll make decisions when we have to."

She nodded.

There was more to say, especially about the powder, but that could wait until later. The main thing was that Tamret and

I had cleared the air, and, suddenly, doing an incredibly stupid thing because we had no choice didn't seem so bad after all.

The conversation with Dr. Roop and Captain Qwlessl was an uncomfortable one. They were both tired of running, and they didn't want to believe what I had to say at first. They knew, however, that I would not make something like this up, and after a couple of convincing demonstrations of the lie detector, they had to admit, however reluctantly, that I was telling the truth.

"How do you want us to cover for you?" Captain Qwlessl asked.

"Whatever you think works best," I said. "You don't want them to suspect you. Ghli Wixxix doesn't really know me, and since she's in Junup's camp, she's probably inclined to think the worst of me. You can keep telling her that I am full of myself and need to be a hero. That will go along with your concerns from the meeting."

"Zeke," Dr. Roop began.

"Don't worry about it," I told him. "You didn't know what I was up to, and I'm sure it looked rude. The main thing is that you anticipate what she's up to and find a way to control what the public knows."

He nodded. "How trustworthy are these Phandic renegades?"

"I think they're sincere," I said, "but they're strange. I don't have any doubt that they really mean to destroy Confederation Central if my plan doesn't work."

"Then it had better work." He put a hand on my shoulder.

"You're not going to use that powder again, I hope."

"I may have no choice," I told him. There was no way I was going to get through this without using the powder and the die. "It's the most powerful advantage we've got."

"I understand," he said, "but make sure you have exhausted all other options."

"I will. I'm in no hurry to get a bad throw."

My data bracelet pinged. Steve was letting me know that he had monkeyed with the engines and we were ready to emerge from tunnel. "I better get out of here," I told Dr. Roop. "You don't want to be seen near me when all of this goes down. They might suspect you've been helping us."

"We can't have that." He nodded. Then he and Captain Qwlessl gave me hugs.

"At some point, things are going to get back to normal, and then you're going to love life in the Confederation," Captain Qwlessl said.

"This is normal for me," I told her. "Maybe normal will seem boring, but I'm willing to find out."

Tamret and I left the room and headed to the shuttle bay. When we arrived, Steve used his bracelet to remotely trigger whatever nasty sabotage he had cooked up. At first nothing changed, and I thought perhaps he had failed, but then there was that odd sensation of dropping out of tunnel. Alarms began flashing, which was natural for something like this. Captain Qwlessl would be going through the standard operating procedure for an unplanned tunnel exit. No doubt the director would review the logs, and she would want to make sure everything looked the way it was supposed to.

We boarded the shuttle. Tamret took the navigation controls

and hacked into the ship's computer to seal the bay from the ship; then she began the process of opening the exterior doors. Meanwhile, I conveyed the coordinates of the renegade base to Steve, who was preparing the tunnel aperture in advance.

Tamret got the plasma field down, and we were on our way. Steve flew evasively, just in case. Captain Qwlessl would raise no suspicions by not wanting to fire at us, but who knew what kind of authority the director might have. I wanted us to be well away before she tried to exercise any of it.

There were several attempts to contact us. Captain Qwlessl was clearly going through the motions to cover her own tracks. We ignored these, and the moment we had our tunnel aperture opened, we were gone.

It would take about eleven hours to get to the renegade base. We would reach our destination around the same time the ship arrived at Confederation Central. We had no way of knowing what was in store for them, and they would be clueless about what we were up to. There were countless things that could now go wrong, and I was expecting to have to deal with every one of them.

Our return to the renegade outpost was uneventful. They hadn't given me any instructions on how to enter the cloaked compound, but I figured I didn't need them. I had the location still recorded on my bracelet, so we flew in low and broadcasted a message announcing who I was. I received a response telling me where to land.

They created a momentary opening in their cloaking shields, and we flew in, while the humans among us gaped at the Old West look of the settlement. We landed next to a few other short-range vessels, which were about the only high-tech things in sight. Otherwise it was all cowboys and nerfs.

By the time we emerged, Convex Icosahedron, Adiul-ip, and a small band of armed guards had shown up to meet us. I took no offense at their precautions. They had no idea why we were there or if we were who we claimed.

I made introductions all around, and if all my friends seemed a little on edge, it was only because we were surrounded by Phands and a guy with a geometric shape for a head and no face. Colors swirled over Convex Icosahedron's flat surfaces and sharp angles as he seemed to regard us.

"As you are here," he said, "I presume your mission to rescue Ghli Wixxix failed, Zeke Reynolds."

"No, the prisoners were rescued," I said, omitting the fact that we hadn't had anything to do with the rescue. The more competent he thought us, the better. "And everything went pretty smoothly on Planet Pleasant. The problem is that your Lasso of Truth gave away Ghli Wixxix's secret—that she's working with Junup." I couldn't be bothered to include his name at the end of every sentence. I hoped this counted as a strategy session so I wouldn't be given a hard time.

The colors of Convex Icosahedron's head shifted more rapidly, which I'd come to think of as something like a nod. "I thought that device might come in handy, Zeke Reynolds."

"If Ghli Wixxix cannot be depended on to restore order to the Confederation," Adiul-ip said, "then we'll have to return to the original plan."

"I have a better idea," I said. "That's what I want to talk to you about. And, hey, we're talking strategy, right? We can drop the names, can't we?"

"A reasonable observation," Convex Icosahedron said, mercifully not using my name. "Let us continue our conversation, but you and Villainic only, Zeke Reynolds. Your associates can await our decision."

"Not acceptable," I said. "They're in on all of this."

"That may be, but I cannot have cacophony in a meeting of such import. Only the two of you, Zeke Reynolds."

Steve shrugged. "It's your plan, mate," he said. "It's up to you to sell it. Though why . . . ?" He jabbed a thumb at Villainic.

I shook my head. "They like him, for some reason, but I don't like the idea of anyone being boxed out." I turned to Convex Icosahedron. "We're a team. Anything we discuss, they need to hear themselves."

Convex Icosahedron appeared to consider this. "As it should be," he said, as though he hadn't proposed separating us in the first place.

We followed the renegades to the building where we'd had our previous strategy meeting. It took a few minutes to gather all the chief advisors, including Colonel Rage, and when he came in, he created a bit of a stir.

"Uh, what?" Alice said when she saw him.

"What's he doing here?" Mi Sun demanded.

I'd had a lot on my mind, so I'd maybe forgotten to mention that the human who had betrayed us back at the Hidden Fortress was now working with the Phandic renegades, and that he was basically trustworthy—as long as he didn't think betraying us again was in Earth's best interests.

"We can trust him, mostly," I said, wearily. Honestly, I didn't have the strength to go over the details. "Enemy of our enemy and all that."

To his credit, Colonel Rage did his best to mend fences, apologizing to everyone and explaining that then, as now, his priority was the protection of Earth. "The fact is," he said, "I've learned that you kids may be better judges of these alien creatures than I am. Maybe it's your youth. I don't know." He rubbed at his eye patch like it irritated him. "If you have something to say that can help us get those monsters off our planet, I'll be happy to listen."

"Nice speech, geezer," Steve said. "Don't cross us again."

"I clearly missed out on some excitement," Nayana said.

"Now that we have that out of the way," the colonel said, "I understand you have new information and a new plan."

I'd lost track of how many times I'd been in desperate situations, life-or-death conflicts in which I'd felt like everything was on the line. I'd been terrified each time, but there was always something that needed doing, maybe a dozen things. I could be scared, but because I had to act, I could put that fear aside. Now here I was, trying to convince these adults that they should drop their plan and follow mine. I needed to convince them that I was right or Confederation Central would be destroyed.

I took a deep breath, reminded myself to speak clearly and decisively, and began.

"You have come up with a way to win this conflict," I said. "You want to put an end to the Phandic Empire. We have the same goal, but we've come up with a different way to do that. We think it's a better way because it preserves Confederation Central. It saves a great city full of millions of beings, a wonder from the time of the Formers. We think the place, and the beings, are worth saving if we can."

I then went into the details. I told them how we would

use their portal to Earth and destroy the Phandic occupation there, gaining access to their computers, which would provide irrefutable evidence of Junup's complicity. Our allies on Confederation Central, meanwhile, would expose both Junup and Ghli Wixxix.

"Not only can we accomplish our goals without having to sacrifice innocent lives," I concluded, "but we show the galaxy that the Phands can be overthrown. We break the alliance with Junup and we humiliate the Phands by taking away a conquered planet."

I struggled to find some clever way to finish, something like *This combination is a winning combination*, but everything that popped into my head either sounded stupid or like an ad for candy. Instead, having made my point, I sat down.

Somewhere in the back of my mind, I suppose I imagined everyone at the table leaping up and cheering. Perhaps there might be a chant of *Zeke! Zeke! Zeke!* This was, admittedly, unrealistic, but I still thought it was a good speech and deserved some kind of acknowledgement.

Instead I got nothing. On Earth we would have heard crickets; here there was only a low, distant humming sound made by carnivorous plants.

"I do not believe you are bringing us anything new," said Convex Icosahedron, finally breaking the endless silence. "We spoke of the idea of fomenting rebellion, and that we rejected it because the numbers didn't support a successful outcome as confidently as the destruction of Confederation Central. What you report, that Ghli Wixxix is in league with Junup, only goes to prove that the corruption is further spread than we feared. I suspect a new analysis of the data will make the liberation of a planet seem even weaker by comparison."

"Weren't you listening?" Tamret demanded. "This plan breaks the Phandic Empire but saves millions of lives."

"I have already explained to Zeke that those lives are merely statistical noise. They are meaningless in the broad sweep of history."

"I do not believe the beings living them would agree with you," Charles said.

"Do your friends still have access to the Former military tech skills?" Convex Icosahedron asked.

I shook my head. "Just me," I said. Sometimes. Only Tamret knew about the system with the powder and the die, and I decided to gloss over the details for now. I didn't want the rest of them volunteering to take that kind of risk.

Convex Icosahedron appeared to think about this. At the very least, colors moved thoughtfully across his head. "Tell me," he said at last. "Did you speak of the plan to destroy Confederation Central to any of your allies?"

Since he was the one who had given me the lie-detecting technology, I had to assume he would know if I told the truth or not. "I told Dr. Roop. I totally trust him."

"Regardless, he is not going to want his city to be destroyed. That means our window to act is closing. We should launch the offensive at once." He turned to one of the Phands. "Alert fleet command to deploy the—"

"Come on!" I stood up. I knew that as a grand strategy, interruption would only get me so far, but I was not willing to let them steamroll me. I could not accept that instead of coming with a plan to save Confederation Central, I'd just sped up the timeline for its destruction. "You can't really believe that this is the right move. Saving Earth not only weakens the bad guys and exposes Junup, but it keeps beings from being killed. How is that not the better choice?"

Convex Icosahedron needed to think about this for a moment. "You are very spirited, and I admire that, but with your plan there is a chance that we will expose ourselves and gain nothing. We shall proceed with our plan. I will promise you that once we have destroyed Confederation Central, we will make the liberation of Earth our next priority. I can guarantee you that your world will be saved."

Colonel Rage nodded. "You can't ask for much more than that."

"I kind of can," I said, slowly returning to my seat. "I get that you want to make sure you win—that makes sense to me— but at a certain point, you have to accept that you are fighting *for* something, not just looking to beat the other guy."

"You seem to have little respect for plans you did not devise yourself," Convex Icosahedron said.

"Everyone keeps saying that I need to be at the center of things," I answered with a sigh. "I really don't. I'll sit the mission out if it means accomplishing the goal."

"Our only goal is to break the grip of the empress," Adiul-ip said.

"But at what cost?" Nayana said.

Everyone stared at her, and she suddenly appeared very self-conscious. "Yes, for those who don't know me, I am Nayana Gehlawat, and I am significantly more intelligent than Zeke. And most importantly, I am a strategist."

"Tell us some more about yourself," Tamret mumbled.

"The point," Nayana responded, "is not how intelligent I am. The point is that, in spite of his limitations, Zeke has struck at the heart of this matter. I understand you depend heavily on your projections of how your actions will affect the future, but I wonder if you have projected the ramifications of the example of the destruction of Confederation Central. Will future generations, when they encounter a potential threat, choose to destroy rather than talk or negotiate because they have learned from the example of the past? Will you, in your desire to sweep the board clear of your enemies, establish a new pattern of bloodshed? Are you, in other words, exchanging one reign of terror for another?"

Nayana's speech, like mine, was met with silence, but this time the quiet felt thoughtful, contemplative, as though they were thinking about what she'd said.

"I think she makes a valid point," Villainic said at last.

"Thanks?" I offered tentatively. Why was Villainic, of all beings, making this pronouncement, like the decision was his?

"Several hundred years ago," Villainic continued, "a culturally important Rarel city called Obvir was almost entirely destroyed in an earthquake. It shocked the entire world, and soon architects began creating buildings designed to survive such disasters. Were you to visit Rarel today—which I highly recommend, for it is a beautiful place—then you would see the effects of that earthquake in the designs of every large city. You can predict what cities will look like in a few hundred years, and you might possibly be correct. Yet, if a visitor in the past had attempted to predict the course of building design before the disaster of Obvir, those projections would have proved false, because a new factor changed everything."

"He's talking nonsense," the colonel growled.

"No, he isn't," I said, looking curiously at Villainic. Inexplicably, he had nailed it. Here I was, arguing that I should participate in a rebellion to get rid of an alien occupation force from my world. A year ago, no one could have predicted that I would do anything like that, but events had changed me. Major events could change entire worlds, entire cultures.

"We don't have the luxury of worrying about future generations," the colonel explained. "A bad plan that works is better than a good plan that doesn't. We have to pursue the lesser of two evils."

"But the plan I'm talking about isn't evil at all," I said. "Isn't that the side we want to be on?"

Colonel Rage looked away. The others—at least those with faces—appeared impatient. Convex Icosahedron inclined his head in my direction, which might have meant anything.

"Your emotions cannot defeat our logic," Adiul-ip said. "I'm afraid we will proceed with the destruction of Confederation Central."

"No," said Convex Icosahedron. He was busy typing rapidly on a plasma keyboard he had summoned. "These beings have pointed out an error in our projections. We did not run all the numbers. We only calculated for political bodies, not individuals. We also failed to factor in how the example of the destruction of Confederation Central would alter future behavior."

I blinked to mask my confusion. I couldn't believe I was right—and that Villainic had convinced Convex Icosahedron that I was right—but mentioning this seemed like a bad idea.

"What does that mean?" Colonel Rage asked. "Are we

going to scrap the winning plan because of the risk of collateral damage? People die. That's a fact of war."

Convex Icosahedron was still typing furiously. "I have always favored the course that produces the greatest possibility of peace. I believed the destruction of Confederation Central was that course, but I now see that such a course may very likely lead to more bloodshed."

"You're going to abandon a clear path to victory because of what some pimply kids tell you?" the colonel demanded.

There was the Colonel Rage I remembered—the guy who would pay any price, no matter how shameful, to complete his mission. He'd seemed reasonable before, when he was getting what he wanted, but now that things were turning in my direction, he was showing his true colors. Besides, my complexion happened to be clear at the moment. His insults were lies!

Adiul-ip looked at Colonel Rage. "We value your martial insights, but we cannot refute the data."

"The data says that a bunch of kids can't kick an invading army off a planet," the colonel said.

"I believe these kids can," Convex Icosahedron said. "If we aid them, I believe they have the skills and the motivation to do precisely what we need." He then stopped typing and looked up at me. Or at least he positioned his head so as to suggest he was looking. "However, you will have to do something very dangerous if your plan has a likelihood of succeeding."

"What else is new?" I asked.

"Give me an hour to prepare a briefing," Convex Icosahedron said. "Then we will begin the final battle against the empress."

The mood in the room had changed. The renegades in general looked confused. Colonel Rage chewed furiously on his lower lip. As for my friends, well, I don't know that we had any idea how to process the information. We had convinced these guys not to destroy Confederation Central, but that meant we were going to do maybe the most dangerous thing we'd ever attempted.

"A moment," Convex Icosahedron said to me as I stood up. "I wish to speak to you in private." He drew me aside to a corner of the room while the others exited.

"You are keeping a secret from the others," he said after they were all gone, "about your Former tech."

"Most of them, yes," I said. "It's to protect them."

"I suspected as much," he said. "But if you wish to continue to keep that secret, then you must commit to a course of action. What you will attempt is much more dangerous than you, or the others realize. You had hoped to minimize your risk, but you cannot—not if you wish to defeat the empire."

Convex Icosahedron told me what I was going to have to do, and really—as these things go—it wasn't so bad. If I could protect my friends and liberate the Earth, I was willing to follow his plan and risk my life.

CHAPTER NINETEEN

s there anything about this that bothers you?" Tamret asked as we made our way to the portal.

There had been another strategy meeting that took more than two hours, and it left me feeling more optimistic than I'd been since learning that Ghli Wixxix was a traitor. We had a solid plan, and Convex Icosahedron had given us some useful tech. The odds of our pulling this off actually seemed pretty good. Even so, I couldn't shake the feeling that we were being set up. Tamret clearly felt it too.

"Plenty," I said. "There's no denying that it's weird that of all the planets they could have built an escape hatch to, it just happened to be Earth. I get that Earth is important to galactic politics right now, but even so. And it's strange that they just happened to recruit Colonel Rage to help them."

"How about that alien having the same shape as the die you have to throw?" Tamret asked. "What kind of being is he?"

"They're called Geometric Upstarts."

"How is that a name for a species?" she asked. "It sounds like a gang of math hooligans."

"Totally," I agreed. "And there's more. Dr. Roop told me that it was one of the Geometric Upstarts who took my father off Earth to begin with. Somehow it seems like we're being toyed with, you know?"

"Do you think they're manipulating us into doing what we're doing?"

"I definitely get the feeling that in spite of all our arguing and persuading, we're doing what Convex Icosahedron always wanted us to do."

"Maybe it's just how his alien mind thinks," Tamret said. "Not all species are going to be as similar as Rarels and humans."

"I suppose that's true," I said, even if I mainly tended to focus on how different we were from each other. As far as I knew, the Geometric Upstarts weren't part of the Confederation. Maybe they'd been left out because they did think differently. Perhaps those differences didn't bother the renegade Phands because they were more alike. Colonel Rage had always been willing to make deals with bad guys if he believed in the cause, so it wasn't strange that he had signed on.

I must have looked worried, because Tamret took my hand.

"You know," I said, "after we win, you could maybe take some time to see if you like life on Earth. If it's not for you, I can take you home."

"You're not going to have access to space travel for years. Remember?"

"Earth won't, but I will. That was part of my original agreement with Ghli Wixxix. If I did what she wanted, I would get my own ship."

She scrunched up her face in a way that suggested she couldn't figure out how I missed something so obvious. "You don't think the fact that she was a traitor, and therefore lying about everything, might alter that agreement?"

"I won't let anyone cheat me," I told her. "They are going

to give me what they promised. And that means I'll be able to look out for you."

"I don't like anyone trying to protect me," she said.

"Not protect," I said. "Look out for. It's different."

She smiled and turned away. "We'll see."

I didn't know that we were done with this conversation, but that was okay. At least we were talking, and I knew what had Tamret worried. I knew that I could make her see reason, and that, provided we survived what we were about to attempt, everything between us was going to be okay.

The portal to Earth was an eight-foot tall metal arch located in the center of town—convenient for anyone trying to escape a planet rapidly collapsing into a black hole. Convex Icosahedron and several other Phands were watching us from about a hundred feet away. I didn't know if they were giving us a respectful distance or if there was some kind of portal wake they wanted to stay out of.

"Let's go over this one last time," I said.

"Seriously?" Mi Sun asked. "It's not as though it's a hastily thrown together plan to defeat the most powerful military force in the galaxy."

"That aside," Alice said, "I can't help but wonder if these guys are being straight with us. I mean, if this plan is solid, why are they sending us to carry it out?"

I shrugged. "Most of us are locals, and we know the lay of the land."

"Colonel Rage is a local," Charles said.

"But we don't trust him, so there's that."

"Do you think they intend to betray us?" Charles asked.

"That would make no sense," said Nayana. "If they wished us captured, they needn't send us anywhere. We are already in their power."

"I agree," I said. "It feels more like we're being tested."

"Yeah," said Steve. "I get that. But I think that if they want to see what we can do, I say we show them."

Everyone but Villainic agreed. He offered no opinion. He'd been much less disagreeable lately, and I wasn't sure why. Maybe I was getting paranoid, but it felt like he knew something I didn't.

"Okay," I said. "Let's review this one last time." I called up some holographic projections from my data bracelet and began to review.

There's a plot device you see in so many *Star Wars* movies that has spilled over to games, comics, and novels: Whatever facility the good guys are fighting is vulnerable at a single point. The thermal exhaust port in *A New Hope*, the droid control ship in *The Phantom Menace*, the Star Forge in *Knights of the Old Republic*, the Starkiller Base's thermal oscillator in *The Force Awakens*. Given that there was a vulnerable spot on Confederation Central itself, these plots had turned out to be surprisingly realistic, but it always felt a little too convenient for me.

I would have gone for that convenience now. The Phands were smarter than their fictional evil-empire counterparts, and they had a system of protective redundancy in place. There were dozens of access points for the subspace energy relay, and they all had to be shut down, almost simultaneously, via an encrypted system. That made a fair amount of sense. Outside of some kind of disastrous emergency, there was no sound reason to shut down the power on which your imperial conquest depended unless you were packing up and going home.

Fortunately, the Phandic renegades had figured out a workaround. Anything that's made to transfer unfathomable levels of energy across a tear in the fabric of reality is going to have the potential to cause a certain amount of damage should such an emergency occur. The trick, then, was to make the Phandic computers think the relay system was experiencing a catastrophic power surge, one with the capacity to short out the entire system. When that happened, the relay could be shut down at two separate locations. A little bit of redundancy was necessary when balancing the risks of a planet-destroying accident *and* an angry population that might not like being conquered.

So, instead of being in dozens of places at once, we only needed to be in three. One so a team could hack into the system and make the computers believe there had been a critical accident, and two other locations to begin the emergency shutdown. Once we cut off the Phandic energy flow, which the invaders needed to power their alien tech, we would send out a broadcast to every television, radio station, computer, and smartphone on the planet giving the people of Earth a heads-up that they needed to pick up a big stick and start swinging at Phands. We would then activate the planetary EMP, shutting down all remaining Phandic—and human— technology, making it impossible for the invaders to restart the system or use their ships, their PPB weapons, or anything else that gave them the ability to dominate a planet using only a couple thousand soldiers.

At that point, we had to hope that the people of Earth would catch on and disarm and capture every Phand they could find. By the time we deactivated the EMP device, the Phands would either be utterly defeated or a battle would then rage for control of the Earth. As for our families and friends in captivity, we had to hope that the Phands looking after them would have bigger things to worry about than exacting a revenge no one would know about.

In order to avoid major chaos, not to mention killing a lot of innocent people, I'd had Tamret hack into the Phandic military communications network and ground all human air traffic halfway through our previous meeting. We agreed that we had to make sure there were no planes in the air when we activated the EMP. The downside was that the Phands would probably decide that the only reason to ground all the humans on the planet was a looming rebellion, so they'd be on high alert.

Steve, Alice, and Charles were in charge of the shutdown station in Beijing. Mi Sun, Nayana, and Villainic were handling the one in London. Tamret had uploaded to their bracelets an algorithm that would basically do the work for them. Their task was to take out any local security by means of a short-range EMP. They'd be deploying the same sort of EMP-insulating technology Ardov had used when disabling our ship, which meant they could still use their weapons and keep communications open. I hoped they would have no problem holding their facilities long enough for us to pull off our operation at the main control station.

The portal allowed us to plug in specific locations, and it was designed with infiltration in mind, so it would find isolated and safe spaces, such as empty rooms or closets, in which to deposit us. The plan was for us to remain in close contact via our bracelets.

"This is probably the most dangerous and stupid thing we've ever done," I said, once I finished reviewing all the logistics. "I hope we don't all get killed."

"That's my kind of pep talk," Steve said.

Steve led his team through the portal to the Beijing station. A minute later Mi Sun looked at me, rolled her eyes, and led her team to London. Now it was up to me and Tamret.

I set the coordinates of the portal. She looked at me, shrugged, and stepped through.

"So, why are we pretending we're in one of these entertainments you like so much?" Tamret asked me.

"It's not pretending," I explained. "It's a safety precaution I learned from a movie—a code. You never know who's listening."

She nodded. "Your planet, your rules."

We'd come through the portal into an empty office in the subspace relay's control station, which had been set up in a building in east midtown. It was a spacious corner office, so I could see the bolt of energy emanating from the Empire State Building while enjoying a charming view of the East River. I was sure the realtor had described it as the perfect place from which to dominate the globe.

I looked through the window at people on the street, the cars slowly inching their way through rush-hour traffic. It might have been just an ordinary day, except I saw groups of policemen sweeping through the pedestrians, checking IDs. All flight traffic should have landed by now, and the imperial government, led by Nora Price, would be scrambling to figure out what was going on that required the grounding of all human air traffic. Security everywhere was going to be high.

I keyed the communications system on my bracelet. "Beijing, you there?"

"Oi," Steve said.

"London?" I tried.

"We're here," Mi Sun said.

"We'll be ready to get started in about two minutes," I said. "I think we'll need maybe half an hour to finish our tasks, so be ready to go on my mark."

"You just love this military talk, don't you?" said Mi Sun.

"Yes," I said, "I do. It makes me feel extra cool. Now stand by."

"We'll need more time than that," Tamret said.

"No, I won't," I told her.

"We don't even know what we're going to be facing."

"It's not going to matter," I said. I took out the little bag containing the sample of powder and the die.

"No way," she said, her eyes wide. She grabbed hold of my wrist. "You can't do that. It's not an emergency."

"Yes, it is," I said, gently pulling free. "Everything depends on this. Everything. Not just my planet, but yours and Steve's. Confederation Central. The Confederation itself, and all the planets under Phandic rule. Nothing we've done has ever been more important than this. Maybe nothing anyone has ever done has been more important than this. We can't risk anything going wrong."

"But it could kill you," she said, glowering. She was clearly unhappy that I hadn't talked about this part in advance.

"I have an eighty-five percent chance of not dying," I said. "And if I get a bad roll, I can still save all those people. If I don't take the chance, we won't get this done, and our chances of getting killed are a lot higher than fifteen percent."

"You don't know that," she said.

"Yeah, I do. Convex Icosahedron told me. He said that it was the only way we were going to be able to pull this off. He knew I didn't want to take the risk if I didn't have to, that I was going to take a wait and see approach about rolling the die. He said if I did that, we would fail. He told me I had to activate the tech tree if we were going to succeed."

She stepped forward. "Let me do it."

I wasn't about to let her take my place. Before she could take a second step, I put a few grains of powder on my tongue and tossed the heavy die on the table. It landed with a hard crack and rolled a few times. I turned away, hardly daring to look. Then I felt a sting of pain as Tamret punched me hard in the shoulder.

"Sometimes you really deserve a smack," she said.

And that was how I knew I'd made my saving throw.

I was grinning. I was in my happy place, and I'm not ashamed to admit it. I had survived my toss of the die—lucky number thirteen!—and now I was running an infrared image of the entire complex through my bracelet to create a 3-D visual. We not only had the layout of the facility, but we knew how many people were inside and what kinds of weapons they had.

We were on the thirty-seventh floor. The control center was on the sixty-eighth. To get there we needed to pass through two security checks. It was no big deal.

Tamret and I strolled down the mostly empty corridor until we got to the elevator bank. Three human guards sat at a station there, looking bored.

"Aura scan," one of them said, not bothering to look up.

Then he did bother to look up, and he saw two kids standing in front of them, one being a cat alien.

Approximately 1.8 seconds later, he and his two companions were unconscious. I used my forging tech to examine and duplicate their security auras, and then pressed the button to call the elevator.

Tamret sighed. "You like showing off, don't you?"

"If everything goes the way it's supposed to," I told her, "I'll never get to use these powers again. Let me enjoy myself. But to answer your question: Yes. Yes, I do."

The elevator opened up on our floor with the second security check. There were ten guards here. It took almost three seconds to deal with them. Then, while Tamret watched, annoyed that there was nothing for her to do, I gained security access for the main control room.

My infrared scan only told me what to expect in the first chamber—another ten guards in there, as well as a couple dozen technical workers. The actual control room, which was basically a giant safe, was beyond that, and would contain more security.

I showed Tamret the projection of what we'd be facing. "There are still some unknowns, but we can expect things are going to get messy. I'm going to hit the EMP as soon as we enter. Be ready to start stunning people. Guards and any other Phands first, then human workers."

She had her pistol out and was activating the anti-EMP insulation that would allow our tech to continue working while the rest of the planet went dark. "Ready." She leaned in and gave me a quick kiss on the cheek. I thought she was being sweet, though I later learned she was trying to distract me.

"Don't blow it."

I opened the door, and it was already blown. I knew that the minute I felt the punch in my face. There was only one hand that could hit me that hard. Also, the furry fingers were a giveaway. It was Ardov, and he was at full power.

CHAPTER TWENTY

I don't know if there is a standard list of things you should be thinking about when you've been sucker-punched by a super-villain, but here's some of what went through my head as I was flying backward, crashing into a wall. First, I'd checked the physiology of the beings in that room, and I'd seen only humans and Phands. Ardov must have known we were coming. The Phands clearly had monitoring systems we hadn't anticipated, and Ardov had cloaked himself. Second, he was powered up, which meant he had taken the time to risk his life by tossing the die—another clue he knew we were coming. Third, if you can't get rid of a guy by knocking him off a spaceship and into the waiting jaws of a giant eel, then you are pretty much never going to get rid of him.

I came to a halt with a sudden, painful crunch as the metal beams in the wall stopped my momentum and kept me from ending up in another office. I shook off the pain and dizziness and tried to get to my feet. Phands and human workers were fleeing from the room, not wanting to get in the way of the cat-alien Hulk. Tamret raised her hand to fire her pistol at Ardov—a useless gesture—and he batted her aside with a swipe of his arm. It was Tamret's turn to fly into the wall, and she didn't have the advantage of augments.

Now I was angry.

My upgrades included bioscans, so I took a few milliseconds

to review Tamret's vitals. Had she been human, she would have suffered at least a few broken bones, but her Rarel physiology had saved her from any serious harm. There was no guarantee she'd be so lucky the next time, though. I had to do everything I could to keep his attention off her.

And that meant it was time for another fight with Ardov. I'd taken some blows the last time, what with him beating my face, literally, to a pulp. I'd come out on top, though only because my friend had run him over with a space shuttle. The bottom line was that he was the one, not me, who had ended up eel food. Victory had not been easy, but it had still been mine. I could win again. I just had to be smart.

"I'm not dead," Ardov observed with a grin. He was wearing loose pants and, inexplicably, an I ♥ NY T-shirt. Maybe he'd taken the time to see the sights.

"Nothing gets past you," I told him as I moved toward him.

"I should have died from the die roll, but I lived," he snarled. "Nothing can kill me."

He seemed to have taken the wrong lesson away from that incident. Instead of realizing I'd been messing with his head, he now thought he was indestructible.

"Not even a giant eel, apparently," I said.

"That?" he asked with a smug grin. "That was nothing. I just forced my way through its digestive tract and made my way out through its—"

"Too much information!" I interrupted. "We'll just say you managed to outsmart a huge fish and leave it at that." I was playing for time, trying to work out what strategy was going to give me the advantage I needed.

"You'll stop joking when your girlfriend is dead," he sneered.

Ardov turned toward Tamret.

So, yeah. Pretty much any rational thoughts or strategies I was cooking up were out the window. I charged Ardov. It wasn't until the last second that I realized I'd fallen into his trap.

I didn't slow time, but it felt like I did. Ardov turned to me, and I thought he meant to land another punch, but his hand was open. He reached out to grab me, and I saw it—the injector in his other hand. I'd been thinking about our fight on Planet Pleasant, when he'd mashed my face. I should have been thinking about our fight in Central Park, when he'd neutralized my upgrades.

That's what he did. Again.

He stepped back and allowed me to move past him as he spun one arm around and slammed me in the back of my neck with the injector. The blow was hard enough to send me sprawling to the floor while the neutralizing agents took effect. My HUD switched off, and I felt myself deflate like a punctured balloon. I hadn't noticed the sensation the first time, being distracted by falling through the air, but I noticed it now. It was like I'd shrunk, turned insubstantial, in just the blink of an eye.

Ardov was standing over me, grinning. I was just an ordinary kid now, and he was a deranged, jacked-up monster. There was nothing I could do to protect myself. Nothing I could say. He had all the power, and I was sure he meant to kill me.

But first he meant to do a whole lot of talking. I'd forgotten about that. He seemed to have become very fond of his own voice. Maybe I could use that to my advantage.

"That stupid scientist at Planet Pleasant required a little convincing," he told me, holding up the injector, wagging it back and forth like the sight of it might make me faint. "She didn't want to give me another anti-upgrade injector, but I convinced her. I knew I'd run into you again."

"I'm flattered you spend so much time thinking about me," I said.

"Oh, I did," he said. "I was ready for you, so I could use this." He held up the injector. A tiny drop of my blood glistened at the tip. "I couldn't wait to find you and turn you into a nothing before I killed you."

"And why is that again?" I asked. "I keep forgetting why you dislike me so much."

He paused to think about it. "Beings like you have always stood in my way. Beings who aren't smarter or stronger, but somehow end up getting everything they want."

"What I've mostly wanted from you is for you not to hurt me or beings I know."

"That's what you tell yourself," he said with some bitterness. Clearly this was something he'd spent a lot of time thinking about. Really, it was nice to see him working through his feelings. His therapist and I were very proud of him. "What you don't understand is that beings like you represent something that's just unfair about the universe. There are beings who deserve to be on top, and beings who should be on the bottom, and when that order gets switched around, everything is thrown out of balance."

"That's very philosophical," I observed.

"Even now, you think mocking me will get you out of this?"

"Seriously, I just want to understand," I said. "I mean, maybe you'll kill me, and before I die, I'd like to know why you hate me so much. What did I do wrong?"

He peered over me as though I were a curious specimen in

a tide pool. Then his eyes went wide with shock.

"He didn't used to talk so much," Tamret said. "It's tedious, but hey, I won't argue with whatever gets the job done."

While I'd been asking Ardov to talk about his feelings and explain his grievances about how bullies throughout the galaxy were being undermined by the beings they tormented, Tamret had snuck up behind him. Lightning quick, she'd grabbed the injector from his hand and jabbed it into his shoulder. She had, in other words, stabbed Ardov with his own neutralizing agent.

Ardov stared, stunned. He looked down at his body, like he was expecting it to do something interesting or surprising, but it was just an ordinary, unpowered Rarel body wearing a touristy T-shirt. In an instant he'd gone from unstoppable to doomed. Having been down that road myself, I knew it was an unpleasant feeling. I also hoped that on some level he could appreciate the irony. He'd been blathering on about how people like me and Tamret undermined him, and, well, that was exactly what we'd done.

Now he had the additional problem of being at our mercy. "Listen," he began.

Tamret shot him with her PPB pistol. With no tech at all working inside him, a single blast on stun should have kept him out for hours, but I wasn't going to take any chances. As soon as we had a moment to spare, I would cuff him, lock him in a room, or do something. Until this guy was shipped off to the penal colony at Rura Penthe, I wasn't going to breathe easily, and maybe not even then.

I held out my hand. "Let me hold on to the injector. You never know."

"Sure thing," Tamret said, dropping the injector into my

palm. She was smiling, but there was something sad in her expression. I knew a few things at once: She had lifted the powder and the die off me and used them.

I also knew, could see in that smile, that she hadn't made her saving throw.

"Tamret, what did you roll?"

"We'll talk when we're done," she said.

"Tamret."

"A three," she said, looking away. "I rolled a three."

I stared at her, unable to speak, unable even to make my mind work. Tamret had gotten out of more scrapes, had come up with more last-second solutions to unsolvable problems, than anyone I'd ever known. How could the luckiest, most resourceful being I knew have rolled a three? Tamret was going to die. What kind of a stupid system was this, anyhow? Who were these Formers, and why had they designed their technology with these obstacles and hoops to jump through? What pleasure did they get from watching inferior beings like us run around like rats in a maze for their entertainment? They were gone, millennia gone, and we were still putting on a show, like actors forced to perform a play with no one watching.

"Tamret," I said again. My voice came out like a croak, something broken and jagged.

She forced another smile. "Let's do what we came here to do. Let's get these Phands off your world and then we'll talk, okay?"

She only had a few hours left before the same technology that had allowed us to survive to this point killed her, and she didn't want to waste it. She was not going to spend her last hours crying or complaining. She wanted to do something that mattered. I wanted to hug her, to cry, to forget about the stupid Phands and their stupid invasion, but I couldn't do that. I couldn't indulge. She needed to complete the mission, and I was going to make sure she did.

"Okay," I said. I gritted my teeth and sucked in a deep breath. "Let's do it."

She smiled at me, and I saw the real Tamret. She'd dropped her guard, let go of her worries about our responsibilities to our worlds. It was just her—the tough, unstoppable, determined girl who had changed my life. I had to press my hand against the wall to steady myself, but I could not break down. Not when she needed me.

"Okay," I said again. "Let's mess up some Phands."

The final, most protected chamber required another round of hacking to access, but Tamret made short work of that. We entered the control room, full of workers. Tamret took about half a second to turn them into unconcious workers. All around us were workstations and consoles beeping and flashing questions at us. This was the power hub of a Phandic colony. Everything that made their occupation possible filtered through this station. It was time to shut it down.

Tamret scanned the room and picked one of the workstations, shoving an unconscious Phand out of the way before she sat down. Her eyes glazed over for a second, and I could tell she was interacting with her upgrades. Then she began typing, her fingers moving in a furious blur over the keyboard.

"This is going to take a few minutes," she said. "It's incredibly complicated, even for me—even for enhanced me. They really, really don't want anyone doing what we are about to do, and they actually bothered to get some programmers who knew their stuff to make it difficult."

"Okay," I said, not sure what she needed from me.

"If I have to stop, even for a few seconds, then everything I've done will reset and I'll have to start over. If that happens more than once, the system will lock me out, and we'll have failed."

"You can do it," I said, making an effort to keep my voice from wavering.

"You're sweet to say so," she said with a slight sneer as her fingers danced over the keyboard. "The main thing is you're going to have to keep the security forces off me while I work. We triggered some kind of alarm. I shut down the elevators and put up some barriers, but they'll be able to break through and start climbing the stairs any second."

"How many are coming?" I asked.

"One hundred and thirty-seven," she said. "And an infrared scan shows a small convex icosahedron. We have to assume one of these guards has got the Former military tech tree. You can't let any of them get near me. You up for this?"

"Not a problem," I said with entirely false confidence. This was, in fact, a huge problem.

Still, I understood what I had to do. There were missions like this in a million video games. Keep the enemies off an ally while she did something important. For the record, I hated that type of mission. It didn't help that I no longer had any of my own augmentations, but I couldn't let that slow me down. Tamret needed me. She was dying, and she needed me to protect her, so that was precisely what I was going to do.

I only had a few minutes to figure out how to hold off more than a hundred bad guys, including one who could wipe the floor with me, literally and metaphorically. I began to scan the space, figuring out how to make my stand. I grabbed several PPB pistols—I'd never had one fail on me, but I'd never had to stun more than a hundred beings before. I wasn't taking any chances.

"How is the one with the die moving?" I asked. "Walking, running, flying?"

"Normally, like a regular being. Just one of the group heading up the stairs," she said. "And stop bothering me. I'm busy."

This was useful information. If this guy was hoofing it up the stairs with a bunch of grunts, it meant he was new to his augments. He hadn't figured out all the cool things he could do yet, and he was still thinking like an ordinary guy. Maybe I had a chance.

With the little time I had left, I overturned several desks, to use as barriers. I wanted to arrange a full set of them, making it necessary for any intruders to have to leap over an annoying number of desks to get close, but there simply wasn't time. The best I could do was to set up barriers at both the main door and the inner door. That gave me two choke points through which no more than two enemies could enter at one time. As long as my aim was decent, I had a shot at pulling this off.

I hid behind a third desk slightly within the main control room. This gave me a good line of sight and a chance to snipe at both blockaded entrances.

I'd only just settled down behind my barrier and taken aim at the main entrance when the first enemies appeared. They were three Phands dressed in some kind of battle armor. They were tall, even for their species, with cruel expressions that suggested a lifetime of battle and violence. Without exchanging a word, all three pushed at the desk blocking the entrance and shoved it aside.

So much for my plan. This was going to be harder than I thought.

Or maybe not. I saw those three Phands and fired off three perfectly aimed head shots. Maybe I'd lost my augments, but I still had my own experiences of battle. I'd faced down bad guys before, and I'd walked away the winner. I'd captured battleships and conquered planets. I'd broken into and out of prisons. Time to show the Phand warriors what it meant to cross Zeke Reynolds.

That's what I told myself to keep from peeing in my pants.

Two of my shots missed, but I still maintain they were perfectly aimed. It wasn't my fault the heads moved. One landed, taking out that Phand. After about twenty more less-perfect shots, the other two were down.

The good news was that these seemed to be the only Phands we were going to have to face. The other good news was that there were now three unconscious Phands blocking the doorway. The bad news was that there was no shortage of humans, and they were now doing their best to step over their fallen buddies and make their way into the room. They wore black Phandic-occupation military uniforms, but they moved like they had real military experience, advancing in tight formation, flashing each other hand signals, and acting in general like a deadly assault on a couple of kids was a typical afternoon for them.

The other bad news was that they weren't just acting like that; they were trying to actually kill us. They were firing guns at me—Earth guns. The kind with bullets. You can't set bullets to stun. I was in real danger of getting killed, but I couldn't let that slow me down. I had to protect Tamret and make sure that she had the time to do what she needed to do. Everything depended on her. Billions of beings on Earth, across the galaxy, needed us to get this job done. Even the future happiness of the guys currently trying to kill us depended on that, though they seemed pretty content at the moment.

At least I didn't have to worry about a stray bullet hurting her. I knew her shielding augmentation would filter anything like that out. All I had to do was keep these people from getting past me, and preferably I should avoid getting shot while doing it.

I began firing my PPB pistol at the soldiers who were coming through the door. Each one who fell only made the bottleneck harder for the enemy to squeeze through. I was able to pick the soldiers off fairly easily, especially the ones who paused to survey the room, take stock of the situation, and make a reasonable effort to kill me. The loud popping of weapons fire was unnerving, as was the clang of bullets hitting the desk I was hiding behind. Most of the shots went wild, though. The ones who tried to take careful shots ended up stunned. The others weren't giving themselves enough time to aim. It was starting to get hectic in there. The bullets theoretically aimed at me were now slamming into walls, furniture, and Phandic computers. Dust from plaster and wood, and smoke from the guns, were starting to obscure their vision. Then a window shattered, letting in a gusting wind. It cleared the air, but papers began to fly around the control room. It was chaos, but I felt sure that the chaos worked in favor of the few making the stand rather than the many trying to prevent us from liberating them.

Then, all at once, no one was trying to get through the door.

Had I gotten them all? I'd never stunned 137 beings before, so I couldn't speak from experience about how long it was supposed to take, but I didn't feel like I could have taken out more than a couple dozen by that point. I certainly hadn't taken on anyone who had been augmented. They were up to something, and I didn't know what.

"Clear!" one of them shouted.

That's when I figured out what they were up to. They were up to making something explode.

Then something exploded.

The blast shook the desk I was hiding behind and filled the air with smoke. It was the doorway. They'd blown away the first bottleneck, sending bits of plaster and wood flying through the air. That was the bad news. There was a silver lining, though. They clearly had explosives, but they hadn't used them on me. Maybe they wanted to take us alive after all. It could explain their lousy shooting.

I wasn't enough of an optimist to think I didn't have to worry about getting shot. I didn't doubt for a second that these guys would be happy to shoot me somewhere just to slow me down. Tough guys in movies could carry on heroically with a bullet in the shoulder, but I wasn't so sure I could. Even if I tried, how long could I really keep stunning bad guys if I was bleeding from a bullet wound? For action heroes, blood loss doesn't seem to have much effect until a dramatically appropriate moment. I couldn't depend on things working that way in real life.

As interesting as these questions were, I had other things to worry about: namely the dozens of armed men moving through their newly made hole in the wall and directly toward me.

I began firing frantically, but there were simply too many of them. They filed into the outer room, crowding like guests at some kind of military cocktail party. I fired through the door, but they were hard to hit. They knew how to avoid me, and they were staying out of sight. That meant they were preparing to blow the second doorway. When that happened, I was going to face more soldiers than I could possibly handle. Once they got through the second door, they would shoot me or at least get past me. They would be able to stop Tamret, and everything we'd done, everything she'd sacrificed, would be for nothing.

Fortunately, I had one shot at dealing with a whole bunch of bad guys in a relatively enclosed space. I lay down some suppressive fire to keep them occupied; then I took Villainic's stun grenade out of my pocket, armed it, and threw it into the outer room.

If they knew what a Phandic stun grenade looked like, and they knew how to disarm it, they would have about a second to get the job done. If the augmented person was in the room with them, it would be an easy task, and I'd be out of luck. On the other hand, if the augmented person was there, why hadn't he just stormed in and disarmed me? He was either holding back for some reason or was really clueless about his abilities. I hated to take a bet on the second option, but it was either that or be overwhelmed.

I threw myself on the floor behind the desk and closed my eyes. An instant later I saw a bright flash through my eyelids and felt the shock wave of the grenade pass through me. That was all very positive, I thought.

I peered up over the side of the desk, pistol out, but saw no movement in the other room.

"How long?" I asked Tamret.

"Ten minutes," she said.

"Ten minutes?" I asked.

"Yes!" she snapped. "I haven't forgotten. I'm almost there."

"I think we're good on my end," I said.

Then I saw the figure emerge through the hole in the outer wall. It was the augment, and her name was Nora Price.

She looked at me and smiled, looking like a CEO in her expensive gray skirt suit. Also, her eyes were glowing red. That is pretty much never a good sign.

"Hey, Tamret," I shouted.

"Kind of busy."

"I know, and I hate to bug you, but can you check real quick to see what it means if your eyes are glowing red?"

There was a brief pause.

"Death-ray eyes," she said.

"Death-ray eyes? That's a thing?"

"Yeah." There was a brief pause as her fingers clattered over the keys. "Seems like kind of an unfair advantage, don't you think?"

"I am thinking that, yes."

"Hello, Zeke," Nora Price said, walking slowly into the room. She didn't bother to hide or take cover. Why should she? She knew a PPB pistol couldn't hurt her.

"Wow," I said. "I get a visit from the viceroy. I must be important."

"Oh, you are," she said, her lips twisted into a cruel sneer.

"You are the most wanted criminal in the entire Phandic Empire, and I'm going to look very good when I hand you over."

"Don't be so hard on yourself," I said. "You've always had a decent sense of style."

She pointed her death-ray eyes toward my hiding place, which suddenly felt completely inadequate. "You're funny. Funny until the end."

"I'm also funny in the after-credits sequence," I said. "Impatient people miss out on that."

"I heard your girlfriend say she needs about ten minutes to finish what she's doing," Nora Price said. "My attack saucers will be here in less than six. I've already won."

"Which is why you're not bothering to attack me and why, after I've taken care of your dozens of goons, you're now just speechifying in my general direction?"

"That is correct," she said. "I don't need to get my hands dirty. I know your pet Rarel could challenge me if she chose, but she will make every effort, no matter how pointless, to complete whatever sabotage she's attempting. So, you see, this is how civilized people use their abilities—to avoid violence, rather than create it."

"I have to tell you, you're really inspiring me to expand my horizons right now."

"You really never change, do you?"

"There aren't a lot of opportunities to put on fresh clothes during intergalactic emergencies," I said.

"So witty," she said. "Especially as you face devastating emotional loss. I also know about the Rarel girl's unfortunate roll of the die. You didn't shut down the surveillance cameras. Very sloppy. So I'm aware that she'd rather go out doing something heroic than waste her short time in a pointless fight with me."

"Yeah, well, there's still me," I said, springing up from behind my desk. I fired a dozen bursts at her. They all hit. They did nothing.

"Did you expect that to harm me?"

"I was hoping I might get lucky," I said, trying to sound disappointed. I needed her to think I had hoped exactly that. I had one chance, and I didn't want to blow it.

Ms. Price had described what Tamret was doing as "some kind of sabotage." That meant she had no idea what exactly we were up to. If she did know, then she would have captured our two other teams by now, which she clearly hadn't. She wouldn't be able to keep herself from gloating if she had them in custody. Our plan was still alive, and I needed to make sure we stayed that way.

I fired a few more bursts at Ms. Price.

"Really, Zeke. What's the point?"

"It's actually very therapeutic," I told her. I fired a few more times. "It relieves the stress. You should try it. Okay, maybe you shouldn't since you have death-ray eyes." I sighed and raised my hand with the pistol, letting it dangle from my fingers so she could see I wasn't about to shoot. I let it fall down on the desk. Then, very slowly, I raised my hands into the air and began to stand up. I would not have been entirely surprised had she hit me with her death-ray eyes, but she probably wanted to hand me over alive. This seemed like a fairly safe gamble.

She squinted her glowing red eyes at me as she tried to figure out what I was doing. "What is this?"

"It's the intergalactic gesture for 'I surrender.' The raised hands are supposed to let you know that I'm now unarmed and can't hurt you. I think there might be a pamphlet around here somewhere to explain it. There are pictures and everything."

"I don't believe you're surrendering."

"I'm unarmed, and my hands are in the air," I said. "I'm pretty sure I'm doing this right."

She continued to consider the situation.

"So, now what?" I asked.

"Now what? Now you wait until my attack vehicles arrive and you're stunned. These are your last moments of freedom, Zeke. I suggest you enjoy them."

"But they don't have to be, right? I mean, you're viceroy and everything. You could cancel those attack vehicles if you wanted to, couldn't you?"

She smirked at me, like this was exactly what she was expecting. "Why would I want to do that?"

I took a step toward her. I moved slowly, nonthreateningly. I slumped my shoulders to signal my defeat, but I also lowered my hands a little. "Come on, Ms. Price. I know you like power and telling everyone what to do, but this is your home planet. Do you really want Earth to be part of the Phandic Empire?"

"You are so naïve, Zeke. Since the Phands have come, we've seen a virtual end of war, crime, cruelty. I understand why you, personally, don't welcome the change, but that's just selfishness. You like the Confederation, and the Confederation lost, so now you're sulking. You must see the truth as it is. Under Phandic rule, humanity will know peace, comfort, and security, but you want to stand in the way of all of that. You're the villain here, Zeke, not me."

"Hmm, that's interesting," I said, taking another step closer to her. "But the Confederation is offering the same thing, only without the enforced reeducation and military oppression. Maybe you can explain how that's not better."

"The Confederation is a temporary blip in galactic history. It can't last. Look how easily Junup was able to take control of their government. A single being was able to undermine their entire political system. The citizens of the Confederation are sheep, Zeke, and sheep always get eaten in the end."

"Or they get sheared. Or is it shorn?"

"I'm not sure I see your point." She was clearly losing patience with me.

"Sheep," I explained, scrunching up my forehead in concentration. "Think about it. Someone comes along and cuts off their wool. And that wool gets turned into a sweater. Maybe a nice striped one. Or a turtleneck."

"Zeke, what are you going on about?"

"Come on," I said. "It's not that complicated. When it's cold, people can put on those sweaters, and they can sit by a fire and roast marshmallows."

"Are you trying to distract me with nonsense?" Ms. Price asked. "I have no idea what you're talking about."

"Marshmallows," I told her. "That's what I'm talking about." My eyes went wide as I worked myself up to a frenzy. "I'm talking about marshmallows!" I shouted. As battle cries of liberation go, this was, admittedly, kind of ridiculous, but my point had been to get closer to her and to put her off her guard. What, after all, did a superaugmented meanie like Nora Price have to fear from an unarmed, idealistic troublemaker shouting about marshmallows? She probably thought the answer was gibberish, but she didn't know that I was concealing an upgrade neutralizing injector in my hand. So now that I was close enough, I jabbed it into her arm.

Nora Price looked at it. Then she looked at me. Her eyes were no longer glowing red.

"I'm talking about marshmallows," I said again, this time my voice low and menacing. I hadn't meant for this to be my cool line, but it was out there, and I was going to run with it. And having said it, I took out one of my spare PPB pistols and stunned her.

The instant she hit the floor, I heard an electronic whir coming through the broken windows. I turned to see two saucers, at least a mile distant, but closing fast.

"How much time?" I asked Tamret.

"Maybe a minute."

I was still pulling a lot of my battle tactics from *Star Trek II*, so I'd asked Tamret to double any time estimates while enemies were lurking. When Ms. Price had said she had attack ships six minutes out, I knew we were cutting things close, but there hadn't been much of a choice. Now things were desperate. We had a narrow window to get things done.

I keyed my bracelet to talk to both teams. "Take care of opposition!" I shouted. "And do it fast! Things are going to be tight."

Both teams acknowledged. I watched helplessly as Tamret's fingers danced over the keyboard. The saucers were moving in. I had no idea how close they had to be in order to stun us. Once they realized Tamret wasn't affected, they would very likely use more aggressive methods to stop her. Maybe they wouldn't be able to hurt her, but they could keep her from completing her task.

"We're good in Beijing," I heard Steve announce.

"All set in London," Mi Sun said a few seconds later.

Finally Tamret looked up. "Done," she said.

She had overridden the security blockades and broadcast the message we'd prepared. Now it was up to the others to kill the power feed.

"Go!" I shouted at them. "Now! Now! Now!"

It took them less than a minute. The bright beam of energy jutting out from the Empire State Building in Manhattan suddenly switched off. The two saucers on the horizon must have known that this meant that things had become critical, because they suddenly sped up. They were moving in on us, and I had no illusions that they planned to stun us. They were going to take this building out.

"Insulate!" I shouted into my bracelets.

"Insulated," Mi Sun said.

"Insulated," Steve said.

I nodded at Tamret. Our EMP insulation fields were up. She hit a few more keys and deployed the massive electromagnetic pulse. Except for the systems within our personal insulation fields, every single electronic system on the planet just went dead. The saucers that had been preparing to fire on us fell from the sky, spiraling into the river. We'd done it.

I looked over at Tamret, who was smiling at me.

That smile reminded me of the price she had paid to complete the mission. We'd done what we had set out to do, but the price had been too high.

Then we heard the alarm sound. Tamret's console had also been insulated from the EMP so she could send the record of what we'd done out into the larger galaxy. Now, however, it was alight. A message flashed along her holographic screen. ELEC-TROMAGNETIC PULSE DETECTED. EMERGENCY RETALIATORY MEASURES INITIATED.

Tamret's eyes went distant. I knew she was trying to pull up data that could explain the message. Then her look turned from blank to alarm.

"They have a protocol for this kind of attack. In the event of an EMP assault that knocks out planetary control, they have a biological response that is designed to target the source of the pulse."

"What does that mean?" I demanded. "What is a biological response? Like a deadly virus or something?"

"Not that. The word I'm getting, it doesn't process through the universal translator, and it doesn't exist in any Earth language but one called Japanese."

"What's the word?" I had a feeling I didn't want to know.

"*Kaiju,*" she said.

I sat down heavily in an office chair. I looked out the window and saw a sudden upheaval in the river. Then it began to emerge—massive and reptilian, and heading directly toward our building. Thousands of gallons of dirty river water rolled off its glistening green body, and it swiveled its massive head, looking for its first target. Then it stopped, and its huge yellow eyes seemed to find mine. It opened its mouth and showed rows and rows of pointed teeth, each as long as a telephone pole.

The Phands were sending Godzilla after us.

CHAPTER TWENTY-ONE

The giant reptilian monster was now entirely out of the river. It must have been four hundred feet tall. It moved closer to our building, pausing only occasionally to sniff the air. It opened its mouth, I assumed to let out the trademark Godzilla screech, but no sound came out. That was strangely disappointing.

"So," I said. "Biological retaliation. That's messed up."

"We need to get you out of here," Tamret said.

I looked at her. She wanted me to get out of there, not us to get out of there. She had already given up on herself.

"There's no time," I said. "That thing is going to bring this building down before we can get to the ground floor. I have another idea."

"I don't even need to hear it to know it's stupid," she said. "My idea is better." She grabbed me around the waist, and before I could object, she ran forward, taking the two of us out the window.

Right. She could fly. I'd forgotten about that.

We were out of the building just as the massive kaiju began to pound its claws against the windows. Glass and dust from crushed concrete rained down on the street below. The monster's head was well below the floor we'd been on, but chunks of building began to fall away from the structure like leaves from a dying tree. Meanwhile, I was gritting my teeth, trying to push back the rush of nausea. Flying is great, but being flown, it turns out, is terrifying.

When we landed on the ground, there was an eight-foot-tall metallic humanoid waiting for us, and it looked unhappy. It had its arms crossed. This wasn't the same synthetic containment unit it had found in the Hidden Fortress. It had either upgraded or the casing was malleable. It was also wearing a business suit that looked really expensive. I didn't care what Smelly looked like; I was just happy to see it.

"Why are you bothering me?" Smelly asked.

I had summoned the AI just before Tamret had grabbed me. That had been my idea—the one Tamret had said was stupid before she bothered to hear it. I was going to get Smelly to stop the kaiju. At least that had been part of my idea. I had something else in mind, and it was a long shot, but I had to hope I knew Smelly well enough to count on its help. It had lived inside my head for months. It owed me.

I gestured with my thumb toward the gigantic, skyscraper-destroying monster. "There's something after me."

The kaiju took a swipe at the building, sending a corner office careening into the river, trailing office furniture and paperwork like a comet's tail.

"That big green thing?" it asked.

"Yes," I said. "That."

"It doesn't seem to be trying to kill you specifically," Smelly said. Its head was elongated on top, moving into a gentle point, and its facial features were vaguely humanoid, though it was weird how its mouth didn't move when it spoke. Maybe it would be weirder if it did. Also, its eyes glowed red, though they were still less creepy than Nora Price's death-ray eyes.

"As soon as it realizes we're not in there, it will come looking for me," I told Smelly. "You have to do something."

"I can handle the monster," Tamret said.

"Your girlfriend can handle the monster," Smelly said. The exposed metal of its hands and face glistened in the sun. It reached up and adjusted its tie and buttoned its coat, like it wanted to make sure it fit in with the other business types in midtown. "I warned you about bothering me with trivial matters. How did you tick off a kaiju, anyhow? You have to be the most irritating being who ever lived."

"*You* are saying that to me? To anyone?"

"I'm not alive in the biological sense," it said. "You can't compare yourself to me."

"Look," I said to it, "Tamret doesn't know for sure that she's up to taking out something like that."

"Neither do I. Let's find out. Call me if it kills her and comes after you. My terms were specific."

"Come on, Smelly. There are beings in that building."

"Phands and Phand sympathizers. Don't look surprised. It seems to you that I appeared instantly, but I actually had to travel here. I had time to review your crisis. I also learned the rules of blackjack, so I'm thinking I'll hit Vegas before I head home. And why is there a game called craps? Am I the only one who wonders about these things?"

I looked at the building. "Maybe they are bad guys in there. Maybe they're just working for them. Some of those people probably had no choice but to work in security. There must be secretaries in that building too, and people in the mailroom and maintenance departments and whatever. The Phands' receptionists don't deserve to die. Go stop the monster."

"That's your one cosmic favor? That's the thing you summoned me from across the galaxy to do? Save the office staff?"

"I thought I was trying to save me when I hit the button," I said. "But while you're here, you can also cure Tamret."

Her eyes widened in surprise. "Can it do that?"

"I was waiting for you to ask." It folded its arms again. "Why don't you understand that I told you not to summon me unless your death was imminent? Not the Phandic janitor's and not your girlfriend's. I'm not your butler. Next thing you know, you'll be asking me to lay out your pajamas before bed."

Another chunk of the building went flying, this time into the street. I had to hope people had cleared out already.

"Smelly, can you do it or not?"

"Of course I *can*," it said. "I mean, if I want to. I'm amazing. Incredible. Remarkable. I'll tell you what, Zeke. I hate to have wasted a trip. I can either stop that monster before it rips apart this city or I can save your girlfriend. You have to choose." It leveled its electronic gaze at me. "Life isn't fair and it isn't easy. One or the other. Make your choice and live with it."

I glanced over at the monster pounding on the crumbling building. I looked at Tamret. She was shaking her head, like I had to choose to save everyone but her. It was an impossible decision. How could I decide? How could I live with myself no matter what I decided?

It was impossible. I couldn't make that choice, but I also didn't think I had to.

"Don't be a jerk, Smelly. Do both, and make it snappy. Please," I added. "Be a pal."

It let out an electronic sigh. "Fine. I only wanted to torment you a little first. Here," it said to Tamret, holding out a piece of what seemed to be some kind of raw vegetable. It looked like pale yellow broccoli.

"I hate [*broccoli*]," Tamret said.

"I know," said Smelly. "I also know it gives you gas. That's why I chose it. Because I'm hilarious. Eat it and you won't die. But you're going to stink up the place. Later, fools."

Smelly flew off, which I guessed was something it could do. It was heading for the kaiju.

"Eat the stupid broccoli, Tamret," I said.

She made a face and popped it in her mouth. She chewed a few times, looking visibly disgusted, and swallowed. "I guess I'm not dying now," she said.

"Do you know that for sure?" I asked her. "Do you feel different?"

"I feel the same," she said. "But the little countdown clock to my death has disappeared from my HUD."

"You had that?"

She nodded.

I hugged her. I didn't know what else to do. I could think of nothing to say. She'd been working to save this planet while her own death had been playing out in front of her eyes, and it hadn't slowed her down, not one second.

"I'm okay now," she said, hugging me back. "Because of you."

I took a step back. "I didn't do anything."

"You got that AI to help me. That's something."

"All I did was ask."

"All over the galaxy, there are billions of beings who need help. It gave that help to you, Zeke. There's a reason. You're always worried about what powers or abilities or technology you have, but those aren't the things that make you a hero."

I shook my head. "I'm not a hero."

"Whatever," she said. "I meant to say idiot. Those are the things that make you an idiot."

Meanwhile, Smelly obviously had some control over the size and shape of its containment suit, as it had expanded to a four-hundred-foot tall version of itself. It grabbed the kaiju and spun it around so they were facing each other. The kaiju glowered at Smelly. Smelly turned to me, opened its mouth, and let out the classic Godzilla screech. It *was* satisfying to hear it.

Smelly then punched the kaiju in the face.

It turned out the monster wasn't so tough. One punch, and it fell backward into the river, and after a long pause, it became clear it was not coming out again.

"That's what I'm talking about!" Smelly announced, fist pumping in the air, its voice carrying like a citywide loudspeaker. "Boom!"

Apparently, this was the sound of the galaxy being saved.

CHAPTER TWENTY-TWO

T hings played out pretty much like we'd hoped. The people of Earth rose up, defeating their Phandic overlords with broomsticks, golf clubs, and, in what I considered a surprising number of countries, cricket bats. With the technological devices down and numbers on our side, it was a pretty simple business. Tamret and I had recorded our own experiences, and once we deactivated the EMP, Nayana, who turned out to know a lot about media software, edited it all together for a galactic broadcast. We sent out beacons to the various quarters of the Confederation and the Phandic Empire. The message was pretty simple: The Phands had been overthrown on Earth. Junup and Ghli Wixxix were evil.

It took a few days, but with Dr. Roop and Captain Qwlessl making sure the news outputs spread the story, the bad guys were soon detained and behind bars. There was a lot of inevitable chaos and confusion in the Confederation government, but reasonable beings were in charge once more, and damage done by Junup was being rolled back. Confederation ships were on the case, making sure the Phandic Empire did not expand, which seemed unlikely. The empress was dealing with world after world, long under Phandic control, rising up in rebellion. Maybe the empire would fall, or maybe it would just shrink, but things were definitely moving in the right direction.

Here on Earth there was also plenty of change. The day

after we shut down the Phands, the *New York Times* front page featured a massive picture of Smelly fighting the kaiju. The headline read ALIEN INVASION ENDS WITH INEXPLICABLE MONSTER BATTLE. There was also a story about the role our team had played in removing the Phands from power. We were all very happy with how they described our efforts, human and alien, to liberate Earth. The story made us look competent and it made it clear that the Confederation—beings of different species working together for the common good—was a great idea. We were all happy about that. The team was less happy that the story was accompanied by a picture of me screaming like a wacko. That headline read "I'M TALKING ABOUT MARSH-MALLOWS!": WORLD SAVED BY TEENS. My argument that it could have been worse was not well received.

Our families and friends turned out to be unharmed. Mi Sun claimed she was still angry with me, but I wasn't buying it, and she couldn't be bothered to work up a realistic level of irritation. She actually hugged me as we waited in an antechamber at the United Nations, where we were to receive a special commendation by the secretary general. It was a long ceremony, and kind of boring, but in the end all of us received medals on ribbons. All of us but Villainic, who stood by the side, looking unsure what to do with himself.

Long and boring ceremonies are always bad news. The party afterward was much better news. I'm not usually a fan of events that require me to wear a suit, but this was an exception. I had probably never been so happy in my life. My mother and father were there, together, with no ticking clock and no crisis on the horizon. My alien friends were on Earth, welcomed as heroes. It was great to meet my friends' families. Nayana's parents, in particular, turned out to be super nice. Her mom kept scolding me for getting her daughter into trouble, but she also kept bringing me food and punch, so I didn't think she was really upset.

"She is much easier to be around since her return," her father told me quietly. "I think she has learned a lesson in humility."

Steve and Tamret were now celebrities. The humans in our group were all famous, sure, but we were boring next to the alien heroes. The world seemed especially to love Tamret—maybe because people tend to find cats more relatable than lizards. Also, in one interview, Steve kept talking about how easy Earth vehicles were to steal. Tamret looked amazing in her lavender long-sleeved gown, and an activist rock star kept flirting with her at the reception. At least she seemed annoyed by it. Every time he spoke to her, she just squeezed my arm and asked who he was again.

I didn't want Tamret to feel abandoned, so I waited until she was engaged in the middle of a long conversation with the First Lady before I slipped away and found Villainic, who was standing by himself, eating a piece of carrot cake. "I am glad your planet was saved," he said. "Otherwise I never would have learned about cream cheese frosting."

I looked over to where Charles, Nayana, Mi Sun, and Alice were talking. Our medals looked big and kind of dorky, but we'd earned them. Charles and I were wearing suits, but he looked more comfortable in his than I felt in mine. Mi Sun looked irritated at having to wear a dress, but I'd made a point of telling her she looked pretty, mostly just to annoy her.

"I'm glad you're having a good time," I told him.

"I certainly am," he said happily. "I am pleased to see more of your world, and I think I look quite nice in this Earth costume." He wore a suit and was now swatting at his tie like it was a cat toy.

I gestured toward the medal I wore around my neck. "Look, I'm the first to enjoy the fact that you've been Chewbaccaed, but that you didn't want one of these pretty much confirms what I already suspected. What I don't know is if there ever was a Villainic, or if it was you all along, whatever your name is."

He narrowed his eyes at me. "I don't know what you mean."

"Yeah," I said, "I think you do. So why not tell me what's going on?"

"Very well," he said with a sigh.

There was a slight shimmer in the air, and the being before me changed shape. No longer was he the blankly handsome Rarel. Now he was a tall figure in a silvery robe with a high collar. Where his head should have been was what appeared to be a twelve-sided die. I figured this being must have been radiating some sort of inconspicuous cloaking field. People noticed him enough not to bump into him, but nothing more. Certainly no one seemed to think it odd that a cat alien had just turned into a Geometric Upstart.

"My name," he said in a voice deep enough to make my teeth rattle, "is Pentagonal Dodecahedron. And yes, there is a real Villainic. He remains on the world where you met Convex Icosahedron. We have offered to return him to his home planet, but he has discovered contentment tending to our population of nerfs."

Villainic had become a nerf herder. My recent sense of the universe being a just place was not shaken by this news.

"Why did you decide to impersonate him?"

"We find the elements of chaos you and your friends create and inhabit to be particularly entertaining. We wished to observe and augment."

"You wanted to make our lives more difficult," I said.

"Perhaps. More interesting. More challenging, I should say. Though I will point out, at times my arguments paved the way for you to pursue your own schemes. You rose to those challenges quite amusingly."

"Thanks," I said. "So you guys are Formers? Is that right?"

"We are, for now, Geometric Upstarts. What we have been in the past, or shall be in the future, is not relevant."

"That sounds like a whole lot of nonsense," I said, "mainly designed to avoid answering my question."

"A question unanswered is its own answer, like a snake devouring its own tail."

"Yeah, you're only proving my point."

"I should like to ask you a question," Pentagonal Dodecahedron said.

"Honestly, you haven't given me a whole lot of motivation to answer, but since I'm probably more reasonable than you, ask away."

"How did you know I was not what I seemed?"

I thought about when I had begun to suspect that Villainic was not himself. "Well, killing those Phands on Planet Pleasant added to my suspicions, but the real giveaway was the business about speaking names at the ends of sentences. I noticed that after Villainic asked to be shown his room. When he came back, he seemed kind of relaxed, but the real Villainic always loved an opportunity to be all fancy and follow forms."

"Honestly, it was a completely made-up rule meant to annoy others," Pentagonal Dodecahedron said. "You'll notice I'm not doing it now."

"Oh," I said. "Well, I was right anyhow."

"Being right in spite of yourself seems to be the story of your life," he said. "It is one of the reasons you are so interesting to us."

"I should probably feel insulted, but I don't really care. Just stay out of my business from now on."

"We shall do so," Pentagonal Dodecahedron said with a slight bow of his die head. "Until it amuses us to do otherwise."

I was about to say something else, probably issue an entirely ineffectual warning, when my father walked up to us, his mouth wide with surprise.

"I don't believe it!" he shouted. "Pentagonal Dodecahedron!"

"Uriah Reynolds!" Pentagonal Dodecahedron answered, equally excited.

The two of them fist-bumped.

"Your father taught me that gesture," Pentagonal Dodecahedron said to me.

"This is the guy," my father said. "He's the one who saved my life and brought me to Confederation Central. I complained about being abducted at the time, but he didn't seem to care too much. And, I guess, when you think about it, it all worked out for the best. If he hadn't alien-abducted me, the Phands would still be on the verge of defeating the Confederation."

"Wait a minute," I said. Things were clicking into place. "These Geometric Upstarts—"

My father cut me off. "I love that name. It's like they're a math gang or something."

"I'm with you," I agreed, "but they're totally into numbers. They like to project things into the future." I turned to Pentagonal Dodecahedron. "Is that why you took my father? Did you predict that his abduction would somehow lead to the decline of the Phandic Empire?"

Pentagonal Dodecahedron lowered its head slightly. "There were nearly five hundred possible outcomes that arose from taking your father, nearly three hundred of which were interesting. That is a very high probability for a worthwhile outcome. That is why we took your father. As it turned out, our investment of time and interest was well rewarded."

My father apparently knew all this, because he seemed more interested in catching up. "Hey, are you and Octagonal Prism still a thing?"

"No, she left me," Pentagonal Dodecahedron said, his colors shifting in a way I felt sure indicated sadness. "For an ixmo."

"Huh," my father said. "I didn't see that coming."

The two of them were clearly strolling down memory lane, so I drifted away, just as the secretary general announced that we had a special guest. The new ambassador from the Confederation of United Planets had, moments earlier, arrived on Earth and wanted to come directly to this gathering.

Steve walked up to me, flicking his tongue suspiciously at a plate of hors d'oeuvres. He hadn't bothered to try to fit into Earth fashions and was wearing one of his usual tunics. He'd told reporters that this was formal wear on his world, but it looked like everything else he'd always worn. My theory was that he'd gotten a kick out of showing up for a dressy event wearing the Ish-hi equivalent of gym clothes.

"You think they'll pick some git for ambassador?" he asked.

"Probably."

I was braced for the worst, but then I saw Dr. Roop enter the room. He was immediately swarmed by politicians and reporters, but he politely made his way over to where we were standing.

"I had to call in many favors to receive this post," he told me, leaning his long neck toward me to better speak confidentially, "but I think I shall enjoy my time here. I hope I will see you now and again, Zeke."

"Whenever you want," I said. "But I understand that you'll be busy."

"No, I mean I hope you will be on Earth."

"Where else would I be?" I asked somewhat nervously.

"That is up to you," he said with a grin. "But you were promised a spaceship, and I have delivered it. The sort of small, long-range shuttle you have grown used to piloting. It is docked at the East Thirty-Fourth Street Heliport and will respond to your voice commands."

Just then my father, who was done talking to his Geometric Upstart friend, walked over and hugged Dr. Roop. He then introduced the alien to my mother. A bunch of politicians moved into the circle, eager to meet the new ambassador, and we got edged out.

"A ship?" Steve said to me with a sly look.

"We could go anywhere," Alice said. She and the others had all wandered over.

"I would still like to see Ganar," observed Charles.

"I have some ideas about how we might reactivate our nanites," Tamret told me. "Get those Former upgrades back for good."

"My parents are smothering me," Nayana said. "I could use some air. I suppose it couldn't hurt to go look at it. Maybe take it for a test drive."

Mi Sun rolled her eyes. "Fine," she said.

The six of us moved toward the exit. I felt Tamret take my hand and brush her shoulder against mine.

"We're not going to go looking for trouble, are we?" I said to her.

She grinned at me. "When have we had to look before?"

It was, I thought, a very good point.

Looking for another great book?
Find it
IN THE MIDDLE.

Fun, fantastic books for kids
in the in-be**TWEEN** age.

IntheMiddleBooks.com

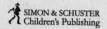